HONOR'S PRICE

By
Mike Rossi

ZMOK
BOOKS

T0243161

Honor's Price
By Mike Rossi
Cover by
Zmok Books an imprint of
Winged Hussar Publishing, LLC, 1525 Hulse Road, Unit 1, Point Pleasant, NJ 08742

This edition was published in 2024 Copyright ©Winged Hussar Publishing, LLC and Mantic Games

PB ISBN 978-1-958872-33-8
EB ISBN 978-1-958872-61-1
Library of Congress No. 2024940524
Bibliographical references and index

1.   Fantasy 2. Epic Fantasy 3. Action & Adventure

Published under license from Mantic Games

Winged Hussar Publishing, LLC All rights reserved

For more information on Winged Hussar Publishing, LLC, visit us at:
https://www.WHPsupplyroom.com
https://www.WingedHussarPublishing.com
Twitter: WingHusPubLLC
Facebook: Winged Hussar Publishing LLC

Except in the United States of America, this book is sold subject to the condition, that is shall not, by way of trade or otherwise, be lent, resold, hired out, or otherwise circulated without the publisher's prior consent in any form of binding or cover other than that in which it is published and without a similar condition including this condition being imposed on the subsequent purchaser.

The scanning, uploading, and distribution of this book via the Internet or via any other means without the permission of the publisher is illegal and punishable by law. Please purchase only authorized electronic editions, and do not participate in or encourage electronic piracy of copyrighted materials. Your support of the author's and publisher's rights is appreciated

Pannithor Timeline

-1100: First contact with the Celestians

Rise of the Celestians

-170: The God War

0: Creation of the Abyss

2676: Birth of modern Basilea, and what is known as the Common Era.

3001: Free Dwarfs declare their independence

3558: Golloch comes to power

3850: The expansion of the Abyss

Ascent of the Goblin King

Tales of Pannithor: Edge of the Abyss

3854: The flooding of the Abyss, the splintering of the Brotherhood, and Lord Darvled completing part of the wall on the Ardovikian Plains.

Drowned Secrets

Nature's Knight

Claws on the Plains

Free Dwarfs expelled from their lands.

3865: Free Dwarfs begin the campaign to free Halpi – the opening of Halpi's Rift.

3865: The Battle of Andro; *Steps to Deliverance*

Pious takes place six months before the events in *Steps to Deliverance*.

Hero Falling and *Faith Aligned* take place several weeks after the events of *Steps to Deliverance*.

Honor's Price begins in early spring and ends in late August.

Pride of a King starts in the winter of 3865, but most of the events take place in 3866.

3866: Halflings leave the League of Rhordia.

Broken Alliance

PROLOGUE

Rhyss' footsteps echoed on the weathered stone tiles as he walked through the halls of Llyngyr Cadw, the seat of Clan Daamuz. He ruefully reflected that all he did these days was bring Lord Drohzon bad news. Today was no different. His rangers had spotted the enemy's advance scouts only a day's march away. The Abyssal Dwarf army would arrive in two, three days at most.

This is where the real smelting starts, he thought. *We're out of time.*

Clan Daamuz had known the fiends were coming for days, and they'd prepared as best they could. They'd spent days harvesting the last of the crops, fortifying the walls, and training every dwarf who could hold a spear, but they were still far from ready. Rhyss was bewildered by the ranger's accounts of the sheer size of the enemy army. Reports of thousands of Abyssal Dwarfs leading hordes of orc and ratkin slaves had been filtering back for days now. It made no sense. How had the enemy become so powerful, so quickly?

He turned a corner and ran into a regiment of dwarfs marching the other way toward the main gates of the keep. Normally they would have stepped aside for the leader of the clan's rangers, but the warriors were too focused on the task at hand to notice Rhyss. And Rhyss was easy to notice, taller and broader than most dwarfs by a few inches, with a shock of unkempt auburn hair that made him seem even taller, and ice blue eyes that pinned people in place when he spoke to them. Rhyss now found himself swimming against the tide of armored dwarfs, and he was forced to slide his way to the side of the hallway to allow the regiment of warriors to pass. Rhyss took the mild disrespect stoically, realizing that the warriors were justifyingly edgy, with little room for niceties.

Rhyss ascended the rest of the corridor toward the great hall, brushing the extravagant tapestries that hung on the walls reverently with his fingertips as he passed. The banners depicted scenes from the storied history of Clan Daamuz, each honoring a noted clan ancestor. Touching the tapestries was a small ritual, but it comforted Rhyss. It made him feel as if the guiding hands of his ancestors were touching his fingers back, offering him their wisdom and courage. Today was no different, and he walked a little straighter as he entered the great hall.

His footsteps echoed on the ornate white and blue tilework, the Daamuz clan colors, as he entered the vast hall. Six columns were arrayed evenly around the edges of the room, supporting a giant dome, over eighty feet across, gilt with silver stars on a deep blue background of lapis lazuli, which highlighted the wealth and status of the clan. A series of shafts had been drilled through the mountain to allow beams of sunlight to penetrate. As usual, Rhyss drew comfort from the touch of natural light deep within the heart of the Red Mountain. His eyes were drawn along the light's path, which alit upon a golden disc high on the western wall that reflected the light and suffused the room with a warm glow. A group of dwarfen thanes was clustered around an ornately carved throne set upon a dais that dominated the far wall. The clan leaders were in the midst of a heated exchange when Rhyss entered, but he couldn't make out any specific words. The thanes grew silent and turned to look at Rhyss, calm and steely eyed, as he approached.

Rhyss steadied himself and kept his eyes locked on Drohzon as he spoke. "My lord, the enemy's advance scouts are less than a day away from Llyngyr Cadw. I believe the main army to be close behind."

Lord Drohzon Daamuz looked sidelong at Rhyss and nodded. "Indeed," the chieftain answered grimly. "It would seem we have less time than we thought."

Drohzon was short for a dwarf but made up for it with an intensity and an air of authority that had been fostered by ruling for almost a century. His diadem sat upon a head of thick black hair, and his eyes were deep brown, almost black. Rhyss had served under Drohzon for over fifty years, and during that time, he had seen Drohzon gain the gifts of wisdom and patience without losing any of his physical vitality. But the last few months had been hard on him, his clan, and on all the Free Dwarfs. The chieftain had physically aged, with gray streaks in his long black beard and more worry lines along his forehead and around the eyes. Drohzon had risen to face the Abyssal Dwarf invasion with boundless energy. As the Free Dwarfs suffered defeat after defeat, as the hold of each individual clan fell, that energy had become more intense, bordering on frantic. Now the devouring armies of their infernal cousins had arrived at Drohzon's home to claim another hold as their own.

Drohzon turned, and his eyes locked on a wizened dwarf with a long white beard, dressed in a blue tonic emblazoned with a stylized red mountain. Rhyss recognized Nygon, the senior stone priest, one of the many dwarfs responsible for communicating with the earth spirits. Drohzon nodded curtly, and the priest abruptly bowed and left. Rhyss watched the exchange with concern.

More secrets. The chieftain's stress was manifesting as an uncharacteristic paranoia. Plans within plans. The thought made him shake his head. Luckily, Drohzon didn't notice as he turned to the remaining thanes.

"Get to your Ironclad and begin the plan. We are to hold them here for as long as we can, to give our people time to escape. Every day we hold those fiends off is a day's head start for our loved ones. Do not engage unless you absolutely must. We hold our positions, defend the gates, and buy time."

Drohzon dismissed them with a nod, and the thanes solemnly marched off to their troops. "We are the lords of stone and fire!" His words echoed off the vaulted ceiling of the great hall as his dwarfs left. "Make them feel the stone of our resolve and the fire of our rage! Dianek and Fulgria watch over you!"

Rhyss appreciated Drohzon invoking the dwarfen goddesses of earth and flame with an almost pleading air. Rhyss waited until the others were gone before he clapped Drohzon on the shoulder. The familiar gesture made the chieftain smile, but Drohzon's gaze was fixed on his departing thanes. Even after the last dwarf had left the chamber, Drohzon's eyes lingered on the darkened doorways.

"Rhyss, are your rangers ready?"

"Yes, my lord. Those that aren't scouting are stationed at the tunnel exits on the far side of the mountain, and troops are hidden all along the southern route. Our people will make it safely to Rhyn Dufaris." The city at the southernmost tip of the Free Dwarf lands was the last bastion of hope for their people. Thousands of refugees had already made the trek to the great chain bridge that led to the relative safety of the Imperial Dwarf lands beyond.

Drohzon nodded and looked pensive. The silence stretched with all the unsaid implications of their situation. How could this have happened? How could the Abyssal Dwarfs have grown so strong so quickly? Their demon-worshipping cousins had always been few in numbers, relying on their mutated and warped slaves to do their bidding. How could they be at the very gates of Llyngyr Cadw, a hold that had stood for almost a thousand years? And what would happen to Clan Daamuz now? Who would keep the clan together and lead them to safety?

Rhyss broke the silence, "How did Din and Dare take the news?"

Dinnidek and Daerun, the chieftain's sons, had been ordered to leave with Rhyss and lead the fleeing warriors to safety. The queen, Brohna, and their daughter, Diessa, had left with the more vulnerable members of the clan a ten-day before. Drohzon had sent all the non-warriors away when the Abyssal Dwarf army had turned south. The citizen levy, the fyrd, had stayed, but the Abyssal Dwarf army was too vast, too strong to resist. Last evening, Drohzon had ordered the fyrd to escape south and reunite with the rest of the clan at Rhyn Dufaris. All that was left at Llyngyr Cadw were the most hardened warriors. They would hold the demons and dark dwarfs here for as long as they could, sacrificing their lives for the good of the clan.

Drohzon grimaced. "Predictably. Dinnidek accepted his duty, but I could tell how disappointed he was. Daerun got angry and argued, swearing up and down that he would stand at my side until the end of days. No doubt he was just saying what Din was thinking. But in the end, I am their chieftain, and they must obey." Drohzon sighed and glanced around at his great hall. His eyes lingered on the ornate bejeweled throne, the giant sculptures, friezes, and tapestries that celebrated the works of Clan Daamuz. "They're too young to rule. I hoped that I would have years to watch them mature into the great leaders and warriors they're destined to be." Drohzon sighed before going on. "But here we are."

Rhyss stood quietly, allowing Drohzon to work through his feelings. After a few moments, the chieftain snapped out of his musing and locked eyes with Rhyss.

"Protect my children, Rhyss. Keep them safe. I will make the fiends pay for as long as I can. The clan must live, and all three of them are the future of the clan. Serve them faithfully the way you've served me."

Drohzon embraced Rhyss, who stood rigid in surprise. The chieftain had never shown this type of affection before. Within two heartbeats, Rhyss softened and returned the hug. Drohzon stepped back, his hands on Rhyss' shoulders. Drohzon squeezed his eyes shut and whispered a single word, his voice cracking slightly.

"Go."

Rhyss turned to leave with a sense of foreboding. He knew in his heart this may be the last time he would see his home, and he glanced back just as he was leaving the hall. He saw Drohzon standing alone amid his seat of power. The chieftain was staring up at a mural of his great grandfather, the founder of Clan Daamuz. In the mural, a stalwart dwarf stood over a slain white dragon, his great axe held aloft, glinting in the sunlight, with the outline of the red mountain of Llyngyr Cadw in the background. Drohzon raised his own axe high in salute to his ancestor. After a heartbeat, he released his grip on the haft of the great axe and caught it quickly, giving it a swift sweep and a flourish. With that, Drohzon hurried from the hall to personally prepare the keep's defenses.

Rhyss watched his chieftain depart, gave the great hall one more last, longing look, and then he left his ancestral home.

* * * * *

Drohzon, lord of Llyngyr Cadw, swiftly led the remnants of his guard out from the darkness of the escape tunnel and into the late afternoon light. In contrast to the choked and smokey halls below, the air up here was fresh, and the wind blew cool against his forehead. The sun was just touching the tops of the mountains to the west, setting the sky on fire. The sounds of the Abyssal Dwarf army echoed strangely from the valley below, and from far back in the tunnel from whence they came. It filled Drohzon with dread. He nervously scanned the mountaintop for enemy troops while the last defenders of Llyngyr Cadw hurriedly filed out of the tunnel, past the old wooden watchtower that stood silent sentinel atop the Red Mountain. The surviving warriors were haggard, wounded, and lucky to be alive. Drohzon nodded to them as they emerged, almost fifty in all. A surprising number, both because so many had managed to survive the final assault on the throne room, and because so few remained from the original defenders.

It had been two ten-days since Rhyss had led most of the clan south. They had held off the fiends for that entire time. A great accomplishment with such a meager force. But in the end, what did it matter?

Nygon was the last to emerge. The wizened stone priest turned back to the tunnel, closed his eyes and gestured with his hand upraised, pointing back into the blackness. The mountain rumbled, and the tunnel collapsed with a great billow of dust. Drohzon nodded grimly in satisfaction and turned his attention to his clansmen. Too exhausted and overcome with emotion for words, he merely gestured for them to form up for march and selected a few of the younger warriors to scout ahead. They wearily obeyed, but their determination fought with their fatigue. Drohzon saw it on their faces and felt it in their shuffling footsteps. One more push.

Nygon sat and closed his eyes again in concentration. A pair of elementals coalesced from the bare rockface of the summit, smaller than the ones that he had summoned earlier to defend the throne room. It was further testament to how weary the old stone priest was. The elementals were weaker, but they would be strong enough. The stone spirits approached the wooden watchtower, and with a great push, they toppled it over, scattering the planks and boards down the mountainside. The noise contrasted sharply with the dwarf's silence. Nygon gestured with his open palms, and the foundations of the tower sunk into the ground, leaving no trace. With this last act accomplished, Nygon wearily stood and swayed a little before regaining his composure. One more push.

Drohzon took a moment to look around one last time at the Red Mountain. His clan's ancestral home. His home. He looked at his warriors, faces covered in soot, grime, and blood. He closed his eyes and let the cacophony of the Abyssal Dwarf army's triumphant cries wash over him. Rage and grief battled within him. So much blood. So much failure. They had killed countless Abyssal Dwarf, ratkin, and orcish soldiers during the siege. It was a small consolation. A wave of weakness shuddered through Drohzon and he dropped his winged helmet onto the bare rock of the mountain. The sound was jarring, and it called the attention of his warriors. Some looked with sadness, sharing their chieftain's sorrow, before looking away in deference or shame at seeing their lord so vulnerable. Some looked with rage upon what had been lost. Most looked dead with blank stares to match their shattered hopes.

After a moment, Nygon gently touched Drohzon's arm, calling him to the necessities of the present. Drohzon tightly squeezed his eyes shut, and his tears traced down his sallow cheeks into his singed beard. With a final nod, he looked up and gestured for the remnants of his clan to march. As long as a single member of clan Daamuz lived, there was hope. As long as his wife and family survived, there would be a chance at redemption. Survival was all that mattered now.

CHAPTER 1

Dinnidek was slowly losing his patience with the Imperial envoy. It wasn't what the Imp was saying that rubbed Din the wrong way. It was how he was saying it. This was the third visit from the envoy, and the Imperial representative had become slightly more condescending with every audience. It was never enough to be overtly insulting, but it came through in his tone. The dwarf spoke as a person who held all the power, and he wanted Dinnidek to know it. The thing that singed Din's whiskers the most was that the envoy was right.

"My lord," the envoy went on, "you must agree that High King Golloch's request for an offering to upkeep the military is not unreasonable." He said it as if Dinnidek had never heard of a tax before. The Imp gently stroked his long black beard as he spoke, which stood out starkly against the white of his tabard, emblazoned with Golloch's seal. Din knew by now that the affectation meant that the envoy thought he was in control. Backed by three attendants, the emissary was resplendent in well-appointed clothes featuring gold brocade. Even his beard was interwoven with gold filigree. He carried the authority of a prosperous and wealthy empire behind him. Dinnidek felt his temperature rise, but he took a slow breath and postured as if he were reconsidering the request.

Din's rising ire was offset by the cool sea air that blew into the Clan Daamuz hall. After all this time, he still couldn't get used to the coastal breeze that swept in from the bank of tall windows along the side wall. He took his time to breathe deeply and focus on the warm spring winds that fluttered the ornate tapestries which hung behind Dinnidek and made the braids of his black beard sway slightly. The low murmur of the waves from the High Sea of Bari crashed below the bustling sounds of the clan settlement in the background.

"...owe the king a great debt..."

The Imp prattled on, but Din's eyes drifted to his own people. A small retinue of guards ringed the outer wall of the hall, dressed in the white and blue of Clan Daamuz. His personal bodyguard, a dour dwarf named Tordek, stood at his side. He was clad like the rest of the guards, and only his closeness to Dinnidek betrayed his station. As usual, Tordek stared straight ahead, looking at nothing and taking in everything.

"...need I remind you of your hall..."

Ah, yes. The hall. The new hall for Clan Daamuz was crafted from the finest timbers in the land and had ornate decorations that reminded Dinnidek of the deep valley of Llyngyr Cadw. To human eyes, it was surely the height of beautiful craftsmanship, but it paled in comparison to the grandeur of the stone vaults of their lost hold. Where before Dinnidek's father had held court in a hall that sparkled with gemstones, precious metals, and the most elaborate marble statues, now Dinnidek's seat was made of less permanent materials of wood, leather, and wool.

In the ten years since their flight from their ancestral lands, Clan Daamuz had survived, but at what cost? In the aftermath of their escape, Clan Daamuz was taken in by the Imperial dwarfs and their High King Golloch, who granted the clan a new home along the shores of the High Sea of Bari. They were assured a voice within Golloch's empire. They had even been promised Imperial assistance to retake their ancestral home from the Abyssals. But since then, Golloch's empire took more and more from the clan, and all that Din and his people had gotten in return were promises. Over time it had become clear to Clan Daamuz that they were, at best, scrap metals in Golloch's empire. None of the Free Dwarf chieftains or thanes had been asked to join Golloch's advisors. The Free Dwarf clans were all being asked for goods and gold for the welfare of the empire but hadn't received much in return besides the initial land grants. Even the land had proven to be less fertile and harder to farm then Golloch's people had made out.

Every year, the king's court requested a greater share of the clan's crops, ostensibly for distribution within the wider dwarfen empire to battle hunger. Din had happily given at first, until some discussion with others in his clan discovered that none of the surplus grain ever reached its way to the Free Dwarf refugees. It had instead been sent to feed Golloch's vast Imperial army. In time, it was obvious to the Free Dwarf clans that, despite all the Imperial promises, they were being exploited.

"...thus, surely you understand why you must comply with the request of the king."

Finally realizing that the envoy had stopped speaking, Dinnidek sat up straighter and addressed the envoy from his throne. "I agree that a *tax*, is most reasonable, especially for pacts of *mutual* defense. But a fifth of our crops is unsustainable. How will I feed my people over the winter and plant the next season?" Din growled low in the back of his throat in annoyance, contemplating how much the Imperials were asking for this year compared to last. The clan had barely been able to afford the tithe last year, and this latest increase would kill any hope of having a winter surplus. He couldn't do that to his people.

"It is a dilemma. But our lord Golloch has many new mouths to feed, and many new people to defend since he graciously accepted you and your clans into the Imperium," the envoy replied silkily. He stroked his beard slowly, then acted as if a new idea had come to him. "In place of your allotted tithe, your clan could perhaps supply Golloch with some of your warriors. A few regiments of your stout-hearted folk would serve well to protect the Empire, and your people, from harm."

Dinnidek felt a flash of irritation at the impertinence of the suggestion. He let the offer hang in the air before he answered. "An interesting offer, but upon reflection, I have to pass. I need my clansmen here to work the farms and delve the mines. I can't afford to lose the dwarfpower during the sowing and the harvest season. And they are best able to protect my clan from harm if they remain close by."

"If you will not give some of your men, then the tithe must stay at a fifth. We must all work together to meet the growing needs of dwarfenkind. There are wide-ranging threats that the Empire must face."

Din bristled at the envoy's words. "I understand that it's incumbent on all dwarfs to help their kin, and I have happily given in the past." Din's frustration boiled over, and his tone became more brusque as he continued. "But in the past two years, not a single coin or ingot of gold has been spent on the invasion against the Abyssals that you keep promising. In fact, the only troops being amassed are out in the western provinces. Why would the High King, in his infinite wisdom, gather his prodigious army near our staunch allies in Basilea? Are there hidden threats in the heartland of the Dwarfen Empire that we haven't heard of out here in the hinterlands? I may be a poor provincial, but if there's some hidden brilliance in these tactics, I certainly don't understand it."

The envoy made a slightly sour face before regaining his composure. "I assure you, Lord Dinnidek, that my lord Golloch has been planning to retake the Halpi region for your kin and the greater glory of the Imperium. But, as you are well aware, the empire is vast, and my lord Golloch has many other pressing matters to attend to. Be assured that he is planning an invasion even now."

"Yes, I believed you the last time you said that, which was... Oh, how long ago was it, Tordek?" Dinnidek turned to his bodyguard, who stood beside the throne.

An exaggerated second later, Tordek answered in a deadpan voice, "One year ago, my lord."

"Why yes, it was a year ago," Din responded. "Hmmm. And in that time, what has actually been done to prepare for this great invasion?"

The envoy gave an exasperated sigh and spoke as if he was explaining things to a toddler. "High King Golloch has been sending spies and scouts into the Halpi Mountains to ascertain the enemy dispositions. It would be suicide to attack without a thorough understanding of the lay of the land."

"Funny," Din responded sarcastically, "if Golloch wanted to know the lay of the land, he could have just asked any of his new subjects. They would have been more than happy to help him in any way they could. But it seems that he can't be bothered to get advice from any of us."

The envoy cleared his throat. "Dinnidek," the envoy gave a small smile as he omitted Din's title in return, "you know full well that only major clans can send representatives to advise the high king. And you also know that none of the refugee clans have been afforded status as a major clan within the Imperium. The next meeting of the Claansvelt is still over a year away, and at that time we can review the deeds of Clan Daamuz and see where your clan ranks within the mighty dwarfen empire."

The Claansvelt was a meeting of the elders of all the Imperial clans. They met every fifty years to discuss the great deeds of the clans and reward the clans whose members did the most for dwarfen society throughout the entire clan's history. On one hand, since the elders took all the works of the entire clan through time into account, it gave ample reverence and respect to a clan's ancestors. But on the other hand, a weak and unremarkable clan could hold onto their favored status for years after the great members of their clan had passed. Din considered the custom the same way he saw many other Imperial customs, as a twisted expression of a noble ideal.

"I'm sure that upon review, the Daamuz clan will be afforded its rightful place within greater dwarf society."

At that last part, the envoy gave a mocking smile, but only for a second, as if to say that the rightful place for the clan would be floating back out to sea.

Din smiled, but it never reached his gray eyes, now stormy in their intensity. "I have heard of these customs that you keep. It seems strange to me that you would value the acts of the dead over the acts of the living. I would think that Golloch would be well served by the best and brightest of his living subjects, but that doesn't seem to be the case." Din delivered this last line while he stared pointedly at the envoy. "On second thought, maybe the High King doesn't need anyone else's advice. He seems to have everything under his direct control after all."

The envoy gave another sour look at the insult and hid his hands within his luxurious black beard that covered most of his tunic. "You may not understand the ancient ways, but you should be thankful that we consider the entire clan history, being as young and inexperienced as you are. I'm sure your father performed great deeds before he failed to defend your ancestral hold."

The hall got deathly quiet. The envoy and his retinue stood haughty and proud. Tension radiated off Dinnidek in waves. Din was completely still, and for a moment, he didn't trust himself to speak. Tordek's leather gauntlets creaked as he tightened his grip on his ceremonial axe. Then, the Lord of Clan Daamuz let out a long breath that spoke of resignation. Din spoke in a low growl, barely above a whisper.

"So, despite your promises from last year, am I hearing you say that High King Golloch will not assist us in retaking our ancestral lands this campaign season?"

The envoy stood a little taller and crossed his arms in front of him in a defiant gesture. "My lord Golloch will not assist you and the other refugees in retaking the Halpi Mountains this year. In addition, as citizens of the Imperium, he would remind you of your duty to the state. He expressly forbids you from attempting any such invasion until he grants his approval. You are to train your soldiers and be prepared for possible reassignment wherever High King Golloch directs you."

"That is dire news," Din said with a tinge of bitterness. "But you believe that his highness will assist us in retaking the Halpi Mountains from the Abyssals next year?"

Dinnidek gazed intently at the envoy, who responded with the same polished voice that he used every time he lied to Dinnidek in the past.

"Yes, I am sure of it. Prepare your people, and Golloch will keep his word to retake Halpi once affairs at home are in order. Definitely next year."

Din knew he was lying. The envoy knew he was lying. And there was nothing that Din could do about it. His clan had lost their ancestral lands. They were refugees who owed their very existence to Golloch and his grand empire. Their only option would be to obey. And obey they would.

"We will return at the end of the harvest season for the fifth. Please be sure to have it prepared for hauling when we arrive."

With that last command, the envoy gave a perfunctory bow. Without Dinnidek's leave, he and his retinue left the great hall of Clan Daamuz. Dinnidek watched them go, glaring daggers at their backs until the delegation had left the great hall.

Tordek relaxed his grip. "Well," the thane said in his usual understated way, "that went well."

CHAPTER 2

For the life of him, Daerun couldn't stop laughing. The joke wasn't even that funny, really. It was how Felwyr had said it. The timing, the funny voice he'd used, and the fact that Daerun had just enough to drink reduced the dwarf prince to a cackling, gasping mess. He and his friends had been at it for just over an hour, sitting in the aptly named 'Ale House,' and the jokes had gotten funnier as the time had gone by.

"The goblin said," he wheezed, repeating the punchline with tears running down his cheeks into his reddish-blond beard, "that's about the height of it!"

He barely got the words out before he started cry-laughing again. Felwyr and the other dwarfen warriors all roared with fresh laughter and pounded the long trestle table with their empty steins. The rest of the Ale House patrons all eyed Daerun's raucous friends in appreciation. The young dwarf's laughter was infectious, and the patrons began to smile and laugh along at the warrior's antics.

"You need to get yourself under control, Dare," said Felwyr, as he wiped the tears from his eyes. He waved his stein vaguely at the assembled crowd in the Ale House. "You're going to damage our reputation as hardworking and dependable dwarfs."

"Ha!" Dare responded with a smile. "Everyone knows no matter how many pints we put away at lunch we're always knee deep in the work again in the afternoon! No one here would call us unreliable, now would they?"

The last part was delivered to the Ale House crowd and was answered with a chorus of "nay's" and raised tankards.

"Our reputation, such as it is, survives intact!" Fel agreed in exaggerated relief before standing to give a bow to the other patrons.

Daerun laughed anew at his friend's antics, even as he thought about his words. Yes, the boys got rowdy every once in a while, but no one would say that they shirked their duties. To do so would have been an affront to the entire clan. All dwarfs knew that 'the clan' wasn't just some amorphous concept, but the clan was actual families, actual dwarfs, who looked out for one other and supported each other. To not give that support when asked was unthinkable.

Daerun was just getting himself under control when the door to the Ale House swung open, and he heard his brother Dinnidek call out. "The next round is on me!"

Dare turned toward Dinnidek with a grin while his dwarfs gave a hearty cheer. Still dressed in his best robes, Din smiled and acknowledged the Ale House patrons as he approached Daerun's table. Dour Tordek followed along in Din's wake. Daerun rose to lock wrists with his brother.

"Thank you, my lord," Daerun loudly spoke, a sarcastic grin on his face and a gleam in his hazel eyes.

Din smiled back, despite himself, "I told you, no 'm'lords' in my presence. I'm going to start calling you 'prince' if you don't watch out. I'll grant you embarrassing titles like 'Master of the Privy Chamber.'" Felwyr broke out in laughter again while the rest of the retinue snickered.

Daerun snorted and rolled his eyes at the threat and graciously took a tankard of ale off the platter that one of his fellows brought back from the bar. "Thank you, Din," he said sincerely.

"My pleasure, Dare." Dinnidek sat down at the end of the long table, opposite his brother. The other warriors shuffled to the far end of the table to give the brothers space and a modicum of privacy. "I owed you a pint anyway."

Dare gave an open-mouthed smile, "Ha! I knew that you couldn't go the entire audience with that Imp without losing your temper. So, what did you say? Was it worth it?"

"My lord told the envoy he was stupid," Tordek chimed in, deadpan as usual.

"Hmmm," Dare mused, "probably true."

"He also said that the Imperial custom of ranking their clans was backward," Tordek went on. Din flushed a little at that.

Dare's eyes widened in mock indignation while he gazed at Din. "Also true. Did my brother say anything else?"

Tordek went on in his understated way. "He intimated that the envoy served a domineering, authoritarian tyrant whose ego was too big to allow him to take advice from anyone."

Din turned and kicked Tordek in the shins to quiet him.

"He did?" Dare gaped from Tordek to Din and back again, a huge grin spreading over his face. "That is undoubtedly true!"

"Not in so many words," Din said, taking an overly long sip from his tankard. "But that was about the gist of it. He left in a huff. Elf-skinned, I guess."

Tordek gave the slightest smile and nod of affirmation.

"So, what about our other bet?" Daerun gazed intently at Din, his mood suddenly shifting to something more serious.

Din shook his head ruefully. "You win that one too. Golloch won't help us retake Halpi this year. The envoy promised next year."

"The same thing he promised last year and the year before," Dare observed.

"Indeed." Dinnidek took another long draught of ale before going on. "Anyway, it was a sucker bet. I knew that Golloch wouldn't help us, just like you did. He's busy posturing like a puffed-up peacock to the Basileans. He doesn't have the stomach to face off against the Abyssals. Too afraid he'll have a hard time and lose face. Not only is he not helping, but the envoy forbade us from attempting anything without Golloch's permission. Do you believe that? His permission! Ridiculous!" This time Din banged his tankard to show his displeasure.

Dare finished off his ale and put the tankard down. "What else can you expect? Our cousins have sold their freedom for a few extra coins and the illusions of security. They're getting to be no better than humans. You and I both know that the clan is fed up with the Imperials. Years now of broken promises for aid, for military assistance, for common respect? You heard the thanes last year, when the Imperials came with empty pockets and empty talk of 'one more year'? They demanded that we do something."

"Yes," agreed Din. "And we listened. You know as well as I that we haven't stood idly by. We made a plan, and we're working the plan. This is the year we go home. We can't rely on the Imps, so we'll do it ourselves. No Imperials, no Golloch, just the Free Dwarfs."

"Good thing we have Clan Helgwin still holding out in Halpi. The Vale of Crafanc is a tough nut to crack." Crafanc was located between the sea and the Ironway, the great trade route that ran along the eastern edge of Halpi and was situated in a fortified vale ringed in on three sides by tall mountains. Their defensible position, combined with their strong army, had allowed Helgwin to resist the Abyssal invasion. "They've been spitting in the eye of the Abyssals for years since the invasion. Any word from Rhyss? He and his rangers have been laying the foundation for weeks now."

"Nothing since their last foray. I still find it strange that he found Halpi empty. It's like all of the fiends went back to their strongholds in Tragar after they looted all they could."

"Empty is a relative term," opined Dare. "They still possess most of our ancestral holds. And their forces roam freely over our lands."

"Yes, but to your point, Helgwin is the key. Once Rhyss snuck past the Abyssals into Crafanc, once we had allies on the peninsula we could coordinate with, we had a real chance. I can't imagine what they've been through the last decade. Living in a state of constant siege, the noose tightening year by year as the fiends get bolder and bolder. Imagine you can't access your fields so you can't farm. What sort of pressure does that put on a people?"

"Good thing you decided to send them help. Those smuggled goods have done more for our fellow dwarfs than all of Golloch's empty promises. And every ship that comes across the High Sea of Bari lets Helgwin know that they're not alone. All that extra food and those weapons not only give them hope, but it's provided a bulwark for us to work from."

"Yep," agreed Din. "Rhyss said Anfynn and his warriors were overjoyed at the prospect of breaking out of Crafanc. They're so hungry to smash the Abyssals for all the destruction that they've wrought. They promised all the aid they could muster to help us retake Llyngyr Cadw."

"We'll need all of the help we can get. We're taking quite the risk, you know. To just up and leave here? To relocate the entire clan to the island of Innyshwylt, in the middle of the High Sea of Bari? And then to force an amphibious assault on the Dewbrock Plain? I would call the plan foolhardy if I didn't have a hand in pulling it together." Dare smiled over the rim of his tankard at his brother. "Diessa has every right to be skeptical."

Diessa, the Daamuz middle sibling, had advised caution, and Daerun knew she wasn't sold on the idea that the invasion was wise, or even necessary.

"Yes, it's bold, but it's also the best we have. Once we establish a beach head, we can join forces with Helgwin and march on Llyngyr Cadw. You know that when Golloch hears that we've disobeyed him, he's going to send his army here to hold the remaining clan members hostage. So, the clan has to depart all at once. I don't want the Imps interfering with the invasion once it's underway. I wanted to give the Imps one more chance before we actually went through with it."

"And see where that got you," Dare retorted, not unkindly. "The whole operation would have been infinitely easier without that pompous windbag's interference. But, as usual, these Imps make things harder than they have to be. Just not as smart as the Free Dwarfs."

"Maybe not as smart, but way more organized. The Free Dwarfs lost their homes because we didn't work together. It just wasn't in our collective nature. But if I've learned anything from Golloch, it's that if the Free Dwarf clans can coordinate their efforts, then we'll be a force to be reckoned with. The days of each clan looking only after their own affairs are over. We have to work as one to meet the new challenges of the world."

Dare and the other warriors had been listening to Din intently, and they spontaneously banged their tankards on the table in agreement. After the moment passed, Daerun lowered his voice and leaned in closer to his brother. "Do you still plan on emptying the treasury?"

Din nodded and leaned in close in return. "We need the money to buy the clan passage back to Halpi. We can't retake Llyngyr Cadw without boats, and boats cost money."

Dare whistled tunelessly and shook his head sadly. "Those riches are the last thing keeping us from starvation if this doesn't work."

"I know, Dare. Don't you think it's tearing me up inside too? But we need the money. We can't stay here." Dare went to argue, but Din cut him off. "The Imps gave us their worst lands out of the goodness of their hearts. Our warsmiths aren't being admitted to the Imperial guilds. Our master miners are being told they need to begin the journeyman process again. They take our crops to feed Golloch's ambition. And now Golloch is demanding troops. Sons and daughters marching off in Golloch's colors, not even under the banners of their clans. You know it as well as I, Dare. There's no future for us here."

Din pushed his tankard across the table in disgust. Dare took in his older brother's frustration silently. Normally he was the emotional one and Din the steady voice of reason. But when Din got hot, Dare got somber, as if to counteract his brother's rare outbursts.

"The clan agrees with you, you know. The thanes said as much. They see it. They feel it, too. The haughtiness of the Imperials grates on all of them. They all long for home, just like we do. And they're ready to go along with your plan." Dare reached up and ran his fingers over the golden key he wore on a chain around his neck. A sizable portion of the clan wore similar keys as symbols of their lost home. They were a silent promise that they would eventually come back to Halpi and cleanse Llyngyr Cadw. Dare reached out with his other hand to touch Din's forearm and held his brother's gaze. "They believe in your vision of smashing our traitorous cousins back to the Abyss, reclaiming our ancestral lands, and shaking off the Imperial yoke that gets tighter and tighter every year. They would rather struggle in freedom than be docile in golden chains."

Dare's voice got louder as he spoke, to the point where Felwyr and the other warriors all banged their tankards on the table in agreement. Even Tordek nodded slightly, with the barest glint in his eye. Din smiled and gazed into the bottom of his tankard as if trying to see the future.

"Despite your brave words, not everyone agrees with us, you know. Deese thinks the entire thing is a fool's errand."

Dare nodded soberly in agreement. Their sister was strong-willed, principled, caring, and stubborn, just like their mother. If she had been born first, she would have made a formidable clan chief. Her standing as a member of the ruling family and her prestige as the clan's stone priestess gave Diessa both power and respect among their people. She had been the spiritual leader of the clan since their mother had passed. Though she had been overruled by the rest of the thanes, her opinion carried a lot of weight. The brothers needed her support to get everyone in the clan on board. The clan wouldn't even consider marching without the blessing of the stone priestess and the earth spirits she controlled. If Diessa opted to stay behind, the invasion was doomed to failure.

"True," Dare agreed, "she doesn't see it the way that we do. But she loves the clan as much as us, and she'll ultimately support whatever decision we make."

"Will she? I'm not so sure." Din looked soberly at his brother. "I'd rather her gladly follow me because I'm right than grudgingly obey me because I'm chief." Dinnidek put his tankard down and looked over to the Ale House door. "Now I just have to convince her."

CHAPTER 3

Diessa was happy with the day's progress. A storm had blown through off the High Sea of Bari during the last ten-day, damaging three of the family holds. Some trees had even fallen, smashing roofs and knocking in walls. Ancestors be praised, no one was injured, but the damage had been extensive. Under Diessa's guidance, the earth elementals had done a remarkable amount of work. They'd cleaned up the debris and placed structural supports for the new walls to be erected.

Diessa raised her hand, and the hulking creatures moved where she directed. The immensely strong stones of its body grinded with every step, the dirt and moss in between contorting as it walked. Diessa sensed the elemental's movements as it easily reached up to set the roof truss for the new structure.

Veit, the clan's master engineer, instructed Diessa on the placement of the beams. He had been Diessa's constant companion for the past few days as the repairs were ongoing. Veit was smaller and slighter than most dwarfs, standing at just under four feet tall. He was constantly moving and thinking out loud, doing calculations on his fingers. He reminded Diessa of a bird, chirping and fluttering the day away. He even tended to cock his head to the side like a bird when he was thinking or listening. She liked working with Veit, who was both free with his knowledge and was always looking to add to it. Veit was endlessly curious about the world and about Diessa's connection with the earth and stone. He had taken advantage of their time together to ask Diessa a myriad of questions. She was impressed with his ability to follow along, even on a subject he had no experience with. Veit had no frame of reference for Diessa's ability to summon and influence the spirits of the earth to do her bidding. To be fair, not many dwarfs did. Being *stone-touched*, as the dwarfs called it, was extremely rare.

She came back to herself, opened her green eyes, and looked at the new building with a smile. Diessa shook her head in delight, causing her thick braid of honey-colored hair to fall from its customary place along her left shoulder to cascade down to the small of her back. The closest earth elemental stood still, holding a four span timber in its giant stone hands. The immediate task complete, it placed one end of the timber down and held it vertical like a spear, with the other end just a few feet above its head. Posed like that, the elemental looked like a farmer leaning against his pitchfork, looking out on his fields in satisfaction. Diessa gave a little laugh of delight, and the elemental turned its gaze to her. The two enormous mica stones that served as 'eyes' glowed and glittered out from a vaguely humanoid face.

"Excellent work, Joro! Thank you for your help." Diessa gave the elemental a nod, and Joro nodded back. Diessa's head was filled with a feeling of satisfaction and pleasure at a job well done. The earth elementals didn't use language the way that dwarfs or humans did. Instead, they 'spoke' with Diessa directly into her mind. They communicated by sharing their feelings, or impressions, directly with Diessa. In a way, it made it easier for Diessa to understand them. It was easy to misconstrue the nuances of language, but it was much harder for her to misinterpret a feeling, especially the raw and direct emotions that elementals tended to use.

Diessa turned to Veit, and her braid fell from over her left shoulder to tumble down her back. "Another couple of hours and we can get the walls up and the room framed in. Think we can get it all done today? Do you mind working with me through to the dinner bell?"

Veit smiled back at Diessa. "That would be great. I would love to work with you for as long as you'd like."

Diessa nodded and turned back to Joro, but she noticed Veit's gaze linger on her face for a few extra seconds before he also turned back to the elemental.

"Looks like we have some more work to do, Joro!"

Of course, Joro wasn't what the earth elemental called itself. The spirit's name was the sound of water slowly trickling through the slim cracks in the bedrock miles below the earth. But that wasn't practical, given the limitations of Diessa's dwarfen speech, so she called him Joro, based on an ancient word for earth in the dwarfen tongue. Joro nodded and gave the impression of seasons slowly grinding by, year after year.

"Yes, I know we have nothing but time," Diessa answered with a smile. Joro and the two other elementals went back to the stockpile of wooden beams, ready to grab more and place them where Veit, through Diessa, told them to go.

Diessa closed her eyes and communed with Joro and the other elementals. She was still aware of her surroundings, but her attention flowed into the spirits, and she saw the world simultaneously through their eyes as well. She was always struck by how the earth spirits were joined together as a collective, while still keeping some of their individuality. She found that the stronger the spirit, the more distinct it was from its fellows; but no matter how great, the spirits were always connected to each other. They shared a common purpose and even a common will.

Seemingly from afar, she heard Veit's commands. She sent her thoughts into the spirits, directing their will and allowing them to do the relatively complex tasks with finesse. The earth elementals did not need Diessa's direct will to move and work, they would do any task they were asked of without Diessa's constant direction. But they were able to perform better with Diessa's active participation. Part of it was that Diessa was able to exert her will on the collective, keeping them on task and more engaged in the work. The spirits were ageless, and the concept of time was different for them. They would do whatever they were asked, but if it happened in three months rather than three hours, what was the difference to them? The other part was that the spirits were unfamiliar with humanoid shapes. They were spirits of the deep earth, after all, and only took this form on rare occasions. Having Diessa as part of the collective gave the elementals some of her confidence and experience using her body. They were able to do more complex and detailed tasks with her 'joining in.'

Within moments, the elementals began to erect the walls around the structure, all of them working industriously while Veit directed the operation. Diessa was one with them as they worked, and they were one with her. She loved the feeling of community, of the many working toward a common goal. It made her feel whole, complete. She missed that feeling when she wasn't communing with the spirits, not as a sense of loss, as if she were incomplete without it, but as an absence, a disconnection. She worked along with the spirits, building physical structures, building up the clan, and improving their lives. Helping the clan was the highest calling any dwarf could aspire to. Bearing this responsibility was a great honor, and one that she took very seriously.

She felt someone shaking her shoulder gently and reluctantly came fully back to herself. She was surprised to find that the shadows of the trees had lengthened considerably, and she felt rather thirsty. The sun had traveled across the sky and was just brushing against the tops of the nearby wood line. She looked up at Veit, who smiled back.

"I'm sorry, I should have woken you sooner, but we were making such great progress that I didn't want to stop you."

Diessa grabbed for her waterskin and surveyed their handiwork. The new longhouse was almost complete, with the walls erected and a new roof in place. Joro and the other spirits stood around the building, looking as if they were enjoying the fruits of a hard day's work. The detail work could be completed by her clansmen, and the building would be complete in one or two more days. She looked up at Veit, who still had his hand on her shoulder, and placed her free hand over his. "It's okay. Thank you for allowing me to work. We make a great team."

Veit let his hand linger for a second, then pulled it back and awkwardly put it on his hip, then his belt, before he finally brushed his fingers through his hair and looked away.

"Yes, I guess we do," he said as he looked at the new building with a nervous smile.

After a second, Veit took a sharp breath in, as if he were about to say something, but before he could get a word out, he was interrupted.

"The longhouse looks great!" Dinnidek strode up to the work site with his customary smile. "Veit, you and Diessa did a fantastic job!"

Veit turned and bowed deeply to his chieftain as he approached, his words left unsaid.

"You too, Joro!" Din waved to the closest elemental.

Diessa felt a flash of a smiling dwarf face and the feeling of warm sun on stone. "He says it was his pleasure to help. I figure that we're done with the major work for now. All the remaining tasks are too detailed for Joro and the spirits to do. The rest of that work can be done by us, right, Veit?"

Veit nodded enthusiastically.

"My lord, I figure it will take," the engineer took a second to count out some figures in his head, mumbling to himself, "sixteen days of work for the building to be complete, and half that to be habitable."

"I'll make sure Dare and his friends bring enough people to get it done tomorrow." The clan chief looked at Diessa, then back to Veit. "Do you mind giving my sister and I some time alone? We have some clan matters we need to discuss."

"Of course, my lord." With that, Veit gave a deep bow to both Dinnidek and Diessa and turned to gather up his plans and his tools.

Diessa walked beside her brother into the wood line, out of the late afternoon sun. The breeze came off the shore and rustled the leaves of the trees, the noise matching the distant sound of the surf on the rocks. She found a comfortable spot and leaned against the bough of one of the taller trees. With a sigh of contentment, she let the tree hold her up and allowed herself to relax after the day's work. Even though she hadn't been the one lifting the beams and building the hall, she still felt drained, as she always did after she communed with the spirits. It was nice here in the shade, and she lifted her braid to allow the cool air to brush against her neck.

Din found a log that let him sit low to the ground, and he grunted slightly as he dropped his weight down. He looked up at Diessa. "I met with the Imperial ambassador today."

She arched her eyebrow at him as if to say, 'go on.'

"He says that Golloch won't allow us to go home. Says maybe next year. He also asked for one fifth of our harvest." Diessa's eyes widened as Din continued. "When I argued that the tax was too much, he asked for troops instead. I stonewalled him and he went on his way, but he expects us to have the fifth ready come fall. We got lucky this year, Deese."

She smirked at that. "Strange kind of luck. At least now you know they won't help."

Din looked out from the shadows of the forest into the sunlight toward the shore. "I always knew, I just needed to hear it from them."

"So that's it for this year, then? You'll rethink this scheme of yours?" They were both silent for a moment before Din spoke again.

He evaded the question. "Every year the Imperials take more, and they give less. It's only a matter of time until they demand one thing too many."

"Yes. But it's better than the alternative."

"Is it?" Din cut in sharply.

"Yes, Din. It is," Diessa responded in an exasperated tone. "We've been over this. Things are definitely hard here. The clan is adapting to these new lands, these new Imperial customs. Adapting to anything new is hard. But there is no war here. No Abyssals. No abominations. No raids."

"No opportunity," Din countered, ticking his fingers one by one. "No voice in their government. No respect for our customs. Those count for something, Deese." She rolled her eyes at that, but Din continued. "You heard the thanes at the council. The clan is frustrated. I saw Dare earlier at the Ale House. Do you know why we keep calling it the 'Ale House' instead of some fancier name? Because the owner won't let us give it a permanent name. He's convinced that we'll be heading back home, so what's the point? Can you believe that? He's worked there for almost ten years, and he is absolutely convinced it's only a matter of time until we pull up these shallow roots and go back home. And he's not the only one. The clan knows we're not getting a fair shake from the Imps. Just ask Veit how he was received by the Imperial warsmiths. He's one of the smartest dwarfs we know, and they laughed him out of the hall because he didn't have the right pedigree. Seeing the way the Imps treat our clan is like a slap in the face."

"Din save your talk about freedom and honor." Din half rose excitedly at her words, but Diessa stared her older brother down until he sat back down in a visible huff. "All of it means nothing if you're dead. Need I remind you that not a single member of the clan has died to violence since we settled here? We've built new homesteads, new farms, and new lives. We've started to regain our confidence and shake off the trauma of the invasion. Despite their discontent, the clan is making a home here, Din. Surely you see that."

Din squinted up at his sister, his hackles still raised. He retorted with a hint of poorly concealed derision. "What I see is that we're running out of time. Golloch won't take no for an answer next year. When he demands troops, and he will, we'll be forced to give them to him. And Crafanc may not last another winter without aid." Diessa frowned in thought at that. She even nodded imperceptibly in understanding as Din went on. "You say that a person's self-respect and honor don't mean anything if they're dead. But I say that a life without honor and respect isn't one worth living. And the clan agrees with me."

Deese leaned away from the tree, planted her feet more firmly underneath her, and crossed her arms. "Yes, they do. You and Dare have been feeding everyone tales about how good we can have it back in Halpi. As if the Abyssal Dwarfs haven't ravaged the lands and defiled our hold while we've been gone. What you call 'home' may not actually be our 'home' anymore. You would lead them back to a wasteland and call it good."

"No, I would lead us back to our lands. *Our* lands, Deese. Our history. We can drive the Abyssals out, retake our home, clean out the filth, and be our own masters again. We may be safe for now, but we will never be truly free as long as we stay here. Golloch will feed us to his war machine and his ambition until there is no clan left. He will grind us out of existence, and I will be powerless to stop it."

Deese stood defiantly but chewed her lower lip as she considered her brother's words. For a moment, she was swept back to the long march from Llyngyr Cadw. In a flash, she relived memories that she had spent the last few years tamping down.

She remembered the hunger, the exhaustion, the constant fear that they would be caught by the Abyssals, and the terror when they finally were. The demons had come upon them while the clan was marching through a defile along the Ironway, sheer stone cliffs to either side. She saw herself and Brohna, her mother, raising the spirits to defend the refugees, buying time to make good their escape. It took time to summon the largest of their kind, but the smaller spirits could be called within minutes. The earth spirits that the queen raised took the form of the clan ancestors clad in stone and stood fifteen feet tall. They crushed the Abyssal Dwarfs' orc slaves beneath their stone boots, mashing and mangling them to a pulp, and sweeping them aside with long swings of rocky axes. They had held them at bay for what seemed like an eternity but was really only a few hours.

The queen had seen their doom first. A horde of grotesque creatures were rushing down the defile, with their Abyssal Dwarf masters behind them, prodding them on. The bizarre creatures were multi-limbed mutants, half mortal, half demon. They were huge and fast, each one a living nightmare. Their numbers and their frenzy were too great to be stopped, and they would surely overrun Diessa and Brohna. They would wash over them and eventually catch their kinsmen. Her mother, and her elementals, waited until the grotesques were fully engaged. Then with a defiant shout, she gestured wide, and the elementals responded. They brought down the very cliff walls around her, and the Abyssal forces fell and were destroyed in the ensuing avalanche. Diessa had barely escaped, as one of the elementals kneeled down over her, shielding her from the falling debris. She relived the cacophony, the abject terror, and then in the aftermath, the sudden silence. She relived the intense joy and amazement at being alive. And then, as she dug herself free in her memory, she relived the soul-crushing sadness when she realized that her mother was gone.

After a few moments, she came back to herself. "You know I don't agree with your plan, no matter the needs, or how much the clan wants it." Diessa felt her temper rise as she spoke, and her words came out more impassioned with every sentence. "Our mother gave her life to lead us all out of danger. She gave her life so that the clan would survive. And we did survive. We defied the Abyssals and crossed the great chain bridge at Rhyn Dufaris. We barely escaped that day, Din, thanks to you and Daerun. But you lived, and mother didn't. And now you want to lead the clan back into danger? You mock her sacrifice."

Din jumped up excitedly at first but then held still as he let his sister's words wash over him. Deese could see the turmoil on his face as he wrestled with the full implications of his and Dare's plan. To be fair, Diessa knew that her brother was trying to protect the clan as much as she was. She also understood that Din was responding to what the clan wanted, what the clan needed. This wasn't just his idea to regain past glory. The clan ached for their freedom, and Din was trying to give it to them, in a way that fed his hunger and desire to put things right. Dinnidek was trying to find the best path forward for the clan, and he had put them first in all things since he had taken on the mantle of clan chieftain. But in this instance, she was afraid that the clan's desire for freedom was feeding Din's desire to redress the clan's failure. It was a vicious cycle. She just wished that the clan could appreciate the second chance they were given to live a peaceful life.

Dinnidek sighed deeply and locked eyes with his sister.

"Mother wasn't the only one to give her life for us." Diessa's eyes filled with tears as her brother went on, his voice husky with emotion. "Father perished as well. They gave their very lives for the clan, so that we would not just survive, but thrive. Please, Deese, trust me in this. We can't stay here. The clan won't stand for it. And I... we, need to lead them back. I am the chieftain of Clan Daamuz, and to lead is to serve the will of the clan. Dare and I can't do this alone, Deese. We need you."

Diessa ran her sleeve across her face and wiped away the well of tears in her eyes. She took a moment to compose herself, then replied in a low voice. "If it's the will of the clan, then I have no choice. I'll go with them to protect them. And I will be there to protect you, too, my lord." Diessa said Din's title with a wry smile.

Din smiled back. "You too? Dare already 'my lord'ed me earlier. You both know I hate that."

"We know. That's why we do it," she said with a full smile and left the moment of reconciliation alone.

They both stood in the woods, the only sounds of the wind in the branches and the murmur of the surf in the distance. Deese took her brother's hand.

"Be careful, Din. I'll follow you and the clan almost anywhere. If you're all dead set on going home, then I'll be there to advise you to the end. Just please make sure you're doing this for the right reasons. Don't put your personal honor and pride above the clan. I won't stand for that."

Din nodded in understanding and hugged his sister tight in a strong, enduring embrace. Deese felt the emotion well up in her brother, and she hugged him fiercely in return.

CHAPTER 4

"You shall address me as 'My Lord,'" Alborz commanded. The slave orc stared back at him, then quickly averted his eyes. It was too late. Alborz casually backhanded the orc across the face. Even though he was almost two feet shorter, Alborz struck the orc so hard that the slave fell to its knees with a split lip. Blood and spittle spattered over the rich mosaics on the floor of the corridor. Alborz waited patiently while the slave slowly picked himself up off the ground. The orc stood before his master, staring pointedly at the Abyssal Dwarf's boots.

"Who am I?" Alborz asked the slave.

"My lord and Overmaster," the orc grunted in reply. His hand came up to dab at his lip. Alborz 'tsked,' and the orc brought his hand back down obediently to his side.

"And how am I to be addressed?" Alborz continued.

"As my lord... My lord" the orc answered awkwardly.

"Yes. I trust you won't forget it," the Overmaster said as he disdainfully turned his back on the slave.

Alborz made his way down the corridor to his brother's workshop as the orc obediently shuffled behind. It was bad enough that the orc had brought ill news. That would have normally earned it a beating. But to not give Alborz due respect should have been a death sentence. Alborz wondered if he was getting soft after a decade as the lord of Llyngyr Cadw.

There's still time to kill it, he thought to himself. *We don't want to let the slaves think they can get away with that. I'll have to make an example of this one later.*

Alborz looked back at the orc and waited until it looked up before he gave it a reassuring smile. The slave nodded and seemed to look relieved while Alborz grinned wickedly on the inside.

Ten years. It had been ten years since he had led his forces to take Llyngyr Cadw and wipe out Clan Daamuz. Since then, he and his brother had contented themselves with solidifying control over the hold. But recently, he had grown restless, and he longed to be back in the Abyssal Dwarf kingdom of Tragar. If he could return to the seat of Abyssal Dwarf power, he'd be richly rewarded for his deeds during the invasion. But he wouldn't return until he could leave Llyngyr Cadw in good hands. He had been grooming his brother, Zareen, to take over in his absence, but things had been slow. Zareen was a genius and master of his craft, but he lacked the temperament to rule.

The Overmaster and his slave came to the door to the laboratory — or was it a workshop? The answer to that question depended on Zareen's mood, or his latest project, Alborz mused to himself. Alborz politely knocked but didn't wait for confirmation before opening the door and entering the room. The orc stayed outside, where it belonged.

Alborz cocked an eyebrow as his eyes looked about the large room. Apparently, today was a little of both.

His brother must have been busy. Tools were scattered around the place, pulled down from the assortment of orderly wall pegs or shelves where they normally lived. Alborz wandered between the chains hanging from the ceiling as he traversed the room, past a group of tables strewn with half-built mechanical parts; weapons, armor, metal limbs — all within easy reach. Heating elements and alchemical tools were scattered over a quartz table, and a small brazier held something that gave off a sickly green fire.

The right wall was composed almost entirely of a brick oven hewn into the stone of the mountain, where an orc slave pumped a bellows on the oven making the coals within glow an angry red. The room was uncomfortably hot, and Alborz began sweating within a few moments. Zareen stood in one corner of the room turning dials and knobs on a giant machine with numerous coiled wires and a set of cranks. A gnorr, a humanoid rat creature, frantically turned the cranks. A low electric buzz crackled through the air, matching time with the frenzied slave's revolutions and making Alborz feel mildly nauseous. A set of wires led from the machine to a dwarf strapped to a stone table. The dwarf was in a drugged stupor, his head lolling from one side to the other as sweat ran down his face. His left arm was tied off with a tourniquet between the bicep and the elbow, and his hand was ashen, almost blue.

If Zareen noticed his brother, he showed no sign, but Alborz was unfazed. Alborz indulged in a cruel smile as he stood back and watched his brother work. Like most Iron-casters, Zareen was highly intelligent, his mind simultaneously able to juggle multiple trains of thought. But once deep into the complexities of his work, Zareen became intensely focused on the task at hand. Alborz had been continually impressed with his brother's vicious ingenuity. And he admired that Zareen had little qualms about experimenting on any creature he could get his hands on. His brother was bound only by the wickedness of his imagination and the limitations of the tools at hand. He pushed the boundaries of grafting creatures together into new grotesque and twisted shapes. The fact that his creations rarely lived beyond a few ten-days didn't matter much to Alborz. They served their purpose, either as shock troops or raw muscle before they perished.

Zareen tapped the rat-man on the shoulder and signaled for it to stop turning the crank. He then walked over to the dwarf and cinched the straps holding it to the table a little tighter.

"Wouldn't want you to hurt yourself," Zareen said to no one in particular before chuckling to himself.

Even after all these years, Alborz still found the sound of Zareen's relatively high, raspy voice unsettling. He put on thick leather gloves, grabbed one of the copper coils, and wound it around the delirious dwarf's arm above the tourniquet.

"We hook the wire to the chosen one, to ensure the blessing works," he spoke to himself in a sing-song way. Once he was satisfied, he turned back to the rat-man. "When I give you the command, you turn that crank. Understood?"

The gnorr nodded in assent and stared at the chosen dwarf in sick fascination.

Alborz had been lucky enough to bear witness to the procedure dozens of times before. The chosen dwarf was being indoctrinated into the Immortal Guard. He had shown undying loyalty to Alborz and had vowed to serve the Overmaster for the rest of his days. In exchange for those vows, the initiate would be rewarded with almost eternal life. Slowly, over time, his weak flesh would be infused with eldritch magics and replaced with ensorcelled metal. The longer he served, the more he would be encased in living armor, and magical viscera would pump through his veins. Eventually, he would be almost completely free from the frailty of his mortal form, and if he was injured, would either magically regenerate or would be repaired instead of healed. The Immortal Guard were the most elite of Alborz's warriors and the unstoppable backbone of his army.

Zareen shuffled back to one of the tables and grabbed a pair of smokey goggles and a leather bit with a long strap. He donned the goggles but left them resting on his forehead underneath his blond hair. Zareen came back to the table and fastened the leather gag to the chosen dwarf.

"Don't want you chewing your tongue," he said as he finished. He patted the unconscious dwarf playfully on the cheek as he went back to grab the next set of components.

Alborz could never really tell if Zareen was truly concerned for his subjects' safety or not. Zareen adored most of his creations the way a master painter would a magnificent landscape. He was proud of his work but had no regard for most of the creatures he used, treating them as nothing more than raw materials. It was only when he worked on other dwarfs that he seemed to show genuine concern, even reverence, for his subjects. Dwarfs were the height of creation, and to be able to enhance something that was already close to perfect was the highest honor.

Zareen returned from the table with a small vial of foamy pink liquid and a larger tin of thick chalky green paste, placing them into his leather tool pouch. Zareen called out to the slave orc by the oven, "You! Take your position!"

The orc obediently stopped working the bellows, picked up a wicked looking axe, carved with runes that glowed evilly in the firelight, and stood at attention next to the unconscious dwarf. Zareen unlatched the straps from the dwarf's ashen arm and pulled it out perpendicular to the dwarf's body, off the stone table.

Zareen held the dwarf's hand almost lovingly, his other hand positioned at the elbow. He looked down on the chosen dwarf with a benign look as his eyes began to widen in excitement.

"Ariagful, the Flame That Devours," Zareen named the Abyssal goddess of fire. "I call upon you to bear witness and to bless your chosen faithful! Stoke his desire! Grant him the strength to smite your foes! Grant him the endurance to faithfully serve your people!" Zareen's voice became more urgent and frantic until his screams echoed off the walls. "Let him be an instrument of your will and a testament to your power! Take this sacrifice and deem him worthy!"

With that, the orc raised the axe high, poised above the initiate's outstretched arm, and swung down with all its considerable might. Zareen screamed in ecstasy as the axe descended, cleaving straight through flesh, muscle, tendon, and bone. The chosen dwarf jolted out of his stupor and wailed in reply. The fires in the oven flared hungrily to life, and a gout of flame erupted out into the room. The arm fell to the ground with a squelch. Alborz thought it may have even twitched for a second, or was that a trick of the light from the fire? Zareen pulled the pink liquid from his pouch and poured it on the arm as it lay on the ground. He said a quick prayer of sacrifice to Ariagful.

"Blessed be the mother in her power. Blessed be the fruits of her anger. She cleanses the world with fire and ash and leaves room for perfection to grow."

He then turned his attention to the chosen dwarf. Zareen pulled out the tin of paste and began slathering it over the stump. The cut had been clean, and within seconds, the magical ointment staunched the wound, though it left the bones and tendons exposed. Satisfied, he went back to the workbench and retrieved a metal prosthetic arm that ended in a fully articulated mechanical hand and a flared forearm guard. It had fasteners that connected at the shoulder, with pins meant to penetrate along the entire length of the upper arm. The arm was elegant, but Alborz knew that it was heavy, and his brother breathed a little heavier while bringing it to the stone table. Zareen resumed his workmanlike manner, and within moments, he connected the metal arm to the chosen dwarf's shoulder. It took longer to fasten the bone to the metal arm, as each tendon had to be stretched and connected into place. Zareen focused intently, and Alborz could tell that his brother's entire world consisted of the six-inch square section where the arms connected. The chosen dwarf had mercifully passed out in shock, and he gave no resistance. Only once had Alborz seen the subject not succumb to the trauma of the ritual, wriggling and cursing until Zareen had been forced to inject a sleeping serum. The Overmaster had made that Immortal Guard one of his personal bodyguards as a reward.

Once all the connections were completed, Zareen turned back to the rat-man. "Turn it! Fast now. Don't tarry. Quickly now. Quickly."

The gnorr obeyed with a wild energy, and within moments the wire began to glow hot, the end gave off slight sparks that singed the dwarf's skin. A lucid dwarf would have screamed in agony, but in its current state, the chosen only grunted and writhed. Within seconds, thin inlaid lines on the black metal arm began to glow, from dull red to bright orange, then angry yellow. The electric buzz of the machine reverberated off the walls, and it droned so deeply that it washed out all other sound. Alborz felt it more than heard it, and it threatened to push all thought from his mind. When the lines shone with a raging white light, Zareen finally signaled the rat-man to stop.

All at once, the room was almost completely silent. The only sounds were the exhausted gasping from the gnorr and the ragged breathing of the newly formed Immortal Guard. Zareen inspected his work one more time. He picked up the metal arm and bent it at the elbow, the wrist, and the fingers. Satisfied, he bent down and carefully picked up the Immortal Guard's severed arm. With his head bowed, he slowly walked to the oven, and with a silent prayer, threw the limb in. The fire within devoured the arm greedily, leaving nothing but ash. Zareen wiped his hands off on a clean rag from his workbench and dismissed the two slaves with an imperious wave of his hand.

Once the slaves were gone, Alborz approached the table and ran his fingers lightly over the metal arm, which still glowed and pulsed with an inner fire. Now that the ritual was over, the heavy arm would feel light and natural to the Immortal Guard, so long as he kept his vow. Zareen stood next to him and gently uncoiled the wire from the flesh of the Immortal Guard's upper arm. He took off the leather gag and gave another loving caress to the sleeping dwarf as he shuffled back to the work bench. Zareen began placing the ritual implements back in their proper place, and with his back to Alborz, he broke the silence.

"What news, Alborz? You seem preoccupied."

The question took Alborz off guard. The Overmaster looked at Zareen's back and grimaced in annoyance, showing emotions that he never indulged in with anyone else. Alborz was always cool and calm, and he prided himself on his disciplined facade. In return, Zareen always had a way of seeing past that façade to know when Alborz was preoccupied with some trouble or other. Zareen may have been engrossed in his work, but he was hardly oblivious when it came to his brother. Now that he'd asked the question, Zareen wouldn't let Alborz lightly brush it off. He would dig and dig until he got an answer. Alborz couldn't outwait him either. He needed to be present for the end of the ritual. He normally didn't like to talk of important matters during this holy time, but there was nothing to be done until the Immortal Guard awoke. It could take minutes; it could take hours. He sighed, composed himself, and against his inclination answered, "I am thinking of returning to Tragar."

Zareen turned to face his brother as a flash of confusion stormed across his eyes. He composed himself with a visible effort of will. "That is surprising. May I ask why?"

"Yes. Yes, you may," Alborz answered as he peered at a shelf crammed with glass vials filled with a chaotic smattering of alchemical ingredients and specimens. He took a deep breath before going on. This was the first time he had put his thoughts on the matter into words. "I have spent ten years in Llyngyr Cadw. In that time, we've gained glory and riches, and made ourselves the undisputed masters of this land. But in the end, we are the masters of only a single, small, insignificant part of the mongrel dwarf empire. I want more, Zareen. We ran a flawless campaign during the invasion and have had constant success since then, due to my brilliance and your ingenuity. But I have been stuck here in this backwater, far away from the center of power. If I return to Tragar, I could claim the honors that are my due and ascend to my rightful place as a high lord of the Abyss."

The brothers stood in silence for almost a minute before Zareen spoke. "I am not surprised. I knew that you were unsatisfied here. As you said, we have succeeded at everything we've put our hands to. We've conquered these lands, and now they seem small to us. It is natural that you would want more." Zareen fell silent, and the only sound was the breathing of the unconscious Immortal Guard. "I have to say, I will miss this place. My work has advanced by leaps and bounds the last few years, due to the lasting peace that you've brought here."

"Yes, but the same peace that has made you successful is slowly killing me. We both know that I am not built for peace. My mind craves conflict, craves new challenges, new battles." Alborz had never thought of himself that way. He certainly never articulated out loud what drove him. But when he said it, he knew it was undeniably true. Alborz felt truly alive during a fight, any fight, of any sort. "The battlefield can be the mountains of Halpi or the political courts in Zarak, makes no difference, but I need a worthy opponent. Not the feeble mongrel dwarfs."

Zareen considered his brother's words for a few moments before going on, "I must ask, are you sure you're not just bored?"

Alborz smiled at that. "Of course I'm bored, Zareen. That's the point. Do you remember when we were mustering for the invasion? We planned to fight the mongrel dwarfs, gain glory and honor and riches, and then return to Tragar as princes and lords. We relentlessly prepared ourselves for a long grueling fight against a strong and cagey adversary that would test our mettle and our intellect. And what happened? We were so successful that it took less than one season to completely break them, to drive them over the sea to cower, destitute, in Imperial lands. We completely gutted them, and they fled for their very lives. There wasn't a single worthy foe among them. It was too easy. That was supposed to be my time to show the world my greatness. But there is no glory in defeating such a weak and pitiful enemy. Ironically, my opportunity was completely wasted because we were too successful."

Zareen stared into the fire of the kiln, seemingly contemplating the implications of Alborz's words. Moments passed, but Alborz stoically waited, allowing his brother's mind to grind through the possibilities. Finally, Zareen's eyes came back into focus. He looked at Alborz and nodded to himself. "When do we leave?"

Alborz shook his head slowly. "*We* aren't going anywhere. *I* am going back to Tragar. You will stay here as the new master of Llyngyr Cadw."

Zareen's eyes widened in surprise. "Me? Why me? Don't you want me at your side?"

"Of course I do, but I need you here, Zareen. We need a power base to work from if I'm to be successful, and I trust you to hold Llyngyr Cadw in my absence." Zareen started to say something, but Alborz interrupted him. "You said it yourself, Zareen, you're thriving here. Out here, away from the jealous eyes of the other Iron-casters, you've been free to run any experiments you like, without them stealing your ideas for themselves. With a little more time, you're set to become as well renowned as Dravak Dalken." Alborz invoked the name of the greatest living Iron-caster, a true mad genius who wielded science and arcane sorcery like no other, knowing the effect it would have on his brother. "I will be leaving you a land under our complete control. You will keep our power base here while I establish our rightful claims back in Tragar."

Zareen considered the idea, but Alborz could tell his brother wasn't comfortable with it.

"I understand your desire," Zareen protested, "but it's very rare for an Iron-caster to lead a hold."

Alborz answered with a hint of growing annoyance at his brother's objections. "Yes, but it's not unheard of. My forces will follow you in my absence. Between the slaves and the abominations, most of them are your creations anyway. You have the intelligence and the skill. You can rule, Zareen."

Alborz didn't totally believe that last part. Zareen certainly had intellect and skill, but he lacked the temperament to rule. Zareen was extremely intelligent and could work out problems faster than Alborz. It made Zareen an excellent Iron-caster. But once he found a workable solution, it became the only solution. Zareen's mind careened from insight to insight wildly, and thoughts turned to certainty then to action in the blink of an eye. But he never bothered to reflect on things. He also took things personally. If something bad happened to their forces, it happened to Zareen. In contrast, Alborz took time to look at a problem from all angles. Where Zareen was tempestuous, Alborz was cold and calculating. Alborz only acted after he'd exhausted every possibility in his mind. That introspective tendency had saved the brothers multiple times from Zareen's rash outbursts. Since taking Llyngyr Cadw, Alborz had only grown more cautious while his brother grew more rash.

His ability isn't the problem, he thought to himself. *If I could just get Zareen to take the long view, I could leave tomorrow with no worries. But I can't wait for him to change.*

Just then, the Immortal Guard stirred. The brothers shifted, one on either side of the table. The dwarf opened his eyes groggily, taking in the room in a haze. He flexed his new arm and brought it up to scratch his cheek. In a flash of realization, he looked down upon it with a look of wonder. Before the guard could say anything, Alborz reached down, grabbed the Immortal Guard's chin, and forced him to gaze into the Overmaster's eyes.

"Blessed of Ariagful, who do you serve?" Alborz intoned the last part of the ritual.

The Immortal Guard locked his gaze on Alborz and rasped, "I serve the lord of Llyngyr Cadw, body and soul, may he reign forever."

"May the Lord of Llyngyr Cadw reign forever!" Zareen recited. "May Ariagful fill you with strength, endurance, and desire to serve for all of his days."

"May Ariagful bless my lord," the guard rasped, "and by so doing, bless me for all eternity."

"Yes," Alborz smiled wickedly, "let it be so."

CHAPTER 5

The wind blew in great gusts that shook the branches of the surrounding trees. *Cold for this time of year,* Rhyss thought to himself. *It's late in spring for Winter to keep her grip.*

Though the wind bordered on bitter cold, Rhyss was sheltered from the worst of it, hidden between the trunks of some fallen trees. He pulled his olive-green cloak a little tighter around him and glanced up at the sky. Looking straight up through the trees was disorienting. The late afternoon light filtered its way through the green canopy and gave the earth a surreal quality. The tree trunks swayed slowly in the wind like the tentacles of some giant sea creature. In contrast, the leaves buzzed and vibrated frenetically like a million little creatures wriggling in their death throes. It made Rhyss think of the fickle menace of the sea. Rhyss hated being on a ship, and each time he and his rangers had made the trip across the High Sea of Bari, he'd kept a white-knuckled grip on the railing.

If things go to plan, I'll never have to be on a ship again, thank the ancestors.

The rustling of the leaves drowned out all other sounds, making it impossible to be heard above a shout. He and his rangers had positioned themselves in a long cordon so that each one could see a comrade on either side. They communicated with each other using hand signals and facial expressions. They were used to operating in silence for hours, sometimes days, so the noise didn't affect them much. Today, it would be a help.

He and his rangers had been hunting the orc patrol for a few days, and Rhyss knew the beasts had camped nearby the last time they came this way. He had studied the movements of the patrols over the winter and into the spring, and he knew their patterns and how far afield the orcs would go. If he was right, his quarry would be arriving this afternoon on their way back to Llyngyr Cadw. His soldiers just had to lay low until then.

Despite being in Halpi for months, the rangers had only encountered the Abyssals and their slaves a few times. At first, Rhyss had given his warriors strict orders to avoid contact at all costs. They had relied on stealth and guile to keep them hidden from the enemy. Rhyss had worked with Kilvar Helgwin and his rangers from Crafanc to prepare the area for the coming invasion by hiding supplies all along the planned invasion route. Sealed barrels full of hardtack and dried meat were stashed away in caves and hollows within the foothills of the mountains. There were also medical supplies, weapons, even whiskey and tobacco. Most troops could only carry about five days of rations with them, and usually only two days of water. Thanks to the rangers, when the time came, the invading army would be well-fed and supplied as they marched inland to Llyngyr Cadw.

It won't be long now, Rhyss mused. When he led his rangers into Halpi, he was told that the invasion would happen on the last full moon before the summer solstice, just over one moon cycle away. It couldn't occur soon enough.

Rhyss had borne witness to how ravaged and barren this once fruitful land had become. The Abyssal Dwarfs were parasites. They were nothing more than vampires, sucking the earth dry of all its bounty. They didn't plant crops. They overhunted the wild game. They looted everything they could with no thought for tomorrow. They were a wildfire that devoured everything in its path, leaving a wake of desolation. Rhyss reviled the orc and ratmen slaves for what they'd done. But he had deep and abiding hatred for his traitorous kin, the Abyssal Dwarfs. They were walking abominations, living mockeries of all that it was to be a dwarf. They served nothing but their vanity and their gold lust. They gave no regard for their family, for their clan, for anyone else. They turned their backs on dwarfen society and cavorted with demons. They bred the orcs and ratmen as slaves. And they had destroyed his home. Their slaves may have done most of the work through weight of numbers, but the Abyssal Dwarfs ordered it all. If Rhyss had his way, he'd wipe every one of them off the face of Pannithor.

But for now, he'd hunt down their slaves. With almost a month to go, most of the supplies were prepared and hidden. The next part of Rhyss' plan was to kill as many patrols as he could and lead the Abyssal forces northward, up into the mountains. Hopefully, he'd pull some of the enemy away from the planned landing spot on the Dewbrock Plain. If he was lucky, he'd link up with the Worm Lord, who was rumored to be hiding in the area. Rhyss hadn't laid eyes on him or his dwarfen warriors yet, but he'd seen the aftermath of their handy work. Clean, efficient, and brutal, the Worm Lord was the righteous hand of Fulgria on earth. Rhyss had spent some time trying to track him and his dwarfs down but came up empty. The ranger shook his head in admiration at the skills required to evade detection, year after year.

Out of the corner of his eye, Rhyss caught a swift signal from the ranger to his right. Someone was coming. Rhyss snapped to attention and stared intently at the area where his comrade had pointed. The howling wind was the only source of sound and motion within the woods, but within moments, a dwarf could be seen slinking along from tree to tree, clad in a deep brown cloak and green leathers. His face was blackened, along with all the metal he carried. His crossbow and weapons were all strapped down to his sides so they didn't swing or make any unnecessary noise. If Rhyss hadn't known what to look for, his eyes would have glazed over the ranger as just another shadow.

The ranger lightly walked among the undergrowth, barely grazing against the leaves of the plants he passed. He came within Rhyss' direct line of sight and pulled back his hood enough to expose his face.

Ah, I should have known it would be Meick. Best eyes in the company. Makes up for his ear. With the hood back, Rhyss could see the great scar that ran up the side of Meick's face and ended in a barren patch of skin where his ear should have been, the price he'd paid at the battle of Rhyn Dufaris repelling a group of ratmen. The healers had done what they could, but the skin remained puckered and red. *At least he still had his head. Three inches to the left and the ratman's axe would have ended Meick for good.*

Rhyss signaled to Meick to report. The one-eared dwarf positioned his hands close to his body to hide his movements from anyone who happened to be watching and gestured deftly to Rhyss in small, precise gestures.

Orcs here. Setting up camp. Near stream. Thirty. Gores. They are careless. Four sentries. We can ambush when ready.

Rhyss nodded in understanding and gestured back. *Take your fist. Hunt sentries. I'll follow. We attack from this side.*

Meick nodded, threw up his hood, and dashed off, tapping one of the dwarfs he passed on the way and signaling him to follow. The rangers were organized in groups of five called fists, comprised of four rangers and a leader who could operate independently if needed. Rhyss waited five minutes, counting out the time on his fingers, and then signaled to the next ranger in line to begin moving toward the stream. Like ghosts, the rangers moved slowly through the woods, up and over the intervening hill between their position and the stream. Rhyss couldn't see the orcs yet through the dense woods, and he couldn't hear them because of the rush of wind in the leaves. Of course, that meant that the orcs couldn't hear the rangers either. A lifetime spent above ground had given Rhyss and his fellow rangers insights into warfare that most dwarfen warriors would never have. Fighting out in the trees and the mountains was different than battle in the close and twisting caves most dwarfs were used to.

A ranger to Rhyss' left signaled to him. *Two sentries dead. All clear.*

Rhyss nodded in understanding and sent the message down the line. A minute later, the signal came back to him that the other two sentries were accounted for. Rhyss waited another minute to see if there was any commotion from down in the camp.

No sign. Good. It's working.

After a moment, he held his fist up in the air. The gesture was mirrored by the dwarfs nearest him, and it rippled out to the farthest dwarf in the company. Rhyss' heart started beating faster in response. He counted to ten and then opened his hand and dropped it down, palm flat to the ground.

With that, the rangers to either side of him began moving down the hill. Rhyss drew two hand axes from his belt and joined them. Like a landslide, the rangers slowly began picking their way down the hillside between the foliage, gathering speed as they went. The wind blew strong on this side of the slope and the trees swayed, their trunks groaning under the strain. Within fifty paces, the camp came into view. The wind covered the ranger's approach so well that even the gores didn't notice them. The orcs were as careless as Meick had said. While a few were lighting their campfires, the rest lounged about. None appeared to give a second thought to the danger surrounding them. The orcs were the masters of Halpi. What did they need to be afraid of? Rhyss smiled as the pre-battle jitters became a fire that arose in his belly.

In the midst of battle, Rhyss always felt disconnected from his body. He stopped thinking and ran on instinct until the fight was over. Get your brain out of the way and let the countless hours of training do its work. When Rhyss was within twenty paces from the camp, his focus tightened down to a single campfire with a group of three orcs around it. One of the orcs happened to look up, and its eyes widened in surprise as it saw Rhyss, then terror as it took in the rest of the rangers storming down the hillside. It yelled a warning as Rhyss left the trees and came to the flat open ground near the stream. The orc fumbled for its sword, but it was only half drawn when Rhyss reached it and swung his hand axe sideways into the orc's abdomen with a sickening crunch. The orc dropped to its knees as Rhyss abandoned his axe in the orc's gut and charged on.

An orc stood on the other side of the fire pit with a stolen dwarfen breastplate strapped to its chest. It stared in panic at its fallen friend, then in doomed realization at the ground where it had left its sword. Within two steps, Rhyss tossed the second axe to his right hand and buried it into the orc's unprotected groin, up and under its breastplate.

The third orc had recovered from its surprise and, squealing a curse, ran toward him with its sword held aloft. One, two steps, and the orc was on him, bringing the sword straight down in a vicious overhand cut. In one smooth motion, Rhyss pulled the axe out of the second orc's groin and pivoted away from the sword stroke on his left foot. The sword thumped harmlessly into the ground. Rhyss continued the motion, whirled around, and buried the hand axe into the back of the orc's knee. It dropped onto its face with a high-pitched scream of agony. Rhyss silenced it with a sharp axe strike on the back of its neck.

With the orcs disabled, Rhyss' attention widened out to the larger campsite. His rangers were pressing their advantage, stepping over orc bodies that littered the ground. Some of the enemy made a break for their mounts, but Meick had positioned his fist on the far side of the camp. They stood up from a dense area of foliage across the stream and shot the orcs down with their crossbows. Their foes fell, some dying instantly from the bolts, while others twisted on the ground in agony. None of them made it to their mounts. A few of the gores had been hit as well and squealed in pain and terror. The orcs that remained alive had rallied near the stream, standing in the water in a small cluster. They were hemmed in by dwarfs on all sides, looking around frantically for escape that wasn't there. They bellowed their battle cries but were rooted where they stood in the cold running stream.

They aren't going anywhere, Rhyss thought to himself. He quickly glanced down at the first two orcs, both writhing in the grass. He finished them off with quick chops of his axe and then headed to the stream.

Rhyss again took stock of the situation. The half dozen orcs continued yelling empty defiance at the dwarfs. If they hadn't acted by now, Rhyss knew they never would.

"Meick, take your fist and look for stragglers. Banwn, have your fist ready their crossbows. Everyone else, keep your axes out in case the orcs find some courage."

Meick nodded and dashed off with his men. Banwn's rangers took out their crossbows and pointed them at the enemy, while the dwarfs on the far side of the orcs moved out of the line of fire. They had danced this dance before.

It took a moment for one of the orcs to realize what was going on. It reacted quickly as if to charge the dwarfs, but it was tripped up by the uneven ground and fell down into the water. The rest of its fellows stayed put, and the orcs and dwarfs watched the orc scrabble around on all fours, trying to stand up while still holding its sword. It was almost comical. The stillness made the brief struggle seem much longer. Just as the orc was standing up, Rhyss nonchalantly stepped forward a few paces and brought his axe up into the orc's chin in an underhand swing. The orc's head snapped back, and it fell dead into the water. Blood mixed with the stream and ran around the feet of the remaining orcs, still paralyzed with fear.

Banwn laughed, breaking the enemy from their trance. They rushed forward as one, but it was too late. Before the orcs could take two steps, Banwn and his warriors filled them with crossbow bolts, and they fell into the water. The rangers' hand axes finished the rest in seconds.

Twenty-five, Twenty-six, Rhyss counted to himself. *I make twenty-seven. Meick left with his whole fist of men, so we're all accounted for.*

Rhyss exhaled in relief. None of his fellow dwarfs were dead or even seriously injured. He always held his breath right after the battle, bracing himself for the aftermath. Luckily, the plan had worked and they took this whole patrol with no casualties. No need for somber songs around the campfire tonight. He hadn't always had good fortune. He had forty under his direct command when they first arrived in Halpi.

With practiced efficiency, the rangers cleaned the camp and finished off any wounded orcs that were still alive. They killed the remaining gores and piled their bodies up in a heap in the middle of the clearing, away from the stream. They pulled a couple gore carcasses to butcher for food, and they put the orc bodies on top of the pile so they could be seen by anyone who wandered by. Rhyss turned to Banwn, who was still chuckling to himself.

"It was pretty funny, wasn't it?" Rhyss asked him. "That orc just splashing away like a fish in the dirt? Just flopping around."

Banwn nodded and his chuckle turned into a full-throated laugh that spoke of both humor and relief. Some of the other rangers joined in, and the clearing was soon filled with laughter. Rhyss chuckled along, keeping an eye out for Meick and his men.

He didn't have to wait long. Still out of sight, Rhyss heard the one-eared dwarf singing a dwarfen tavern song loud enough to be heard over the wind. He smiled. Meick always sang right after a battle. It was his way of getting out the post-battle jitters, and it told Rhyss that everything was clear. Meick's song ended as he approached Rhyss.

"We found one that slipped away during the fight. Shot him down easily. The rest of the woods are clear of any trace of orcs."

Rhyss nodded.

"Excellent work, Meick." Rhyss raised his voice so the whole company could hear. "Let's gather up whatever goods we can and get moving. I want to hit the next patrol in a few days."

The rangers all replied confirmation and began filling their waterskins in the stream and looting the orc bodies. Most of the orcs' belongings were of poor quality, and their food rotten and inedible. However, occasionally one of them would have stolen dwarf goods to be reclaimed. One of the rangers called in excitement when he found an old flask of dwarfen whiskey in a saddlebag. Excitement turned to disappointment when he was reminded that an orc had put their mouth on it. The ranger regretfully ditched the flask in disgust.

Rhyss picked up a large flat piece of shale from the stream bed and carried it to the base of the mound of bodies. He used another rock to scrawl a dwarfen 'R,' a picture of the moon's phase, a few numbers, and an arrow on it. Once satisfied, he looked one last time at the clearing and nodded in satisfaction. Rhyss would let the dwarfs rest here for an hour, then they'd move north and west along the stream. It would bring them closer to Llyngyr Cadw and give them more patrols to kill. They had just over three ten-days to draw the Abyssal Dwarfs away, then double back to meet the invasion force when they landed on the Dewbrock Plain.

Hopefully, Din and Dare got the ships they needed from the Imperials.

Rhyss had confidence they'd pull through. He couldn't wait to be reunited with his clan when the invasion force arrived. But Rhyss would take advantage of the time he had. He intended to cause a world of trouble between now and then.

CHAPTER 6

"Well," Din said as he gestured out toward the dozens of boats anchored just offshore, "it's not how I pictured it, but I'm impressed, Dare."

It was a motley armada composed of mostly wide and stable cog trading vessels, but there were a few sleek sloops and even a small warship in the mix. None of the ships flew the same banners, so the harbor was a riot of different colored sails, hulls, and pennants waving bravely in the breeze.

Daerun smiled in satisfaction. "Yep, it looks like a right mess, but it will do. You always wanted the Imps to help, but I figured it was a fool's errand. So, I went on my own and found a fleet for us instead."

Din shook his head at Dare's words. He had never seen so many boats together in one place, but to call this motley collection of ships a 'fleet' was pretty generous. Still, the brothers had been hiring dwarfen traders to transport goods to Innyshwylt for the past few months in preparation for the invasion, but this was metal of a higher purity.

Dinnidek clapped his brother on the shoulder and grinned with genuine joy. They were one step closer to going home. He thought back to the day the clan first arrived on these shores. Din and his siblings had set about building houses, digging wells, laying out fields for planting, and widening out the nearby mines. It was Veit who saw the potential of the sea. The clan had no idea how to build boats, but they knew stone. Within a few ten-days, Veit had begun laying out the stone jetty with Diessa and Joro. After a year, they had established a safe harbor and enough mooring space to dock eight ships. Trade had picked up quickly and brought with it a level of prosperity to the clan that Din hadn't thought possible.

Damn Golloch and his greed, Din thought to himself. *We could have made a good home here.*

The brothers made their way down the causeway, Tordek a respectable distance behind, and headed toward the ships moored along the piers that protruded like fingers out into the water. One ship dominated the little harbor. It was an actual warship, taller than the other ships, with a full panoply of cannon and sails. There was only one real naval power in the area besides the Imperial Dwarfs, and that was the Hegemony of Basilea; and while the humans and dwarfs had a tentative alliance, Daerun wasn't that big of a fool... Was he?

Din pointed to the brig and looked sideways at Dare. "You hired Basilean help? Golloch will have a fit of apoplexy."

"If I thought that would do it, I would have done it sooner," Dare answered with a smile. "Nope, those aren't Basileans. But that's the captain's ship."

Dinnidek's eyebrows knitted in consternation. Anyone with enough money could put on a big hat and call themselves a captain, but that didn't make someone a leader. These sailors were opportunistic and untrustworthy smugglers at best. An ugly thought occurred to Din. *Oh gods, what if they're not dwarfs?* "So, you're not bothered by the fact that these are pirates?"

"Not really," Dare answered. He stopped and faced his brother. "It's a little late for second thoughts now, isn't it?" he asked playfully. "Din, you gave this responsibility to me. I performed a miracle in just a few ten-days."

"Well," Din corrected his younger brother, "you did say that you'd been working on it since the first frost. So, technically you had more than a few ten-days."

Dare looked exaggeratedly aggrieved, though his eyes twinkled playfully.

"Don't cloud the issue with facts. Listen, I was completely justified in my lack of faith with the Imperials. So there." Dare pointed out to the fleet for emphasis. "We have enough Free Dwarf trade ships to get our entire clan over the High Sea."

"No, it's not that. It's just..."

"It's just what?"

Din looked slightly sheepish. "They're pirates, Dare. They make a living from stealing. Aren't you afraid that they'll double-cross us once we get out to sea? What if they turn on us? *They're pirates!*" Din threw up his hands for emphasis.

"So, what if they do? We're warriors." Daerun gave Din a maddeningly confident wink and continued down the wharf. Din shook his head in exasperation and followed him. "Anyway, it's not like the whole fleet is full of pirates. Most of them are Free Dwarf traders who are happy to help us. I hired a group of smugglers to guide us to the best landing spot. I vetted the captain and the crew. They come highly recommended by everyone I spoke to. You know how we've been running goods to Clan Helgwin? That's one of the ships that's been doing it. They've never been caught, never had to ditch their cargo, and always smuggled their goods on time. They are the best there is."

"Well, that's good. We definitely can't be late this time. We have a rendezvous to keep."

One moon cycle away from the landing date. In the next three ten-days, they had to relocate the clan to a temporary camp on Innyshwylt, prep for the landing, and then proceed with the invasion. From there, they would meet up with Rhyss and the forces from Clan Helgwin, and march on Llyngyr

Cadw.

The jetty widened out with enough space to offload cargo. Carts, piled high with crates of food and goods for the trip, were lined up in an orderly row along this section. A few dozen dwarfs gathered around the empty carts, talking amongst themselves. The dwarfs were dressed for travel in well-worn clothes and hooded capes of green and gold. They carried long rifles, each one a master-crafted work of art. Din noticed one that had a stock carved to look like a dragon, with the barrel of the gun protruding from its open jaws. The gun barrel had been tempered in the fires to glow with a bluish sheen and etched to give the impression of a stream of fire erupting from the dragon's mouth. From a distance, Din could tell that these dwarfs carried themselves with the confidence and easy manner of veterans.

"Who are they?" he asked Daerun.

"I had some extra money of my own," Daerun said with a hint of pride, "and I figured that it wouldn't hurt to take out insurance. You know that we'll be short on cannon because of the trip overseas, and we may have a hard time transporting artillery quickly over land. So, I hired a group of sharpshooters. They've served time abroad fighting up north, and they've worked for the traders in the area guarding caravans."

Dinnidek slowed down and took in the dwarfs with a new, critical eye. On second look, he noticed how some of them had been keeping an eye on him and his brother as they approached. Their gear was in perfect condition, and the rifle firing mechanisms looked shiny and well-oiled. Their packs were arrayed in orderly lines, ten to a row, and none of the rifles were laying on the ground. He couldn't help but nod in satisfaction at their discipline and professionalism.

The owner of the dragon rifle had been watching Dinnidek rate the riflemen, and he approached as Din nodded. "So, we pass your test, I hope?"

He was relatively tall, blond, dark blue eyes, and his beard closely cropped, coming down just to his collarbone, which was odd for a dwarf. Like his fellows, he was dressed in a green cloak with gold brocade around the edge. His leathers were stained green and tan, and he carried a satchel with a journal and writing implements peeking out. He spoke with an Imperial accent, his words short and clipped, with emphasis on some of the consonants, in contrast to the Free Dwarf dialect with its longer vowels and more lilting cadence.

"Greetings, Lord Daerun," the rifleman addressed Dare with a nod before extending his hand to Dinnidek. Tordek stood closer to Din in response. "Allow me to introduce myself. I am Rorik Baranu, captain of the Green Wyverns. You must be Lord Daamuz."

Din obliged Rorik with a strong handshake, which was heartily returned. "Pleasure to meet you, Rorik. And yes, your soldiers are very impressive. My brother says that you and your band are professionals. Where have you served?"

Rorik smiled at the praise. "I formed the Wyverns when we had that little issue with the Abyss a decade ago. Found that demons react the same way to bullets that most things do. Since then, we've been traveling around, making a name for ourselves up in Ardovikia. We've even done some work for Golloch's nephew Rordin out west."

"Impressive," Din said. "If I may ask, what makes you better than my units of Ironwatch riflemen?"

"Riflemen, you say?" Rorik's voice got louder so that the other Wyverns could hear. "You call your gunners riflemen, but do you see these long rifles we carry?" Rorik gestured forcefully at his long rifle as he spoke, emphasizing each point with a shake of his finger. "Each one is a masterwork of technology. They shoot as far as a cannon, and the rifling in the barrels makes us far more accurate than any of your Ironwatch. We use ammunition that can punch through any armor. We can cut down units of knights and monsters before they can get close."

At this, the other Wyverns nodded in appreciation, and a few of them called out 'yes' in response.

"We can kill enemy commanders during a battle, cutting the head from the snake. My sharpshooters have the eyes of hawks and are as steady as the mountains. Your cannons and Ironwatch are blunt hammers, Lord Daamuz, but my marksmen are scalpels."

Din waited a moment to make sure Rorik was finished before responding.

"That's excellent, Master Rorik. I stand corrected. My brother and I are honored to have you with us." Din smiled graciously then turned to address his brother. "So, what are the terms of the agreement?"

Dare replied, but Din noticed that his brother kept eye contact with Rorik while he spoke. "Rorik and his Wyverns will fight for us, under our command, until we retake Llyngyr Cadw or until the three Daamuz siblings are dead. Did I get that right?"

Rorik nodded. "That's correct. We'll help you kill the Abyssals and retake your home. Half paid up front and the other half upon completion of the quest."

Din squinted his eyes at that. "Pretty confident in yourself, Master Rorik? I'm surprised you didn't want all of the money up front."

To be fair, Din was also relieved that they only wanted half the money. It made it easier to keep Rorik and his troops loyal if they had money on the line. He was momentarily taken aback by this line of thought. When did he stop trusting everyone? The answer came quickly. When he became responsible for the entire clan. The thought was unsettling.

Rorik's face became all business. "Lord Daamuz, if I may, my sharpshooters and I are the very best there is. If I didn't think we could help deliver you and your clan to your ancestral home, I wouldn't have taken the job. I also must confess that this will only add to our growing reputation. I hope to become so well-known among your people that the Wyverns can secure more contracts with your Free Dwarf kin. It also helped that Lord Daerun offered an enticing price."

Din glanced sidelong at Daerun as if to say, 'how high a price is an enticing price?' Dare gave a tiny shrug in response, and Dinnidek turned back to Rorik.

"As I said before, we are grateful that you've decided to join us. I look forward to talking more with you over the coming days. In the meantime, please excuse my brother and I. We have an appointment with the captain."

Rorik bowed to Dinnidek. "Of course, my lord. The pleasure is mine. I look forward to giving our demonic kin the what-for." With that, Rorik turned on his heel and sauntered back to his men.

"Well, what do you think?" Daerun said, turning from the mercenaries and back to his brother.

"Has a high opinion of himself, doesn't he?" opined Tordek.

"Seems to," said Dinnidek. "But if he's half as good as he says, we'll be lucky to have him."

"We'll see," Tordek stated in his monotone. "Thunder makes all the noise, but lightning does the work."

"Yes, Tordek," replied Daerun. "We all know that you're lightning incarnate."

Din chuckled despite himself as Tordek glared at Dare's back. The guard took the opportunity to give the brothers space as they proceeded toward the ships.

Now that they were closer, Dinnidek was taken aback at the size of the massive brig. He had little experience with ships. Most of the ones that he had seen in Estacarr were small cogs or trading ships, and he hadn't been on a boat since the harried flight from Rhyn Dufaris almost a decade ago. At that time, he had been crammed onto a small longboat that clung to the massive chainway as it crossed the Great Cataract. He'd never seen a ship this tall. The sails and the masts reached up to the sky like the trunks of giant trees. The sides of the ship were immense, even taller on the fore and aft like a pair of twin fortresses. They towered over the dock and shielded the jetty from the mid-morning sun.

And this is a smaller warship, he thought in wonder. Traders had spoken of truly huge Imperial dwarf dreadnaughts. *Shame we couldn't have gotten a few of those, but you can't find ore without a pickaxe.*

At this distance, Dinnidek could see that what he'd taken as Basilean decorations from afar had been subtly replaced by dwarfen iconography. Din craned his neck upward to take in the intricate woodwork along the railing carved to resemble an undulating mountain range. Each of the numerous gun ports along the sides of the ship had a hatch carved with reliefs of dwarfen warriors. Grandest of all, the sunburst signets on the sails, though the same color and shape as a Basilean ship, were all composed of a giant monochromatic mural of a dwarfen hold inset on a mountainside. It was all so skillfully done that you had to be close to pick out all the intricate details of clouds, waterfalls, animals, and individual dwarfs atop parapets.

As they approached the gangway, Dinnidek saw someone big enough to match the ship. An ogre stood in the midst of the deck, calling out orders to the sailors who rushed about in choreographed chaos. The crew was a varied lot, with dwarfs, men, even an elf, and what looked like a salamander. Some were busy hauling ropes attached to cranes that stood along the dock side of the ship, while others carried stores manually from the jetty into the ship's hold. The ogre was tall and muscular, like most of his kind, with skin well-tanned from long hours in the sun. He was dressed in a long white shirt, a pair of black leather belts that crisscrossed his hips, black knee-length breeches, and leather boots. He wore a bright orange bandana to protect his head from the sun that contrasted starkly with the blue bandanas the rest of the crew wore.

Dinnidek stopped at the bottom of the gangway and called up to the ogre. "Hello there, Captain! May we come aboard?"

The ogre continued to call out to the sailors. *Maybe he didn't hear me,* thought Din. He took a step up the gangway and called out, even louder this time.

"Captain! I'm Lord Dinnidek Daamuz!" At this, the ogre stopped what he was doing and turned to look at the dwarfs. Din continued, "Ah, yes. Captain, may my brother and I come aboard?"

The ogre shot a confused look at Dinnidek, then turned to look behind him, as if he was searching for someone. *That's odd,* thought Din. *He must have seen us. We're standing right here.* When the ogre failed to look back, Din started fidgeting and looked down at himself to make sure he hadn't miraculously turned invisible.

A few awkward seconds later, a silver-haired elven sailor up in the crow's nest leaned out to look down on the deck. He called down to the ogre, "Sunny, you idiot! The dwarf thinks you're the captain!"

Din blushed a little at that, and he heard Daerun snort from behind him. Din turned to his brother, who was trying to stifle a grin.

"You knew, didn't you?" Din accused Daerun in an exasperated whisper. "And you just let me make a fool of myself?"

Daerun just spread his hands and smiled. "To be fair, I made the same mistake the first time I met Saorsi and her crew. I figured it was only fair if I shared the experience with you."

Din rolled his eyes and turned back to the deck.

The ogre, who was apparently named Sunny, shielded his eyes from the mid-morning glare with his hand and peered upward into the crow's nest. "Pipe down, Moon, I knew what he was thinking. I was just looking for Saorsi was all."

"Sure! Sure, you did," Moon said sarcastically. The elf seemed to espy something, and his face abruptly disappeared from view.

Din looked back down to the deck and caught sight of a dwarfen woman approaching them. Probably the ship's healer, he mused. From where they were standing, her head came into view first, followed by the rest of her body as she approached. Her dark brown hair was arrayed in a hundred tiny braids cascading down her back and framing her face. Her deep green eyes stared up at the crow's nest where Moon had just been before, then fixing her gaze on the Daamuz brothers. She was thin and wiry for a dwarf, and her short frame was all muscle and sinew. She was wearing a black halter top and black billowy pants that cinched at the ankles. As she passed by Sunny, she only came up to the ogre's hip, but it was now obvious to Din that she was the captain. She radiated an intensity with the way she carried herself, and Dinnidek found himself inadvertently standing straighter in her presence.

"You must be Captain Saorsi," Din stated, slightly chagrined.

"Yes, and you must be Lord Dinnidek," replied Saorsi. "Welcome to the *Maiden's Revenge*. Let me personally thank you and your brother for placing your trust in me and my crew."

She spoke with a sincerity that took Dinnidek by surprise. The captain waved her hand to beckon the three dwarfs aboard, and she turned her back to them and headed to the middle of the deck.

By the gods, this ship is hers, thought Din in wonder. *She's in command. On a warship, of all places!* Males and females nominally held equal status in dwarfen society, but their responsibilities were separated by gender roles. Females were the masters of hearth and home. They usually led in education and caring for the members of the clan, and they held equal ground in religious matters. In contrast, males were the masters of crafts, of law, and of war. They were builders, merchants, and war leaders. In most clans, female warriors were not uncommon, but it was very rare to see a female general, or a ship captain.

Saorsi walked back to the ogre and slapped his leg as she approached. "When you get this stuff stowed, Sunny, I want you to look over the cargo allocations for the rest of the fleet, as we discussed. Make sure you spread the food, stores, and munitions evenly amongst all the ships just in case we lose some during the assault. Get Arvind to help you."

Sunny nodded and headed to the forecastle of the ship. Saorsi turned to the dwarfs.

"So, you met Sunny. He's my right hand. I think you met Moon as well, up in the crow's nest. Arvind is our wizard. Comes from way up north. You'll meet the rest of the crew once we get underway."

Din nodded along, taking note of the crew and their nicknames. He replayed the last few seconds from a fresh perspective, ticking off the points in his mind. *She seems to have everyone's respect. She's a thinker. And she has a presence that speaks command. If she were a man, I wouldn't have thought twice.* He shook his head in exasperation at himself, and at the world. Dwarfen society was changing, in some ways for the worse, but maybe in some ways for the better. *When the cave-in happens, sometimes new jewels are revealed.*

Dinnidek and Daerun walked up the gangway to the deck, with Tordek following close behind. Daerun was unabashedly fascinated with the activity going on all around and was genuinely trying to take in everything at once. Tordek kept his eyes on Saorsi but would occasionally sneak a quick glance at the other sailors on the deck.

Saorsi continued, "For security reasons, each of you will be on separate ships when we make the crossing. I don't want to lose all of you if the Abyssals get lucky and pick the right ship to blast when we attack. Same thing goes for the supplies and your troops."

Din nodded in appreciation at these precautions. *All of this seems prudent,* he thought to himself. *Glad to see that she's a planner too. Can't be too prepared.*

However, at this, Daerun startled. "Captain, when I hired you, you said that we'd be making a safe landing at a secret spot. So what's with this talk about ships sinking?"

Saorsi smiled at Daerun's question. "Can't be too prepared, Master Daerun. If things go according to plan, we won't see a single Abyssal Dwarf the entire time. However, I always plan for the worst. I've smuggled tons of cargo into Crafanc and Clan Helgwin, and these precautions are the reason my crew and I are still alive."

"It probably helps that the *Maiden's Revenge* looks like a Basilean brig from afar," observed Din. "How did you capture the ship in the first place?"

Saorsi laughed delightfully. "Thank you for the vote of confidence, Lord Daamuz, but I didn't capture it. Despite appearances, there's no way I would be daft enough to try to capture a Basilean warship. The colors may be the same, but the lines are all wrong, and anyone who knows anything could tell the *Maiden's Revenge* isn't Basilean. There's no holy icon on the bow, the masts aren't spaced the same, and the forecastle is too low. But from far away, it hopefully makes Golloch's dreadnaughts think twice before getting close enough to find out. Anyway, when I first found the *Maiden* I didn't have my own ship to battle with at the time. So, Sunny, Moon, and I stole it honestly," she said with a smile. "I've been making my way ever since. You'll find that the world is a big place. Plenty of opportunity if you surround yourself with the right people and pursue the right causes."

She sighed and went on.

"To be fair, I didn't have much for most of my life. Always chafing under other people's expectations. I left Caeryn Golloch when that wretch declared himself high king, and I've never looked back. Like you and your clan, Lord Daamuz, there's no room for me in Imperial society. That's why I'm so keen to help you and yours."

Dinnidek nodded in appreciation at the sentiment. "So, you've spent your time smuggling for the Free Dwarfs? That's a cause my brother and I can get behind."

"Smuggling," answered Sunny in his deep baritone, "a little raiding, some thieving. We hit the Abyssal Dwarfs, Basileans, even some Imperials. But Saorsi never preys on the True Dwarfs, as she calls them. She says they're the only dwarfs that keep their word anymore."

Saorsi squinted up at Sunny, then looked back at the brothers. "That's true. The Imperials act more and more greedy and grasping every day. The gold lust is getting its grip on them. And if it ain't money, it's status. Pretty soon, they'll be getting like the Abyssal Dwarfs, with everyone only serving themselves. I intend to be far away from here before that happens."

"So do we," said Daerun, "thanks to you."

"It's nothing, Master Daerun. I'm no saint. I'm still getting paid, ain't I?" Saorsi gave a lop-sided smile, and Daerun snorted in response.

Dinnidek brought the conversation around again, "So, you know a hidden place where we can land our people safely?"

"Yes," Saorsi said, "I do. There's a spot along the Dewbrock Plain where the water is deep close to the shore, with a spit of land that juts out like a natural dock. I've used the spot plenty of times to offload smuggled provisions. If we time the landing when the tide is right, we should be able to get the ships closer to shore and minimize the time your people will be exposed on the longboats. And if we approach during the early morning, the Abyssals will have no idea we're coming until it's too late. The timing will be the key."

"Hmm," Din grunted in understanding. "We'll need to find a place near the staging area to practice. I don't want the invasion to be the first time we attempt a sea landing."

"Agreed, Lord Daamuz. I know just the spot. It's not exactly the same, but we should be able to do a dry run a few miles north of the temporary

Mike Rossi

camp your clan has set up."

Of course, she knows of a spot, Dinnidek thought. *She thinks of everything.*

Saorsi went on, "Like I said, you and your brother have my word. I'll get you and your clan back home, no matter the cost. Sunny knows, I may lie, cheat, and steal, but I never go back on my word."

Something in the words Saorsi used struck Dinnidek. *Never go back, huh? What an appropriate turn of phrase to use. Never go back. I don't know if that's a good omen or not,* he thought uncomfortably. *If it were just me, I wouldn't be on the lookout for signs and omens. But I have the whole clan on my shoulders now.* He glanced over at Daerun, who was busy talking with the captain. He felt a little surge of pride in his brother. He had come through admirably when Din needed him. *Well, maybe not just my shoulders, after all.*

CHAPTER 7

The gnorr slave bowed deeply to Zareen. "My lord, your bath is ready."

It kept its eyes to the ground as it stepped aside to allow the Iron-caster to enter the chamber. Zareen gave the servant an affectionate pat on the shoulder as he walked past the slave and into the small grotto that was nestled deep within the bowels of the mountain hold, shaped like a teardrop. A hot spring bubbled up into a pool in the far end of the room, filling the room with mist that mixed with the soporific smoke that wafted lazily from a brazier set near the side of the pool.

Zareen shed his robe and waded into the pool up to his chest with a sigh of contentment. He allowed the warmth of the water to settle into his bones, and he felt his heartbeat slow in response. He breathed deeply through his nose and held the incense in his lungs for a few seconds before exhaling. As he did, he dropped his entire body into the water and waded to the deepest part, where his slaves had carved a bench for him to sit on. He took his usual place, closed his eyes, and let the different sensations wash over him. Zareen had run experiments on the spring waters and had found that they contained all sorts of essential and rejuvenating salts. Between the incense and the salts from the water, Zareen felt calmer after spending time in the grotto. His mind, which normally sparked relentlessly from idea to idea, became more serene. Zareen had better focus and could work through problems easily after an hour in the spring. Some of his greatest breakthroughs had occurred while meditating in this room. It wasn't a stretch to say that this room had literally changed his life.

After a few moments, he opened his eyes and began talking to himself, as he was prone to do. "The Lord of Llyngyr Cadw," he stated to himself with a sigh. His voice reverberated through the room, coming back to him with different intonations and making it seem as if he was speaking with himself.

"The Lord of Llyngyr Cadw?" the room asked.

"It's not something I ever wanted." The room echoed his musing back to him. "I would have been happy with Alborz running the hold while I continued with my experiments. There's still so much work to do." Zareen closed his eyes and brought his cupped hands up over his head to pour the warm water down his neck. He rubbed his hands through his hair and then ran them down over his face.

Zareen had become a master of creating new abominations, of stitching creatures together into new forms, new potentials. He had created rites that channeled Ariagful's blessings in innovative ways. He was gaining notoriety for his work among the other Iron-casters before the invasion. Unlike his brother, the time away from Tragar had been a blessing. Alborz had been right about that. The Iron-casters were both jealous of their secrets and prone to stealing each other's ideas, usually to the detriment of their work. But out here on the frontier, Zareen had been free to work, to explore, and it had paid off in spades.

He had dabbled in so many experiments. He bred countless orcs and ratmen to be slaves. He was particularly proud of the abominations he'd created, twisted amalgams of disparate creatures fused together through sorcery and surgery. Some of his greatest works had lived for months, and he'd even gotten one to last a year in a semblance of life. His most stable creations had been the dwarf-demon halfbreeds. With the upper half of dwarfs, they were as intelligent and driven as any of his brethren. The bottom half was usually a demonic quadruped of some sort, which gave the halfbreed supernatural strength and speed. He had even bound unwilling spirits to living obsidian, creating giant golems with the strength of mountains and the cruelty of demons. It was rare for an Iron-caster to be proficient in more than one of these endeavors, but Zareen had mastered all of them.

"I've pushed the limits of sorcery and science about as far they'll go."

The room agreed. If that was true, if he had truly attained mastery of his craft, then he'd have to channel his drive and genius into new endeavors. And one of them could be the lordship of Llyngyr Cadw. If Alborz was looking to test his mettle and meet new challenges, then why couldn't Zareen? The idea rolled around in Zareen's mind. He tried to envision ruling the hold. Telling people what to do. Keeping order across their lands. No, not their lands. *His* lands. The prospect was daunting. But with Ariagful's guidance, nothing was impossible. He reviewed his many accomplishments in his mind, taking pride in each one. He had served Ariagful diligently for decades, and she had rewarded him handsomely in return with long life, unnatural vigor, and flashes of insight.

"Is this just another reward for my service?" he mused.

"Is this just?" the room asked.

"Just another service," the room mused.

"My just reward," the room stated.

Zareen sat in silence, eyes closed, letting the thought wash over him. Alborz was right that most of the denizens of Llyngyr Cadw would follow him with no reservations. He had bred the orc and ratmen slaves to serve. And he had directly created most of the others, either the dwarf-demon halfbreeds, the towering golems made of obsidian, or the Immortal Guard. His handprint was on so many of the lives here. If Alborz was the law-giving father, then Zareen was the caregiving mother. With Alborz's blessing, the rest of the Abyssal Dwarfs would fall in line. And Ariagful would give him the insights and wisdom he needed to serve her in his new role.

"To Her eternal glory," he said. "And mine as well."

He sat in silence, holding on to his decision, stretching the moment out for as long as he could and savoring the feeling of it. It was truly his right to rule, and he would do it skillfully. He would keep order here, and Llyngyr Cadw would thrive under his oversight. The hold would become a hub of arcane lore, and other Iron-casters would come on pilgrimage from Tragar to learn his secrets. All for a price. "There is always a price," he said out loud.

"Price is all," the room answered.

Just then, Zareen heard footsteps outside the cave. *Foolish slave,* he thought to himself. *It isn't time yet to retrieve me. I will have to let him know his er-...*

Zareen abruptly stopped his train of thought and sat up straighter as Alborz entered the cave.

Alborz was dressed in his usual finery, and the low light in the cave twinkled off the many rings on his hands and the jewels embedded in his beard. He looked like his normal, passive self, but Zareen could tell that he had something on his mind. The little crease at the corner of his brother's eyes always gave it away.

"Come, Alborz, sit," Zareen said. Alborz nodded and slowly sat on the floor of the cave. He took a deep breath of incense and slowly blew it out of his nostrils like a sleeping dragon. Zareen waited a few minutes for Alborz to say why he'd come, but the silence stretched on. Finally, Zareen gave in. "What brings you? It's rare for you to ever come down here, and you've never interrupted my ruminations before."

Alborz composed himself and answered, "Another orc patrol has failed to report. We believe it's been ambushed." Alborz spoke quietly, with no sense of anger or loss, his words only carried a statement of facts.

A flash of rage stormed across Zareen's eyes, but he too composed himself, though it took a few moments.

"That is unfortunate," Zareen said between clenched teeth. "That's the third patrol we've lost in the past ten-day."

"Yes. Yes it is."

The brothers sat in silence for almost a minute before Zareen spoke. "I intend to double the patrols. We need to find who is responsible. Our forces encircle the Vale of Crafanc, so it is not them."

That wasn't entirely true. The Imperials had been smuggling food into Crafanc. If food could be smuggled in, then rangers could sneak out, though not in great numbers. Alborz had slowly been strengthening the siege around Crafanc, but until recently, they couldn't spare the forces necessary to wage a full-scale assault on the hold. Alborz had been prepared to attempt it a few years after taking Llyngyr Cadw, but he had been stymied by a new player in the field; a dwarf who called himself the Worm Lord. The enigmatic leader of a group of renegade dwarfs, the self-styled Worm Lord had been waging a guerrilla war against the Abyssal Dwarfs since a year after the invasion. His forces melted into the wilderness and struck unsuspecting patrols without warning. The brigand commander had raided and destroyed all the stores for the assault on Crafanc, so the brothers had been forced to bide their time.

"If it isn't Crafanc," surmised Zareen, "then that leaves the Worm Lord."

Alborz narrowed his eyes at the mention of the name and thought through the problem out loud to his brother.

"The patrols were all lost within the past ten-days, but the first patrol that we lost and this last one were stationed far to the west, within the great mountain wilds. We've lost patrols there before, and we both believe that's where this Worm Lord and his forces are hiding. But the one we lost five days ago was supposed to be patrolling to the east, toward the Dewbrock Plain. The Worm Lord could not have covered that much ground in so little time." Zareen nodded in understanding. "Therefore, it's someone else. Either Crafanc, or a different group of rangers from another hold, maybe Helgarth to the north. Though it doesn't make sense they'd be this far south. They have nothing to gain by being down here."

The brothers thought in silence for a few moments before Alborz went on.

"What would you do, Zareen? Soon these decisions will be yours to make."

"Let me send some of my forces north along the coast. This will cause Clan Helgwin to recall their forces and keep them cowering in their hold. I can burn everything between the mountains and the sea as an offering to Ariagful and starve them all out."

Alborz smiled at the suggestion as he took on a paternalistic tone. "Zareen, you always err on the side of bringing overwhelming force to solve a problem. This is your greatest strength and your greatest weakness. No, we can't just destroy everything in our way. We need to know what is happening, especially if there is a new player on the field. Our response requires intelligence, a trait your creations sorely lack. They have a cruel malice, but little initiative besides the drive to kill and destroy."

Zareen felt rage flare up inside him at his brother's words. How dare Alborz malign the very troops that had secured him victory after victory. He let his anger surge through him, and he took some deep breaths of the soporific smoke within the cave. When he had calmed himself, he began to look at the problem clinically, like Alborz would have. Yes, the abominations and slaves were miserable scouts. They didn't have the temperament or the discipline. But not all their minions were so helpless.

"I see your point, Alborz. What if, in addition to sending fresh forces to Crafanc, we were to send the halfbreeds and the gargoyles? They are our fastest warriors, and they can cover ground quickly. They're also smart enough to be effective as our eyes and ears."

"Yes, that could work. Send the halfbreeds to the place where the patrols were lost and see if they can track down the ones responsible. But I want you to send the gargoyles out to the sea."

"The sea?" Zareen couldn't hide the incredulity from his voice. "Why there? Why not just send them with the halfbreeds to find the enemy from the sky?"

"Because I think there's more to this than just a few missing patrols. I think this is related to the food that is getting smuggled into Crafanc. Call it a hunch. I would like you to scour the High Sea along the Dewbrock Plain and see if you can catch sight of these smuggling ships. If we can cut them off, then we can combine that with your scorched earth tactics and starve Clan Helgwin out once and for all."

Zareen considered his brother's plan. It made sense and would be another step toward removing one of the last holdouts of mongrel dwarf resistance. And once Crafanc was taken, Alborz would be free to pursue his destiny in Tragar, and Zareen could rule Llyngyr Cadw undisturbed. He nodded to his brother.

"I'll give the orders. My forces will set out this afternoon." He was going to say that he'd come to Alborz the moment he heard anything, but he stopped himself. If he was going to lead, he had to take on the mantle. "I'll let you know our next steps when they report back."

Alborz nodded in approval. "Yes. Yes, do that. In the meantime, I want you to meet me in the throne room this evening. We can discuss what we know about Crafanc and Clan Helgwin. Then we can forge a plan to take Crafanc once and for all."

"I will."

Alborz stood up, brushed off his clothes and gave Zareen one last considering look before he turned and left the cave. Zareen considered the problem of the missing patrols, his mind racing through dozens of strategies. His thoughts were like a flock of birds, screeching and flittering among the branches of a great dead tree. He breathed deeply and forced his mind to slow down, forced the birds to land, to consider each option completely before rushing to the next one.

His mind clear, he took a final deep breath. "It's time that I harnessed my will and learned what I need to rule the hold."

"Will to rule?" the room asked.

"Need to hold," the room replied.

"Rule the will," the room whispered.

CHAPTER 8

Daerun's longboat was on its way to the shore, but his nerves were making his stomach churn, and his insides fought against the rocking of the vessel as it plowed through the waves. Despite the breeze blowing across the open water, he had broken out into a sweat that had nothing to do with the temperature. He felt the tell-tale tightness in the back of his jawline, and it took an effort of will to keep the bile in his throat down. He was seasick. He had heard from Sunny that the key was to keep his eye on a spot on the horizon, and he diligently stared at the proposed landing spot on the shore as the boat plowed through the waves.

Doesn't feel like it's helping, but how can I really tell? he thought miserably to himself.

The sand of the beach shone bright white in the midday sun, and Daerun had to squint his eyes because of the glare. The surf was up, which was a mixed blessing. It made the boat heave to and fro on the waves as his dwarfs worked the oars, which didn't help. But occasionally the sea-spray would assault him in his place in the bow of the boat, and the cool water felt good on his flushed face. *Hooray for small miracles,* Daerun thought. It was a temporary reprieve from the queasy feeling in his gut, and soon he felt the welling in the back of his throat again.

He turned toward the side of the boat, just in case he lost it, and despite himself took in the magnificent vista. The midday summer sky was a deep azure color, with hardly a cloud in sight, and the breeze was strong heading in toward the shore. The sea, in contrast, was a steely gray, with white foam atop the waves that matched the white sails of the trading cog from which Daerun and his Ironclad had disembarked. Four rowboats, long and shallow, kept pace with his longboat in the race toward the shore. Each held three dozen warriors, all decked out in armor and rowing as if their lives depended on it. Due to the tides, the longboats were absolutely flying, and some of them were kicking out white foam along their prow.

But the tides were the only reason the ships were making much headway, despite the fact that each of the boats had a few seasoned sailors from the main ship on board to keep the amateur oarsmen on time. The warriors had all practiced working the oars before setting sail with Saorsi and her flotilla, but it hadn't been enough. Mostly they had sat on benches with oars bolted to wooden railings, and only some of them had the opportunity to work with real boats. It had been enough to learn the basic skills for how to keep timing and manipulate the oars, but learning and doing were two very different things. Thank the ancestors this was a dry run.

The boat lurched to the side as one of the warriors mistimed the catch of the oar. The dwarfs behind tried to compensate, and their oars all banged together. As they attempted to recover, one of the oars ricocheted off an errant wave and bounced back wildly above the side of the boat. Felwyr, who was sitting behind, cursed and ducked out of the way just in time to avoid a broken nose.

"All stop!" Moon yelled out to the crew. The silver-haired elf was perched lightly in the back of the vessel with a look of equal parts smugness and exasperation. He sat crisscross with his feet pulled up out of the water that had begun pooling in the bottom of the boat. "Alright, we start again on my cadence!"

The warriors all did as they were trained and pulled their oars up out of the water, ready to restart on Moon's signal. The elf raised his hand and then dropped it as he began the song he used to keep time.

> Coin it rules the navy
> Coin it rules the sea-ee
> If you're looking for some gold
> You'll be waiting 'til you're old
> You'll get no coin from me!

Moon's voice emphasized the motion of the oars, with the loudest syllables where the oars caught the water and the softer ones as they came out of the stroke. The warriors all took up the chant and reestablished their rhythm. With everyone in sync, the boat surged ahead through the waves. Daerun smiled and pumped his fist in appreciation.

"That's it, boys! That's how it's done!"

Dare craned his neck to look away from the cog and check on how Din was doing. Far off in the distance, he saw the five boats with his brother's regiment crashing along with the surf on their way to the shore. *No way to know how fast they're going, really,* he thought to himself. *But he's not way ahead, so we're still in the race.*

Daerun had placed a friendly wager with his brother that he and his soldiers would be the first to form up in ranks on the shore. Din had agreed to the bet with gusto. Not only was fraternal honor at stake, but the loser's regiment would set up the camp for the winners for a ten-day.

"C'mon, boys! I want to see the look on their faces when I ask them to set my tent flaps and fluff my pillows!"

The dwarfs pulled the oars with all their might, struggling against the waves and their own breastplates. Since they would be wearing armor on the day of the invasion, the warriors had decided to make everything as realistic as possible. Saorsi had advised them against it, but the dwarfs had been adamant.

Moon continued chanting at the warriors, his arms swinging back and forth to keep the time.

Jewels they rule the navy
Jewels they rule the sea-ee
If you're looking for some gems
Just go and ask your friends
You'll get no jewels from me!

The warriors were getting the hang of it. The oars were plunging into the water as one, and Daerun could feel the boat surge forward as they all pulled through the entire stroke. Moon kept his arms moving in time as he called out specific pointers, "Keep time now! Watch my hand and listen to my words! Left side, pull a little softer, we're drifting to the right. That's it! Keep time now. One, two, three, four! Set, catch, stroke, finish!"

Daerun felt his stomach lurch as a larger than normal wave picked up the prow of the boat, and he clutched the rail in response. He stared down at the bottom of the boat and saw the water sloshing around the boots of the warriors. He tried to block out his stomach as he concentrated on Felwyr's boots and breathed deep. Meanwhile, Moon called out the cadence and the boat kept pace toward the shore.

"Set, catch, stroke, finish!"

Dare felt the blood rush to his face, and he missed the next verse of the elf's song.

It took a few minutes for Daerun to control his breathing and allow the rush of blood in his ears to subside. Once Daerun told his guts who was in charge, he spared a look around. The landing site was much closer, and they were near enough to shore for him to clearly see the seafloor.

"Okay, five more strokes then we're stowing oars and jumping out," Moon instructed. "Five, five, five, five, four, four, four..."

Daerun gathered up his shield and slung it across his back. He stood up in the boat and placed his left foot on the bench in front of him. He pulled out his battle horn and gave a long blast to signal for the warriors to vault over the sides into the surf. The warriors stowed the oars on the bottom of the boat, gathered up their weapons, and splashed into the water as the longboat's bottom scraped across the seafloor. Dare felt the boat lurch under him with the shift in weight, and he grabbed the side of the ship before vaulting in.

The air had been warm, but the water was cold, as frigid as a mountaintop pool on his thighs. The shock of it shot right through Dare's body, and he felt his clothes quickly get heavy and waterlogged. He started marching through the water.

"Come on, boys! Almost there!" Daerun looked ahead at the white sand. It was close enough where he could easily walk there on dry ground in less than a minute. But even though the water was shallow, the waves kept pulling at him, making him lose his balance. The water fought him with every step, and after a few paces, he began breathing heavily with the exertion. He heard some of his soldiers cursing and grunting with the effort. Another minute, and he was gasping for air. His legs felt like lead, and he had gotten some saltwater in his left eye, making him squint. He powered through a couple more strides, and the water got shallow enough where it was to his mid-thigh. The wading got easier, and he pointed his war hammer forward. "There's the shore, boys!"

He ran the last few steps out of the water and felt the sands shift slightly beneath his boots. It was a strange sensation, but it was better than fighting the waves. He raised his hammer in the air, "Form up on me! To me! To me!" The dwarfs were gaining the shore now, and they ran over to Daerun, forming up in neat lines facing toward Dinnidek's landing place. Daerun glanced over to see how his brother was doing. It seemed that he had just made the shore. "To me! Quickly now!"

Daerun turned his attention to the other boats. Four of the five of them had already disembarked, but the fifth was still wallowing out about one hundred yards from the shore. Even from here, Daerun could tell that the oars on either side were out of sync with each other, and the bow of the boat waved from left to right. As Dare watched, a wave caught the boat in the rear just as it was turned to the left, and it amplified the turn so that the boat was sideways to the shore. With its broadside to the waves, it rocked crazily to and fro, and one of the warriors was pitched over the side.

Dare felt dread in the pit of his stomach as he watched helplessly from the shore. One of the human sailors was calling out instructions to the men to turn the ship while another jumped into the water to see to the fallen dwarf. Despite himself, Daerun took a few steps toward the water, as if there was something he could do. Dare held his breath for what seemed an eternity. Finally, a pair of heads crested the water and bobbed along with the waves. Daerun exhaled in relief as the sailor swam toward the shore with the dwarf in tow. After a few moments, they both were standing up to their necks in the water. In the meantime, the boat had righted itself and was angling back to the shore. *Thank the ancestors.*

Daerun kept his hammer raised for his soldiers to assemble, but he watched the warriors who were wading toward the shore intently. He imagined what it would be like to defend against this type of assault against long rifles. The dwarfs would be completely at his mercy. And if he only had melee weapons, where would he set up his warriors to repel the attack? Would he set them right at the furthest reach of the waves to slay the exhausted warriors as they finally broke from the sea's embrace? Probably.

The gods help us if they're waiting for us, he thought with concern. With a shudder, he switched his attention back to his brother's men. Even though he had landed second, all of Din's boats had landed closer together. Dinnidek had formed up on the beach about a quarter-mile away, and he saw the last few of his Ironclad sprinting toward the formation. He looked back at the soldiers from his last boat, and they were just reaching the shore when he heard a great shout from his brother's regiment. He looked back to see his brother's troops formed up in square. Dinnidek himself was in the place of honor in the front right of the line, with his axe held high in the air. He had even unfurled the Daamuz clan banner, with the white dragon on a blue background, in the front left.

Show-off, Dare thought in admiration. *Good for him. But I'll be damned if I'm going to set up his camp for him. I'll tell Tordek to do it.*

That brought a smile to his face as he shepherded the last of his bedraggled stragglers into line. The last ashore was the unfortunate dwarf who had almost drowned. Dare came out of the ranks to greet the soldier and pat him on the shoulder as he passed. Like the rest of them, the warrior was completely soaked, but his face was pale with exhaustion, and maybe a lingering terror, as he passed. Dare looked for the sailor who had saved him, and he spied him swimming back out to his longboat.

Amazing, he thought in admiration at the sailor's ability to navigate the water.

Daerun came around and put his arm around the warrior as they rejoined their regiment. The warriors ranked up bravely and faced Din's troops. At Daerun's urging, they gave an answering shout in salute. From behind him, he heard more shouts as additional units made it to shore and joined their regiments. Within the next ten minutes, the entire dwarfen force had formed up in regiments and companies, just as they had trained. Daerun continued to keep his hammer in the air and began calling out to the neighboring regiments to take their spots in the formation. Further away, he could hear his brother doing the same.

The entire affair had taken maybe half an hour from when the landing craft had pushed off from the main ships to when the last regiment marched into the battle line. Daerun was struck by how strange time was. Parts of the trip had felt like an eternity, while other parts felt like they had taken seconds. He couldn't get a bead on how long each stage of the landing had taken. Would that be important? His mind came back to how vulnerable his soldiers would be as they attempted the landing. The timing would be very important. How could he reduce the amount of time his soldiers were wading? And which was worse, having a small number of boats to shoot at, or a dispersed line of dwarfs advancing through the water? He just didn't know. He would have to hammer out some options with Din and the rest of the clan leaders. As if on cue, he saw Diessa and Veit coming down the beach toward them.

Daerun motioned to Felwyr, who was standing nearby. "Round up the boys and get them back to camp. I'll be along in a few." Fel nodded to obey, calling out to his sodden clansmen to form up in ranks. Now that the landing exercise was over, and his adrenaline had subsided, Daerun began noticing the cold. His boots squished with each step, and his clothes were heavy with water. His pants and sleeves clung to him and impeded his movement, and the wind cut through his wet clothing and made him shiver a little.

At least my stomach has calmed down, he thought. Even the padding under his breastplate was soaked and began chafing his skin. He unconsciously scratched at the metal where his chest itched but sheepishly pulled his hand away when he caught Veit watching him with a smile.

In contrast to Daerun, Veit and Diessa were both dry and warm, having watched the whole operation from the shore. The wind was cold for early summer, and Diessa was dressed practically in pants and a long tunic, with a heavy hooded cape adorned with leaves stitched along the hem. Her hood was thrown back and her dark blonde hair waved in the breeze. She met Daerun with a smile and a hug.

"Be careful, I'm soaked!" Dare warned, but Diessa kept him in a stubborn embrace.

Meanwhile, Veit stared out at the dwarfen forces arrayed along the beach. "That wasn't bad, but your warriors were very vulnerable while wading to the beach."

Daerun extricated himself from Diessa and turned to face the sea. "I was thinking the same thing. We'd be sitting ducks if the Abyssals were waiting for us."

"Yes," said Veit, "that's true. The entire landing from the time you disembarked from the rowboats to the beach took almost seven minutes. That's a lot of time. Can we tell the soldiers to stay in the boats longer? Maybe wait until they get stuck in the sand before you all jump out?"

"Maybe," said Daerun, "but then are we trading slag for scrap? If we stay clumped in the boats, then we'll make easier targets for any long-range artillery the Abyssals may have."

Veit nodded but continued to stare out at the main boats far off the coast. "Think we can bring some counter-battery fire to bear off the main ships?"

"I'm not sure," said Daerun thoughtfully. "You saw the one longboat got crosswise to the waves and started bucking. Figure if one of the bigger ships came close enough to bring their cannons in range, then they'd have a hard time aiming."

"We're lucky that no one drowned," observed Diessa. "From what I can tell, the weather today is about as good as it can be, and we still had the near miss. Goodness knows that we probably won't be so lucky on invasion day."

"Then we'll have to keep practicing," said Daerun. "You two will be joining us next time, right?"

"That's the plan," said Veit. "We'll have to do a dry run eventually." At that, Veit paused and smiled to himself. "Ha! Dry run... what an odd phrase to use in this instance."

Diessa gave the engineer a bemused look while Veit chuckled to himself.

Dinnidek arrived, Tordek following close behind. Like Dare, Din was soaked through, but despite that, he had a giant smile on his face.

"Pay up, Dare!" Dinnidek could barely contain himself as he quickly hugged Diessa and nodded excitedly to Veit.

Daerun, meanwhile, shook his head in mock indignation. "We had you beat except for my one straggler."

Diessa punched Daerun lightly on the shoulder and admonished her brother. "Careful, Dare. That was almost a tragedy."

"Yes, it was," agreed Din. "We got lucky. I want to send a gift to that sailor who saved the warrior's life." Tordek nodded in acknowledgment. Daerun knew the dour bodyguard would take care of it at the first opportunity. "Veit, how do you think it went, based on what you saw?"

Veit and Daerun told Din their observations about the need for more practice with the ships and their concerns with how exposed their people were while wading to the shore. Dinnidek's demeanor grew serious as he listened. "What about counter-battery from the ships?"

"Veit and I already discussed it," said Dare. "We'll have to talk about the limitations of the ships and the cannons with Saorsi."

"That's Captain Saorsi to you and me."

Daerun smiled at that. "True. She wouldn't let me forget she's the captain," he said admiringly. In response to Dare's tone, Diessa gave Din a bemused smile, to which Din gave a grin and a wink back to his sister. Daerun narrowed his brows, ignoring whatever game they were playing.

Dinnidek thought for a moment before addressing Veit. "I want you to look at building some sort of pavises or shields on the front of the longboats to protect us from fire during the landing. That should help us get the ships closer before we jump into the sea."

Veit nodded, his mind already chewing on the problem. "They'll have to be strong enough to stop arrows and bullets, but not so heavy that they drag the nose of the boat down into the waves. And you don't want to obstruct the coxswain's view. Let me think on it and I'll let you know what I come up with after dinner."

"Diessa," said Daerun, "can you call up Joro and some other elementals to wade along in front of us?"

"Sadly, no. The elementals take time to summon, and even if I did, the sand isn't the best earth for them to use. They wouldn't be able to keep their forms for very long. The less solid the earth is, the more energy and willpower it would take for me just to bind them, let alone have them move around. That's why the spirits prefer stone and rock that stand the test of time."

The group was silent for a while, thinking about the invasion. The only sounds were the rush of the wind, the crash of the sea, and the occasional call from a seagull. The birds brought another issue up in Daerun's mind.

"What about the gargoyles? The Abyssals used those flying demons to track us during their invasion. How will we stop them from seeing the ships as we approach?"

Veit was the one who answered first. "You could have your sharpshooters dispersed throughout the fleet. If Rorik is as good as he says, his troops should have no problem shooting the gargoyles out of the sky, yes?"

"That would work," Din said. "We'll just have to be extra vigilant. And anyway, if Rhyss does his job, the Abyssals will be turning their attention away from the Dewbrock Plain and in toward the mountains. Hopefully, by the time the Abyssals know we're coming, we'll have already landed."

"Let's hope," said Daerun. "We'll need a couple of waves of ships to land the troops and all of the supplies for the invasion. If the initial landing doesn't work, we'll be calling this island home for the rest of our lives."

"True," said Din, "we aren't going back to Golloch, that's for sure. There isn't a lot of room for failure."

"Yes," agreed Diessa, "but partial success may not be much better. If we take Llyngyr Cadw, Golloch won't just cheer and applaud us from his throne for a job well done. He won't want to lose the rest of the Free Dwarfs or have them think that they can just up and leave his empire. So, he'll spread lies about us. He could say that he supplied us with help, which most people will know is a lie. He may also say that we were in league with the Abyssal Dwarfs all along, and that's the only reason we were successful without his help."

Daerun felt his heartbeat faster at the insinuation that Clan Daamuz would ever join forces with the Abyssals.

"If we aren't successful," Diessa continued, "we'll be forced to fall back to this island. We may be able to make a go at it here. It wouldn't take much to turn the temporary village we've built into something permanent.

But without Llyngyr Cadw, we'd still be only slightly better off than in the Empire. Sure, we wouldn't have to send treasure and soldiers to Golloch, but we'd be exposed and alone out here until someone with a fleet gets the same idea as us. Can you imagine waking up and seeing a fleet of Imperial Dreadnaughts floating off the coast? Golloch won't give us a second chance."

Daerun began nibbling his pinky nail as he contemplated how that metal would bend. Would Golloch attack a fellow dwarf clan? Of course, he would. If Golloch thought Clan Daamuz were traitors, he would just portray them as Abyssal Dwarfs to the rest of the Imperial clans. It wouldn't take much. The idea didn't sit well with Dare.

"And there's nothing to say that even if we do retake our home that it will be the same." There was fire and stone in Diessa's voice. "But this is the chance we're taking. The chance that the clan is taking. So, we'll do our best for us and them. It's all we can do."

Daerun nodded, but he continued to chew. All this time, he'd only been looking at the problem as a Free Dwarf. He'd let his disdain for Golloch's empire blind him to the eventuality that he and his clan would be branded as traitors by other dwarfs, even if those other dwarfs were only Imperials.

I guess this is what it feels like to be an outlaw.

Daerun found that he didn't like the feeling at all.

CHAPTER 9

Rhyss' breath was starting to come ragged, and he could feel the fatigue building in his muscles. Despite the growing ache in his legs, he kept going, eyes locked steadfastly on the ground before him as he ran over the rough terrain. He and his rangers had been on the run for three days straight, leading the Abyssal forces further and further north up the Rimebrook River. Rhyss had spent the last ten-day getting the Abyssal's attention, with multiple raids along the Ironway. The plan had worked perfectly. So perfectly, in fact, that the Abyssals had sent a sizable force after him. Besides the halfbreeds that were on his tail, Rhyss knew there were regiments of ratmen stationed to the south along the Ironway to prevent his escape. At first, Rhyss had been happy that he was drawing such a large force away from the Dewbrock Plains, but as the enemy numbers continued to grow, he'd realized how much trouble he was really in. It was odd that the enemy would bring such overwhelming force to deal with him. Usually, the Abyssal commander was more precise and judicious with his forces. He wasn't sure what this change in tactics meant, but he didn't have time to dwell on it.

Yesterday, he had left the river and led his rangers into the Rimethorn Woods, up toward the mountains between Crafanc to the east and Cwl Gen. The woods were dense, with lots of pines and thick underbrush. The rangers had spent almost their entire lives in the woods, and their mastery of woodcraft allowed them to navigate through the thick foliage easily. In contrast, even though the demonic halfbreeds were faster over open ground, they had trouble finding the winding paths through the forest. Rhyss would have easily eluded the halfbreeds and the ratmen, but the Abyssals had a few grotesques with them. These particular monstrosities were a weird mixture of demon, wolf, and maybe bears? He couldn't be sure, but they had excellent senses of smell, and they had unerringly tracked Rhyss the entire time. Even the normal tricks of crossing running streams or doubling back through marshland to hide their scent hadn't worked for long. His rangers were outnumbered, but Rhyss had been cagey, refusing to engage the enemy.

Rhyss ran through the woods with the rest of his fist following behind. To his right, he saw another fist keeping pace. They moved at a good clip, taking long strides that ate up the ground. Rhyss didn't bother trying to hide his tracks. They needed speed. The ground sloped upward as they went further up the side of the mountain. As he ran, Rhyss kept his eyes dialed in on the ground in front of him. His mind took in the ground, the roots, the branches, and processed all of it. In response, each footfall landed in the best spot to avoid tripping or turning an ankle. His gait varied as he went, sometimes cutting a stride short to place his foot on a flat spot of bare earth, sometimes reaching with his leg to clear an intervening root.

Rhyss had spent almost two centuries traveling through these woods. His woods. His mountains. Since returning after the invasion, he had looked at the land with a new perspective. He and his rangers had mapped out every hiding spot and defendable position in their minds. They knew of every location where they could safely rest and hide from the enemy. Rhyss now led his rangers to one of those hideouts, a system of caves and tunnels in the side of the tallest mountain in the range which the rangers had affectionately nicknamed Mount Drohzon.

The path grew steeper, and they were now half running, half climbing. As they gained elevation, the trees grew shorter and scrub bushes became more prevalent. Rhyss felt the wind blow stronger now, and the temperature became colder as they left the shelter of the woods below. With a last push, the rangers broke above the treeline. The sun shone bright and cold from a clear blue sky, and Rhyss could see the entire valley for miles back to the Rimebrook. At any other time, he would have stopped to marvel at the view, but not today. Up above, the wind howled over the rocky crags and the bare mountain slopes, while down below, the howls of the grotesques grew ever closer.

Rhyss looked around and espied the cave entrance. It was a narrow slit in the side of the mountain, with a small shelf and a protruding boulder nearby that looked like a dragon's head. The actual entrance was hidden from below, practically invisible to anyone who didn't already know of the cave. He scrabbled the last few feet to the entrance and squatted by the side of the small ledge. He quickly pulled a small bullseye lantern out of the side of his pack and lit it with a piece of flint that was attached to the side. Meanwhile, the dwarfs of his fist had caught up, and along with some other rangers arrayed themselves behind cover and faced back toward their pursuers with crossbows at the ready. The remaining fists all arrived and started entering the cave. He handed the lantern to one of the rangers as they wound their way into the cave entrance and out of sight. The rest of the rangers followed close behind, with each fist leader producing a similar lantern for their troops to use. As usual, Rhyss counted them as they passed by.

Twenty-seven, twenty-eight, I make twenty-nine. Everyone is here.

As the days went by, the number of rangers with Rhyss had slowly diminished.

Of all their hideouts, Rhyss had purposely chosen this location to retreat to. The caves themselves were pretty narrow and hard to navigate, with rocks protruding wildly out from the walls. The tunnels snaked this way and that, and it was impossible to see more than a dozen paces in any direction. The cavern had a couple of splits and side caves, but the main tunnel ran from where Rhyss was standing to a second entrance down in the lower slopes. That entrance was hidden in a thick copse of dense foliage and would be impossible for the Abyssals to find. The tunnels were big enough to allow the halfbreeds to enter, but they'd feel cramped, and wouldn't be able to bring their numbers to bear.

He and his warriors still stationed outside the cave would hold the halfbreeds here for as long as they could to give his rangers inside time to get in position and set the trap. He regretted having to use all the gunpowder stores, but he was happy to put it to good use. He turned back to peer down the cave and saw the glint of lantern light reflected on the jagged cave walls. One of his warriors further in used the narrow beam of the bullseye lantern to signal he was in place. Rhyss took his sword and used the flat of the blade to reflect the daylight back to a location deep within the cavern. The spot of light bobbed on the cave wall like a will-o-the-wisp. Once he had it in place, he moved his sword this way and that. The projected dot of light blinked on and off a few times before he left it in place for a three count. The lantern light blinked in response to his signal. Rhyss read the signs and nodded to himself. His rangers were in position, but they needed time to finish the triggering mechanism.

He turned his attention outside and gave his eyes a second to adapt to the relative brightness of the late day sun, which was close to touching the mountaintops to the west. He nodded in approval and called to the rangers around him on the hillside.

"Hold steady, men. You know the plan. Our boys inside need a little more time to set the surprise, so we hold them here for as long as we can." The warriors all raised their fists in acknowledgment of the command.

Rhyss took out his war horn and blew a long blast that reverberated down into the valley - a clarion call that rang in challenge to the filth down below. He blew again and again, daring the Abyssals to come and face him. After his third blast, he stopped, and the last echo faded away, leaving only the sound of the wind.

Into the silence came the howling of the grotesques and the war cries of the fiends. A moment later, Rhyss caught sight of the first halfbreed as it came over a small undulation in the ground, and it made him recoil inside at the unnatural sight. The hybrid was a walking nightmare, a dwarf fused with a quadrupedal demon, like some infernal centaur. It stood taller than the surrounding scrub trees, with only the lower demon half obscured by the foliage. The dwarfen part was dressed in cruel blackened plate mail with spiked gauntlets and a horned helmet, which gave it an insect-like aspect. The armor mercifully hung down below the creature's torso and covered the place where the dwarf fused with the demonic lower half, which was a deep red color, covered in iridescent scales.

"I see you, demon!" Rhyss called in challenge to the abomination. The halfbreed locked eyes with Rhyss and raised its spear in return as it moved to charge up the hill. Rhyss froze inside as the twisted amalgam of flesh came fully into view. The foe charged forward recklessly but floundered as its cloven hooves slipped on the rocky ground. The rangers took advantage and fired their crossbows with deadly accuracy to bring the creature down with an inhuman roar. Rhyss exhaled in relief, not realizing he had been holding his breath in anticipation.

The dwarfs' victory was short-lived as another dozen halfbreeds come crashing through the brush. Rhyss' rangers calmly reloaded their crossbows, unshaken by the impending charge. They placed a foot on the crossbar and bent over to place the string into a small metal hook that hung off their belts. When they stood up, they cocked the strings taut. Their speed and efficiency reflected years of practice and thousands of repetitions.

Rhyss aimed his crossbow at the closest Abyssal, shooting for the lower torso, just under the breastplate. It sailed true and buried itself right in the hip. The halfbreed crashed down with a scream. Two seconds later, the other rangers fired their volley while Rhyss reloaded. A couple of the bolts bounced from armor plates or got stuck on shields, but a few of them landed. Undeterred, the halfbreeds cleared the foliage and began galloping up the rocks.

"Hold!" Rhyss yelled to his men. "We keep them here until we get the signal."

His rangers acknowledged the order, and the closest warriors pulled their axes as the ones further upslope reloaded for another volley. Rhyss took aim at the leading halfbreed, which was charging toward one of the dwarfs hunkered behind a rocky outcropping. The dwarf cringed back and feebly raised his axe as the demonic creature bore down on its prey. Rhyss fired and the bolt struck the halfbreed a glancing blow in the side of the head, clanging off of its helmet and dropping it to the ground in a daze. The ranger wasted no time and jumped forward to bury his axe in the halfbreed's neck.

Rhyss quickly bent over to reload his crossbow, his ears straining for the signal that the trap was ready. The mountainside was getting crowded with the enemy, and the ominous howls from the grotesques were getting closer. He stood up and efficiently placed the next bolt in the crossbow as he surveyed the field. Other halfbreeds had weathered the hail of fire and closed with the rangers, and a wild melee had begun. Some of the rangers further upslope were still free to fire into the enemy, but the rest were busy fighting for their lives against the much larger foes. Rhyss stole a quick glance behind him at the cave entrance. What was taking them so long?

"Tighten up!" Rhyss exhorted his men. "Fall back!"

He holstered his crossbow and rushed headlong into the fray to give his rangers some time. A pair of halfbreeds had cornered one of the dwarfs, who was desperately taking cover behind a large boulder. The demonic hybrids had cunningly split and were flanking the ranger from both sides, spears poised to skewer the hapless dwarf. Rhyss drew his axe and sprinted the last few feet toward the closest enemy, hoping that they would be so intent on their prey that they wouldn't see him coming.

The halfbreed pulled back its spear to strike down the dwarf. Rhyss wouldn't get there in time.

"Hey!" he yelled, and mercifully, the halfbreed turned at the sound.

Rhyss closed the last few feet and recklessly flung himself forward at the enemy, jumping up to strike at the fiend's face with his axe. The halfbreed raised his spear shaft just in time to deflect the blow, but Rhyss' body barreled into the enemy, and they both went down in a heap. Rhyss and the halfbreed scrabbled to regain their feet, but Rhyss was faster. The demonic centaur was still pushing up with its forelegs as Rhyss attacked again, and the ranger savagely struck it in the neck, bringing the fiend down.

Beside him, the other dwarf grunted in pain as the second halfbreed sunk its spear into the ranger's shoulder. Rhyss pulled his second handaxe and threw it in one smooth motion. The axe flew true and struck the halfbreed in the leg. The demon bellowed in pain and pulled back its spear to thrust at this new threat. Rhyss ran forward and viciously hacked at the halfbreed's other front leg, sending it crashing to the ground. Rhyss savagely chopped until the foreleg was almost severed, the halfbreed finally passing out from the pain. He knew that some of these beasts could regenerate their wounds, but it would take a long time to grow a new limb back.

Rhyss pumped his fist as he heard the horn signal from inside the cave. Finally. He turned to tend to the wounded ranger, who was leaning shakily against the boulder, his good hand pressed on his wounded shoulder to staunch the blood. Rhyss gently hooked the dwarf around the waist and pulled him along, back toward the cave entrance.

"Time to go, boys," Rhyss commanded. The rangers that weren't engaged fired one last volley into the taller halfbreeds, while those in melee made an orderly retreat back toward the cave entrance. It was just in time. Some of the fallen demons, lying almost dead upon the ground just moments ago, were beginning to twitch and move, their wounds slowly stitching themselves back together with infernal magics. Meanwhile, the living halfbreeds were still pushing their way up the hill in a frenzy, desperately trying to come to grips with the fleeing rangers.

One of the slower dwarfs lost his footing while rushing toward the cave and fell to his hands and knees. The closest halfbreed veered toward the downed dwarf while the unfortunate ranger scrabbled to stand back up.

Rhyss raised his handaxe and shouted to the demon. The halfbreed spared a glance for Rhyss just in time to catch the axe in the face. It reared on its back legs in agony and fell backward, crashing down the rocky slope. Meanwhile, the ranger made it to the cave entrance and ducked inside.

By now, the mountainside was full of halfbreeds charging up the slope toward Rhyss' position. The ranger captain called out to them, "Well, it's been fun!" He gave them a genial salute goodbye and followed his fellow dwarfs into the cave.

Rhyss moved quickly down the tunnel. The residual light from the entrance was just enough to allow him to see the uneven floor. He ducked his head to avoid an outthrust rock and twisted his body to snake around a small, sealed keg lying behind a boulder. He kept his eyes sharp for the thin wire that ran from the keg deeper into the tunnel. It wouldn't do for the keg to get jostled. It wouldn't do at all. Rhyss caught the glint of other wires running along the tunnel floor to multiple crevices and crannies, and nodded in satisfaction.

From behind, he heard the halfbreeds milling around the entrance and the howls of the grotesques as they came closer. The ranger in front of him turned the corner, and Rhyss stopped to look back. He could clearly see two of the dwarf-centaurs in the entrance, talking to each other, with a large group of them behind. Rhyss waited a few seconds, but when he saw the grotesque's legs through the opening, he knew it was time to go. The trap was set, now it was time for the demons to take the bait. Rhyss waited until one of the halfbreeds dared to enter the tunnel and shot his crossbow. The halfbreed caught the bolt on its shield and roared in fury as it charged into the cave.

Rhyss fled and called out to his rangers positioned further down the tunnel with words from a dwarf children's game, "Buck Buck, number five's coming!"

He rounded the corner to see his soldiers positioned behind cover a dozen yards down the tunnel, near the next turn. This part of the cave was wider, and he moved a little faster. As he passed the rangers, they uncovered their bullseye lanterns and aimed them along with their crossbows down the tunnel behind him, blinding the halfbreeds. Rhyss took position just behind his men, and one of the rangers handed him a loaded crossbow.

It didn't take long for the first halfbreed to turn the corner. It was so tall that its head practically scraped the tunnel ceiling. As if from an unspoken command, the rangers all fired at once, and the halfbreed screamed in pain. It slumped against the wall of the cavern and the legs on one side thrashed wildly. A second halfbreed came around the corner and tried to jump over the body to get at the dwarfs, but the roof of the tunnel was too low to allow it. The halfbreed clumsily tripped and was shot in the chest for its trouble.

The body landed on the first halfbreed, effectively trapping it in place.

Rhyss taunted the Abyssals, "You'll have to try harder than that!" He could hear more of the halfbreeds grouped around the bend and out of sight. Just a few more moments. The trick would be to catch as many of the demons as he could before igniting the charges.

Moments later, the sounds outside changed. Deep raspy breathing, punctuated by low rumbling growls, echoed down the tunnel. Rhyss heard feet shuffling, and the grunts from the halfbreeds went from aggressive to more subdued. The light from outside dimmed as something large and menacing entered the cavern. Rhyss tapped the warriors on their shoulders and silently ordered them further down the cave. They retreated quickly as Rhyss raised his horn and blew a quick staccato note. It was the signal to blow the charges.

Rhyss knew he should have run with the rest of his rangers, but a small part of him, the piece that burned with such fierce hatred for his Abyssal cousins, forced him to stay and bear witness. Once he'd given the signal, the rangers further back should have connected the wires and triggered the explosion. But as Rhyss waited, his anticipation changed to concern as the seconds ticked by. Surely, they'd heard his signal? Had something gone wrong? He could hear the grotesque's footsteps getting closer, now seemingly steps away from the turn in the tunnel.

Despite himself, Rhyss stubbornly held his ground, waiting for an explosion that wouldn't come. With morbid fascination, he was held mesmerized as one of the grotesques came into view. Rhyss could clearly see the hulking creature in the lantern light, and he could discern a head and torso like a bear with two lines of tentacles growing from either side of its spine. The legs were abnormally long and ended in gripping claws that widened out to give it excellent balance. The eyes glowed with an inner malice that lit the cave a wicked shade of green. Despite himself, Rhyss' mouth became dry with fear. He knew that he had to keep calm.

He also knew it wasn't working.

The wounded halfbreed's screams grew more frantic as the grotesque came closer. The monster looked down and dismissively raked its front claw across the halfbreed's head and smeared it across the cavern floor. The screaming abruptly stopped, and the only sounds were the grotesque's snuffling and the whoosh of blood in Rhyss' ears. The grotesque caught Rhyss' scent and stared directly at the ranger, despite the darkness. Its eyes were shot with a green glow and held a malicious intelligence. Its gaze never faltered as it pulled the halfbreed carcasses out of the way. Rhyss' insides turned to jelly and despite himself, he was pinned in place by fear. The grotesque took a step closer and fully turned the corner. Its entire body filled the cavern, and its tentacles writhed in agitation at being confined. The smell from the creature filled Rhyss' nostrils and made him nauseous. It took another step closer, slowly stalking its way toward Rhyss and his rangers.

His rangers! What had happened? The signal!

Just as Rhyss began to shakily raise the horn to his now dry lips, there was a 'WHOOSH!' and the tunnel entrance filled with flame. It roared around the turn and up the passageway toward Rhyss in a wave of destruction. The inferno sucked the air out of the tunnel, making Rhyss gasp as he instinctively crouched down behind a nearby rock for cover. The fire flashed above his head, and it dissipated just as quickly as it had arrived. A cacophony of screams and the smell of burning fur assaulted him in response. He took a few moments to catch his breath before slowly standing up, his hands groping on the boulder to support him. He blinked a few times as he opened his eyes to get the white spots to clear from his vision. The explosion had been meant to bring the tunnel down onto the heads of the demons, but Rhyss and his men were no engineers. The explosion had torn the enemy to shreds, but the mountain had proved stronger. The tunnel, strewn with debris, had refused to collapse. Through the residual spots, and the dust floating in the air, he saw the grotesque rolling on the floor of the cave, its skin a smoldering ruin. It slowly regained its feet and shook the stone debris from its shoulders. Rhyss could only stand transfixed as he marveled at how tough the creature was. It just wasn't fair.

The grotesque snuffled the air, and slowly turned toward Rhyss. Further down the tunnel, he heard one of his rangers cry out for him, and he snapped out of his paralysis. He turned and ran as fast as he could. As he did, he heard the grotesque spring after him. He turned the corner and saw some stragglers standing along the tunnel, their crossbows half drawn. Rhyss eschewed any pretense at stealth, and urgently yelled to his men.

"Go! Go! Go!"

He pointed frantically down the tunnel as the grotesque crashed into the narrow turn where he'd just been standing. The rangers all eagerly obeyed. Some of them had the presence of mind to fire their crossbows before running, while one of them just dropped it and fled. None of them stood their ground against the frenzied death machine bearing down on them.

The tunnel twisted to the left and sloped sharply downward. Rhyss nimbly slid from rock to rock as he descended further down into the mountain, his rangers running ahead of him. In contrast, the drastic changes in the cavern floor forced the grotesque to slow down its pursuit as it navigated between rock outcroppings and boulders. The fleeing rangers carried Rhyss' warning forward, and as the captain fled, he saw fewer and fewer of his troops in front of him. He knew they were running for their lives to the lower entrance. Rhyss could hear the surviving halfbreeds yelling to each other in pursuit behind the grotesque.

Rhyss could feel the grotesque keep pace with him as he raced through the tunnel. He instinctively ducked as one of the grotesque's tentacles lashed out toward him, smashing against the tunnel as it missed, and sending small chips of stone flying. He turned sideways to maneuver through the narrow end of the tunnel, which opened into a wider room. Hopefully, that narrow spot would slow the grotesque down.

Rhyss practically flew into the room, which was shaped like an oval with a small fissure running along the walls and ceiling in the middle. A fist of rangers was arrayed along the far end of the cavern, crossbows cocked and ready. Rhyss spun around and peered intently at the tunnel opening. He had expected the grotesque to be right behind, but oddly there was no sign of the demon. For a brief moment, Rhyss allowed himself to relax, hands on his hips as he stole some deep breaths. Between gasps, he kept his eyes nervously on the dark tunnel behind. One of the rangers went to speak, but Rhyss raised his fist for silence, his ears straining to catch any sign of the grotesque. He took a half step forward and caught a glancing green glint from far back down the tunnel. It was all the warning he had.

The grotesque rushed forward and smashed its body into the narrow opening, shattering the rock around the tunnel entrance and spraying debris everywhere. Rhyss inadvertently flinched backward and fell to the floor as the monster landed heavily over him. The grotesque stood dazed for an instant, and it took a moment to shake off the impact. That brief pause saved Rhyss' life. The rangers cried in amazement at the sheer power of the creature and reflexively fired their crossbows. The bolts sunk deeply into the creature's flesh. The grotesque roared in pain and bounded over Rhyss toward the rangers.

"Run, you idiots!" Rhyss shouted as he pulled his last hand axe and rushed after the demon.

The grotesque's tentacles lashed out at the rangers. Most of them were able to dodge the dazed and wounded monster's attacks, but one of the dwarfs was swatted backward against the cave wall, his helmet making a sharp clang sound at the impact. Rhyss jumped up onto the creature's back and chopped down with his axe as the rangers ran to tend to their dazed comrade. He could feel the heat from the monster's burnt body, and the reek of its flesh made Rhyss gag. The blade landed once, twice. The grotesque roared and bucked wildly. Rhyss grabbed at one of the tentacles and held on for dear life. The grotesque craned its neck backward, trying to snap at Rhyss with its jaws, but it couldn't contort its body enough. The tentacles flailed at him, but Rhyss stayed low to the creature's back, and the grasping tendons barely missed him.

Finally, in frustration, the creature spun and tried to push its back against the wall to scrape Rhyss off, but luckily the grotesque pushed against the fissure, and Rhyss contorted his body to avoid the rocky walls. He let go of the tentacle as the creature pulled back to the middle of the room and pushed against the walls to keep his balance.

Rhyss tumbled out of the fissure and landed on his feet. He quickly scanned the room for his fellow rangers, but they had all wisely fled. With his men relatively safe, Rhyss turned back to the serious business of getting the heck out of there. He dashed toward the exit and got there just as the grotesque turned slowly back toward him. The demon was starting to show the effects of all of its injuries. Rhyss sprinted down the tunnel, shouting "Go! Go!" to his men, though he knew that most of them must have made it to the exit by now. It was only a little further.

He turned the last corner where the tunnel corkscrewed down steeply in a sudden drop, and he recklessly jumped downward from boulder to boulder. Above him, he heard the grotesque rushing just behind. Ahead he could see the faint glow of daylight reflected from the exit just around the next bend. The grotesque tried to stop at the sudden drop, but it was too massive. It had too much inertia, and its claws scrabbled for purchase on the stone floor to no avail. Rhyss heard it yowl as it fell, flailing in blind panic, and he jumped in desperation away from the monster's body. He was still in midair when he felt it crash into the boulder where he had just been. Rhyss landed oddly and went down hard, wrenching his knee in the process. He yelled and reflexively reached for his leg, which was on fire from the pain. For a brief moment, both he and the grotesque writhed on the ground, trying to stand up. Rhyss found his feet first, but his leg was having problems following directions.

"Fulgria, that hurts!" he yelled in frustration. He had only taken a few steps before the grotesque also stood on all fours, ready to finish the chase.

A ranger was there to meet Rhyss on the last turn. The warrior reached out and pulled Rhyss forward, almost throwing him out of the narrow exit and into the last of the late afternoon sun. He landed flat on his stomach and turned over just in time to see the warrior dive out of the narrow crevasse after him. From flat on his back, Rhyss could see a dozen rangers arrayed around the cave mouth, crossbows drawn and ready. The grotesque crashed against the cave exit but was blessedly too big to fit, and this time, the stone of the mountain held. It roared in rage, and it glared balefully out at the rangers now shooting into the cave. The grotesque's yowls echoed off the cave walls within and the mountain slopes without. It turned its body, and a few of the tentacles from its back snaked out and coiled around the downed warrior's outstretched ankle. Another ranger stepped forward with a great axe and began cutting them away. Once they were severed, the tentacles shot back into the cave, leaving trails of black ichor that steamed and smoldered on the ground. The grotesque kept throwing its body against the cave exit like a battering ram. With each crash, the ground on the outside of the mountain shook, and the dirt around the entrance rippled. The rangers kept shooting their crossbows whenever they could see the creature's body, and after a few moments, the 'thumps' from inside the cave grew weaker and weaker until they stopped altogether.

Rhyss stood up, brushed himself off, and went to the warrior to clasp arms with him in an unspoken gesture of thanks. Rhyss gingerly moved his leg this way and that to gauge how much damage his knee had taken. It felt 'off,' and there was a flash of pain if he twisted on it, but for the most part, he could still walk. From deeper in the cave, he heard the guttural speech of the halfbreeds nearing the exit. They must have seen the dead grotesque blocking the way and put two and two together. One of them approached the exit, and the rangers drove him back with their crossbows. The surviving halfbreeds within the cave were little threat, now that the trap was sprung, even if it didn't all go according to plan.

Rhyss heard the muffled sounds of battle from higher up the mountain, toward the upper cave entrance. He smiled and gave a little fist pump in triumph at the sound. Just then, two dwarfs came running down the mountainside from upslope near the treeline. One of them called out to the captain as he closed the distance.

"Rhyss, we've engaged the enemy!"

As he came within the circle of rangers around the entrance, the messenger pulled back his hood and revealed a scarred ear and a big smile.

"About time you showed up, Meick!" Rhyss exclaimed.

The second dwarf walked up to Rhyss and clapped him on the shoulder. "What am I, old mushrooms?" he asked with a smile.

"Kilvar!" Rhyss hailed the other dwarf with a giant grin. "Ha! Great to see you again, my friend."

Kilvar was shorter than Rhyss, but just as muscular. He had a rugged square face, with unkempt blond hair that stuck out wildly from under his helmet, which was crafted to look like the face and jaws of a hunting hound. He was dressed in worn leathers, with a tunic and cape dyed various shades of red.

"Glad we didn't miss the fun," Kilvar responded. "It was hard to break the Abyssal encirclement around Crafanc, but I was able to lead a hundred of my rangers over the mountains. For all that they've been here for a decade, the Abyssal slaves just can't navigate the mountain passes the way we do."

Kilvar spoke softly with a low gravelly voice that rumbled from deep in his chest. Rhyss found that he had to concentrate when Kilvar spoke to make sure that he caught everything that was said. It contrasted with the commanding tone he used when he was leading his warriors and his mastiffs. Clan Helgwin were renowned as excellent dog trainers, and their forces were usually accompanied by packs of hunting dogs.

Rhyss responded to Kilvar, "It's a blessing that they haven't mastered the mountains yet, or you'd be in some tough shape."

Kilvar nodded in agreement before changing the subject. "When you have a chance, I received word from your clan. They've relayed the proposed invasion site to me."

Rhyss nodded to Kilvar and turned his attention to Meick. "Give me a full report."

Meick's report was interrupted by one of the halfbreeds, which had come too close to the cave exit. The rangers fired their crossbows into the slim shaft and drove the abomination back into the cave. Meick waited patiently until there was a break in the action.

"The Abyssals have been corralled around the upper entrance. Some of the halfbreeds are currently trapped within the cave. The ambush killed one of the grotesques, but we haven't been able to find the others."

Rhyss motioned toward the nearby cave entrance. "There was one more, but we took care of it. Its body is in the cave by the exit."

Meick's eyes widened in surprise. "I didn't think something so big would fit through the cave entrance."

"Neither did I," Rhyss answered with a wry smile.

Kilvar gave Rhyss a sidelong glance. "Is this another one of your overly complicated plans that sort of worked?"

Rhyss shrugged sheepishly. "The plan was flawless. We lured the enemy into a trap, like fireflies in a bottle. We were going to collapse the tunnel to cork it up, but you and your rangers served the same purpose. See, it all worked out."

Kilvar raised his eyebrow but said nothing while Meick continued with his report.

"Our rangers met up with the forces from Clan Helgwin three days ago and made for Mount Drohzon, just like we planned."

Rhyss had originally landed with two hundred rangers under his command and had sent them out in bands of ten fists each to cause trouble. Since then, he'd been in loose contact with his men, and they had left signs and runes carved on rocks for the other groups to find. The original plan had been for his forces to meet up with Clan Helgwin's rangers further to the south. But when the halfbreeds had begun hunting him in earnest, he had sent Meick out to change the rendezvous site and gather up the other ranger groups to set the trap. The addition of some of Clan Helgwin's rangers was a welcome blessing. Knowing now how big the Abyssal force was, he didn't think that his forces alone could have pulled this off.

"The halfbreeds around the upper entrance are being driven further and further up the mountain by our forces. Most of us are stationed just below the treeline." Rhyss nodded at that. Unlike the towering demon centaurs, the dwarfs could take cover in the low scrub trees and harass the halfbreeds with their crossbows. Meick went on, "That being said, we don't have the numbers to stop every one of them from escaping."

"That's okay," said Rhyss, "we want a few of them to get away and report back. Hopefully, the Abyssal commander will send more forces this way to continue the hunt." Rhyss turned his attention back to the cave exit. The rangers could hear a commotion rising from the halfbreeds inside the cave. Apparently, they had figured out that they were trapped and were getting desperate. Rhyss turned back to Meick. "So the upper cave entrance is under control?"

"That's right," answered Kilvar in his low rumble. "We have ten fists stopping anyone from exiting the cave. The rest of our collective forces should be driving off the remaining Abyssals as we speak."

"Excellent," said Rhyss. "Get four fists and station them here with the rest of my men. I want fifty rangers at each cave exit. We'll spend the next few hours making sure the mountains are clear. I figure the halfbreeds can exhaust themselves all night trying to escape." He savored the idea of them squeezing out of the exit in single file. "Once morning comes, we'll go in and root them out cave by cave."

Meick nodded and ran back up the slope, Kilvar not far behind. Rhyss turned back to the cave exit and joined his men. This had worked better than he could have hoped. Now that he had combined his forces with Clan Helgwin's, he should have this sorted by tomorrow evening.

Then we head to the Dewbrock Plain.

* * * * *

On the mountainside to the north of the battle, a lone dwarf stood hidden in some scrub trees, watching the ambush unfold. He had seen the dwarfs spring their trap and took note of everything that had happened. The sun had fallen completely below the mountaintops to the west, and the stars were just beginning to show themselves. In the darkness, the dwarf couldn't see much, but he could still sense the situation. Even now, the sounds of fighting began to diminish as the ambush was winding down. The dwarf closed his eyes and listened, trying to glean any other information he could before he headed back to the Worm Lord to report. Eventually, he couldn't discern anything meaningful over the sounds of the wind and decided it was time to go. He opened his eyes, pulled his ragged cloak tight around him, and dashed away down the mountain.

CHAPTER 10

Rorik basked in the simple glory of a perfect summer day. The sun was just hot enough to make him feel warm, while the sea breeze kept him from sweating. The weather had finally caught on to the fact that it was nearing the summer solstice, and it had warmed up considerably during the last few days. From his place on the bow of the ship, he felt the roll of the sea as he rose and fell with each wave. It was comforting to him. He heard the sailors singing in the rigging over the creak of the ropes and the flap of the sails caught by the wind. He unconsciously hummed along as his eyes swept the skies, his rifle cradled in his arm. One of his riflemen was stationed above in the crow's nest, keeping a second set of eyes on the horizon. At Captain Saorsi's orders, the riflemen were spread throughout the fleet to keep watch and neutralize aerial Abyssal spies. Naturally, Rorik had claimed a spot on the *Maiden's Revenge*. What was the point of being the leader if he couldn't be on the best ship in the fleet?

The ships were sailing together in a close formation, in an attempt to make them harder to find. The *Maiden's Revenge* led the way, speedily sailing westward with the wind. The flagship was positioned bravely in the front of the fleet, her sails shining resplendently in the sun. From his vantage point in the bow, Rorik couldn't see most of the fleet, hidden as they were behind the *Maiden's* massive sails. However, the other lead ships to his left and right were close enough that he could see the individual sailors bustling to and fro. The *Maiden's* sailors were busy too, and Rorik could clearly hear Sunny calling out orders to the crew. Rorik kept his focus out to sea, but in his imagination, he could see Sunny waving his orange bandana for emphasis. The day was clear, and Rorik could see for miles before the line of the sea faded into the sky above. He could just make out a small sliver of land to the southwest, one of the long atolls that sheltered the shore of the Halpi Peninsula.

It would be nice if the rest of the mission went like this, Rorik thought. An easy landing followed by an easy walk, capped off with an easy battle. He knew that it was an unrealistic fantasy, but there was no reason to ruin such a magnificent day with dour thoughts. Reality could wait. Rorik spared a quick look around at the other ships, packed with dwarfen warriors, extra boats for the landing decorated with the warrior's shields, and barrels of food and munitions. He was struck with just how ambitious, how borderline crazy, this undertaking was. Rorik's fingers idly traced the filigree on his rifle scope as he thought about what lay ahead.

Footsteps behind him pulled him from his reverie. He glanced back to see Captain Saorsi standing a few feet away, gazing out to sea. She was dressed in her customary black outfit, but today she had foregone the hat, and her myriad braids waved in the breeze. Rorik kept his attention to the west but addressed Saorsi all the same.

"Good day, Captain. What can I do for you?"

Rorik could hear the smile in Saorsi's voice. "Nothing today, Rorik. I'm just taking in the sun." Rorik noted Saorsi's habit of omitting his title, but he didn't mind. He knew there was only one captain on Saorsi's ship.

A few moments went by with each of them intently looking at the sky. Saorsi broke the silence first.

"You have to hand it to them, the audacity to move their entire clan all at once." She motioned toward the nearby trading cogs. The ships were packed with warriors hunkered down on the deck or sheltered under makeshift tents they'd erected to keep out the sun. The Daamuz clan banner hung on all the other ships, a white dragon rampant on a field of blue. "To have that much resolve. It's truly admirable."

"If you ask me, it borders on folly. They could have stayed in the empire and lived their lives in peace."

"Sure, they could have," Saorsi said with a tint of iron in her voice. "But they would have to give their wealth, their men, their sons to Golloch. Those are the kinds of compromises that a Free Dwarf can't abide."

Rorik snorted at that.

"Life is full of compromises. It's what allows civilization to work." He kept his gaze stolidly westward but motioned with his hand for emphasis. "If everyone just did whatever they wanted and didn't bend to the will of the greater good, it would be anarchy."

Saorsi began to say something, but Rorik continued.

"I'm not saying that everyone would be completely selfish given the chance, but we spend our lives choosing which compromises we're willing to make."

Saorsi considered the point for a bit. "True, but some concessions just can't be made. I spent my first seven decades being told to compromise my wants and desires by a society that didn't care to give me anything in return. I finally left. Since then, I've tried extremely hard to live an uncompromising life. I worked my way up to being the true master of my destiny. And now that I've tasted true freedom, I'm never going back."

Rorik smiled. "Yes, but even if you started with nothing, you are now the owner of a ship, with a crew at your beck and call. From where I sit, prosperity and riches give you freedom. When I have enough money, then I can also do as I please."

Saorsi laughed at that. "Strong point, Master Rorik. Strong point."

Rorik smiled in return but kept his focus out to sea.

"It really is madness. There's no going back if this doesn't work." He shook his head in disbelief. "What a giant leap of faith."

Saorsi thought about it for a moment before answering. "I would agree with you if they were hoping for help from someone else, or even divine providence from the gods. But they aren't doing that. They're not looking for a miracle. They put their faith in each other, and in the help from Clan Helgwin. Have you ever seen anything like this in the Empire?"

"Can't say that I have. The refugees call themselves the 'Free Dwarfs,' and I never understood the name. How can you be free when you're subservient to the clan? But after being with Clan Daamuz for the past month, I think I'm beginning to understand."

"Yes, it isn't that they all give up their free will to Dinnidek or Daerun. They're not all sitting around waiting to be told what to do. It's that they all serve each other. It's ingrained in them. They're living the ideals the Empire pays lip service to." Saorsi paused in thought before going on. "Rorik, I'm curious. You left the Empire for a life of adventure, but you haven't left the Empire entirely. Why is that?"

After a moment Rorik answered, "I still serve my clan. Clan Baranu has been loyal to the Empire for generations, no matter who was on the throne. When that weakling Kludis Foesweeper was king before Golloch, we put duty first and served him loyally. And my clan will stay loyal to Golloch. He's not who we would have chosen, but Baranu is a minor clan, and we didn't get a say. Captain Saorsi, my clan will never be known as disloyal, and neither will I. The clan lives on through the ages. In a way, the clan gives us immortality. The things we do today reverberate into the future, through our clans. We bring the clan glory, and the clan's glory gets reflected in us."

Saorsi snorted at that. "I was told the same thing when I was younger. But it always rang hollow to me. You see, it was always the clan elders telling me how important tradition was. But for a maiden under Golloch? Tradition means being subservient to men. Females aren't supposed to lead in war or trade, and that's what the dwarfen empire is all about now. There's no room for education or caring for the poor. Even religion has fallen by the wayside. Dianek is a quaint concept in the capital, and Fulgria is only worshipped because of her ties to money and manufacturing. It's all in what they can get from the gods, not what the priests can do with the gods for dwarfen society."

Rorik nodded in agreement. "Yes, the alloys have changed under Golloch. The last Claansvelt was more cutthroat as the clans jockeyed for status. There are more feuds between the clans as well. Golloch's supporters would say that iron sharpens iron, and that the competition is pushing all the clans to greater and greater achievements. The empire has never been so prosperous."

"But how do you measure prosperity?" countered Saorsi. "Yes, there is more wealth, but it's being held by fewer and fewer of the clans. It's a hold built on sand, Rorik. Did you know that Lord Dinnidek organized the relief effort for Clan Helgwin? He asked the other Free Dwarf clans for help, and they gave. I've been running goods to Crafanc for years now, all because the free dwarfs help each other. You won't catch the Imperial clans doing that."

"Maybe, maybe not," answered Rorik. He thought about how Clan Baranu had been scrambling for prestige over the last decade. It seemed that every action the clan had taken was weighed to see how much advantage could be squeezed from it.

I'm lucky I'm the sixth son, he thought. *It gave me the freedom to strike out on my own. I guess I've always played the game too. Every contract I take has been to gain glory for myself, and by extension for my clan.* He had always taken for granted that what he'd done was right, but Saorsi was making him reconsider. *What good is gaining status for the clan, if I'm hurting my fellow dwarfs in the process?*

He didn't like the feeling, so he tried to change the subject. "We're planning to land on the Dewbrock Plain. Do you think the landing will be contested?"

"I don't know. How would they know we're coming?" she asked rhetorically. "From what I understand, Lord Daamuz has his people causing trouble far inland, to keep the Abyssal forces away." Saorsi chewed her lip while envisioning a contested landing. "If they're waiting for us, it will get messy."

Rorik saw rows and rows of Abyssal warriors in his mind, backed up by infernal cannons and grotesque abominations. He shuddered at the thought.

"The *Maiden's Revenge* is armed with cannons. Why can't we just bombard them from the sea?"

"Compared to the Abyssal cannons and mortars, our guns are just too small. Their artillery outranges my cannons. We'd have to get pretty close to shore to bring the guns to bear, and once you're that close, you're out of options. The sea bed is unpredictable, so we'd be in danger of running aground, and then we'd be in real trouble. We'd be a sitting duck for their artillery. Not to mention that the *Maiden* is the only ship in the flotilla with real cannon. The rest have small bore guns that are used as a last resort. Those are there to make the crew feel good, as opposed to making the enemy feel bad."

"Indeed. Though I've found that careful aim makes up for the size. That's why my sharpshooters are so feared. These rifles can be just as effective as cannons, in the hands of an expert."

"Really?" answered Saorsi wryly. "Sounds like magic."

Rorik was about to answer when he caught the sound of gunfire from the southeast. *The southeast? Why would anything be coming from that direction? There's nothing back there besides the great sea.* Then Rorik looked back to the south. The long spit of land that he had spied earlier was way behind him. They had passed it as he and Saorsi had been talking.

The truth dawned on him just as Saorsi sprang to action and began yelling out orders. "Sunny! Get the men on high alert! Pass it on to the rest of the fleet. Looks like we have company from the southern atoll."

Rorik shook his head in disgust at his oversight. His only solace was that he wasn't alone in his mistake. He had assumed, along with everyone else, that trouble would be coming from the shores to the west.

"Aye, Captain!" Sunny answered. He began barking out orders in his booming voice.

The crew of the *Maiden's Revenge* jumped to action. Men ran to their stations and pulled pistols from their belts and crossbows from racks set neatly by the masts. Rorik gazed intently to the south. He heard more shots and answering shouts of alarm from that direction. His rifle was already loaded, so he primed the firing pan with a pinch of gunpowder and cocked the flintlock back. He raised his rifle and rested the butt lightly against his shoulder, his finger near, but not on, the trigger. He took a few deep breaths to steady his nerves, and he waited.

Rorik didn't have to wait long, as he tracked a group of stone-skinned gargoyles as they soared up and over the sails of a nearby ship on their leathery bat-like wings. He raised his rifle to aim and peered through the scope. He swung the end of the rifle in a small circle until one of the gargoyles came into view. Through the scope he could see the gargoyle's beastlike snout and red eyes. All four of the beast's limbs ended in vicious claws. The gargoyle's gaze locked on to a sailor in the small trading cog's crow's nest.

"We can't let any of them escape! Take them down!" Saorsi shouted to her crew, but Rorik kept his focus on his target. The gargoyle's wings shifted, and it hung in the air for a moment before it began its attack dive. At over one hundred yards, the range was much longer than most of the Ironwatch rifles could manage, but Rorik was right at home at this distance. He breathed out and pulled the trigger. His long rifle gave a loud crack as the fire in the pan flared. The bullet flew true. The left side of the gargoyle's head exploded, and it fell lifeless onto the deck of the ship below.

"Even if you think you've killed it, keep shooting!" ordered Sunny. "These fiends regenerate their wounds! A single cut or shot won't do it!"

Rorik smiled to himself. *Not that one. That one's a goner.*

Rorik lowered the rifle and began reloading as he looked for another target. He pulled out a cartridge from the front pouch of his satchel, behind his journal. He ripped the paper cartridge with his teeth and poured the gunpowder into the barrel of his rifle. He dropped the rest of the cartridge in after the gunpowder. He pulled out the ramrod from below the long barrel of his rifle and used it to press the bullet down deep into the gun. Four gargoyles flew low and fast over the bow of the *Maiden* and swooped to attack the ship to the north. Rorik reprimed the pan and took aim. The entire process had taken him less than twenty seconds. He saw one of the fiends approach a sailor climbing down from the rigging. Rorik breathed out slowly as he tracked the gargoyle's trajectory. He assessed its speed and led it along, aiming a little low to compensate for the kick of the rifle. He released his breath and fired. The shot hit the gargoyle in the back, and it careened wildly into the mast with a sickening 'thunk'. The gargoyle's body fell to the deck, and the warriors on the ship were waiting for it. Armed with axes and hammers, they crushed it to a pulp. But that was only one of the fiends. A second one grabbed the unfortunate sailor with its hind claws and dragged it up into the sky. The sailor wailed in panic as the gargoyle flew high into the air and dropped its victim. The screaming abruptly stopped when he hit the deck.

Rorik kept loading and looked for another target. A great shout went up from the south, and the sharpshooter heard dozens of muskets going off at once. He grinned as he bit down on the next cartridge.

Looks like those Ironwatch have gotten their act together, he thought. *Good. More metal in the air is a good thing.*

Looking calmly for another target, he took in the details of the battle. Moon, the elf with the silver hair, was standing on the raised aft deck brandishing two pistols and firing at anything that got close while screaming oaths in elvish. In contrast, Arvind stood next to Moon, a bastion of calm amid the din, dressed in brown breeches and a fur vest, his blond hair wild in the wind. The northman waved his hand languidly in the air, and with a sudden motion, aimed his palms at another cluster of gargoyles. A blinding flash of lightning arced from his splayed fingers right through two of the fiends. The air smelled like ozone and burnt flesh as the gargoyles fell limp and lifeless into the sea.

Rorik raised his rifle and fired at the same cluster with similar results. The sound of battle could be heard throughout the flotilla, along with the wails of the wounded and cries of the dying. Saorsi was shouting encouragement to the men. The dwarfs were getting the best of it, but they weren't coming out unscathed. Rorik calmly reloaded his rifle. This was the rhythm of battle. Load, assess, aim, track, breathe, fire. If things went well, he would repeat the sequence until the battle was done. If things didn't go well, then he'd improvise. He'd rarely needed to use the hand axe hanging from his belt, but it had happened more than once.

Eventually the sound of battle subsided. As the shouting ceased, relative silence fell over the fleet, broken now and then by the grunts and sobs of the wounded. Rorik stood ready but allowed himself to breathe deeply and relax his tense muscles. He heard Saorsi shouting for a report. Rorik looked around and espied his man still up in the crow's nest. He waved up at him, and the dwarf showed him three fingers. Rorik gave him a thumbs up and showed him the sign for five. His man gave an answering thumbs up and went back to keeping watch. Sunny was in the middle of the deck talking to Saorsi in his bass rumble.

"Sounds like we had two or three escape. No help for it, now."

Saorsi cursed aloud in at least four different languages.

Rorik agreed with her. Three days until landing, and they'd been spotted. Things just got a lot harder. A tense sail, followed by a hard-fought landing, a long march, and an apocalyptic showdown with the denizens of the Abyss. Reality had found a way to ruin a perfectly good day.

CHAPTER 11

The sound of music echoed hauntingly within the great hall of Llyngyr Cadw. A chorus of slaves clustered in one corner of the hall were singing an old dwarfen hymn to Fulgria, rearranged in a minor key. The tone of the music matched the shadowed lighting that barely illuminated the maroon walls and the red and white tiled floor. Multiple races were represented in the choir, with orcs singing the lower ranges, a few humans the mid-range, and ratmen for the higher notes. Alborz thought they sounded particularly lovely today; he'd have to commend the surgeon on his work. The slaves' vocal cords had all been altered so that they could only sing a single note. It removed the possibility of being out of tune, so the only thing the slaves had to worry about was keeping the cadence. Regular beatings had taken care of that.

Within Alborz's easy reach was a table laden with food that filled the room with a sumptuous aroma. Despite how appetizing the food was, Alborz barely touched any of it. Some days he wasn't hungry, but he liked having the food on hand just in case.

Alborz's hand swayed absently back and forth with the rhythm of the music, as if he were conducting the chorus, while he studied a giant map of the Halpi Peninsula laid out on a table in the middle of the hall, surrounded by lamps that bathed Alborz in a tight circle of radiant light. The map was made of thin layers of metal, stacked to give a relief of the topography. Small tokens made of precious metal and gems were strategically placed on the map to represent dwarf holds and troop locations. The token colors represented the different forces at play in the area. Silver and gold fillagree depicted major roads and important underground tunnels. The regions of the map were displayed in appropriate colors, blue steel for the great seas; green patina on copper for the forests; and the Abyss, just on the northern edge of the map, a deep blood red.

Alborz was gazing intently at the area between Llyngyr Cadw and Crafanc. A marker, shaped like a centaur, was lying on its side in the mountains to the north. A small orange token, shaped like a mastiff represented Crafanc. It stood in a ring of mountains, and multiple black tokens formed a cordon around the southeastern opening in the mountain range.

The slaves finished their hymn, and Alborz let the silence stretch before pointing to the chorus. At his signal, they began a new song. This one was faster, reminiscent of an old dwarfen tavern song, but the notes were louder and harsher.

As the chorus sang, Alborz stopped keeping time and instead began moving the black pieces from the outlying territories to the Ironway near

Llyngyr Cadw. A few markers were already placed there, including a few noticeably larger than the others. He mumbled to himself as he positioned a few units to face some green and brown blocks located in the underground tunnels.

This should hold off the wretched goblins infesting the tunnels while we deal with more important matters.

Alborz's finger caressed the wooden centaur. The loss of some halfbreeds had hurt, but at least the Worm Lord wouldn't be able to interfere in Alborz's plans. He would flood the northern passes with ratmen slaves to keep the Worm Lord busy for the rest of the season.

With these distractions tied down, Alborz was finally able to bring most of his forces to bear against Crafanc and Clan Helgwin. He surveyed his miniature armies arrayed along the Dewbrock Plain. Zareen had followed through on his plan, and the whole area was ringed tightly with Abyssal Dwarfs and orcs. The troops had burnt the land and were pushing step by step closer to the mongrel dwarf keep of Crafanc. Zareen's forces would pin Clan Helgwin in place, and Alborz would lead the second wave, currently assembling outside of Llyngyr Cadw, to take Crafanc once and for all. Further out to sea a small, winged token stood on the southern atoll along the Plain. As of today, the gargoyles hadn't reported anything back.

Meh, Alborz thought, *it had only been a hunch. I'll be happy to be wrong this time.* Alborz hummed along with the music as he stepped back to survey the entire landscape. Things were falling into place. He'd be in Tragar come winter.

The large doors of the great hall opened as Zareen strode purposefully into the room, disrupting Alborz from his thoughts. One look at his brother told him that Zareen was bringing bad news. He raised his hand to the chorus. The singing stopped in mid note.

"Leave us," Alborz ordered imperiously.

The slaves quickly filed out of the room, leaving only Alborz's personal bodyguards stationed around the outer walls of the hall. Once the last of the choir had departed, Zareen approached the table, across from his brother. Alborz kept his attention on the map for a moment, then took a deep breath and locked eyes with Zareen.

"Brother, you look like you swallowed a coal. Please report."

Zareen cleared his throat. "Brother, my gargoyles have returned from your mission. They encountered some ships approaching from the east. They engaged the enemy to discern more information and took heavy losses." Zareen spoke the last words with some bitterness, but it didn't bother Alborz. Those creatures were tools to be used. Nothing more. "The ships were discovered yesterday. At that time, they were four days out to sea and were headed to make landing on the Dewbrock Plain. A few of the surviving gargoyles are shadowing the fleet from a distance, and they will be able to pinpoint the landing site sometime tomorrow."

Alborz processed the information in brooding silence. He gazed down at the table for a moment, then placed a small bundle of grapes from the food table into the sea on the map, north of the atoll. Alborz weighed three or four possibilities. Was this a major Imperial invasion? Not likely. The Imperials would be foolish to land on the Dewbrock Plain without securing the Jarrun Bridge to the south. Was there a matching land force approaching? He hadn't heard anything from his northern spies near Helgarth. And there had been no word of an invasion from Rhyn Dufaris. Strange.

"Tell me more about the ships. Were they all warships? Imperial dreadnaughts?"

"No. From what my troops report, there is only one warship in the fleet, flying Basilean colors. The rest are trading ships and blockade runners."

Alborz considered this. A Basilean ship? Operating this far north in the High Sea of Bari? Surrounded by civilian ships? It seemed unlikely that the Hegemony would have any interest in the area. "What can you tell me about the troops?"

"Mostly dwarfs, with a smattering of humans. The flagship is crewed by a mix of ogres, dwarfs, and elves, though I'm not sure how reliable that report is. One of my gargoyles mentioned that most of the ships were flying a blue and white banner, with a serpent or bat insignia."

Alborz narrowed his eyes at this. He didn't recognize the symbols. *Bats? Snakes? It doesn't make sen-...*

He looked up over Zareen's shoulder at the mural that dominated the great hall. Today it was a panoramic view of the Great Abyss, as seen from the high tower of Zarak. But when he had first conquered Llyngyr Cadw, it had depicted a dwarf lord slaying an ice dragon.

"Could this symbol have been a dragon, mayhaps? A mixture of a snake and a bat?"

"Sure. That would make sense. Why is that important?"

Alborz pointed to where the mural had been. "It would appear that the mongrel Daamuz clan is coming home."

Alborz smiled and clenched his fist in anticipation. He studied the map, and his gaze locked on the Dewbrock Plain and the orange mastiff. He began considering the possibilities.

"How would you assess the situation, Zareen? Assuming I'm right, when the Daamuz clan arrives, how do we respond?"

Zareen studied the map for a moment before answering. "They are coming with enough soldiers to make a play for Llyngyr Cadw. But even so, they have to know that they'll be outnumbered, so they'll be counting on help from Crafanc." Alborz nodded in acknowledgment, and Zareen went on.

"We won't have time to take Crafanc the way that we wanted to."

"No, to handle both the invasion fleet and the stronghold at Crafanc, we'd need more time, which we don't have, or overwhelming force, which we don't have."

Zareen grimaced at that, but Alborz kept his face stoic while his mind kept formulating and rejecting plans.

"If I were Daamuz," Zareen said, "I would land, raise the siege of Crafanc, and then combine forces to assault us here in Llyngyr Cadw."

"Yes, that would seem to be the wisest course of action. That would make sense if they were free to land. But what would happen if we gathered our forces to meet them?"

Zareen considered the map. "We only have a few days before they arrive, so we'd have to send the troops around Crafanc to the landing site. This would lift the siege and give Helgwin free reign to move against us." Alborz watched as Zareen caught up to where he was. "So, either way, Crafanc will be relieved," Zareen said. Alborz nodded in appreciation. "Given that, it would be best if we moved our forces to deal with a threat, as opposed to keeping them in place and waiting be attacked."

"My thoughts exactly."

He began weaving the disparate threads of his thoughts into a tapestry of a plan. Alborz studied the black markers on the map, and his gaze came to rest on the overturned centaur. Like his brother, Alborz had a habit of thinking out loud when he became engrossed in a problem.

"Our decision to send the chosen halfbreeds up into the mountains made sense at the time. Now, we'll wish we still had them near Crafanc." He picked up the centaur figure and considered it before putting it back on the table. "We have some nearby, but not nearly enough. We may not have enough troops to fully stop Daamuz from landing their forces. But I don't want them to land uncontested. Hmmm."

Zareen stood by silently, giving Alborz space to think.

"Clan Daamuz will be here in three days. We need to simultaneously repel them and take Crafanc at the same time. How can we do this? We don't have the forces required to destroy both armies."

Alborz studied the map intently, shifting pieces around in his mind, moving troops across the landscape. Alborz was aware of Zareen's attention, his brother's gaze shifting nervously between Alborz and the map. There was something there in the back of his mind. The frayed edge of an idea.

"Do my forces need to destroy them? Or could I let hunger and the elements do my work for me? Crafanc has been under siege for months and is slowly being starved out." The idea became firmer in his mind as he circled around it. "I don't have to destroy the two armies. I just have to remove their options." Alborz spoke with more urgency as the idea gained momentum.

"I can move most of our besieging force to the south to block Daamuz from landing. I'll need to leave a portion of our forces around Crafanc to make it seem like the siege is still ongoing, and to pin Clan Helgwin's forces in place. This will provide us with time."

"But if we don't have enough troops to stop them, why bother fighting them?" asked Zareen. "We could scorch the earth and make their lives miserable until they flee back to Golloch on their ships."

"I could, but if they escape, they'll just come back next year. I don't need to win on the beach. I have all the time in the world to win. I want to trap the invaders and destroy them utterly. If I'm correct about Daamuz, they are coming to Llyngyr Cadw. They'll need to take this stronghold by the equinox or else the cold and the lack of food will force them back over the sea. But what if they can't flee? What if I destroy their ships so they can't escape?"

Zareen had caught up to Alborz's train of thought. "They'll have to retreat to Crafanc."

"Yes, and we'll reestablish the siege and close the door behind them. How will Helgwin deal with so many more extra mouths to feed?"

"Not well," said Zareen.

"Not well at all," said Alborz with a smirk. "So, we can't stop Daamuz from invading or the siege from being lifted. I can't destroy the ships out at sea because I don't have a fleet. And I can't just send the rest of our gargoyles to destroy them at sea because they're full of warriors. So, I'll wait until the warriors are on the shore." Alborz moved the grapes to the Dewbrock Plain. "Once the ships are relatively empty, we'll have the gargoyles attack and set fire to as many of the merchant vessels as we can. This will destroy their provisions as well."

Alborz plucked a grape from the bunch and dropped it on the floor.

"We'll inflict what damage we can as they land."

He picked another grape from the bunch and nodded to himself in satisfaction before continuing.

"They'll need artillery to breach the walls of Llyngyr Cadw."

He moved the remaining grapes inland to the Ironway.

"So, I'll destroy that next. If they bring them as part of the initial assault, I'll make that a priority target for our troops. If they keep them on the ships, we'll send the cannons to the bottom of the sea. If they do happen to have any artillery after the initial invasion, I'll engage them in a set battle to destroy it."

He plucked another grape and moved the sparse remains to Llyngyr Cadw.

"I'll destroy their artillery and the mongrels will be left to starve outside of our fortress."

He picked the last few grapes from the bunch, leaving only a single fruit and a stem.

"From there, I'll wait them out until they inevitably retreat. Follow them and harass them all the way to Crafanc, where I'll seal both clans in their tombs."

He nonchalantly crushed the last grape with his thumb. Alborz looked up from the map with a fiery fervor in his eyes.

Zareen smiled maliciously in response to his brother's intensity. "I'll have my remaining gargoyles send the word to our troops around Crafanc to execute the plan. I would assume that we'll keep amassing our troops here to deal with whatever comes next?"

"Yes, we'll gather our might here. If the Daamuz pups make landfall with any hope left, we'll crush it out of them." Zareen and Alborz nodded to each other at the same time, which made them both smile. Alborz gestured to the door, and Zareen left to put the plan into motion. Alborz looked down at the map again. He was being handed a chance to destroy both of his foes. What infernal providence. He thought about how desperate the Clan Daamuz must be to attempt something so risky. What would drive a leader to endanger his position like that? *He's probably under intense pressure to provide military success to his people to maintain his power.*

He gazed again at where the old mural had once been. The mongrel lord had stood proud and strong in the painting. *Maybe the old blood runs in this mongrel chieftain's veins. Maybe he's as good as he thinks.* Alborz remembered how easy the invasion had been. How they'd pushed Clan Daamuz into the sea. How he'd been robbed of his chance for honor and glory.

I actually hope he is.

CHAPTER 12

Dinnidek chewed his mustache in concern. Two days had passed since the gargoyle attack, and Din knew that the invasion was in trouble. The Abyssal Dwarves knew they were coming, and all hopes of an easy landing had been dashed. Since then, he'd mulled the situation over in his mind, studied it from all the angles he could think of. He'd talked himself into and out of a dozen plans, but none of them had offered a clear solution. Thankfully, today he'd be able to discuss the issue with the other thanes and hopefully find some clarity. As bad as the tactical situation was, Dinnidek had more pressing things to worry about.

Dinnidek's ship sidled alongside the *Maiden's Revenge*. The sea was relatively calm today, and the ships quietly rose and fell with the waves. As the ships got closer, Din noticed how his ship rose as the *Maiden* sunk down. The asynchronous motion of the two ships disoriented Dinnidek and made him feel a little nauseous. Thankfully, unlike some of the other warriors, he had avoided getting seasick so far. To be fair, he also hadn't eaten much since sailing for the invasion. Din had almost lost it during the practice landing, which would have been bad, since Daerun would never have let him hear the end of it. In contrast, Daerun never seemed to suffer from little things like seasickness. It made Din just a bit jealous of his younger brother.

By Fulgria, I'll be happy when we're back on land, he thought.

Like his first impression on the docks, Dinnidek was in awe of the sheer size of the ships. He had never seen ships sailing so close together, and it made him nervous. He would have thought the ships would want to stay far apart so they didn't accidentally bump into each other and sink. A part of him knew he was being silly. Ships weren't that fragile. But during his first few days on the ship, he realized that the only thing that stood between him and drowning were a few planks of wood. The thought made him anxious, and since then, he'd tried to push the idea out of his mind with varying degrees of success depending on the day.

Today wasn't looking good.

The crew of the trading cog were rigging up a small crane that they used to load the ship from the dock. It consisted of a boom that swiveled out away from the deck with a net attached to the end. The crew were replacing the net with a small chair that could hold him and Tordek. The captain assured Dinnidek this was a standard way of transferring people from one ship to another. Din acquiesced with good grace on the outside but was apprehensive on the inside. His only solace was that Tordek seemed to be doing worse than he. The stalwart bodyguard stared stonily straight ahead, as if he were trying to block out his impending doom. Normally Din would have been there to cheer up his friend. But not today. Today Din was too nervous to reassure anyone convincingly.

The captain approached the two dwarfs with a smile. "The rig is complete, my lords. Please come and seat yourselves."

Din's heart sped up, but he nodded to the captain and steeled himself. He gave Tordek a sidelong glance and saw a flash of terror in his eyes, but it quickly fled as Tordek caught Din watching him.

"Come on, Tordek, it will be fun," Din lied.

Tordek looked straight ahead and approached the rig like someone going to the gallows. Dinnidek knew he didn't look much better. Both dwarfs were quickly secured into the rig, their arms entwined in the ropes, their bottoms on a slim plank of wood, and their feet swinging freely in front of them. The captain smiled at the two and motioned for his sailors to hoist the rig. Dinnidek nodded. Before he could thank the captain, the makeshift chair soared into the air, and Din's stomach fell to his toes. He looked down to his feet, but he saw the deck rushing away from him. That wouldn't do, so instead he looked across to the *Maiden's Revenge*. That helped for a moment, but as the rig swung wide of the cog, he was certain he would be flung toward the *Maiden's* masts. He flinched and looked back down to see the water churning between the two ships. Now he was going to be drowned and crushed to a pulp against the unrelenting hulls. As the rig plunged down to the *Maiden's* deck, he gave up his dignity and just squeezed his eyes shut as hard as he could. He clenched the ropes so tightly his hands hurt. He heard Tordek whispering to his ancestors to take him home.

Within two breaths, the rig stopped descending and hung relatively still in the air, swaying lightly back and forth. Din opened one eye and saw that he was only half a span above the deck. He slowly looked up to see Daerun standing a few feet away with a giant smile on his face. Diessa was trying unsuccessfully to hide her grin behind her hand. Veit stood nearby as well, but in typical fashion, he was engrossed in studying the boom and the rig.

He gave Tordek a gentle elbow nudge, and the bodyguard opened his eyes and exhaled.

"Thank the ancestors, that's over," Tordek exclaimed as he began untangling himself from the seat.

"I agree," Din said under his breath, loud enough for only his bodyguard to hear. Dinnidek unceremoniously hopped down, landing solidly on the shifting deck. Tordek stumbled a little as he landed next to him. Din purposefully ignored Daerun and instead went to the railing to signal to the captain that they had survived the harrowing trip and could retract the boom.

The captain signaled back and said, "We'll wait nearby until you're finished with your meeting, then we'll use the rig to bring you back on board."

Dinnidek waved to the captain with a forced smile.

I hope this meeting lasts three days, he thought.

Din turned and walked past Daerun on his way to the captain's quarters in the aft. As he passed his brother, he heard Dare chortle with barely suppressed amusement.

"Oh, give it a rest," Din said in a tone just loud enough for Dare to hear. Daerun dropped any pretenses and fully gave in to his laughter. Din slapped his brother lightly on the shoulder. "You're brutal, you know that?" Despite himself, Din smiled as he tried to salvage what was left of his dignity. "It wasn't that bad, was it? I mean, I didn't squeal like a goblin or anything."

"No," said Dare, regaining control. "It wasn't that bad."

Daerun pointed over his brother's shoulder. Din turned to see Diessa pantomime clutching ropes with her hands as she scrunched her eyes as tight as she could.

"Brutal," said Din with an exasperated smile. "I'm never gonna live that down, am I?"

"No," said Dare and Deese in unison. Dinnidek decided that retreat was the better part of valor, so he purposely turned away from his siblings with a flourish and studiously examined the door to the captain's quarters.

The three Daamuz siblings entered the cabin with Veit and Tordek in tow. Having been onboard the smaller trading cog for a ten-day, Din noted how relatively spacious the captain's quarters were. A bank of windows dominated most of the back cabin wall and added to the roomy feel. The space was sparsely furnished, with a small writing desk attached to the right wall and a built-in bookshelf crammed with books, maps, scrolls, and mementos. The middle of the room was dominated by a heavy wooden table laden with small plates of food. Unrolled maps were held down at the corners with mugs, daggers, and a pair of candelabras. A ring of chairs consumed the remaining space. Saorsi was seated at the head of the table, Sunny standing to her right, his head just barely missing the rafters. The captain was dressed in a full black waistcoat with a high collar. She acknowledged Din with a slight nod and winked past him at Daerun. Rorik sat a few chairs away with a mug of dark beer in front of him.

Din placed himself opposite Saorsi at the far end of the table and waited patiently while the rest of the entourage took their seats. Tordek purposefully stood behind Din's chair. He took a wide stance and rested his hand on the back of the chair to maintain balance. Sunny was the last one to sit on a solid massive bench, and as he did, Saorsi spoke.

"Welcome, honored guests," she said, in a formal tone as she gestured to the small plates of food and the cask of ale by the door. "Please, make yourself comfortable and help yourself to refreshment. Lord Dinnidek, Chieftain of Clan Daamuz, has called this council to discuss our upcoming strategy."

Dinnidek took a breath to clear his head before starting. "Thank you, Captain. As you are all aware, Abyssal spies discovered the fleet and even now are shadowing our progress toward Halpi. This is correct, Rorik?"

Rorik had taken a pull from his tankard and took a moment to put down his mug before answering. "Yes," he said ruefully. "The gargoyles can be seen through our scopes, staying out of range but close enough to track us. They'll be able to lead the Abyssal forces right to us when we make shore."

Din nodded in acknowledgment. "So, it looks like an easy landing will be out of the question. Now that we'll be fighting our way to shore, I want to discuss our situation." He looked to his brother. "Daerun, what are you hearing from the warriors?"

Daerun glanced to Diessa before he spoke. "From what I've seen, and from what Deese has told me, our clansmen are confident. There was discussion among the warriors on my ship, and they believe the Abyssal Dwarfs have grown soft in the past decade. They believe that we're stronger because we're fighting for a cause. In short, their blood is up and they're ready for a fight."

Diessa nodded in agreement before adding, "Yes, the warriors on my ship think the same. They look forward to taking revenge. I should also note that they have taken to giving each other personal tokens, so their friends can deliver them to Llyngyr Cadw if they don't survive the assault."

"Lots of keys being passed back and forth," added Veit, referring to the talismans the refugee dwarfs were wearing. Daerun, who had taken up his tankard for a drink, banged it down on the table to show approval, just like he did at the Ale House. He took the chain that held his key from around his neck and held it in his hand.

Diessa's voice sounded quiet in the cabin, and Din had to strain to hear it. "This is a sign of our clan's resolve, it is true. But they are also acknowledging the dreadful price they may pay. I feel I must ask again, are we sure we want to go through with the landing if the fiends are waiting for us? It could take a heavy toll, and if we lose too many of our clansmen in the landing, there may be no reason to push on."

The room fell silent. Din took in his companions' demeanor. Most of them were looking at the table, the floor, or the rafters, as if avoiding the sight of their friends would remove the possibility that any of them would be lost. Only he and Saorsi were watching the others.

There's a thin line between courage and bravado, thought Din. *There will be plenty of bravado the next two days as the clansmen keep their spirits up. The true courage will come out when they're in the thick of it.*

Din locked eyes with Saorsi, who gave him a slight nod as if she was reading his thoughts. Din nodded thoughtfully in return and took a deep breath in. That seemed to signal everyone out of their thoughts and back to the conversation.

Daerun broke the silence. "Being spotted was certainly bad luck, but I think we have to continue on. The clan's confidence is high, and as I said, they're looking for a fight. If we turn back now, we consign ourselves to waiting for Golloch to come and have his way with us. I'd rather die fighting the Abyssals than my fellow dwarfs, no matter how misguided the Imps are."

Tordek and Veit grunted in agreement. Even Sunny said "aye" and pumped his fist in a small motion, at least what was a small motion for him. Saorsi, in contrast, gave no sign but kept looking at the other dwarfs. Diessa nodded her assent at last but kept her eyes down in her lap.

"That settles it, then," said Din. With that, he motioned to the map laid out on the table. "Captain Saorsi, you selected the site for the invasion. Could you please walk us through the terrain?"

Saorsi stood and addressed the group.

"If you look at the map, you'll see a portion of the eastern coast of the Halpi peninsula, between Jarrun Bridge and the southern reaches of the Dewbrock Plain." Saorsi picked up a rapier from the table to use as a pointer. She highlighted a section of shoreline with a spit of land that jutted out like a finger into the High Sea. Handwritten notes were scrawled all around the shoreline in small and tidy script. Black and red lines were laid out in the blue portion of the map that seemed to Din to have something to do with the water. Saorsi placed the point of the rapier on the spit of land. "This is the southern reach of the Dewbrock Plain. I've been using this spot for smuggling goods to Crafanc for the past two years. This headland to the north forms a natural jetty that should keep the seas relatively calm."

"Relatively," remarked Daerun. "It could be tough if the winds don't cooperate."

"Indeed," agreed Saorsi. "That's why we're going to do the assault in the morning, so we have the sea breeze at our back. You see the solid lines along here?" she pointed to the black lines drawn in the sea. "These show your depth at high tide, which occurs right around sunrise at this location. This will also allow us to bring the ships closer to shore to lessen your time in the longboats and offer some fire support."

Dinnidek noted the water was deeper along the southern side of the spit of land. He pointed to the spot and asked, "Captain, if I'm reading your map correctly, the water in this area seems pretty deep. Is it deep enough to moor a ship and disembark our troops without the longboats?"

Saorsi smiled at Din and shook her head 'no.'

"The water isn't nearly deep enough for any of the ships we currently have, except for in the one spot south of the spit. If we tried, we'd just run the ship aground, probably too far from shore to disembark easily. It's too shallow for the bigger ships, so we'll have to stick with the longboats."

Saorsi motioned to Sunny with her free hand, and the ogre stood and reached across the table. He moved a plate of scones to a spot offshore.

"We'll bring the fleet as close as we can before the landing craft disembark. This gives us the best chance to beach the longboats while avoiding rocks that could snag or sink you."

Sunny removed some of the scones from the plate and pushed them across the map to the corner of land just south of where the spit pushed out into the sea.

"You'll want to avoid landing on the spit. You don't want the enemy to form up on the mainland and bottle you up there. We'll instruct your warriors to row for a spot south of the spit here. This should give them all a common spot to aim for and allow you to amass your soldiers into battle formation faster. Once the landing craft have been launched, the transport ships will turn and head back out away from the artillery fire." Sunny took the now empty plate and pushed it back off the map. Saorsi gauged the room before asking, "Any questions?"

Din waited a moment, and hearing none, he moved on.

"Thank you, Captain. We'll be sure to brief our clansmen on the plan." He turned his attention to Veit. "Speaking of rowing, Veit, you've done a good job retrofitting the ships." The clan warsmith smiled at the compliment. The engineer had built a low lattice across the front of the longboats, where the warriors could place their shields while they rowed. "You've field tested the longboats and they don't become imbalanced?"

"Yes, my lord, we ran live tests with the men. We found that if we shift two of the warriors to sit further to the rear of the boat, the weight distribution remains the same. That being said, the shields won't be of much use against Abyssal Dwarf artillery, but it's better than nothing."

"No," said Din, "the artillery will be a problem, no matter what we do."

At this, Saorsi spoke. "Since the *Maiden* won't be transporting warriors, we'll be free to approach the shore and provide counter-battery fire. That should help some. However, if I can reach them, they can reach us, and we'll be a bigger target."

"I appreciate the offer, Captain," said Din, "but hopefully you won't be in harm's way for long. Rhyss and his rangers are supposed to rendezvous with us at the landing site. If he arrives in time, he'll know to target the guns first."

"Yes," said Rorik as he reached for a pastry ship and held it before him, "if he makes the rendezvous. However, there's no guarantee he'll make it." With that, he took a bite, as if to show the trouble they would be in.

"No," acquiesced Din, "there's no way to be sure. But Rhyss has never failed to come through. He'll be there." Daerun banged his tankard for emphasis. Rorik arched his eyebrow and went back to his beer. "Anyway, that's out of our control. I trust Rhyss to follow through. He trusts all of us to be there too. In two days' time, I intend to be shaking his hand on the shores of Halpi."

The rest of the Daamuz clan banged their tankards in approval.

That, thought Din to himself, *may have been bravado.* He pursed his lips. It had been months since he'd laid eyes on his old friend. A lot could have gone wrong in the past month. That didn't bear thinking about.

Rhyss, he thought silently as he stared down at the map, *don't make me a liar.*

* * * * *

"I know it sounds like I'm lying," Rhyss exclaimed to his mates around the campfire, "but I swear that stupid orc fumbled around in the stream for like two minutes. It was the most bizarre thing."

The rangers from Clan Daamuz all smiled at the memory. One of them chimed in to say it was closer to three minutes. The dwarfs of Clan Helgwin all looked skeptical, but they listened all the same. In total, a couple dozen dwarfs were gathered around a small, sheltered fire that had burned down to coals, so it no longer gave off much light or smoke. Rhyss had posted sentries in a wide perimeter. The campsite was surrounded by high rocks and dense foliage that would screen them from enemy scouts that snuck past his men. Most of the rangers were smoking pipes, and the clearing was full of the sweet smells of burning tobacco.

Rhyss continued his story. "And so he trips, and that dumb orc is sloshing around in the stream, and all of us are just standing around, waiting for him to get up. I mean, *everyone.* Even his stupid slave buddies were standing there with wet feet like, 'C'mon, Slag, get it together!'"

Rhyss delivered the last line in a low growly voice, and the rangers chuckled at his orc impression. The ranger captain was really warming up to his story now and stood up for the next part.

"So, by now, I've lost my patience, and just as Slag picks his stupid face out of the stream, I walk up with an underhand swing that just smashes him." Rhyss took a step into the circle and pantomimed the strike, as the rest of the rangers chuckled. "I spattered Slag's teeth all over his mates. I mean, I got Slag bits all over their clothes, their hair. It's a good thing they were already standing in a stream. And then it occurs to them that they're surrounded by dwarfs and they should probably do something."

"And how did that go?" asked Meick exaggeratedly in an obvious setup.

"Great for us," answered Rhyss, "and bad for them." The rangers all laughed in appreciation.

The laughter was short lived, and silence settled in again. Kilvar spoke in his quiet voice from his seat near the fire, "What do you expect from slaves?" Kilvar held an elaborate pipe featuring a pack of dogs racing along the stem after a fox, whose tail made up the bowl. His other hand was busy scratching behind the ears of a great black hunting mastiff named Boon. Boon nuzzled his head up into Kilvar's hand and thumped his tail back and forth in happiness. "They're bred to follow orders. Can't think for themselves. By Fulgria, I'd rather have a pack of hounds than a group of slave orcs any day."

"Hard to argue," agreed Rhyss. As usually happened when everyone agreed, the conversation lulled. The rangers collectively embraced the quiet. The only sounds were the occasional crackle from the coals and the accompanying hiss of a dwarf drawing on a pipe. Kilvar slowly rubbed Boon behind the ears. In response, the mastiff gave a contented 'shnuff' and laid down at his master's feet. Rhyss savored these moments of peace with his friends. Before the Abyssal invasion, he had taken them for granted, but the last decade had taught him how precious an evening of laughter and stories truly was. Add in a few pulls on a flask or draws on a pipe, and it created its own kind of magic.

I sound like a halfling, Rhyss ruefully thought to himself. But hard times reinforced what was truly important, especially when good things became scarce.

As if he was reading Rhyss' mind, Kilvar waved his pipe in the air.

"Rhyss, I want to thank your dwarfs for the tobacco. We've hardly had any leaf for the past few years." He took a long draw on his pipe for emphasis, and he slowly blew it out of his nostrils. The smoke pooled around his beard and made him look like a dragon in deep contemplation. "The clan has been rationing everything since the invasion started. The minute we got back from Rhyn Dufaris, we set a watch all around the mountain vale. First few years weren't too bad. We could still farm in a few pastures, hidden from Abyssal eyes. Two years later, we had to seal the underground tunnels. Too many goblins and ratmen."

Boon's head came up at the word 'goblin,' but Kilvar rubbed his head, and the great hound settled back down.

"Interesting thing about the ratmen," Kilvar continued. "We fought off multiple underground incursions since the invasion, and we usually thrash them good. You burn them up or kill their leaders and they flee back to where they came from. Last time we were attacked by a new breed of rat. These were fiercer and grittier than the Abyssal slaves we usually see. Seems like some of the rats have declared themselves independent from the Abyssals and are making a play at carving out their own warrens."

Rhyss spat into the fire at the news. "What's that human saying? The enemy of my enemy is my friend? That's a load of mushrooms. The enemy of my enemy is just another enemy." A few of the rangers chuckled at that.

Kilvar went on, "So we sealed the tunnels. The next year, the Abyssal raids got so bad we had to abandon the mountain vale. Five years in and we slammed the great gates of Crafanc shut, and we haven't been able to go out in force since then. The underground farms barely supply enough food for the people we have, and anything else besides food and water is a luxury. Crafanc would have fallen months ago if it weren't for Daamuz and the other Free Dwarf clans smuggling food to us."

"It's the least we can do," answered Rhyss. "The clans must pull together, or we'll get crushed one by one. Rhyn Dufaris taught us that."

"Rhyn Dufaris taught us plenty of lessons," agreed Kilvar with a tinge of bitterness. "We just learned them too late is all." He stared into the fire for a moment and then shook his head. Kilvar took a long pull on his pipe, and the ember inside the bowl lit up and reflected off his eyes as he spoke. "I hope I never have to be on the receiving end of those guns again. Rhyn Dufaris was enough for me."

"You fought at the Great Cataract?" Rhyss asked, surprised. "I thought your clan had been cut off in the retreat "

"Yeah, I was there," said Kilvar, a faraway look in his eyes. "It was a close-run thing, and we barely escaped after the battle. But we slipped away back north, pursued all the way by grotesques and halfbreeds." He took another long pull on his pipe. "Do you remember the sound those demonic guns make?"

"I'll never forget," said Rhyss. "Normal cannons make this whistling sound after the boom. The Abyssal shells make this low whine and growl as they cut the air. Sounds like a great beast hunting for you." He shivered as his memory relived the last battle, outside of Rhyn Dufaris.

* * * * *

Rhyss was pressed in among the surviving Free Dwarf warriors. The Abyssal Dwarfs had pushed the remnants of the Free Dwarf clans to the southernmost tip of the Halpi peninsula, where they hurriedly tried to make their escape across the Chainway over the Great Cataract. During their desperate flight, the warriors had been separated from their clans and had fallen into the battle line wherever they could. The Free Dwarfs were packed together, shoulder to shoulder, a living wall of steel determined to delay the Abyssal Dwarfs for one more day. In this place, in this moment, individual clans meant nothing. The only thing that mattered was that dwarfs were protecting dwarfs. Clans that had been rivals for centuries now gladly shed their blood for one another in the face of a common enemy that came with hate and spite and fire.

Rhyss was standing in the line, axe in one hand and a long spear in the other. He was next to Meick and a pair of dwarfs from the Thistledew Clan. The night was shrouded in smoke from the artillery and lit from below with the red of innumerable fires. Constant booms and explosions assaulted his ears, and he could barely hear the orders coming from down the line. A horde of ratmen were forming up in front of the battle line, backed by giant obsidian golems, jet black silhouettes against the nightmarish red background.

"Hold fast, boys!" Rhyss turned to his right and saw Daerun standing on a rocky outcropping in the front line, bolstering the men. Nearby, Din stood tall with his shining helm held aloft. Tordek stood solidly between them as always, the Daamuz clan standard planted against his right foot and flying bravely.

"For your kin!" bellowed Dinnidek. "For your wives! For your daughters! Your sisters and your parents!"

At each phrase, the warriors in the line yelled their defiance at the ratmen. A group of shells screamed low overhead and burst behind Rhyss. He flinched momentarily, ducked, and scrunched his eyes shut while clods of dirt and debris rained down on his head. He looked up in time to see the ratmen beginning their charge toward him, a mass of claws, rusty weapons, worm-like tails, and glowing red eyes. He felt the low thumps in the ground as the obsidian golems slowly plodded behind them, driving the ratmen forward.

Scanning the line, Rhyss saw a group of larger ratmen, dressed in better armor, heading for the spot between Rhyss and the Daamuz brothers. It looked like they were going to try to drive a wedge and break the dwarf line.

"Dinnidek!" Rhyss called out to get the clan chief's attention. Din turned and saw where Rhyss was pointing. Din nodded in understanding and patted Daerun on the shoulder. Dare took the Daamuz clan banner from Tordek and hoisted it high in the air. Rhyss turned back just in time as the ratmen gave a great war shout and closed the final gap between the lines. He stole one last glance at Dinnidek. The prince raised his axe high in salute. After a heartbeat, Din released his grip on the haft of the great axe and caught it quickly, giving it a quick sweep and a flourish.

Looks just like Drohzon when he does that, Rhyss thought.

With that, Din dove forward into the ratmen, Tordek a half step behind.

The ratman slammed into the dwarfen line. The dwarfs locked shields and prepared to repel the charge. Rhyss tightened the grip on his spear and stood just behind Meick, who held a great round shield and a short stabbing sword. He placed his left hand on Meick's back to support him as Meick took the impact of the rat's sword stroke on his shield. Rhyss switched his spear to an overhand grip and thrust it over Meick's right shoulder. He caught the ratman in the face with the point of the spear. The rat's head snapped back, and its leather helmet flew into the throng behind. Rhyss pulled the spear back and quickly chose another target. Another thrust buried the spearpoint in a ratman's shoulder, and it went down with a screech.

Rhyss tapped Meick on the shoulder and bellowed into his ear from behind.

"Push to the right!"

Meick nodded and turned his body to begin the push. Meick took a half step forward to take the space where the ratmen had been standing, thrusting to the right with his short sword under the leather chest plate of another rat. It coughed up a spurt of blood and dropped. Rhyss could see the knot of shock troops before him. They had driven a wedge a few feet into the dwarfen line, and the Ironclad line here was thin.

Rhyss turned to some of the Ironclad behind him and yelled to them. "We're gonna cut them off!" he said, pointing at the shock troops. "Come behind us and protect our flanks!"

The Ironclad acknowledged him, and Rhyss turned back to Meick, who was holding his ground.

"Ready?" he yelled above the din. Meick nodded, and Rhyss yelled, "Go!"

With that, Meick put his head down and pushed forward, Rhyss thrusting his spear at the enemy with every step. Rhyss felt the dwarfs behind him rush forward to fill the gap they'd made in the line. Rhyss took two of the shock troops from the side before the enemy knew they were in trouble. The elite rats had been swarming around Daerun and the clan banner. The prince was keeping them at bay with wide sweeps of the banner pole, and he called to his Shieldbreakers to hold fast while Dinnidek drove his own counterwedge into the ratman line.

"Come on, boys! They're nothing but slaves! This isn't their fight! This is our fight! We are the Free Dwarfs! Daamuz!"

Three of the largest shock troops attacked Daerun at once. The prince parried one of the attackers with the banner and used the motion of the parry to clip another enemy in the side of the head - but the weight of the pole threw Daerun off balance. The third shock troop raised his halberd high to strike Daerun. Rhyss hoisted his spear and threw it with all his might. It landed true, driving through the ratman's back, the end buried in the ground, pinning the vermin's writhing corpse in place. Daerun recovered and drove the butt of the banner pole into the last ratman's face. He gave a quick wave to Rhyss in acknowledgement for the help.

Rhyss pulled his hand axe just in time to see a ratmen dive recklessly into Meick with a vicious overhand stroke with its sword. Rhyss pulled Meick back and the sword clanged against the side of Meick's helmet, instead of cleaving the ranger's skull in half. Meick dropped like a rock and Rhyss stood over his friend's body. From behind the line of rats, the obsidian golems were approaching, giant black shadows against the red sky.

* * * * *

Rhyss shook himself and came back to the present. The sounds of battle in his memory were replaced by silence, and the infernal landscape faded away. The moon in the clear night sky cast a cold light over Pannithor. It was two days from full.

"The Abyssal Dwarf forces are heading from Crafanc down the coast as we speak," Rhyss said. "Looks like they know about the invasion fleet. Not long now. Two mornings, and we'll be at it."

"Yep," Kilvar nodded from across the coals as he pointed at Rhyss with his pipe. "Two mornings. And with the siege lifted, our forces will be free to come out and play. In the meantime, we'll keep shadowing the Abyssals and follow them to the landing site. If we keep our heads down, they'll never know we're there. Those orc outriders are no match for us. Brutish. Obvious. The bluntest of instruments. They're as easy to evade as they are to spot."

Rhyss smiled back at Kilvar. "It would be amusing if the stakes weren't so high."

He looked around the fire at the dwarfs from the two clans. Kilvar was right, they had learned the lessons of cooperation too late. But they had learned them all the same. It was time to teach the Abyssals some lessons of their own.

CHAPTER 13

Dinnidek sat on the end of his bunk and tried to clear his mind. It was an hour before dawn, and he wished that he had gotten more sleep. He was alone in the small captain's cabin with nothing but his thoughts, the slow motion of the ship, and the sounds of his soldiers gathering on the deck. He had spent the night immersed in equal parts excitement to be returning home and anxiety about the battle to come. It hadn't left much room for rest. Despite the early hour, he was dressed in his full battle armor, his white and blue tabard draped about him and his dragon helm on the cot by his side. He knew he should be on the deck, but he wanted to savor the precious moments of peace. They would be the last he'd have for a while.

He closed his eyes and spoke aloud. "Father, I promised you that I'd return and lead our people back home. That your sacrifice wouldn't be in vain. That I'd protect the clan in your name until we could stand again in our ancestral halls." He felt emotion welling up in his throat. "It took us years, but we've come to fulfill that promise. Through it all, Deese has been my rock and Dare has been my fire. We miss you and Mother so much. We've done the best we can to live up to your ideals and to make you proud."

He paused again to fight back a sob. In a voice shaky with emotion, he continued.

"Please, watch over the clan. May you and all of our ancestors guide us and protect us."

He took a few last deep breaths to compose himself, opened his eyes, and stood up. He smoothed his tabard, held his helmet under his arm, and took a step toward the cabin door. Pausing with his hand on the doorknob, he finished, "I love you, Father." Then he opened the door and strode onto the deck.

The ship was crowded with warriors gathered near their assigned longboats, and Din could feel the tension in the air. The dwarfs were speaking in hushed tones as if their need to connect with each other was fighting against their reluctance to break the stillness of the midsummer night. The air was warm, promising a hot day ahead. The soft glow of false dawn graced the eastern horizon as the stars shone bright and clear in the vast western sky. It reminded Din of how the sky looked from the mountaintops when he scaled the heights around Llyngyr Cadw in his youth. He took it as a good omen.

The Ironclad fell silent as Din strode up the steep stairs to the upper deck. He placed his hand on the rail and swept his gaze over every one of the warriors, making eye contact with as many as he could. The moonlight reflecting off their eyes was mirrored in their helmets and breastplates. It made them look ephemeral in the darkness, like ancestral spirits called to battle. Din raised his hand and addressed them.

"My clansmen, my family, my friends, our ancestors look upon us now with pride." Din spoke quietly, and the warriors gave Din all their attention. "We have come to take back what is ours. To fulfill our sacred oaths. To reclaim our homes and our honor. I know you've yearned for this day, just as I have. The filth that stains our realm and sits, fat and lazy, in our halls has no place in Halpi. These mountains and streams call to us to cleanse the land, to push the clanless betrayers, their mindless slaves, and their demonic minions back into the Abyss. They are many. But we are one. Let us go now, and fulfill our destiny, as one united clan. Look out for each other. Protect each other. Our ancestors walk with us. Together, let us wipe the betrayers from the face of Pannithor." Din slammed his mailed fist against his breastplate, and the sound reverberated through the night. He shouted to the heavens, "DaaaaaaaMUZ!"

The warriors all raised their fists and responded as one. "DaaaaaaaMUZ!"

Din smiled and raised his hands to the sky, soaking in the energy of the moment, the power of his clan. From the next ship over, he heard the clan name taken up by hundreds of throats.

"DaaaaaaaMUZ!"

He could see Diessa glowing in the lamplight from her spot in the ship's prow. She shone like an emerald with her green cloak and silver armor, warhammer held aloft. The clan name erupted from his left and he turned to see Daerun's ship plowing ahead. His brother stood in the middle of the ship, on a set of barrels by the main mast, surrounded by his men. Further away and slightly behind, the *Maiden's Revenge* was silhouetted against the rising sun, just breaking above the horizon.

Din turned back to his warriors and chanted the clan name again. The dwarfs roared their pent-up anger and rage into the morning, and the ships turned toward the shore.

Their shore.

* * * * *

Saorsi stood at her customary spot on the aft deck, Sunny next to her on the wheel. She was dressed for action in form-fitting black leather armor, high boots, wide-brimmed hat, and three belts festooned with daggers, a pair of pistols, and her rapier. The sun was just peeking above the eastern sea when the fleet erupted with battle cries. She smiled and let the moment wash over her. She'd never experienced anything like this, and she figured she never would again. A female dwarf leading a fleet of ships? It was unthinkable just a few decades ago. A female leading an invasion? Madness.

She turned to Sunny with a glint in her eye. "You ready to make history?"

Sunny smiled back but made no reply. He turned back to guiding the ship, but Saorsi could see him mouthing the word 'Daamuz.' Saorsi was glad to see it. She had been concerned when she first took this commission that the rest of the crew wouldn't go along. This wasn't their fight. Smuggling food and goods was one thing. But sailing into cannon fire? That was something else entirely. As usual, Sunny had understood Saorsi's motivations. He'd checked with the crew, like he always did, and got them to believe the vision as well. They had all been castoffs from their homes. A crew of misfits that had found common cause and purpose in each other. It was time to pay some of that good fortune forward. If they could help Clan Daamuz return home, that was worth fighting for. If they could put a black eye on the Abyssals, so much the better.

She knew this was something she had to do. To show that she wasn't some willful runaway with a trumped-up sense of her own ability. She was a damned good captain and an excellent leader, and her sailors knew it. Now it was time for the world to know it as well. She wouldn't let the invasion fail. Her honor demanded it.

"Alright, Sunny. Let's bring her around and start guiding them in."

"Aye, Cap," said Sunny as he turned the wheel. Once he set course, Sunny reached out with his giant hand and laid a few fingers on Saorsi's shoulder. His voice rumbled just loud enough for her to hear. "The lads believe in them, you know. They know we're doing right. The last year of smuggling made us lot believe that goodness can win. If we don't stand against evil here, then where? If we let it grow, where will it end? So yeah, they know this is right. They believe in the dwarfs. And the few that don't believe in Daamuz believe in you."

Saorsi reached her hand up and squeezed Sunny's fingers in acknowledgment as she looked up into his solid, square face. "Thank you, Sunny."

He grinned and kept his sights on the shore. "Anyway, our part will be over soon. We just have to get through the morning. Maybe those rangers have taken care of the guns for us."

As if on cue, Saorsi heard the distant sound of gunfire from the shore, followed by a low whining growl as Abyssal shells flew toward the fleet. They landed a thousand yards ahead of them, marked by white plumes of water. A small puff of smoke bloomed from the ridgeline back from the sandy shore.

"Well," said Sunny blandly, "there goes that."

Saorsi called out to her crew. "Alright, you dogs! Let's show these freaks what we're about! Moon, keep an eye on the shore and let me know when you see the puff of smoke from the guns. We'll see them before we hear them."

"Aye, Captain!" replied Moon from the crow's nest. His spyglass was out and trained on the shore, silver hair blowing behind him; one of Rorik's sharpshooters stood to his left, ready to snipe anything that got too close.

"Sunny, when Moon calls, you crank starboard. Next time, crank hard to port. Got it?"

"Aye, Captain," Sunny responded, loud enough for the rest of the crew to hear.

"Arvind, you keep the sails full until I tell you to stop, got it? Don't want us running aground when we get near the shore."

"Yees, Captain," the northman replied in his strange accent. He was seated cross-legged in an elevated spot at the very rear of the ship. He had foregone his fur vest and was bare chested, dressed only in breeches and a faded blue rag tied about his head. His eyes were closed as he wove his hands this way and that in a sinuous dance. Every few seconds, he gathered the air and pushed it forward to the sails. A gust of wind erupted from his palms and the ship surged forward. The *Maiden* began gaining on the trading cogs around them.

Moon called down from the crow's nest, "Now, Sunny!"

Sunny responded by cranking the wheel hard to the right, and the bow of the ship responded like a living thing. Saorsi counted to herself.

One, Two, Three, Fo-...

The shell landed with a splash, this time only a few hundred yards ahead. Saorsi nodded to herself. At the current speed, they would be within range to return fire soon. The key would be to not expose the broadside of the ship until they had the enemy artillery in their sights.

"Guns ready! Keep the gunports closed until my signal!"

The crew shouted back that they had heard the order. The *Maiden* wasn't transporting any of the landing force. Her role was strictly to coordinate the other ships and provide cover for the longboats. The trading cogs would drop their landing craft and then turn back out to sea to minimize time under fire. In keeping with the plan, the majority of the sharpshooters had been placed on Saorsi's ship. They wouldn't be part of the initial landing, and onboard they could offer long range support. She could see Rorik and the Wyverns clustered around the bow of the ship, their weapons at the ready.

"Keep us steady, Sunny," she said to her first mate, "I want to give those Abyssal guns something to think about."

* * * * *

Diessa nervously scanned the shoreline for the tell-tale smoke of the artillery. Every time the Abyssal guns fired, she searched the sky for signs of the shells. What had started as a few sporadic shots had grown into a near constant bombardment. Low booms sounded every twenty to thirty seconds. With each one, Diessa looked back at the wheel of the *Celestian's Smile*, where Captain Therngeld stood with an oversized longsword hanging from a belt that was cinched too tight. Despite his long human legs, the sword dragged on the deck and looked like it might trip the captain if he dared to walk anywhere. It was an apt metaphor, thought Diessa. From what she could tell, Captain Therngeld was an excellent trading ship captain who was out of his depth. The problem was that none of his crew had bothered to tell Therngeld that being a good sailor didn't make him a good soldier.

Diessa could see Dinnidek's small force of five boats already making a beeline for the sand, the warriors rowing with all their might. The makeshift wall of shields at the front of each boat bobbed wildly with the waves. She looked up at Therngeld, who was intently guiding his ship and monitoring the sails. She turned back as the artillery boomed with another volley. Therngeld had seen what the *Maiden* was doing and was imitating the motion, setting a zig zag pattern through the water.

Diessa felt Veit brush against her shoulder and lean in to whisper, "Do you think we should be boarding the landing craft? When will Therngeld give the order?"

Diessa turned and shook her head in exasperation. "I don't know. The soldiers are getting restless, and frankly, so am I."

She looked at the fleet and saw even more of the landing craft had pushed off from their transport ships. Still Therngeld didn't give the order to board. Diessa's eyes flicked to the group of Ironclad once more. She noticed some of them edging their way to the railing, and a few impatiently standing with their arms and feet on the rail, ready to spring at the slightest indication from the captain.

Finally, Diessa gave in and walked back to speak to Therngeld. He kept his attention on sailing the ship but addressed Diessa as she approached.

"My lady, what can I do for you?"

Therngeld was as polite as always, but Diessa could tell he was feeling the stress of the situation, putting up a brave face while under fire. Diessa felt for him - this probably wasn't what he'd envisioned when he'd signed up to help. It softened her attitude toward him for the moment.

"Captain," Deese began deferentially, "should I tell the warriors to disembark? The other ships have already offloaded their landing craft."

"Not yet, my lady," Therngeld replied. "I want to get the *Celestian* closer to shore before you disembark. I want to limit your exposure to those guns, if I can help it, and my ship can move faster through the water than those longboats." The artillery sounded again, and the captain turned the wheel in response. "With the sun behind us, the Abyssal Dwarfs will have a hard time seeing us in the glare."

Diessa nodded and turned back to Veit. The captain's reasoning seemed sound to her. But the other ships had already disembarked. Why hadn't they also followed the captain's reasoning? She just didn't know. She gathered some Ironclad on her way back to the bow, including their commander, a short dark dwarf named Bruon.

"The captain will give the signal to board shortly," she said. "He wants to get the ship closer to shore to limit our time in the water and get us to land faster." The warriors around her nodded thoughtfully. None of them had any experience at sea, so they were all at the mercy of the captain and his expertise.

Or lack thereof, Diessa thought.

* * * * *

"Excellent job, boys!" yelled Daerun from his spot in the bow. "Just like we practiced, one, two, three, four; one, two, three, four."

From his vantage point in the coxswain's position, Daerun could sporadically make out the spot on the shoreline where they would make their landing. When the boat crested a wave, the wall of shields blocked his vision, but when it came down, he could see groups of orcs and ratmen forming up to meet them. Rockets screamed overhead and burst on the waves all around the boats. Daerun was intellectually aware that there was only a tiny chance of any one shell hitting his little boat, but he cheered inside every time a shell missed and a plume erupted into the air. He breathed an extra sigh of relief, thankful that he wasn't seasick at the moment.

Felwyr called out the cadence to the men, with new lyrics to the same song they'd been using to train.

> When I reach the shore, lads
> When I reach the shore
> I'll find the closest slave
> And put him in his grave
> He'll bother us no more.

The warriors all took up the song, singing the second and last lines. Meanwhile, Dare kept his eyes on the landing site, nestled between the main beach and the spit of land. That spot of land remained empty.

"Come on, boys!" Dare shouted. "Just a little further!"

The scream of a rocket flew close overhead, and Daerun flinched down. The explosion from the shell was close enough to shower the warriors with sea water. The rowers lost their cadence, and the ship foundered for a second before Felwyr got them back on track. Daerun clenched his teeth tightly; he'd rather be fighting a million demons than be stuck out here in this stupid boat. Out here, he and his troops were helpless, at the whim of randomness and chance. All they could do was row faster to bring this nightmare to an end.

"Come on, boys," he yelled to his men. "Let's get this part over with! I'm bored and want to crush orc skulls."

Another volley of rockets whined and growled their way overhead, and he heard a great explosion from behind the *Maiden's Revenge*. Was that one of the transport ships getting hit? No way to know.

"Keep rowing! One, two, three, four!"

* * * * *

"Hold now, Wyverns," Rorik ordered. "Hold your fire. Almost there. Almost within range." Rorik watched through his scope as the enemy formed battle lines along the shore, waiting for the dwarfen longboats that were barreling recklessly toward them. Luckily for them, the artillery seemed more focused on the transport ships than the landing party. He found it odd, but he couldn't spare too much thought for it. A shell struck the water less than one hundred yards off the starboard side, and Rorik felt the explosion reverberate through the ship. That one had been close, but compared to the warriors on the landing craft, he was as safe as the mountain. It would take multiple hits with those shells to bring down the *Maiden*. Rorik took it for granted that Saorsi would do everything she could to protect her precious ship if they got into real trouble.

Through the scope of his rifle, Rorik swept the northern horizon and saw troops of gargoyles flying in the distance. Strange that they were keeping so far out of the fight.

"Looks like they're keeping their distance," Rorik muttered to himself. "Learned their lesson last time they tussled with us." He turned his scope to the shore. The ratmen were amassed near the bend, with the orcs to the left. It looked like they were trying to repel the invaders piecemeal, using the orcs as the anchor for that flank.

He thought for a moment then made a decision. He turned and shouted back to Saorsi as he pointed toward the horde of orcs that had formed a living wall. "Captain, do you see those orcs portside? I think we should head in that direction and target them with our broadsides. Give Lord Dinnidek a chance to take the shore."

Saorsi turned, spoke with Sunny, and then shouted back. "Thank you for the suggestion, Master Rorik. I need to get close enough to silence those guns, and if I turn broadside too soon, we'll be a juicy target. You'll have to use your amazing rifles to do what you can." Another shell burst to the starboard side, this time a little closer. Saorsi cursed up at Moon to keep his fool eyes open.

Rorik shrugged in mild annoyance. Who cared about those shells? They hadn't hit much of anything so far. Meanwhile, the orcs were a real and imminent threat. He ordered his sharpshooters to target them and cause as much havoc as they could.

"You know the drill," he said, "aim for the biggest ones in the bunch. Unless you can pick out an Abyssal Dwarf in the mix, then end him quick."

He turned to check the range once again when a shell screamed by, just missing the top of the mast and striking the side of one of the transport ships. Strangely, this one had started offloading soldiers later than the rest. Two of the landing craft were just pulling away from the ship, filled with warriors. The shell smashed the other two longboats to pieces, with half of the aft landing craft hanging uselessly from the ropes that fastened it to the railing. The explosion tore a giant hole in the side of the ship, sending splinters of wood flying everywhere. The wooden shrapnel left a deadly swath in its wake.

Rorik could hear the sailors and warriors scream, some in panic, some in pain, and he felt a heavy dread in the pit of his stomach. He was rethinking his attitude toward the artillery. Saorsi was right, the guns had to go.

* * * * *

Dinnidek heard the explosion, and his head whipped around in time to see the aftermath. Debris from the cannon shot flew through the air, and shards of wood and metal rained down into the sea. He heard the yells and screams carry over the water, and his blood ran cold as he recognized the ship.

"Oh no," he moaned aloud. "Deese!"

He shouted his sister's name as he involuntarily stood. He took a half step to the aft, as if he would dive into the sea and swim to Diessa.

Tordek grabbed him around the waist and pulled him back down. They landed hard together on the bench, Tordek's oar hanging limply in the water. The rest of the Ironclad had stopped rowing at Dinnidek's outburst. Tordek held tight to Din and glared at the warriors.

"Don't stop, you fools! Keep rowing! Our lives depend on it."

Dinnidek heard Tordek take command, but everything felt far away. Din was completely numb. What had he done? He felt Tordek hold him tight, and Din half-heartedly struggled to break from his friend's grip. Tordek leaned in close, speaking so only Din could hear.

"I know what you're thinking, but the ship isn't sunk yet." Din squeezed his eyes shut and clenched his fists in pointless anger. "A few of the landing craft have disembarked. She may be on one of them. You don't know she's dead, so we have to act like she's alive, understand?"

Din opened his eyes, breathing ragged, but thankfully facing away from the other warriors. He got himself under control enough to nod to Tordek. A wave of boiling rage surged through Din. Could Deese be alive? Perhaps. But either way, the Abyssals would pay. They would pay dearly. Dinnidek grunted and turned his attention to the shore where the Abyssal Dwarf foes were waiting for them. Lines of ratmen and orcs. The Abyssal Dwarfs hadn't even had the stomach to come and face him. They'd sent their lackeys instead. Pathetic.

He addressed his warriors with cold steel in his voice. "You heard Tordek. Keep rowing!"

Din picked up Tordek's oar and pulled. He let the repetition of the motion wash over him, push his emotions down, and give him something to focus on. The artillery continued to rain down, but Din kept his eyes firmly on the Ironclad on the bench in front of him.

Tordek yelled to the crew, "A few more pulls." Din heaved the last few strokes and the ship ground to a halt against the sand below. "Prepare to disembark!"

Din stood and turned to face the shore, which was just paces away. Tordek handed Din his shield. Dinnidek took it, drew his war axe, and jumped over the side. The water came to his thighs, and the buoyant waves lifted him slightly while his armor weighed him down. It was a weird feeling. Around him, other landing craft ran aground in the shallows. He took a few strides away from the ship, making room for the rest of his warriors to disembark.

The orcs stood in the sand, at the edge of the waves. Din noticed his Ironclad rushing to the beach, and he called out to them. He raised his axe and rallied them to his position.

"To me!" Din commanded. "Daamuz, to me! Form up on me, then we take the beach." His Ironclad obeyed and the warriors gathered in a great horde about him. Tordek stood a few paces away, holding the clan banner high in the air. "To me! As one! As one!"

The clan stood shoulder to shoulder, the waves pushing them step by step to their home. Din let out a mighty shout, "DaaaaaaaaaMUZ!" Over a hundred throats joined him. The Abyssal slaves unconsciously clustered tighter together in response, even as they roared back. Din called out the clan name again and led his people slowly, inexorably, out of the sea. More landing craft were disgorging dozens of Ironclad to join the line all around him. The orcs held their positions, not wanting to fight the dwarfs and the waves at the same time. When the water was just below the top of his boots, Dinnidek called the charge and broke into a run. The clan followed, a madness in their voices as they screamed their war shouts.

Dinnidek took the last few yards in a sprint and closed with the orcs. He pushed forward with his shield held up to block a descending swing from the closest enemy. Momentum brought him inside of the orc's swing, and he caught his foe's forearm on the metal rim of his shield. The sword stroke had lost all its power, and the weapon clattered harmlessly off Din's shoulder pauldron. He continued to push and knocked the orc off balance. It fell back into the press of his fellows, spoiling their attacks and disrupting the line. Another slave came with a low stab from a rusty sword. Din took a stutter step backward and brought the bottom rim of the shield down hard on the sword as the orc overreached. The sword clattered harmlessly to the ground, and Din swung his war axe down onto the top of the orc's head. The blade glanced off the side of the enemy's leather helmet and buried itself in its shoulder. The orc faltered and instinctively reached out for Din to keep itself standing but Dinnidek pulled the war axe out of the slave's shoulder blade and brought it down with a quick chop onto the top of its head. It fell face down into the sand.

Din felt the press of the Ironclad formation as more warriors joined the line and the dwarfs pushed forward. The warriors here had successfully formed a beachhead. Din let out another cry and thrust forward into the orcs. He would make them pay.

* * * * *

Diessa opened her eyes, or at least she tried to. All she saw was blackness. It was odd, because the last thing she remembered, the sun had been up. A persistent ringing in her ears muffled the sounds around her. She shook her head from side to side and got her bearings, but she was in a daze. She realized she was lying prone, face down, and she felt heavy. No wonder she couldn't see anything. She pulled her hands underneath her and pushed herself up gingerly from the deck. Something held her down, but she squirmed forward to get out from under it. She opened her eyes again, and this time it worked. Sort of. One of her eyes was stuck shut. Diessa brushed lightly across her eye socket and the fingers came away sticky and wet. She put her hand in front of her working eye as she came to her knees. The fingers were covered in blood.

Ah, she thought in a detached way, *that explains it.*

Her breathing came quicker as she realized that the blood was hers. She ran her hand through her hair, and she felt the cut across her hairline.

Thankfully, it didn't feel deep, but it was a mess. What had happened? She urgently tried to stand but only got to one knee before she fell back onto the deck in a wave of dizziness. She closed her eyes and waited for the world to stop spinning, taking slow, deliberate breaths to keep her growing panic at bay. She pressed her palm to her head to put some pressure on the wound and breathed through the pain. Finally, after what felt like an eternity, she opened her eye again to survey her situation. Bodies, and parts of bodies, were lying everywhere. Wood splinters were strewn across the deck, some as big as her forearm, and the ship looked to be torn apart from the inside out.

On the aft deck, Therngeld's lifeless body was draped across the wheel. She remembered now. She had heard the screaming of the approaching shell, then a flash of light and she was thrown to the ground. Pieces of wood had eviscerated the dwarfs climbing onto the landing craft. The last thing she experienced was the deafening sound of the explosion and something landing on top of her. She craned her head to the left and saw Veit lying next to her on his back with a piece of wood stuck in his lower leg. Diessa snapped out of her haze, and she gasped in mild panic at the amount of blood around the wound. Her breathing came fast as she moved to check on Veit, but she felt him shudder and shift his body. He was as dazed as her, but he was alive, thank Dianek. Her eyes widened when she realized what had happened – had Veit shielded her from the explosion?

"Veit," she called to the engineer. "Veit!" this time more urgently.

"Deese?" he answered.

It was hard to hear him above the ringing in her ears, and his voice sounded like he was speaking through stone.

"Oh, thank the gods, you're alright." He rolled on to his side to look up at her. "I'll be okay. My leg got caught in the shrapnel from the explosion. But you're safe."

Diessa smiled weakly at Veit as she tried to stand on wobbly legs. Now that she knew Veit was alive, she took stock of the situation. Even though the captain was lost, the survivors outnumbered the dead. Lots of dwarfs were still alive, crawling dazedly over the deck or clutching wounds. The *Celestian* listed to the side, and she heard a deep groan from belowdecks. Veit maneuvered himself so that his back was to the main mast, and he sat up with a groan of his own.

"The ship," he began, then winced from pain. He started again, taking shallow breaths between each phrase. "The ship is sinking. I think there are survivors... below decks... but the landing craft... were all destroyed..."

Diessa stood up and stumbled to the rail. Water poured through a gaping hole in the side of the ship. The back half of the last longboat hung there in mockery. Clansmen were crying in pain over the ringing in her ears. Veit was right, she had to find a way to get the boat to shore. She shuffle-walked to the aft deck and gingerly climbed the stairs to the wheel. Up close, Diessa could tell that Therngeld hadn't seen the end coming. A shaft of wood from the deck had buried itself in the captain's head. Diessa gently disentangled the captain's lifeless arms from the wheel and pushed his body away. She tried the wheel, but it wouldn't spin. She gave it a kick, but it wouldn't budge. She felt the adrenaline pulse through her muscles, forcing her to action. She gave the wheel another kick as she looked out past the ship toward the shore, which was close, but still too far away. Panic began rising within her, but she took some deep breaths and tried to tamp down the rising feeling of dread.

She made her way back to Veit and weighed her options. The *Celestian's Smile* would continue sailing into the middle of the bay until it sank. She couldn't steer it – nor did she know how to - and she couldn't make it go faster. If only there was a way to move the ship to the shallows in time. Panic began nibbling away at the edge of her mind, but she ruthlessly shut it down.

I survived, she calmly explained to herself, *so that I can help the others survive. What can we do to get the boat to the shallows?*

In a flash, it hit her. If she couldn't get the boat to the shallows, she'd have to bring the seafloor to her. She kneeled next to Veit and held his face in her hands.

His eyes locked on hers, and he smiled. "Thank the ancestors you're okay."

Diessa smiled back at him, shakily. "Thanks to you." He sighed and closed his eyes, but reopened them as Diessa leaned in close. "Listen, Veit. I'm going to try to save the ship. I need you to stay with me. I need you to wake me up if I black out. Can you do that?"

Veit's eyes flashed, and he grabbed for Diessa's hand. "What are you planning?"

"I'm going to summon Joro and ground the ship." Now that she said it, she realized how risky it was. Earth elementals needed rocks and stones to hold their power. Sand was the hardest material to use, and Deese would be drained to the core as Joro tried to hold his form. But what choice did they have?

Veit squeezed Diessa's hand. "We talked about that... It won't work... You said so yourself."

"Yep." Deese answered with a tired smile. "I'm doing it anyway."

Veit sighed in exasperation. "Okay. I can't stop you... How will I know if... you're in trouble?"

She smiled at him.

"Trust me, you'll know. Now hush and keep an eye on me." She leaned forward and gave Veit a kiss. It was quick, almost chaste in its brevity, but Veit's eyes widened in surprise all the same. Veit went to say something, but Deese raised her hand. "Later."

With that, she felt around her clothing and found the pouch containing Joro's summoning stones and placed them before her on the deck. The ship was listing heavily now, and she had to hold the stones down with her free hand to stop them from sliding away. With her other hand she etched a rough circle into the wooden planks of the deck with her dagger. She placed the dagger in the circle, not because she needed it for the ritual, but because the dagger wouldn't roll, and it held the stones in the circle while she chanted. She closed her eyes, took a breath, and began.

* * * * *

"Come on, boys! Daaaaamuz!" Daerun bellowed the clan name as his Shieldbreakers stumbled through the waves to his position. He had finally beached his longboat just south of the headland, near the bend. He took the time to gather his Ironclad in his front line, great round shields at the ready. Behind him, Felwyr was organizing the Shieldbreakers, armed with two-handed axes and mauls, into battle groups that could reinforce the line or push the enemy back once the hand-to-hand fighting began. In the rush to the shore, Daerun had lost his shield, but he had exchanged weapons with one of the Shieldbreakers and now wielded a great hammer with a long haft. A horde of ratmen were coming down the beach from the bluffs behind, led by Abyssal Dwarf slave drivers. The vermin were dressed in ragged padded armor with rusty weapons and helmets. What they lacked in quality they more than made up for in quantity. The beach was covered in ratkin, and they weren't in organized formations; they were just arrayed in mobs. Daerun looked to the north and saw that the spit was clear, but he couldn't lead his soldiers there. The water there was too deep and, as Saorsi had said, they would end up being stranded and picked apart. No, he'd have to lead his warriors onto the shore here.

He heard Felwyr coaxing the last of the stragglers into position. The Abyssal slave drivers answered by screaming at the ratmen and whipping them into a frenzy on the beach. Daerun wondered how his soldiers would be able to press forward against so many enemies. The decision was taken from him when the rats suddenly surged forward into the sea and charged the dwarf formation.

Daerun started in surprise. They were charging? He smiled brazenly as he turned to his clansmen and raised his axe in anticipation.

"Ha!" he yelled to his men. "The slaves want to welcome us home. Let's show them what a real homecoming looks like!"

The dwarfs tightened their line, weapons at the ready. As the ratkin rushed into the water they foundered against the waves and lost the momentum they had gained from charging on the beach. "Send it over, vermin!" Daerun taunted. "Daaaaaaaa…"

"MUZ!"

The dwarfs bellowed their war cry just as the rats made contact with the line. There was a great crash of iron on wood and steel as the dwarfs locked shields and stopped the ratmen advance. A few unfortunate Ironclad fell from spear wounds or lucky dagger thrusts, but they were replaced as the second line of Ironclad stepped forward to fill the gaps. Daerun swung his great hammer in a wide arc and buried the metal head into the side of one of the rats. There was a sickening crunch, and the slave crumpled to the ground. A few ratmen thrust their spears at Dare, but Felwyr covered the prince with his great shield. Daerun hefted the great hammer and swung it high, striking another slave in the head. Blood sprayed from the ratman's long snout and spattered all over his mates. Daerun stepped back for another swing, and Felwyr stepped forward to shield them both from attack.

"Daamuz!" Dare cried, as the ratmen in front of him regrouped for another push. He heard a great shout from his right and spared a glance. The Ironclad regiment had repelled the vermin advance, and they now allowed the Shieldbreakers to move through the line to take their place. It was a tricky maneuver to execute and a testament to their discipline and training. The Shieldbreakers splashed forward through the surf and came at the enemy with a fury. Their great weapons swung through the air and landed like meteors from the heavens. The rats on the front line fell like grain at harvest time, but there were so many of them that the dwarfs couldn't carry their momentum any further. A fresh press of slaves halted the dwarfen advance, and a vicious melee ensued.

Past the Shieldbreakers, further to the north, he could see Abyssal Dwarf regulars forming up along the spit of land. They would be in the flank of the dwarfen line, but the same deep water that stopped Daerun was also too deep for the Abyssal Dwarfs to cross. A great squeal snapped his attention back to the ratkin who were charging once more.

"Here they come again, boys!" he shouted as Felwyr stepped to the side. Dare swung his hammer overhead in a wide arc in front of him, and the rats hesitated. One foe tried to stop but was pushed forward by the troops behind, and he took the hammer stroke on the top of his iron helmet and fell into the surf. The hammer skipped up off the helmet and continued through its trajectory. Daerun, still facing the enemy, let the momentum carry the hammer over his head and brought it around for another strike. It landed with a satisfying thud into the side of another vermin. Like an intricate dance, Felwyr stepped forward and pushed the remaining enemy back with his shield to give Dare room for another strike.

Dare looked up the beach and saw row upon row of ratmen. Individually, they were no match for the dwarfs, but there were so many. They wouldn't be able to take the beach as long as the rats pinned them in place.

"Lots of 'em, boys! But it's no matter," he said as he took another swing that crushed a vermin's skull. "We have all morning!"

* * * * *

"I want a crew on the longboat now!" Saorsi shouted from her customary place on the aft deck. "Cast off and get me any survivors from the *Celestian*!"

She pointed to the sinking trading cog with her spyglass for emphasis. A trio of sailors jumped to the task, swung the landing craft away from the deck, and started lowering it to the sea. A pair of shells growled and whined as they whizzed by. The artillery barrage was so intense now that Sunny was ignoring Moon and simply turning the ship by instinct. Saorsi peered through her spyglass and zeroed in on the artillery. The ridgeline was clouded with smoke from the demonic guns, and she couldn't make anything out through the stagnant gray-black haze. Small puffs were coming hot and heavy now.

She gritted her teeth in annoyance. The rangers were supposed to have taken care of the guns by now. At this rate, they wouldn't last much longer. Another shell exploded fifty yards off the bow. If she lived through this and met Captain Rhyss, she swore to punch him right in the mouth.

At least some of the trading ships had begun turning back out to sea. So far, the fleet had lost four ships total. Not bad, considering how heavy the bombardment had been. Saorsi scanned the skies around the *Celestian's Smile*. The cog was taking on water and listing heavily. She figured the ship had only a few minutes before it would capsize.

She trained the spyglass to the west to see how the warriors were doing. A few of the longboats were still making their way toward land, but for the most part, the warriors had made it to the shore.

Saorsi looked to the southern shore and saw Lord Dinnidek's troops making good headway against the orcs. The Daamuz clan banner was waving wildly in the sea breeze, and she could see the footprints in the sand where the dwarfs had gained ground. Between Dinnidek to the south and Daerun's forces to the north, there was a space where the clansmen and orcs were scattered thin, and the fighting was more fluid. The remaining longboats were headed to that section of shoreline, and it seemed that the Free Dwarfs would be able to easily close the gap. From the number of craft remaining, another couple hundred warriors were still to land. To the north, the enemy commander was trying to push Daerun's force back into the sea with little success. The beach was teeming with ratmen, but Daerun seemed to be holding his own. It was only a matter of time before the vermin lost heart and broke. They could only handle casualties like that for so...

Saorsi's blood ran cold as she turned the spyglass onto the headland. The sandy spit of land was full of Abyssal Dwarfs — holding blunderbusses. At first she only counted a few, but more were rushing to fall into formation. She lowered the spyglass and saw the full situation. Daerun's troops were being pinned by the ratmen while the Decimators were preparing to fire into their flank and mow them down. The prince and his soldiers were as good as dead if they didn't do something.

If *she* didn't do something.

She looked at the waves and her trained eye saw the deep part south of the headland. In a split second, she made her decision. She checked to make sure that the longboat had cast off, and then she turned to her first mate.

"Sunny!"

"Aye, Captain," he responded while turning the wheel sharp to the left.

"I want you to go full sail and make for a bearing seventeen degrees to the right."

"Aye, Captain," Sunny reflexively responded. Then he stopped and looked at her. "Wait, what?"

Saorsi glared at Sunny with eyes like steel. "You heard me, Sunny. Seventeen degrees right, full sail."

Sunny looked like he was going to argue, then he peered into the heading. After a few tense seconds, he nodded in understanding.

"I see now, Saorsi," he said in a low tone. "Sorry." He turned the wheel and started bellowing in his low baritone. "Moon, get down from there and unfurl the sails full."

Moon's head poked out from the crow's nest and gave a cheery wave. The elf patted the sharpshooter with him on the shoulder and, with the grace afforded him and his kin, clambered under the metal hoops that served as a rail. He swung out onto the spar for the sail and began working the ropes. Meanwhile, Sunny set the new course.

Saorsi did some quick math in her head and yelled back to her mage.

"Arvind, once Moon has those sails open, you give me one more wind blast. Once that's done, prepare to drop anchors on my signal." She pointed down to the deck at the sailors gathered there. "You lot, get below decks and prepare the guns on the starboard side. I want them primed and ready to fire chain and grape on my order. The rest of you, prepare the ship for grounding."

Most of the sailors jumped to obey, but a couple of them hesitated at the last order. Saorsi bellowed in anger, "What are you waiting for? You see those Decimators on the shore? They're gonna butcher Daamuz where he stands. By the salt in my veins, we're not gonna let that happen. Now prepare the guns and do as I say, or I'll leave you here when we're done!"

That got the sailors' attention, and they ran quickly to obey. Saorsi gripped the rail tight. This was going to be close.

* * * * *

Rhyss crept forward through the scrub trees and bushes near the shore. Meick and Banwn were to his right, Kilvar and Boon to his left, the rest of the rangers trailing behind. The foliage here was short and sparse, and it clung desperately to the thin sand for life. Luckily for the rangers, the thick smoke from the Abyssal Dwarf guns shielded them from view, just as the relentless thunder of the rolling artillery fire shrouded any sound they made. Rhyss furrowed his brow in annoyance that they couldn't have arrived earlier, but what was done was done. His rangers had been forced to deal with an errant halfbreed patrol, and though it had been necessary to ensure their secrecy, he cursed the delay.

He stopped and peered ahead through the smoke. He could see the closest guns, silhouetted against the morning sun. The artillery were twisted constructs of metal and bone that stood almost ten feet tall, towering over their crew. The gun chassis were designed to look like cavorting demons holding up mortar barrels that resembled fiery cauldrons or leering demonic faces. He could make out a group of Abyssal Dwarf warriors guarding the artillery and the baggage train. It was hard to reckon numbers, but it looked like a couple hundred warriors were arrayed in a wide arc. Some were facing inland, but most of them were watching the battle on the beach below.

Rhyss motioned for his rangers to halt, and he mimicked shooting his crossbow. He normally would have used hand signs, but Kilvar wasn't part of his clan, and he didn't know the intricacies of the clan's dialect. Rhyss looked back and saw the rangers emerging, spectral, from the smoke. Kilvar froze and kept a strong hand on Boon's collar.

The artillery kept up a steady fire. Over the explosions and sounds of metal-on-metal, Rhyss could hear deep guttural growls and groans coming from the war engines, punctuated by screams echoing from the depths of the Abyss. It unsettled Rhyss' nerves and made him jumpy. He shook his head in anger at himself. Despite the urgency, he didn't want to act rashly. If he came at the Abyssal Dwarf guards piecemeal, they'd destroy his force. He'd have to wait until he had a critical mass.

Rhyss whipped his head around as he heard an enormous explosion out at sea. The Abyssal Dwarfs cheered and gave a loud war whoop in celebration. Rhyss could see a great gout of fire erupt far out in the bay. From the sounds of it, the gunners had scored a direct hit on one of the landing craft. Rhyss felt anger swell up inside him. They couldn't afford to wait any longer.

Rhyss signed to Meick. *Hold line. On my sign fire three times. Then we charge.*

Meick nodded and sent the signals down the line. He crawled over to Kilvar to let him know the plan. The hound master was crouched low and peering back inland. He still had a tight hold on Boon's collar. The hunting mastiff was standing stiff at attention, ears pointed straight up and eyes focused on the Abyssal Dwarfs. Rhyss tapped Kilvar's shoulder and spoke into his ear.

"Our rangers will pepper them, then charge on three. Sound good?"

Kilvar nodded, then turned his head to speak into Rhyss' ear in return. "Got it. I'm going to send in the dogs on the second volley. Disrupt the line and give us cover for the charge."

Rhyss gave him a thumbs up and went back into his position while Kilvar issued his orders back to the dwarfs who were straggling to the line. Rhyss signaled to Meick, *Dogs on two. Aim high on three.* Meick nodded and sent the word back.

Rhyss waited tensely and counted to sixty to give his rangers time to receive their orders and get into their final positions. At sixty, he raised his hand and shook it toward the Abyssal line, one finger, two fingers, three fingers, flat palm gliding across his torso.

With that, he raised his crossbow, aimed at the closest target through the haze, and fired. His crossbow string thrummed with the shot. A half second later, he heard the cries of alarm from the Abyssal Dwarf line. He reloaded, picked another target, and fired again. This time, the target's body spasmed before falling to the ground. He felt the wind of the great mastiff's passing as Boon ran swift as an arrow toward the Abyssal line. He watched in appreciation through the smoke as the hound bounded across the dunes and landed like a shadow amidst a cluster of Abyssal Dwarf sentries. They had barely raised their weapons before Boon pounced on the closest one and latched onto its forearm with vicelike jaws. Rhyss fired his crossbow at one of the other three sentries, and a metallic clang rang out as the bolt bounced off the Abyssal Dwarf's helmet. He slung his crossbow, drew his hand axes, and ran toward the dazed enemy with a wordless shout.

Rhyss sprinted across the dunes with his rangers, sparing quick glances this way and that to check on them as they advanced. As he ran closer, he could make out more details through the smoke and the haze. To his left, a pair of hounds were worrying away at an Abyssal Dwarf body. Behind them, a knot of Abyssal Dwarfs were fighting fiercely in a small circle, surrounded by rangers. Boon had overborne his quarry and was trying to bite down on the Abyssal Dwarf's neck. The fiend had used his other arm to shield him, but Boon crunched down into the forearm, and the Abyssal Dwarf screamed in agony. Rhyss raised his hand axes in front of him as he ran the last few feet toward the dazed warrior that he'd shot in the helmet. The fiend was still gazing at the ground and had just straightened his helmet when Rhyss arrived and savagely chopped across his body to smash him square in the face.

Rhyss caught the third Abyssal Dwarf sentry moving out of the corner of his eye, and he barely turned in time to catch a sword stroke on the end of one of his hand axes. The impact wrenched the axe from his grip, and it fell to the ground at Rhyss' feet. Rhyss instinctively swung his second axe around, but the sentry deflected it with his shield. Rhyss recovered and squared off against the Abyssal warrior.

A tense moment went by as the two foes sized each other up. Rhyss bent his knees in a feint to grab at his axe on the ground. In response, the Abyssal Dwarf took a step forward and thrust his sword out at Rhyss' abdomen. Rhyss stepped back and parried, but the fiend was now standing on top of his dropped weapon. He knew that he was in trouble. The Abyssal Dwarf had longer reach with his sword, and he had a shield and strong armor to deflect Rhyss' remaining hand axe.

The Abyssal Dwarf saw Rhyss glance down at the ground and smiled at him in mockery before stepping in and attempting to bash Rhyss with his shield. Rhyss desperately backpedaled out of the way, but his injured knee from the cave gave out. He landed flat on his back and the air whooshed from his lungs. He locked eyes with the Abyssal Dwarf as the monster smiled broadly in triumph. The fiend stepped forward and pulled back his sword for a final stab, and Rhyss feebly brought up his hand axe in defiance.

Just before the Abyssal Dwarf could land his blow, he was tackled from behind by Boon. The jet-black mastiff landed like an omen of doom and rode the Abyssal Dwarf's back as his prey landed face first in the sand next to Rhyss. The ranger rolled away, recovered his second axe, and stood. He turned quickly to defend himself, but he needn't have bothered. Boon's jaws were firmly buried in the back of the Abyssal Dwarf's neck. A torrent of blood erupted from the wound and was greedily soaked up by the sand.

Rhyss exhaled in relief at his escape, and his vision expanded to the battlefield again. The incessant sound of the artillery had ceased, replaced with the more mundane cacophony of battle. The Abyssal Dwarfs had recovered from the initial shock of the charge and were trying to regroup. The rangers were picking off the stragglers at the fringes, but there were still enough enemy troops to offer stiff resistance. Most of Rhyss' soldiers were busy hacking away at the infernal machines and their crew. He saw one of the guns, the bodies of its crew lying dead all around it, actually buck in place like a living thing and shoot a gout of fire from its barrel. The rangers flinched back from the flames, but one of the unfortunate souls got caught and went up instantly, the fire clinging to his skin and hungrily consuming his flesh. The air was full of the smell of sulfur and burnt hair. The rangers redoubled their attack, burying their axes into the exposed bone and leather sections of the great war engine. The demon inside the machine howled in rage as the fire within the monstrosity flickered and died.

Rhyss ran toward the rangers assaulting the engines and got their attention. "Form line! Form line!"

Rhyss pointed frantically to the closest group of Abyssal warriors who were rallying for a counterattack. The rangers fell into a thin line facing the enemy and loaded their crossbows. The Abyssal Dwarfs were shouting war cries and getting into a coherent formation as more of their force rallied together, and they'd be ready for a counter charge any minute. The rangers aimed their crossbows and awaited the order from Rhyss.

"Fire!"

The volley tore through the Abyssal Dwarfs. A few of the more unfortunate ones fell dead, while others were wounded or stunned by the impact. The rangers loaded for another volley as the Abyssals milled around in shock. From further inland, Rhyss could hear the enemy war horns desperately trying to rally the Abyssal troops closer to the beach. Rhyss and his men efficiently reloaded their crossbows while the fiends were shaking off the effects of the volley. With a desperate cry, the Abyssal Dwarfs clustered together and charged toward the rangers.

"Fire!"

The second group of shots was devastating. The fiends fell to the sand, clutching their chests, legs, and faces where the bolts had struck them. Some of the ones that were lucky enough not to be shot instinctively dove to the ground for cover, and the charge faltered. The psychological effects were devastating. In the face of the crossbow fire, the remaining Abyssal Dwarfs turned and fled down the dunes toward the sound of the horns, ceding this part of the battlefield to the rangers.

The rangers had loaded their crossbows and were preparing to fire, but Rhyss focused them on the task at hand.

"Let the curs run! Now we have to finish off those guns!"

With that, he charged toward the closest demonic mortar, his rangers close behind. The dwarfs yelled their battle cries, shouting the clan names of Helgwin and Daamuz. Rhyss grinned in satisfaction at finally striking back against the Abyssal Dwarfs. He laughed in a mixture of exultation and bloodlust. He'd spent the last year killing their slaves and constructs. Now he had struck a blow against his infernal kindred, and it felt glorious.

* * * * *

Rorik swore out loud as his shot went wide. Through his scope, he could see his target – an Abyssal Dwarf armed with a thunderpipe and an ornate helmet – flinch as Rorik's shot struck the dwarf next to him with a splatter of blood. He 'tsked' in annoyance as he methodically went about reloading his rifle and spared a glance around the ship. From his place in the bow, he hadn't caught the specifics of Saorsi's orders, but the sailors were urgently rushing around while the ship picked up speed toward the shore. He hoisted his rifle and searched for his target amid the press of Decimators.

"There you are," he said out loud as he zeroed in on the pesky Abyssal commander. To be fair, he couldn't be sure that his target was a leader; but in his experience, commanders had more ostentatious clothes to set them apart. You couldn't go wrong sniping at the soldier with the biggest hat. He carefully took aim and exhaled as he pulled the trigger. This time his shot hit true despite the rocking of the waves; the Abyssal Dwarf fell to the ground and out of his scope's field of vision.

Rorik took down his rifle and noticed just how close they were getting to the shore. He peered through his scope to see if the artillery were within range. He smiled in satisfaction as he saw the swirling melee all around the ridgeline.

"Yes!" he exclaimed. It was one less thing to worry about. Rorik spared a glance at the rest of shore, which was still getting closer, despite the fall of the artillery. He turned to the aft and saw that the sails were completely full and sailors were frantically tying loose cargo down across the deck. Rorik looked back at the spit of land and could tell that the ship was bustling along at a good clip. He saw Daerun's forces savagely fighting the ratmen in the waves, Decimators arrayed in their flank. From behind, he heard Saorsi commanding the sailors to ready the anchors on her signal. His brain replayed the last few minutes, and it finally put the pieces in place.

"Sweet Fulgria," he exclaimed. He slung his rifle across his back and grabbed the railing in growing panic. "She's gone mad!"

* * * * *

Daerun's instincts told him that the ratmen were close to breaking. The vermin had relentlessly pushed against the dwarfs, but Daerun's soldiers had been implacable. Even though they hadn't been able to gain any headway, the Shieldbreakers were slowly grinding the enemy down. The cries and exhortations of the slave drivers grew more and more desperate as they clung to whatever control they still had over the mass of slaves. The two sides in this part of the battle paused as the ratmen regrouped for another charge, and the dwarfs tightened their formation in response.

Dare's breath was heavy, and his arms were getting tired from the constant battle. His legs were fatigued from fighting the continual motion of the waves. His boots were soaked, and his feet felt like they were made of stone. Felwyr stood stalwartly nearby. His oversized round shield had a few notches cut from along the upper rim but was still serviceable. Daerun sized up the ratmen. He could tell that they were losing their enthusiasm for the fight, and if they were repulsed one more time, then a concerted dwarf push would scatter them. If the rest of his troops felt like him, then they wouldn't be able to mount a sustained charge with legs like lead. He'd have to time it just right.

Dare was about to issue orders to the warriors when he heard the sharp crack of massed gunfire from his right, followed by cries of panic and pain. He glanced quickly to that flank, and his blood ran cold. The ratmen were fully engaged with the Ironclad on that side of the line, pinning the dwarfs in place. Just beyond them, in the distance, he could see Abyssal Dwarf Decimators through a haze of smoke that had come from their thunderpipes. They were arrayed in formation along the headland and had fired into his flank, striking the dwarfs and ratmen alike. The rats there screamed in panic and tried to retreat, but the dwarfs cut them down as they turned to flee. The Decimators prepared another volley and fired into the mass of bodies. Warriors from both sides fell indiscriminately to the barrage of shrapnel. Daerun yelled in dismay at the carnage. His troops were trapped between the sea, the ratmen, and the blunderbusses. There would be no escape.

Luckily for him, the foe before him had also stopped in response to the gunfire, and it gave Dare a moment to react. He grabbed Felwyr's sword arm and yelled at him to follow as he ran northward to take command.

"Ironclad to the north! Form shield wall! Shield wall!"

At Dare's order, the dwarfs were reforming to face this new threat, but the water, the floating bodies, and the sand slowed their progress to a crawl. The Abyssal Dwarfs raised their guns and fired again. Ironclad frantically hunkered down individually behind their shields to deflect the hail of bullets. Some of them knelt in the water to shelter themselves, but it was to no avail. The bullets struck a wide swath of the line, and dozens of dwarfs fell to the relentless fire.

The dwarfs let out a groan of dismay as Daerun splashed toward his men. "Form wall! Form wall! Shieldbreakers, to me!"

If he could pull them back, he may be able to make a concerted push in the middle and gain the beach. But even with the protection of the shield wall, they were sitting ducks. The water was too deep for the Ironclad to reach the Abyssal Dwarfs to the north.

"Hold, boys!" Daerun screamed to bolster his troops in the face of certain death. "Hold!"

He cringed in anticipation as the Decimators again raised their weapons.

He inhaled in surprise and gaped, slack-jawed, as the *Maiden's Revenge* plowed into view. He let his hands drop to his sides as the great white and blue ship sailed straight between his soldiers and the Abyssal Dwarfs. The great hull towered above the battlefield, and the bow shielded the Ironclad from the line of Decimators. He heard the shouts of sailors as they held onto the railings, and Rorik clinging white knuckled to the bow, yelling "No, no, no!" Above them, all he heard was Saorsi's strong voice shouting out orders as her ship came to a grinding halt. The bow of the ship pushed up into the air as the hull struck against the sandy sea bed. Some of the sailors lurched forward at the sudden stop, others were barely able to hold fast. Through it all, Dare's gaze was transfixed by Saorsi, standing calm and in command.

* * * * *

Rorik braced his legs and arms tight as the *Maiden's Revenge* careened through the water. The sailors dropped anchors behind the ship and turned the sails wildly to get them out of the wind. The *Maiden* had slowed considerably over the past fifty yards, but it was still moving fast when it ran aground. A great shudder went rocked the entire vessel that shook the masts and jolted Rorik to the core. He was thrown forward, along with some of the unfortunate sailors and anything that hadn't been battened down. He caught himself against the rail and took a second to steady his nerves. The ships listed to his right, the mast leaning toward the spit of land and the Abyssal Dwarfs below.

Saorsi didn't waste any time to begin shouting orders.

"Dammit, Moon, get below decks and elevate the guns! Sunny, get down there and help him! Arvind, fry those bastards!"

Rorik couldn't help but grin as he watched the Abyssal line scuttling to reform amid the confusion from the sudden appearance of a warship out of nowhere. The enemy commanders were attempting to restore order when a bolt of lightning arced from the *Maiden* into the Abyssal Dwarf formation. Rorik smelled the tell-tale odor of ozone and heard the Abyssal Dwarves shriek above the crash of thunder.

The lightning bolt shook Rorik to action, and he brought his rifle up and peered down his scope. A quick sweep and the fancy cloak of his target filled his sights. He followed the cloak up to the Abyssal Dwarf captain's head. He exhaled and pulled the trigger. Blood erupted from the Abyssal Dwarf's collar, and his prey dropped out of sight. Shots from his fellow sharpshooters whizzed through the air like wasps. He pulled his scope down and his vision expanded again to show the whole beach. The Decimators had recovered from the initial shock and raised their thunderpipes to aim at the *Maiden's* decks. Rorik reflexively dropped down onto his back for cover, and a hail of metal sliced over his head. Small chips of wood splintered into the air where the bullets hit the wooden railing. Rorik calmly loaded his rifle while he stared up at the sky.

"What was Saorsi thinking?" he complained to himself. "This is madness!"

He rolled onto his stomach and poked his head above the deck. He saw the Decimators reloading their weapons, their commanders ordering them to hold their ground. Rorik stayed prone, propped up on his elbows. He went to select another target through his scope, but as he did, he saw the Abyssal Dwarfs raise their weapons toward the Maiden. He pulled down the rifle and quickly rolled away onto his back again as the crackle of gunfire rang out, answered by cries of pain from the ship's crew.

Rorik rolled back to his stomach and took aim. As he did, he heard what he assumed were the gunports opening up. The crew was shouting from below decks as he took a bead on an Abyssal Dwarf banner bearer. The standard featured a stylized thunderpipe crossed with a lightning bolt. The standard bearer himself was partially concealed by the banner, and Rorik waited patiently for the breeze to shift the cloth enough to give him a clear kill shot. He could distinctly hear Sunny's deep baritone, "A little more. Little more. Keep cranking the screw. That will do it!"

The Abyssal standard bearer turned to offer encouragement to his troops, and his helmet came into view.

Rorik relaxed his shoulders, peered through the scope at the top of the dwarf's helmet, and exhaled as he pulled the trigger.

Sunny yelled, "Now! Fire!"

Rorik's shot dented the standard bearer's helmet, and the Abyssal Dwarf fell like a stone as a shower of his own blood washed down over the right side of his face.

The deck shook violently under Rorik, and the explosions that followed were deafening. He grasped the railing post to steady himself and he stared in dread fascination as the Decimators simply ceased to exist. Grapeshot and cannister tore through the Abyssal Dwarfs, shredding the unit to pieces. Bodies were strewn everywhere, blood and gore spattered all over the ground where the thunderpipes had once been. The beach was full of the guttural screams of the injured and the moans of the dying. The few foes that remained were momentarily stunned at the extent of the wreckage around them. Likewise, Rorik was frozen, stupefied, at the destruction.

"I'll be damned."

* * * * *

From his vantage point, Daerun saw the *Maiden's* cannons unload upon the Decimators and heard the deafening sound of the broadside. Rapid flashes reflected off of the water as the guns fired, and he watched transfixed as the close-range cannonade threw up gouts of sand and hurled Abyssal Dwarf bodies into the air. In a single moment, the *Maiden's Revenge* had eviscerated the Abyssal Dwarfs from that part of the battlefield. Daerun, his Ironclad, the Shieldbreakers, even the ratmen, all stared in mixtures of fascination and horror at the Abyssal Dwarf remains.

As if waking from a dream, the dwarfen warriors sent up a wild cheer filled with relief and elation. Daerun shouted in joy with the rest of his clan before coming to his senses. The ratmen were beginning to slowly step away from the dwarfs as they realized the danger they were in. The dwarfs had to take advantage right now if they were going to finally gain the beach. He pulled at the soldiers around him and started bellowing orders.

"To me! Shieldbreakers form up for the charge! To the shore! To Halpi!"

The dwarfs were energized with renewed vigor. It was as if the last hour of fighting against sea and swarms had never happened. With a frenzied war cry, the dwarfs stormed the beach, and the ratmen melted away. Those that tried to fight were relentlessly slaughtered. Dare finally ran out of the water and onto dry land. It was a glorious feeling.

Once they had gained the shore, Dare raised his hammer high in the air, and his warriors began clustering around. From the north, he saw the remaining Decimators who had escaped the initial cannon barrage trying to regroup on the mainland, outside of the arc of the *Maiden's* guns.

"Felwyr, take the Ironclad and head westward. Keep the pressure on those ratmen and don't let them rally, understand? Shieldbreakers, with me! The captain sacrificed her ship to save us. We're going to head north and provide her with some cover. We'll drive into the remnants of the Decimators and scatter them to the four winds."

The soldiers acknowledged the orders with enthusiasm at the prospect of revenge. Felwyr began designating warriors to gather the troops and follow behind as he and the immediate Ironclad tore off after the ratmen.

Daerun shouted the clan name and ran north, the Shieldbreakers keeping pace. He was afraid that the Decimators would stand their ground and fire into his men, but the Abyssal Dwarfs had no more stomach for fighting. They turned and ran for their lives. Some even dropped their guns in their haste. When he saw that the Abyssal Dwarfs no longer posed a danger, he slowed his run to a trot, then a walk, and surveyed the field. His Ironclad had taken the beach, and the clan warriors owned the entire field from the spit of land south to where his brother was pushing back the orcs. The guns on the bluff above were silent. Dare saw a mass of Abyssal Dwarf warriors gathered to the west. It looked like the enemy commander was pulling his remaining dwarf forces back and sacrificing his slave troops to cover his retreat. It would be nice to destroy them once and for all, but Daerun knew he had to consolidate his forces and sweep the beach before they could indulge in chasing the enemy inland.

Dare glanced up at the *Maiden's Revenge*. He shook his head in astonishment at the last few minutes. *Thank the gods for Saorsi,* he thought. *We'd be dead if it weren't for her.* His eyes swept the decks, and he saw the captain standing proud near the wheel. By chance, she looked in his direction and caught his eye. Dare stopped walking, and he raised his hand in salute. Saorsi raised her hand in return, then blew him a kiss before striding out of sight. Despite himself, Daerun felt self-conscious. He smiled a little too broadly and felt his face get a little hot.

I'm being a sap. Diessa will never let me live this down. Now that he wasn't fighting for his life, he wondered how Diessa had fared during the landing. *No way to know now. I'm sure she's fine. Probably landed safely with Veit somewhere south of here.*

* * * * *

Dinnidek fought like a berserker against the slave orcs. He had channeled the loss of his sister into an unrelenting rage that threatened to turn him from a trained warrior into a mindless killer. He fought with an intense savagery that his foes couldn't match. He had recklessly thrown himself into the fray, and where he went, the orcs fell. Throughout it all, Tordek had shadowed Din, guarding his flanks and protecting him from the enemy and from himself. Finally, Dinnidek began to reach the edge of his endurance. His emotions couldn't overcome the growing weariness in his limbs, and he was moving slower and taking deep breaths in between his attacks. After the latest engagement, the orcs pulled back to regroup, and Tordek barked at the soldiers to stay in formation and hold their ground.

Once he was sure that the Ironclad were in good order, Tordek took the opportunity to stand in front of Dinnidek. The stoic bodyguard pulled Din in close so only he could hear.

"My lord, rest a moment. We have them on their heels. No need to get yourself killed now that we're home."

Dinnidek stared blankly at Tordek for a few deep breaths and slowly came back to his senses. He took stock of how tired he was. As the anger subsided, it was replaced again with the deep sense of loss. He understood now how a dwarf could give in to rage and despair and lose himself in the path of the berserker. It was an easy way to bottle up his emotions and dull the pain. He took a few more breaths and looked at the Ironclad around him. They were regarding him with a mixture of awe and apprehension. He looked back toward the waves and saw the trail of orc bodies that lay strewn in the sand. He couldn't seem to remember the last few minutes. His mind registered that Tordek had been giving orders to the men. He squeezed his eyes shut for a second and concentrated on regulating his breathing. Two deep slow breaths and he felt more like himself.

While his eyes were closed, he heard the dwarfs around him murmur in astonishment. He opened his eyes in time to see the *Maiden's Revenge* sail pell-mell for the shore, then he gasped as the ship ran aground. He hadn't put any thought into how the rest of the invasion was going. He saw Daerun's troops pressed into the sea against the masses of ratmen. He shook his head in shame. Tordek was right. The clan needed a commander, not a killer. The wary looks from his Ironclad reinforced the feeling. In the distance, he heard the crackle of gunfire from the Decimators. Past the *Maiden*, out in the bay, Din saw the *Celestian's Smile* listing and slowly sinking below the waterline. Another round of distant gunfire echoed down the beach.

Din clenched his fist in anger at his impotence. He should have been able to keep Diessa safe. He knew that the sentiment was completely ridiculous, but in that moment, it didn't matter.

The beach north of the *Maiden* erupted in fire and steel, followed by the cheers from his soldiers. He saw the ratmen break and run for safety. The Ironclad around Dinnidek shouted in triumph and turned toward the slave orcs. The enemy, so savage just moments ago, began to lose their resolve. They clustered together and tentatively stepped away from the dwarfs.

Din smiled at the closest orc and yelled his clan name in defiance. The orc flinched back as hundreds of dwarfs shouted in response. Dinnidek raised his war axe and rushed forward against the shaken enemy, and his warriors followed as one. The dwarfs locked shields and ruthlessly pushed the orcs back. Here and there along the line, the orcs tried to hold their ground, but the dwarfen shield wall left no room for the orcs to counterattack. Where before the orcs had relied on their ferocity to stop the dwarfs, now they had nothing. They were slaves, nothing more. They lacked any sense of purpose besides killing, and without the upper hand, they were wilting. The slave orcs gave one last hopeless push but were repulsed easily by the dwarfs. Tordek and Dinnidek pressed forward and cut down three of the orcs in rapid succession. It was more than the orcs in this part of the line could endure. The orcish retreat went from a steady walk to a panicked rout as the dwarfs rushed forward into the gap. The panic spread down the line, and within seconds, the orcs ceded the field, turned tail, and fled inland. Tordek shouted the clan name and led the Ironclad in chasing down the fleeing foe.

Din ran forward, swept up by the rest of his troops, but after a few strides he slowed his pace and eventually stopped. Now that the enemy was fleeing, Tordek's words dawned on him.

They had done it.

They had come home.

Din was overwhelmed with emotion, and he fell to his knees in the sand. Ten years of pent-up anger and anxiety welled up from inside of him. With ragged breath and shaking limbs, he dropped his axe and his shield and covered his face with his hands. He kept his eyes closed and soaked in the moment with his other senses. He felt the sand of Halpi beneath him, smelled the sea, heard his warriors shouting their triumphant war cries over the sounds of the waves. After a minute, he lowered his hands and opened his eyes. He was looking up into the merciful sky, and he let his gaze fall back down onto the *Celestian*.

In that moment, all the satisfaction that had burned like a fire within his breast went cold. He saw the ship, slowly sinking. Only, on second look, the ship wasn't sinking. It was in the same position it had been in a few minutes ago. He wondered if the ship had run aground or was just taking a while to succumb to the waves. He focused intently on the ship, and he saw the sails shifting back upright. Dinnidek slowly stood as he watched in disbelief. The ship was righting itself and was actually rising in the water. How was that even possible? He stared in wonder as the ship slowly moved toward the shore. As it came closer, the water got shallower, and the ship continued to rise above the waves. From this distance, Dinnidek could just make out the head and arms of a giant humanoid shape sticking out of the water. Joro laboriously pushed the ship through the surf to the safety of the earth.

Dinnidek shouted in delight. "Diessa!" Her name was a prayer of thanks to the generations of his ancestors. "Yes!!"

His eyes welled up with tears as he ran up the beach to see his brother and sister.

* * * * *

Rorik couldn't believe what he was seeing. The damaged trading ship was being half dragged, half carried through the waves by a giant earth elemental. The goliath was mostly submerged beneath the waves, but Rorik was close enough to make out a myriad of strange and fascinating details. The elemental rose slowly from the waves, water cascading down the stone, sand, and coral of its body. The sand that made up its form kept sloughing away, as if it couldn't keep its cohesion, and its head was a bulbous lump on top of its oddly shaped body. Rorik saw a small fish flop to and fro from a crevasse near the goliath's shoulder before finally dislodging itself and falling mercifully into the water below.

The *Celestian* was a ship in name only. Its hull was fractured, and water was pouring from the hole in its side. The back of the ship was a mess of splintered wreckage and bodies, both alive and dead, laying on the deck. Shouts of relief and amazement arose from within the vessel. Rorik noticed a pair of dwarfs huddled together near the main mast. He recognized the stone priestess and smiled at her resourcefulness. The earth elemental gave one last great heave and pushed the ship up and out of the waves toward the shore. With that, the elemental seemed to melt as the sand that held the stones together succumbed to the ocean waves and dissolved into the surf. The ship gently ran aground and slowly settled into its final resting place. Rorik looked down at the *Maiden*, beached as it was on the headland, and wondered if the stone priestess could do that trick again.

* * * * *

Veit sat near the mast, cradling Diessa's head in his lap. He gazed intently at her face and gently stroked her blonde hair. He was careful to avoid the cut on her head. He felt the *Celestian's Smile* glide to a stop, but his gaze never wavered. He was softly calling Diessa's name, and a few tears tracked through the dust on his cheeks and into his beard. Diessa's breathing was ragged, and blood was trickling from her nose. She had fallen unconscious a few moments after Joro had arrived. He felt her pulse race as the elemental dragged the ship to shore.

Now that Joro had been released, the tension in her face softened, and she fell into a deep sleep.

"You did it," he whispered to her. "You saved them. You saved us."

He heard the survivors stirring. They were speaking to each other in hushed tones about the miracle that had just occurred. Still, Veit kept his eyes on Diessa. He leaned over and kissed her lightly on the forehead.

"You are amazing," he whispered.

The survivors began to gather around Veit, keeping their distance out of respect and awe for what Diessa had done. Now that the ship was safe, Veit's leg throbbed in intense pain that was harder to push aside. He tried to straighten his limb, but it was frozen in place. His muscles near the wound just wouldn't relax. He'd have to see a healer, after Diessa, of course. He would make sure she was okay first.

CHAPTER 14

Dinnidek stood on the beach of his homeland and listened to the dwarf camp from a distance. His warriors had finally settled down after a long morning of battle and a longer afternoon of toil. The camp had been laid out, tents erected, fires lit, and the dwarfs had allowed themselves to enjoy their hard won victory. But instead of joining in their elation and relief, Din had refused to share in his clansmen's joy. Instead, he had spent the afternoon in a blur, knee-deep in all the minutiae of administering to the clan. He'd ordered the soldiers, secured supplies, established a field hospital for the wounded, set watch, and sent out scouting patrols. He'd attended to the dead and personally led the warriors in caring for the bodies. That had been the hardest part of the day, harder than the fighting. He'd made sure to acknowledge every fallen warrior in a small way. He collected their keys, said their name, and gave a small prayer to their ancestors for each clansman as they were carried to their final burial place.

Dinnidek knew he was using his responsibilities as a shield. He was trying to drown his feelings with work but was only partially successful in blocking out the guilt. Every time he came close to stopping the self-accusations, to getting his mind right, the look of apprehension on his warriors' faces during the beach assault came unbidden to his mind. His loss of control and the resulting uneasiness he saw in his clansmen's eyes justified every ounce of self-loathing he could heap on himself. He was no berserker, and he had no desire to become one. But he was confronting a part of himself that he did not like. He hadn't stopped moving since the battle ended. He was like a baby who craved the soothing motion of his mother, swaying back and forth while she held him close and told him everything would be okay. But now that the work was done, he was left alone with his thoughts. Since sunset, he'd walked beside the shore, but now Din stopped and forced himself to be still. The warm sea breeze, the sounds of the waves, and the moonlight all combined to center Din and calm his mind.

Upon reflection, he had been subconsciously avoiding everyone, except for Tordek of course, whose duty demanded that he stay near Din at all times. But Tordek felt Din's need for space and obliged by keeping his distance as much as he could. Even now, Tordek respectfully stood far enough away to not intrude, but close enough to intervene should something happen. As he watched, another dwarf approached Tordek. Din couldn't hear their exchange over the sound of the waves, but as the dwarf came closer, Din recognized the confident stride. Rhyss respectfully stopped a few paces away, but Din motioned him closer and gathered him in a strong embrace.

For a moment, the two old friends just stood and smiled at each other. In the whirlwind of the afternoon, Din hadn't had a chance to really reconnect with Rhyss. They had both been too busy with clan affairs. Din hadn't spoken with him in months, and the ranger's presence reinforced his feeling of calm and quiet.

"Rhyss." The name was all Din could manage before he was overcome with emotion. Rhyss nodded in response, seemingly struck speechless as well.

Finally, Rhyss broke the silence. "We finally did it. It took ten years, but we did it. We came home."

"Yes. We still have a long way to Llyngyr Cadw, but we've come home to Halpi." They silently shared the moment together, savoring the words. "You did excellent work, Rhyss, securing supplies, gathering our allies, and destroying the Abyssal artillery. I knew I could count on you."

Rhyss frowned at that and gestured vaguely toward the silhouettes of the shipwrecks out in the bay. "I should have been here sooner. If I had done better, we wouldn't have lost so many."

"You were spectacular, Rhyss. You can't hold yourself responsible for the timing of the battle. Thousands of decisions led us to this morning. You couldn't be expected to know where the enemy patrols were. When you found them, you dealt with them quickly and moved on, like a true leader. You're not a god, Rhyss." Din slapped Rhyss affectionately on the shoulder. "You're just an amazing mortal, and a slightly above average dwarf!"

Rhyss chuckled at the last part and then gave Din a long look. "You okay? Tordek called for me and told me you needed a friendly ear."

"Oh, did he now?" Dinnidek looked over Rhyss' shoulder to where his bodyguard was standing. If Tordek couldn't see him, he'd hopefully still feel Din staring daggers at him. Dinnidek reflected before answering. The day had been a maelstrom of emotion for them all. "Yes... And no. We won, Rhyss. We scored a great victory today. I should be happy. I should be like Daerun, celebrating with the men. But I can't shake the sadness at seeing what we've lost. To be honest, I've never experienced this mix of emotions before, at least not so strongly. My only taste of real battle was during the Abyssal Dwarf invasion, and that had been a string of bitter defeats. In some ways, it's easier to lose and see the dead and the wounded. It's more... consistent? But to win, to know that today was a great day for our people, and to know that our exile is over... I feel so satisfied, so happy. But right there, right underneath that joy, is this nagging guilt that keeps pointing to the casualties, the destruction. How dare I feel any semblance of happiness when my fellow clansmen lay dead? Is the price of our victory, the price of our clan's honor... my honor, too high? I keep thinking of what I could have done to save more of them."

Rhyss stepped closer to Dinnidek.

"Din, you can be sad, you can mourn, but you can't put their deaths on your shoulders. That weight will crush you. Yes, we suffered. Scores of our warriors will never walk the earth again, scores more will live with their injuries for the rest of their lives. But this was the price the clan was willing to pay. You can't have a battle without loss." Rhyss paused to assess Din's demeanor, and his voice got gentler. "It took me years to learn that lesson. I worry over every ranger that I lead, but I can't stop the hand of fate. Neither can you."

Dinnidek smiled ruefully. "I know, Rhyss. It just hurts to see it."

"Of course it hurts. You'd be no better than our bastard cousins if you weren't moved. You can hurt. You *should* hurt. But you're no more responsible for their deaths than I. You're not a god, Din. You're just an amazing mortal, and a slightly above average dwarf." Din chuckled ruefully at having his words brought back to him. Rhyss pressed on. "You know I'm right, Din."

"Yes, yes," Din said dismissively, "I understand that, Rhyss. But to know something isn't the same as seeing it. I spent so much time planning things out, trying so hard to think of every detail, search for every edge I could give us to keep everyone safe."

Rhyss smiled. "You did. But that's not how this works. Death is a part of war. It's a fact. You can't plan your way out of it. And I know that you'll always judge yourself more harshly than others. You just commended me on how I led my men, and all I see are the flaws. It's our nature. It's one of the things that makes a good leader."

Din snorted. "Good leader? How can I call myself chieftain when my decisions almost doomed the clan?"

"Nay, not doomed," replied Rhyss. "This was a victory, Din."

"Yes, we won, but if Saorsi hadn't..."

"We won," Rhyss stated bluntly. "Despite all the catastrophic scenarios running through your mind, the fact of the matter is that we won. All the 'what-ifs' just don't matter. They aren't real. Yes, it was close, and things could have gone different. But they didn't. The Daamuz clan has come home, just like we said we would."

Dinnidek frowned at the ground and clenched his fist.

"You're right. But it goes deeper than that." Unbidden, he saw Diessa's ship explode, relived the terror, and felt the utter powerlessness. "The landing was successful, yes, but not because of me. In some ways it was successful despite me. You, Daerun, Saorsi, Tordek, all led the clan to victory. Meanwhile, when I thought that Diessa was dead, something inside of me snapped. All my meticulous planning counted for nothing. I was powerless to save her, the same way I was powerless to save my parents, the same way

I was powerless against the Abyssal Dwarfs, and the Imps. I hated myself for how weak and impotent I was, and it drove me mad. I vented my hatred on the orcs. Tordek was left to lead the warriors. In that moment, I failed, Rhyss. I spent years preparing for this day, and in the moment of truth, when my people needed me to lead them, I threw it all away. The clan trusted me to be their chieftain, their protector, their steady hand that led them to victory. I betrayed that trust, pure and simple."

Din took a few deep breaths to regain his composure.

"Are you done?" asked Rhyss with a smile. Din glared at Rhyss, but the ranger didn't waver. "First of all, you're talking down about my chief. Could you stop the Abyssal Dwarf invasion alone? Were you going to talk reason to Golloch? Could you deflect the cannon shot so that it missed Diessa's ship? No. You're not powerless, you're just mortal." Rhyss paused to let his words sink in. "You think you failed? I've had a chance to catch up with the lads around camp. Let me tell you what the clan is saying. Word is that you prepared the army and forged them with discipline and determination." Rhyss held up his fingers and ticked them off one by one. "That you personally led them in countless hours of drill. That you learned how to row alongside them and feel their unease on the water. That you gave them poise in the line of fire."

Din scoffed, but Rhyss persisted.

"After our exile, you helped us rediscover our confidence and our purpose. You showed us a vision of what was possible and gave us a path forward. It was your planning that allowed us to be successful. There are supplies waiting for us right now because of you. There are lads from Clan Helgwin to assist us because of your foresight. How can you honestly say that all this work was in vain? Din, we're standing here in Halpi because of you. The clan trusts you. They don't need you to shelter them from all the evil in the world."

Din considered that for a moment. Everything Rhyss said was true. All his preparation, his planning, had been key to their success. Was he being fair to himself? Of course not. Somewhere along the way, he had conflated leading the clan through hard times with shielding them from hard times. As if he alone had the power to make everything right in the world. He had irrationally taken on the responsibility of keeping everyone safe. Now that he said it out loud to himself, it sounded like madness. What arrogance! What ego!

Din shook his head at his own folly, and Diessa's words came back to him. She had warned him not to put his needs above that of the clan. Not to serve his ego. And yet, here he was. Din had assumed that her warning was about taking all the glory for himself, but that was never going to happen. However, vanity was only one facet of how his ego could drive him. He had been reluctant to share the responsibilities, and the resulting burdens, of leadership. By putting the weight on himself, he thought he was shielding the rest of his loved ones from the worry, the anxiety, the sleepless nights. But he was wrong. No one dwarf could be responsible for the well-being of the entire clan. The clan functioned as one, an extended family, spreading the burdens across many backs. For Din to put the weight of the clan solely on his shoulders was the height of hubris.

The clan didn't need Din to suffer *for* them, they needed Din to suffer *with* them.

Rhyss went on. "I remember how your father looked toward the end. He was a steady and confident chieftain, but the string of defeats had made him nervous, anxious. He put all of those losses on himself, and it broke him."

Din recalled his father's face when he sent his sons away from Llyngyr Cadw. A mixture of sadness and manic exhaustion reflected in his father's glassy, haunted eyes. Din had always assumed that it came from the strains of fighting the invaders. But maybe it wasn't that at all. Maybe it came from personally feeling every loss and not having anyone to share the pain with. He had sent his closest confidant, his wife, away for her safety, and he had carefully hidden his pain from everyone else. The strain must have been too intense for him to bear.

Din sighed deeply. To survive what was to come, he'd have to let go. He'd have to trust that his loved ones were strong enough to endure the price of victory. If he didn't, he would lose himself again.

Rhyss embraced Din. "You're not alone. You're a member of the clan. Yes, you're our leader, but that doesn't set you apart. We're part of something much greater than ourselves, Din. The clan survived for thousands of years before us and will survive long after."

They stood silently for a while, the young chieftain and the old veteran, with nothing but the timeless roll of the waves and the spontaneous sounds of celebration in the distance. Din opened his eyes and saw the moonlight reflect off the rolling waves. It reminded him of the glint of armor and weapons, and he thought he saw hundreds of his ancestors striding row upon row from the sea. In that moment, his spirit was reassured.

Finally, Din locked eyes with Rhyss.

"Thank you."

Rhyss clapped Din affectionately on the shoulder in response and Tordek took the opportunity to walk over to join Din and Rhyss. For a long moment, they stood gazing out at the vastness of the High Sea.

"Your head on straight?" Tordek asked Dinnidek tentatively.

"It will be," replied Din. He smiled at his friend's solid presence. He would recover. And it started with this. "Thank you, Tordek. You led the troops when I could not. You kept your head when I lost mine. And you protected me from myself."

Din patted his longtime friend affectionately on the back. In typical laconic fashion, Tordek simply nodded in acknowledgment.

"Let's get back to the camp," suggested Rhyss. "The clan needs its chief."

The three walked slowly, savoring the moment of relative solitude before diving back into the maelstrom of activity. As they approached, Din saw dozens of small fires that his clansmen had lit up and down the beach, away from the main camp. Warriors from Clan Daamuz mingled freely with the Clan Helgwin rangers, the Green Wyverns, and the *Maiden's* sailors. A few soldiers saluted the three as they passed, but most of them were too focused on their comrades to notice. The warriors were busy telling stories, drinking, singing, and laughing. It was as if the army had respectfully moved the celebration away from the camp, to not disturb the somber proceedings going on there. Din felt his clansmen revel in their victory. There was a mixture of relief and joy in the air that captured the moment perfectly, and in a way, honored the clan's fallen warriors.

"There you are!" Daerun bellowed from his place at the fire as he caught sight of Dinnidek walking by. "It's 'bout time you came to join us, my lord!"

Din reddened as the warriors around the fire stood and bowed to him. Dare was the last to bow, and he made sure to give Din a sly wink before bending low with an exaggerated flourish.

"Oh, get up!" protested Din with a chuckle. "That's enough. Come on, everyone up."

Dare was the last to straighten, joining the general laughter from the soldiers as he approached Din and embraced him. Now that they were close, Din could smell the whiskey on his brother's breath.

"Where did you get the spirits? I didn't think we had much in the supplies?"

Dare looked around, as if he were guarding a precious secret.

"You're right, there were only a few barrels that actually made it to shore. But it's all in who you know," he replied slyly. "The boys from Clan Helgwin were carrying a portion each, and they were willing to share." Dare grinned impishly as he went on. "And Saorsi had some on her ship, and she's a generous type, so here we are."

"All in who you know?" said Din with an arched eyebrow.

"Exactly!" Dare beamed.

"Saorsi is a generous type, huh?" Din asked skeptically. "Anyone else get a portion from her stores?"

Dare raised his finger, as if he were making a critical point in a debate.

"Nope!" His grin widened further. "I mean, she gave some to me, but she didn't say I couldn't share it, so I've been doing the good work of spreading cheer, if you know what I mean. And the boys, well they could use some cheer, and so here we are."

The meandering stopped as Dare lifted a sizable waterskin, which seemed near empty. He offered the waterskin to Tordek, who politely grabbed it and took a token pull before closing his eyes in pleasure. Dare slapped Tordek on the shoulder.

"That's for keeping my brother safe, you miserable bastard."

Dare tried to feign seriousness, but he burst into laughter at the end. Din and Rhyss chuckled along at Dare's antics while Tordek smiled self-consciously and passed the waterskin to Rhyss, who took a small sip before returning it to Daerun.

The four dwarfs headed toward the camp. They passed a few more fires, soldiers gathered around. In one group, Din heard a great clamor of music coming from a makeshift band. Soldiers had produced reed flutes, a small drum, and one of the Wyverns even had a small five-stringed instrument with a pair of striking sticks. They were playing a reel at a furious pace, and Sunny, of all people, was dancing in the middle of the circle, trying to keep up with the ever-faster tempo. The ogre had doffed his orange kerchief and was waving it wildly over his flushed head while a hunting mastiff cavorted next to him. The four watched as Sunny finally had to stop in a fit of laughter, and the crowd erupted in appreciative applause.

The last fire they passed had the biggest crowd around it. Ironclad mixed freely with rangers, sharpshooters, and sailors sharing stories of their experiences earlier in the day. Rorik was seated on an overturned longboat, sketching in his journal while he laughed with the men. Din heard the sharpshooter finish his story amid the other choice snippets from the crowd.

"...I was so proud of myself after sniping the leader, then BOOM, the beach just disappeared. I shouldn't have bothered! After the mess those cannons made, I'm going to trade in my rifle for one of those!"

"...missed me by that much, I swear..."

"My feet will be sodden for months..."

"I thought we were goners, but the next thing you know, I see this giant shadow sail up and blot out the sun."

"I've never seen anyone fight so hard. Lord Dinnidek was relentless. Killed almost a score of orcs by himself, I tell you!"

Din felt self-conscious at the last comment and walked a little faster to distance himself from the story, but Rhyss caught Din's eye and pointed back at the storyteller with a smile as if to say, *see?*

They left the beach behind and ambled into the camp. A group of sentries hailed them on the way, but the watchmen became flustered when

Din and Dare came into view. Rhyss gave the password and commended the sentries as they passed through the makeshift gate. The dwarfs had dug a trench and berm encircling the camp, obscuring the light from the bonfires on the beach and muffling the sounds. In contrast to the rollicking celebration, the army camp was orderly, quiet, even somber. Their mood shifted to match the subdued energy of the camp. Din felt a welcome peace settle on him. They walked amidst orderly rows of tents, and warriors spoke in hushed tones. The camp felt like some sort of holy place, a temple to the ancestors. Din had ordered the infirmary placed in the middle of the camp to protect the clan's most vulnerable in the event of an attack. It was also conveniently close to Din's command tent and sleeping quarters.

Din noted a cordon of warriors stationed around the hospital tent. It was odd. He didn't remember stationing so many guards here. On closer inspection, Din noticed that most of the soldiers were injured, with bandages or splints. But despite that, they were all armed and alert, and one of the Ironclad hailed Din's retinue as they approached. Din recognized him as Bruon, the leader of the soldiers on the *Celestian's Smile*. Bruon was dark and stocky, with brown eyes, tanned walnut skin, and wild black hair and beard that gave him a disheveled air. The sergeant's right arm was in a sling, but he still held his hammer close to his chest. All the soldiers around the tent were from the *Celestian*.

"Bruon, it's good to see you up and about," Din said with a smile. Last time Din had seen these dwarfs, they were patients inside the tent, not outside guarding it. "I'm trusting that you and your troops will be getting some well-needed rest?"

Din's question was delivered as a strong suggestion, but Bruon shook his head in response.

"Not yet, sir," he said sheepishly. "Beg pardon, my lord, but my fellow brothers and I have taken an oath to guard the priestess Diessa until she's well." The other guards stood up straighter at mention of their oath, belying the exhaustion on their faces. "We owe the priestess our lives, sir, so it's only right that we protect her life in turn."

The warrior's dedication and sense of honor made Din well up inside with emotion, and he didn't trust himself to speak. The silence stretched, but Daerun rescued Din by bowing low to Bruon. When he rose, he clasped Bruon on his good forearm and locked eyes with him.

"My brother and I are honored at your gesture. However, we can't have you and your troops falling to exhaustion. You need your rest if you're to effectively guard the priestess."

Bruon went to argue, but Dinnidek raised his finger to interrupt. He motioned to the guards.

"Gather round! Come close." The guards clustered around him expectantly. Din saw the look of pride in their eyes, which belied their injuries. "You have taken a sacred oath, but you have also taken an oath to fight for the clan. You cannot serve two masters. Therefore, Bruon, I propose that you and these warriors take a new oath. You will be Lady Diessa's honor guard. You will do as she commands, and you will protect her to the best of your ability. The only restriction I give you is that no matter what she says, you must continue to stand by her until your last breath. As you know, my sister is very humble, and the thought of having an honor guard may not sit well with her. Do you understand?"

"Yes," Bruon said, bowing deeply to Dinnidek, followed a moment later by the rest of the warriors. Din waited for them all to rise before continuing.

"Do you solemnly swear, on your honor, by the Earth Mother Dianek, and with your ancestors as eternal witness?"

"Yes!" The warriors responded as one, with quiet voices, reflecting the seriousness of their oath.

Din smiled as Daerun took charge and addressed the warriors. "Alright then, Bruon. I would suggest you leave four of your number here while the rest of you get some sleep. We're in the middle of the camp, so four sentries should be more than enough. Take the watch in two hour shifts, and all of you should have enough rest before we march tomorrow. If Deese isn't awake by the morning, you'll need your strength to carry her," he finished with a chuckle. Bruon bowed again and began issuing orders to his troops while the four leaders entered the hospital.

As they entered the dimly lit tent, the iron odor of blood, combined with the smell of aromatic herbs and potent alcohol, assaulted Din's senses. He took a moment to get his bearings and swept his gaze around the space. He couldn't see an empty cot, all were filled with his fellow clansmen. So many. Din exhaled softly and bowed his head in respect as he carefully made his way between the injured dwarfs laid out on blankets on the ground. Gingerly, he moved toward the only source of light in the vast tent, a pair of portable lanterns set in the corner by a stack of crates and a small table where a lone dwarf was standing with his back to them. As Din got closer, he could hear the dwarf singing quietly to himself, engrossed in mixing herbs in a mortar and pestle beside a haphazard pile of bloody bandages and jars of alcohol filled with scalpels, saws, and knives. Coming around, the dwarf's face was further illuminated by a small fire burning in a bowl situated on the floor nearby, and Din could smell the astringent odor coming from the steaming pots suspended over the flames.

"Cormak," Din quietly hailed the healer. Cormak turned and beckoned Dinnidek in with a tired wave of his hand. The healer was slight for a dwarf, with brown hair pulled back and a beard bound up in two large braids, the ends loosely tied behind the back of his neck. Cormak stopped grinding the herbs and wiped his hands off on a towel.

"My lords Dinnidek, Daerun. Master Rhyss. Tordek. It's a pleasure to see you again." Despite speaking in a whisper, there was deep respect in Cormack's deep and resonant voice as he addressed each of the dwarfs in turn. He gestured to the dwarfs sleeping all around. "Today has been tiring, but it could have been a lot worse. Most of the warriors who survived today suffered minor injuries. Luckily, they'll have stories to tell and the scars to prove it. These ones here are in the worst shape. I've done what I can for their injuries, but for now I'm relying on strong valerian tincture to help them sleep. Captain Saorsi plans on taking most of them with her when she leaves tomorrow for Innyshwylt."

"Excellent work, Cormak," replied Dinnidek. "You truly are a miracle worker."

Cormak shook his head. "No, my Lord, the true miracle workers are the healers that can use magic to bind wounds and cure the sick. I do the best I can with the herbs the Earth Mother has provided."

He gestured to where Deese was lying peacefully on a cot, covered in a light blanket. Veit was seated on a pillow on the floor, his back propped up against the head of the cot. His lower leg was heavily bandaged, and he was snoring lightly.

"Lady Diessa is still in a deep sleep," he said as he led the entourage to her bedside. "Veit told me that she passed out on the ship and has yet to awaken. I cleaned and bound her head wounds, and washed the blood from her face, but she barely stirred."

He pointed down at the engineer.

"I did extensive work on Veit. The wood stabbed deeply into his calf, and he will walk with a limp. I did the best I could, but he'll probably need a cane from now on. Despite that, he's rather lucky. If the wood had struck his thigh, he would have perished from the blood loss."

Din gazed fondly at Veit. The Ironclad from the ship had told him how the engineer had saved Diessa from the blast. "We'll have to honor him in some way, Dare."

"Yes," agreed Daerun, "we will. But I don't think our gratitude is what he's after. I think Diessa is the only one who can grant him what he wants."

Din smiled as he focused on his sister.

Cormak went on, "I am somewhat concerned about Diessa. She's been completely unresponsive since she arrived. However, she doesn't seem to be brain-addled. She seems weary, like she hasn't slept in days. Here, let me show you."

Cormak lifted a small lantern and held it over Diessa's face. With his other hand, he opened her eyelids. Diessa didn't react. She laid still and her breathing didn't change. However, her pupils constricted equally to the light, and her eyelid twitched a little before he released his hold. Cormak put down the lantern and spoke, as if he were giving a lecture to an assistant.

"You can tell by the way her eyes respond to the light that her brain isn't injured. She's just exhausted. I would imagine she poured her vitality into summoning the elemental in such harsh conditions, and it drained her." He took Din's hand and pressed it to Diessa's wrist. Din felt her pulse, stout, but terribly slow. "Her pulse is strong, despite the sluggish tempo, which tells me that for all other purposes she's healthy."

Din nodded in understanding, and Rhyss asked, "How long will this last?"

"I don't know. I've never seen this before. It could be hours. It could be days. In the meantime, she'll have to stay hydrated and kept warm. How do you plan on taking her with you on the march?"

"We'll leave that up to Bruon," said Din. "He's the leader of her new honor guard after all. We probably won't be leaving for another day or so. Hopefully, she'll be awake by then."

"We'll see," said Cormak, somewhat skeptically. "If my lords could excuse me, I'd like to finish my work and get some rest before tomorrow."

Din thanked Cormak and the retinue departed the hospital tent, leaving the healer to grind away at his herbs. Din noticed that there were only a few of the honor guard stationed by the tent flap. It seemed like most of the soldiers had taken his advice and searched for some rest.

As they continued through the camp, Daerun spoke, "Din, I'm surprised that you didn't insist that Diessa leave with the other wounded on the *Maiden's Revenge*."

Oddly enough, the thought hadn't occurred to Din. Now that he was confronted by it, he wondered why not. After some consideration, Din answered, "It's true that I feel odd about bringing Diessa with us, but if I try to send her home, or if she wakes up on the *Maiden's Revenge*, she'll never forgive me. She vowed to serve the clan, just like us, and we'll need her if we're going to succeed. For me to take that opportunity, that choice, away from her, it wouldn't be fair to her... or to us. The clan will look after her, the same way they look after all of us, probably more so. They love her, and they'll literally carry her until she's well again."

The soldiers meandered further inland and climbed the bluff overlooking the beach. The ground here was less sandy, with clumps of small scrub trees clinging to the soil. Dinnidek lagged behind the other three, and as his companions' silhouettes were outlined against the moonlit sky, Din was struck by how much he loved these three dwarfs, all in different ways. Rhyss was a mentor, with years of experience to share. Tordek, his steady right hand and constant companion. And Daerun, his brother, who knew him the way only a sibling could. And even though she wasn't with him, Diessa was his conscience. He was lucky to have them.

Din heard a host singing in low tones from up ahead. A throng of dwarfs circled around the army standards, which had been planted into the ground in front of a freshly dug mound. The breeze blew softly, causing the white and blue dragons on the banners to flutter lazily in the night air. Din had presided here when they had buried the fallen warriors in the dirt of their homeland. He had said prayers and given his blessing to them and their descendants. Instead of celebrating, some of the survivors had opted to stay, singing their fallen comrades to their final rest. Clansmen had been rotating in and out as the night wore on. As they neared the holy site, Din and his companions each showed their respect in different ways. Daerun saluted to the ground, finished off the whiskey, and slung the skin over his shoulder. Rhyss pulled his hood up to hide his face. Tordek slowed his pace until he walked beside Din and joined the crowd in song.

The music was deep, with long low tones that rumbled in Din's chest and invoked the underground halls of Dianek. The music had no words, but the chorus of dwarfs joined their strong voices to make a powerful song. Din beheld his fellow clansmen all around him, heads bowed as they called on the Earth Mother's blessing through the music. The dead would be greeted by the clan's ancestors to take their honored place among them. They would join the countless fallen warriors in protecting the clan into the future.

Occasionally a lone dwarf would sing a few spontaneous verses to celebrate one of the fallen, while the chorus continued to provide a base solid as the depths of time. As Din watched, the soloist finished his verse, walked to one of the army standards, and hung a key on a long chain from the top of the banner pole. The banners were festooned with dozens of keys, trinkets, or other personal effects.

We're taking their personal tokens home, Din thought solemnly.

Each remembrance of the fallen was a promise that their spirits, through their tokens, would finish the journey.

Tordek, Rhyss, and Daerun joined the clan in mourning, their voices added to the depth of the funeral hymn. Din contemplated the tokens in silence. He reflected on his earlier conversation with Rhyss. Each of those keys was a warrior who laid down his life for the clan. Din mourned every loss deeply. But he didn't feel as deeply responsible for their deaths. No, their blood wasn't on his hands. The Abyssal Dwarfs were responsible for the death, the destruction. He couldn't have stopped their passing. But for the clansmen who remained, he could do better. He could celebrate with them and amplify their joy. He could share in their pain and diminish their sorrow.

Din was powerful, not because he was greater than the clan, but because he was part of it.

Din melded his voice with dozens of singers to make a single, powerful voice that shook the earth and rose to the skies. As he sang, his eyes misted over. Letting the emotion of the music wash over him, he felt tears track down his cheeks, and he finally allowed himself to cry.

CHAPTER 15

Rhyss squinted to shield his eyes from the late afternoon sun. Like the other warriors, he had spent the day after the battle preparing for the long march to Llyngyr Cadw. The hours sped by as the dwarfs packed up their camp, tended to the wounded, and secured their supplies. With no carts on hand, every warrior was tasked with carrying their full equipment, food, and water. In addition, the general munitions, hospital goods, and other equipment were evenly distributed amongst the men. The planning had consumed most of Rhyss' time, and he hadn't been able to catch up with the other thanes. Now that evening was close, they only had one more task to complete.

The day had been warm and sunny, but a bank of clouds creeping over the western mountains promised an overcast evening. The sun was a baleful eye that hung between the mountains below and the clouds above, setting them both on fire. It would soon sink below the horizon, mirroring the tide. According to Saorsi, this afternoon's high tide gave a small window of opportunity to return the *Maiden's Revenge* out to sea. If they didn't get this to work now, they'd have to wait until morning, and the chance of saving any of the other transports would be lost.

The *Maiden* was still run aground, mast tilted toward the sandy spit of land where it had leveled the Decimators. Ropes radiated from the ship in every direction. Lines were attached to anchors placed behind the ship in deeper waters. Others were held by masses of dwarfen warriors clustered to port and starboard. With all the ropes, the ship looked like a giant white spider in the midst of its web. Saorsi was on shore, directly in front of the *Maiden's* bow, with Arvind standing nearby. At her signal, Arvind waved his hands and Saorsi spoke, her voice magically amplified.

"Alright, everyone, to your lines!" Saorsi's voice boomed over the sound of the waves.

Rhyss, along with the rest of his rangers, found their footing and grabbed on to the rope with a solid grip. Further down the spit, Daerun and his fellow dwarfs picked up their lines and braced themselves, and past them, Kilvar and his rangers. Rhyss knew that Dinnidek and scores of dwarfs were standing in the waves to the south of the ship, ready to pull.

"Sunny," Saorsi called, "you start ketching on my signal, got it?"

Sunny stood tall in the *Maiden's* bow, and despite the difference in height, Rhyss could see most of his upper body. He waved his orange kerchief to acknowledge the order. Saorsi had instructed the dwarfs earlier that day on the plan. Ketching relied on the crew to use block and tackle to pull anchor lines while masses of dwarfs used their ropes to rock the ship from side to side. This would break the suction of the sand on the hull and hopefully allow the ship to move freely.

"Shore, are you ready?"

Rhyss and his dwarfs gave a resounding 'yes' in response.

"Surf, are you ready?"

Rhyss heard the fainter yell of Din's troops from the other side of the ship.

"Surf side, now!"

Rhyss waited and held the rope slack while Din's troops strained at the lines. Rhyss' rope bowed from the ship to where it dragged on the sand. Sunny bellowed for the sailors to begin cranking the blocks.

"Shore side, now!"

Rhyss and his dwarfs hauled back on their lines while Din's side released their ropes and let them slide. Rhyss dug his feet into the sand and hauled back on the rope, the rangers working as a unit to pull it taut.

"C'mon, boys! Put your backs into it!" Daerun encouraged. Rhyss was too busy straining from the exertion. It was like playing tug of war with a mammoth. After a thirty count, Saorsi called for the surf side again. Rhyss gasped for breath in the small respite before Saorsi called on the shore side to haul again. Back and forth they went, switching on Saorsi's command. The intervals became shorter until they were closer to fifteen counts. The mast began to slowly oscillate. The movement intensified until the ship was wiggling back and forth like a living thing. But the Maiden still hadn't moved backward at all. Sunny was yelling at his crew, half in encouragement, half in frustration.

Rhyss' feet sunk further and further into the sand. The dwarfs around him were holding their breath, straining at the ropes, scrabbling their feet, their faces red from the exertion. He heard Daerun yell 'Sweet, Dianek, let go!' as he pleaded with the Earth Mother in frustration. Saorsi called for the surf side to pull, and Daerun's prayer seemed to do the trick. Rhyss felt something give, and the mast straightened into the sky as the Maiden finally crept away from the shore and out into the open sea. The dwarfs gave a great cheer as Saorsi yelled excitedly through Arvind's spell.

"Let go the lines!" she commanded triumphantly.

Rhyss unceremoniously dropped onto his butt in the sand and smiled wearily. He took a few deep breaths and straightened his back. His hands began to throb. He enjoyed the simple pleasure of not pulling anything for a few moments before he slowly stood up. He walked over to Daerun, who was seated in the sand next to Felwyr, blowing on one of his hands. "What, no gloves?" asked Rhyss.

"No," Dare replied as he grabbed a glove from Felwyr and put it on. "Fel forgot to bring his, so I let him borrow one." After putting the glove on, Dare realized he didn't need it any longer and began to immediately take it off. "Now we both have one ripped up hand. Luckily for me, mine is my left." Dare slapped Felwyr on the shoulder. "Good luck wiping your bum later, Fel!"

He burst out in laughter at his own joke while Felwyr grunted and rolled his eyes. Rhyss chuckled and held out his hands to help Dare and Fel up.

"Gods, you're both as heavy as the ship," he said as the two stood and brushed themselves off. Kilvar, with Boon loping alongside, joined them.

Work finally done, most of the dwarfs were heading back to camp to rest up before the march west tomorrow. Rhyss and his companions stayed behind and slowly meandered to meet Saorsi and Dinnidek.

"I didn't spy your face until the afternoon, Dare. You busy all morning?"

"Busy all night, more like," said Felwyr.

"Is that so?" Rhyss asked Dare slyly. "What were you doin'?"

"Nothing," said Dare. But Rhyss noticed he glanced at Saorsi as he said it. "Nothing worth talking about with you, anyway."

Rhyss smiled knowingly at Daerun. "Good for you," he said, but he didn't push it further. Dinnidek was speaking with Saorsi as they approached, and Rhyss didn't want to embarrass the captain.

While the Daamuz clan had spent the day preparing for the long march to Llyngyr Cadw, Saorsi had paced the beach, her fiery temper aimed at her crew and the Ironclad volunteers as they ran lines and cared for the ship. Now that the *Maiden* was out to sea, she seemed visibly relieved. She was all smiles as she greeted the dwarfen thanes. Dinnidek, in contrast, seemed pensive.

"My lord," Rhyss saluted Dinnidek before bowing deeply to Saorsi. "Captain, I owe you an apology." Saorsi's eyes widened in surprise. "If my rangers and I had hit the bastards sooner, we would've stopped the Abyssal artillery and saved you a lot of grief." Saorsi nodded her acceptance. "And thank you for placing your ship between the prince and those damned Decimators. Without you, we would have lost Master Daerun and his clansmen. The Daamuz clan owes you a deep debt of gratitude."

Rhyss respectfully bowed again to Saorsi, and Din and Dare both followed suit. Saorsi waited for them to rise before answering.

"Thank you, Captain Rhyss," she said humbly. "I accept your apology… though I do remember telling Sunny I should lay you out for taking your grubbing time." Now it was Rhyss' eyes that widened in surprise. Saorsi smiled at him disarmingly. "It was my honor to fight alongside you."

Her gaze swept the rest of the dwarfs as she spoke. Did Rhyss notice her gaze linger on Daerun for a split second longer than everyone else?

"How is Diessa?" Rhyss asked Dinnidek.

"Still recovering. Cormak says she's stable, but she may be asleep for days. Bruon took your suggestion, Dare, and his soldiers will be carrying her on the march until she awakes."

"Good," said Saorsi, "your sister deserves it. The way she saved those soldiers, I've never seen anything like it."

"Agreed," said Dare, with a hint of pride. The group stood in respectful silence for a moment, each saying a prayer for her quick recovery.

"We lost a lot of ships," Din observed ruefully.

"Yes," grumbled Saorsi. "It seems the gargoyles were waiting out at sea to strike the ships during the landing. They used alchemical fire to burn most of the transports when I went in to help you. That's why they stayed out of the battle for so long. Apparently, the Abyssal commander planned to trap you here in Halpi."

Din grunted in response, "It would seem so. And it explains why the artillery was so focused on the transports, even after the troops disembarked. How long until you can return from Innyshwylt with supplies and reinforcements?"

"I will need to find the surviving transports and lead them back safely. I'm sure some were able to escape the gargoyles, but we may only have a third of the fleet remaining. It will take a ten-day before we can return, and with reduced stowage capacity, it could take months to bring everyone over. I'm sorry, Master Dinnidek, but you won't be getting much help from me the rest of the way."

"That's grim news," Din said thoughtfully. "But as Rhyss said, you've already done so much for us. The clan is in your debt."

Saorsi smiled in return.

"Clan Helgwin will help as it can," Kilvar said in his low gravelly voice. "A scouting party from Crafanc arrived this afternoon. The army we thrashed yesterday was mostly troops that were besieging the hold. When you landed, Lord Dinnidek, you pulled them away. Clan Helgwin is now free to move, and they're sending their forces to join you at the southern tip of our mountain range, along with cannon to help breach the gates of Llyngyr Cadw. They should meet your army in three days' time."

Dinnidek grinned broadly while Daerun pumped his fist at the good news. Rhyss felt heartened. The additional troops would be welcome, but the artillery was key to retaking their ancestral hold. The original idea was to have the transports drop off the clan's artillery after the troops had successfully landed and the Abyssal guns were neutralized. With the gargoyles burning the boats, they were only able to secure a few smaller cannons from Saorsi's ship. The support of Clan Helgwin gave the clan a fighting chance again.

"Speaking of help, Rhyss," continued Kilvar, "my people tell me that there's been no sign of the Worm Lord for the past few ten-days, since before we left Mount Drohzon."

Dinnidek gave the two rangers a quizzical look, and Rhyss filled him in on the little he knew of the Worm Lord and his mysterious army in the mountains.

"It's good to know some of our people survived the invasion," said Din. "I can't imagine living secretly in the wild for almost a decade. Madness. It's a shame we can't contact this Worm Lord and seek his aid."

"I've tried," said Rhyss, "but he can't be found if he doesn't want to be. I have a feeling he'll show himself if we make a big enough mess."

"Let's hope so," said Dare.

Saorsi bowed and took her leave, promising to be back as soon as she could. Dare followed her to the waiting longboat, Moon in the prow. Rhyss smirked in admiration at Dare's back.

"Good thing she's leaving tonight," said Din. "Give him a chance to get some rest before tomorrow."

Rhyss snorted. It was meant as a joke, but Din was right. Everyone would have to be at their best. The army had won yesterday, but without ships, they had only one chance at taking the hold. If they failed, the survivors would be forced to retreat to Crafanc.

If that happens, it will get cozy very quickly, Rhyss thought to himself as he watched Dareun and Saorsi walking the beach. *And not in a good way.*

CHAPTER 16

"Come on boys, it's a few hours until your nap time!" Daerun joked with the dwarfs in his column. "As for me, I don't need any rest!" Daerun exaggeratedly boasted to the warriors all around him, who chuckled in response. The brave front hid the emotional weariness that Daerun was carrying around. Now that he was finally back home, he found that it didn't feel like home anymore.

Clan Daamuz had been on the march for three days, pushing to make their scheduled rendezvous with Clan Helgwin. Like the rest of the dwarfs, Daerun carried his personal effects, provisions, weapons, armor, and various tools. In addition, each dwarf was allotted a share of the communal goods, such as tent parts, tarps, ammunition, and healing supplies. In typical fashion, Daerun had taken an extra portion to carry. He had a second pack piled high with tent parts on top of his personal backpack, and two bags full of vials and bandages for Cormak, which made him look like a tinker who had lost his cart. The heavy, bulky bags caused him to walk with a weird gait as he marched along.

Due to his station, Dare started the day at the front of the column, but he made sure to march with each regiment over the course of the day. Since the extra load made him a little slower than everyone else, it all worked out. Currently he was in the middle of the column, behind the artillery train. Veit had done a great job salvaging parts from the longboats and the wreckage of the Abyssal Dwarf carts to make carriages for the clan's few cannons. Where he could, he had made the wheels extra-large to let the carriages move easier over the rolling plains. When Dare had asked him why so big, Veit mentioned something about rolling resistance or somesuch. Daerun had nodded politely and pretended to understand. But now that he saw them in action, he got what Veit was talking about. The height allowed the warriors shepherding the guns to move them easily once they got going.

Dare glanced back down the column and saw Veit stumping along with his cane amid Diessa's honor guard. Bruon and his troops had created a makeshift litter to carry Deese, who was still asleep. Like the gun carriages, it was solidly made of leftover parts, but the honor guard had decorated it with strips of blue and white cloth to give it a more regal feel. Teams of six took turns carrying the litter, and they made sure everyone received a go. Veit, for his part, had made a canopy to keep Diessa out of the sun.

He really cares for her, thought Dare. He and Din had noticed Veit hanging around Diessa more and more before the invasion, but he didn't figure it meant too much. After the landing, however, Veit hadn't left Diessa's side, which meant a lot. *Who would have thought?*

Dare wasn't surprised that Veit was sweet on Diessa. He thought very highly of his sister, after all. However, he was surprised that his sister would express any feelings in return. She had always struck Dare as too wrapped up in her role as stone priestess to let others in. *Well, if it works out, Diessa could do a lot worse.*

Veit marched as best he could, his leg in a splint, amid the heat and dust of the day. *Have to hand it to him,* thought Daerun, *Veit's as tough as he is smart.*

The column wound its way somberly through the land, the mountains encircling Crafanc visible to the north. The landscape near the shore was green and vibrant in keeping with the season, and the dwarfs had sung songs and talked freely as they marched. But not now. Just a day's travel inland, the land took a sickly turn. Daerun had heard stories from Rhyss about how the Abyssal Dwarfs and their slaves had ravaged the land, but hearing and seeing were two different things.

After just a decade, the land seemed... withered? Like a bear in late summer that hadn't eaten in months. Or thirsty, maybe? Daerun was having problems putting it into words. The foliage looked diminished. The leaves on the trees were smaller, there weren't many flowers, and the green seemed less... green. It was like the world was faded. Even the very stone was affected, the rocks more jagged and cracked. The ground was parched, and it easily kicked up dust that choked the dwarfs near the back of the column. After the first day, Dinnidek ordered the regiments to rotate their place in line after every rest to spread the misery around. That had been smart, but it only partially helped. The grime clung to everything and, combined with the heat, caused sweat to run in brown rivulets down the dwarfs' faces. The dust obscured sight and gave the sun a red tinge as it traveled across the sky. Dare was reminded of a red eye that beheld the world below and hated everything it saw.

He gazed on a burnt-out copse of trees in the distance, the bare black trunks looking like a skeletal hand clawing at the sky. It occurred to him that reclaiming their home went beyond thrashing the Abyssal Dwarfs out of Llyngyr Cadw. Retaking the hold was only the first step in healing the land. The clan had started the march talking amongst themselves and singing songs. But the further inland the army marched, the more the clan's excitement had ebbed. Now the troops spoke in hushed tones amongst themselves at the devastation. A few of the troops started boasting about what they would do to their fiendish cousins, and a slow simmering ire was starting to burn within the breasts of the warriors. Some sang old dwarfen songs of triumph and glory while they marched.

Even though the clan seemed more somber, Dare noted with some pride that their resolve was clearly stronger. The next time they met their traitorous kin, there would be a reckoning. The feelings were amplified because there was no going back. They'd left Golloch's empire far behind. Even if they wanted to leave, there weren't sufficient boats to rescue them now. Hopefully Saorsi would scrounge up enough survivors to bring over the rest of the clan before Golloch learned of their exodus.

If anyone can make something out of nothing, it's her, he thought, admiringly. *She's got enough will to change the world.*

Daerun hadn't spoken of Saorsi since she sailed away. He was normally gregarious and open with others, but he kept a few things to himself. It didn't feel right to talk about her when he was drinking with the boys. Anyway, the point wasn't for him to talk, but to listen. Dare made sure to talk to as many people as he could to get a clear picture of how the clan was doing. In return, the warriors shared their hopes and fears freely with Dare about the return home, the upcoming battle, the trials of the march, and their loved ones back on Innyshwylt.

Daerun and his brother had been raised by their parents to rule the clan. Where Din had been forced to follow his father around to endless meetings and functions, and Diessa had spent her time with their mother learning to work with the stone spirits, Dare had been free to indulge in building common bonds with his people. Daerun liked to think this gave him a more personal leadership style that reflected his ability to bond with anyone. Nowadays, he spent most of his time immersed in the clan. Working alongside his fellow dwarfs built trust and let them see him as one of their own. Time spent playing and drinking, besides being therapeutic for him, gave him plenty of opportunities to hear how they were really doing. Unlike Din, who wore the mantle of leadership like a suit of armor, Dare's way was more intimate, and he relied on shared experiences to inspire his clansmen. Din planned, Diessa nurtured, and Dare listened. With their mix of personalities, they had been able to keep the clan alive.

As far as Dare was concerned, Dinnidek was inspirational in his own way. His method of planning and organizing things gave the clan the structure they desperately needed after the invasion. He was constantly coordinating and communicating to make sure everyone was working toward the same goals. Din was always looking for ways to improve the dwarfs' daily lives, and the clan trusted him to keep them all marching in the same direction. Despite his brave façade, Dare was one of the few people who saw the toll it took on his brother. Since their exile began, Dinnidek had shown an increased need to control things. He had taken more and more on himself, keeping most of the clan at a distance. Dare was still surprised that Din had let him secure a fleet for their invasion.

Not that he'd had much choice. Daerun had avoided the issue by not telling his brother what he was doing. It was the type of thing that Dinnidek would have put on himself to do. Dare had warned him about taking on too much, about the need to delegate, but Din hadn't listened. However, something seemed to have changed in his brother since the landing. It was hard to put a finger on, but he seemed more free, less fretful. *It will be good for him if it sticks.*

Dare saw a group of rangers trot past toward the front of the column, ignoring prodding questions from the marching warriors. Dare wasn't concerned - if it was something important, they would have made sure to pull him aside. Meanwhile, the dwarfs around Dare indulged in wild speculation about the news the rangers carried, most of it borderline absurd and designed to stave off the boredom of the march.

Eventually the call to halt was carried down the line, and the column slowly came to a stop.

"Well, gents," Dare said to the warriors around him, "it's been a pleasure walking with you today. I'll see you around the campfires tonight."

A few of the troops grinned at him and clapped him on the shoulder as he headed off to the front of the column. He arrived to see Din, Rhyss, and Kilvar speaking with a group of dwarfs, dressed in the red and gold of Clan Helgwin, accompanied by a small pack of hunting hounds. Their allies had arrived first and were encamped around the southern foothills of the mountains. Daerun sized the warriors up with a deep respect. The rough environment had taken a toll on the Clan Helgwin army. The troops looked both ragged and rugged, their gear a mixture of well-worn and well cared for. Their clothes were faded and frayed in spots, but the weapons and armor seemed serviceable. The real story was around the eyes, which belied a mixture of haunted determination and steely resolve. If they'd been through fire, then it hadn't burnt them, it had just forged them into something stronger.

As Daerun approached, Boon left Kilvar's side and trotted over to push against his legs in greeting. Dare spared one of his hands to scratch behind the mastiff's ears while he extricated himself from his bags. He grunted in relief as he put down his backpack. He hadn't realized how heavy it was while he was moving, but once he stopped, he was glad to be rid of it for a while. He shrugged his shoulders to loosen them up and rolled his neck, which made little popping noises. He sighed in relief and joined the circle of dwarfs, Boon leading the way.

"Lord Anfynn," said Din, "may I introduce my brother, Daerun. Dare, this is Anfynn, war leader of Clan Helgwin."

Din shot a small gesture at one of the three Helgwin thanes to give Dare a clue as to who was who. Dare slyly winked at Din in thanks before bowing low. Anfynn showed the same wear and tear as the rest of his troops.

He was dressed in plain, but well-kept, armor and clothes. The only nods to his station were a helmet adorned with rubies, and a maroon cloak with golden brocade trim depicting a hunting scene. His hair and beard were a deep red that matched his clothes, and his eyes were light gray.

"My lord," said Dare as he rose, "we are in your debt. Please accept my thanks on behalf of the Clan Daamuz for your support in our time of need."

"You're thanking me?" said Anfynn incredulously. He spoke with a passion that was infectious, and Daerun couldn't help but smile in return. "No need, Lord Daerun, no need. Without your help, Clan Helgwin would have perished years ago. No, there's no need for that. We're honored to help you fight our Abyssal kin. My warriors haven't roamed free in quite a while, and we're all howling to take it to those traitorous bastards. With our two clans united, they won't know what hit them. When we saw the ratmen and orcs march away, I knew we had to seize the opportunity, so I brought the full might of the clan with me." He swept his arm to take in the entire hillside teeming with dwarfs.

Dare was elated to see the reinforcements. Anfynn was right, together their combined host would be a match for the Abyssal Dwarfs. But Dare noticed the serious look that came over Din's face when Anfynn spoke, and it caused him to reconsider the war leader's words. The full might of their clan? Even with only part of their army present, Clan Daamuz was marching with twice their number.

He looked again at the Helgwin forces with a more critical eye, and he saw a clan that was diminished. Clan Daamuz were blessed compared to these ragged warriors. The last decade spent exiled to Golloch's empire may have been odious, but it had allowed the clan to regroup and regain their strength. In contrast, Helgwin had been at constant war for all of that time. No peace. No rest. No wonder they were so happy to see Clan Daamuz.

Dare's mind came back to the conversation to hear Rhyss speaking. "I've sent out the lads in all directions to keep us from being ambushed, but we've given Kilvar's rangers the honor of locating the Abyssal Dwarfs."

Dare nodded in satisfaction at the arrangement. Kilvar's troops had been scouting this land for years and presumably would be familiar with all the changes since the Free Dwarf exodus. It was also smart politically, because such an important assignment honored Clan Helgwin.

"My scouts will be back soon," Kilvar said in his low baritone. "The land is clear between here and Llyngyr Cadw, with rolling hills and sparse forests. There are only a few defensible locations closer to the hold. With their stone-cracked slaves, the Abyssal Dwarf army can cover more ground than us. We won't be able to tell where they'll set until we get much closer, which puts us in a bind. I'm hoping that we'll find the enemy and have some idea where they're heading."

"Yes," Din said, "but the Abyssal commander knows the land as well as we do. And his gargoyles will be sweeping the skies to find us, which gives him a huge advantage. Sadly, he'll know our location long before we know his."

At Dinnidek's words, a quiet fell over the group. To be successful, an army needed to know where the enemy was while hiding their own movements in return. Flying scouts meant the Abyssal Dwarf commander would have both at his disposal. It was a sobering thought.

"Lord Dinnidek," said Anfynn, "once we take Llyngyr Cadw, what then?"

Din stroked his beard as he contemplated the question. "To tell you the truth, I haven't thought about it much. We still must reclaim our home, and I didn't want to put the cart before the pony, if you know what I mean. A lot will depend on how much support we get from the rest of our clans."

"I think this will be the spark that lights our forge." Anfynn spoke with fervor and urgency, as if willing it to be true. "This will be the beginning of a greater Free Dwarf push to retake Halpi once and for all. With you to our west, we'll be free to come out from underground and remake ourselves under the sky. Our two holds will form a bulwark against the Abyssal Dwarfs and allow our people to finally come home."

Din smiled and nodded along as Anfynn painted a picture of the dwarfs reclaiming all that they'd lost. Dare saw it in his mind and wanted to believe in it, but the vision was replaced by the skeletal trees under the red-hot sun. They had a long way to go. They had to defeat the forces around Llyngyr Cadw now and be strong enough to hold it in the future. Even if Clan Daamuz won today, there was a chance they'd find themselves in the same boat as Helgwin, trapped in their mountain hold, waiting desperately for a lifeline from their kin still in the Empire.

Dare's dour thoughts were interrupted by a Helgwin ranger running toward them, a hunting dog keeping pace by his side. The scout approached and gave an informal salute to Anfynn before speaking between breaths.

"My lord, we weren't able to find the bastards. We reckon they're gathering on the Ironway, about three days west of here, but we can't get close enough to see 'em. The blasted open ground makes it impossible to hide from their gargoyles." The scout's frustration was evident in his voice. "Our rangers will shadow them from a distance, but we won't know their numbers or where they're headed."

Daerun tried not to be dejected at the news. It would be tough to make plans when they didn't know the enemy's movements. They had to find them before they could kill them, after all.

* * * * *

"Our name is Diessa."

The realization came as a shock to them. Like striking a match in a dark cave, it separated the light from the darkness.

They hadn't remembered a moment when they were separate, but they must have been at one time.

"We are a dwarf."

They remembered now. There was a ship, and it was sinking into the water. She came and held the ship up until it was back on land. No, that wasn't quite right. They had been on the ship, not under it. She had been hurt before she summoned them. Then they were one.

"But before that, I was Diessa."

They were aware of being in motion, without moving. They felt the warmth of the sun on her skin.

She couldn't open her eyes. No, that wasn't true. She opened her eyes, but she couldn't see. The heat on her face meant there should have been light, but everything was darkness.

She couldn't hear. She just felt every vibration as it traveled through her. No, that wasn't true either. She heard the murmur of dwarfs all around her, echoes from far away. If anything, she heard too much. While she was 'they,' she didn't notice, but now... She closed her eyes and tried to drown out the echoes. With a force of will she focused, and the myriad sounds slowly subsided.

"What happened?" she asked aloud, her mouth painfully dry. Surprisingly, a chorus of impressions flooded her mind in response, and she gasped at the onslaught. "Too much," she mumbled aloud. "Too much at once."

The images stopped, leaving only a single vision of a giant earth elemental carrying a ship through the waves before eroding away to nothing. Her mind was thrown back to the moment when the ship was saved.

She remembered Veit stroking her hair, the sun and wind on her skin, the pain in her head. She tried to awaken, but she was too weary. The summoning had taken too much from her, and she knew she was dying. Her spirit flickered and she gave in to exhaustion, satisfied that she had done one last thing for her clan. She felt herself floating, peaceful and serene as the pain, the purpose, all faded away. Suddenly she was grasped by a pair of hands, then a dozen, then a hundred. They held her reverently in a strong embrace, and she let herself be enfolded into a deep communal consciousness. The last thing she remembered was an intense feeling of joy that she had returned.

She had been subsumed by the chorus of spirits, made part of the collective. Now that she had reemerged, she was having problems separating herself.

"I am Diessa," she asserted, in an attempt to regain her individuality. "I. Me."

She was only partially successful. She sensed things as if through a fog. Now that the non-stop images had ceased, she opened her eyes and saw broad strokes of light and darkness, but that was all. Sounds came from far away. It was as if her dwarfen senses had been muted.

They were... no, she was... disoriented and couldn't explain why she felt motion.

She saw a vision of a group of warriors carrying a female dwarf on a fancy litter. With a start, she realized the dwarf was her.

Why am I being carried?

In response, she saw the warriors they had saved, and she felt a deep feeling of love and respect. She knew that she'd been asleep for days. No, asleep wasn't right. She was hit by a wave of feeling, as if she were back in the collective consciousness again. She realized that the earth spirits from Halpi had saved her. They had sheltered her spirit while she healed.

Joro's smiling face came unbidden to her mind, and she knew that her old friend had been the catalyst. He had roused the spirits to her, and they had gladly heeded the call. She was again inundated with memories, but this time, she was able to focus and control them. The Abyssal Dwarfs had taken a toll on the very earth, and the infernal energies of the Abyss ran like veins of corruption throughout the Halpi peninsula. She felt the land, drained of its vitality, crumbling to dust and ash. When the dwarfs were forced to flee, their symbiotic relationship with the earth spirits of Halpi was broken. The spirits were bereft, left to the mercy of the Abyss. The small pockets of Free Dwarfs that remained became tiny oases in a sea of decay. The earth itself had missed the dwarfs' presence, and when Diessa and her clan washed up on shore, the spirits flocked to her in desperation and joy.

The intensity of the feelings began to fade, and her hearing became more acute. She slowly roused herself and sat up. As she shifted her weight, she heard one of the flaps on the litter open and a dwarf gasp. A great commotion went up from the warriors all around her and she was slowly lowered to the ground. When she felt the earth below her, the collective grasped her mind again, and she was almost subsumed. She took a few deep breaths to keep herself calm as she repeated her name, gaining more confidence with every repetition.

She heard the canopy open again. "Diessa," Veit said quietly, "you're awake."

He sounded as if he had witnessed a miracle, and it made Deese smile. Without waiting for a response, he enfolded her in a soft embrace. She held on to Veit silently in return and breathed deep to steady herself. She had lived. She was herself. It was a miracle.

"Veit, thank the ancestors," she whispered through parched lips. She breathed deeply, emotionally, before continuing. "It worked."

"Yes," he responded. "Yes, it did."

She could hear the smile in his voice. He tried to say something else but couldn't get the words out. She felt him tremble as he silently wept for joy. She squeezed him tightly and half cried, half laughed in response. She wanted to see his face so badly but could only see an indistinct haze of light. She squeezed her eyes shut in frustration.

A foreign consciousness brushed against her mind. She felt it gently tug on her psyche, and her vision shifted as a small earthen shape emerged from the ground next to her, under the cloth of the litter. She instinctively turned toward the sound as the elemental ripped the fabric and poked its small head up next to Diessa's foot. As it came into the light, Diessa saw a vision in her mind of her and Veit hugging beneath the blue and white canopy. They both looked worn and disheveled, and Veit's injured leg stuck straight out in front of him while he sat on the ground beside her. All of this was superimposed on the blurred whiteness of her own sight. She realized that she was seeing through the small elemental's eyes, as well as her own. She closed her own eyes and the blurred vision ceased, leaving only the elemental's view. Seeing herself in the third person was disorienting, causing the elemental to turn its head to look away in response. She giggled in delight and called the elemental to her.

It obeyed, and she saw Veit turn and scramble back a bit as it approached. "Don't worry. I can't see yet, but the earth spirits are helping me. This little one is lending me his eyes." The elemental turned its head to Veit and nodded sagely.

Veit glanced at Diessa in wonder. "How?"

She told him how the elementals had saved her by joining their consciousness to hers, and how she was still regaining her senses. She also told him about the land dying under the Abyssals, and how the spirits were powerless to stop it once the dwarfs left. As she spoke, she tried to reconcile seeing the world from the elemental's perspective. She kept her eyes on Veit and tried to 'focus' on him as much as possible. In response, the elemental slowly walked closer and closer to the engineer until it was right at his feet. Veit listened intently, considering the implications of her story. Once she was finished, he looked from Diessa to the elemental with wonder.

"I've never heard of such a thing happening," he said. "In fact, I don't think anyone has."

"Neither have I. Yet here we are."

It struck her that the phrase was something her father used to say. It seemed appropriate, somehow. She saw a vision flash across her mind of a dwarf standing on a mountaintop, dressed in singed clothing, his great axe held loosely in one hand, and a grand helmet in the stylized form of a dragon in the other. As she watched, the dwarf dropped his helmet onto the rocks at his feet. She tried to hold the scene in her mind, but it was gone as quickly as it came, fading as if she were waking from a dream.

She realized that she was ravenous and thirsty. She turned her head to find a waterskin, but her vision didn't track. A second later, the elemental turned its head the same way, but the lag was noticeable.

"This will take some getting used to," she said self-consciously.

Veit handed her his waterskin, and she had to grope around to grasp it due to the strange perspective. Veit placed the waterskin firmly in her hands and set off to find her some food, caressing her hand as he left. Diessa picked up the elemental and placed it in her lap.

If we're going to be tied together for a while, little one, she thought to the spirit, *I'll have to come up with a name for you.*

She thought for a moment and settled on Gwel, an ancient dwarf word for sight. The elemental nodded solemnly in approval at the name. She experimented with the sight, looking this way and that as she waited. If she kept the elemental close to her head, her vision was only slightly out of sync. She fared better when she could see her own hands. She tried picking things up, even tossing objects from hand to hand.

She was just getting the hang of it when the canopy flap was withdrawn, and she felt the midday sun on her face. Without the shade, the light should have changed, but Gwel's sight didn't respond to the added light. She reflexively moved her hand in front of her eyes to shield them from the sun to see if her sight would change, then remembered that she wasn't seeing through her own eyes anymore. She shielded Gwel's eyes instead. Still nothing.

Diessa noticed with a start that she was surrounded by dwarfen warriors. She sheepishly brought her hands away from Gwel's face down to her lap and turned her head to take in the dwarfs. A second later, the elemental followed suit. At some unspoken command, the dwarfs knelt before her, heads bowed. Diessa waited patiently for them to rise, but they continued to kneel. She felt her cheeks heat in embarrassment and finally broke the stalemate by clearing her throat.

"Rise, fellow clansmen, rise." Some of them looked up but no one moved. "Get up, I insist."

She recognized one of the dwarfs as Bruon, the Ironclad commander from the *Celestian's Smile*. In fact, all these dwarfs had been with her on the ship. What had the earth spirits shown her? A group of dwarfs carrying her out of gratitude, that was it.

"Bruon," she said, "have your dwarves stand. I won't have you kneeling to me like that."

The dwarfs stood as they were ordered, but still none spoke. Diessa sighed. "Alright, you're the dwarfs that have been taking care of me since the landing?"

"Yes," Bruon said with a smile as he motioned to the Ironclad around him. "It's our honor, priestess. We've been with you since you rescued us, and we intend to be with you every step to Llyngyr Cadw."

Diessa would normally have squinted at Bruon incredulously. Instead, she let her voice make her point. "I appreciate your help, and am truly humbled by your men's gesture, Bruon, but now that I'm recovered, I won't be needing you to carry me anymore."

As she spoke, Diessa tried to stand to prove that she was okay, but she was overcome by a wave of dizziness and nausea, forced to sit unceremoniously back down again. A couple of the Ironclad stepped forward to help her, but she raised her hand. "I'm okay. Just a little dizzy is all. I'll be right as the mountain in a few minutes. I just need a little food."

Multiple warriors offered her food from their packs as she vainly protested that there was no need for any of that.

"Please, priestess, allow us to help you. It's our duty."

Diessa tilted her head in mild aggravation, and Gwel cocked its head to the side in imitation. She was undeniably hungry, and they were sharing food. There was no harm in it. Why was she being stubborn about this? She grabbed for some hard tack and her waterskin while she mulled it over.

"Thank you, Bruon. Thank you all. I appreciate everything you've done, including the food." Her stomach cramped with anticipatory hunger pangs as she took the first bite. By the ancestors, this was the best thing she'd ever eaten.

The warriors stood by respectfully while Diessa ate. She made a show of outwardly ignoring them as she mulled over the situation in her mind. As the clan's stone priest, she was used to being shown the respect due her station. She also understood the warriors' desire to show their appreciation. But the fact that they'd taken oaths to serve her went beyond gratitude to border on veneration, and that felt uncomfortable.

She felt the hot summer wind and heard the warriors marching and talking over the squeal of the artillery carriages. She thought about how they'd carried her for three days. The pragmatic part of her understood the need for it. They couldn't just leave her on the beach. But the thought of her people carrying her didn't sit right with her. They were bowing to her, calling her by her formal title. She'd have to put a stop to that before Dinnidek caught on. He'd never let her live it down. She sighed and 'looked' around again at the litter. Her eyes lingered on the decorations, and it made her self-conscious again.

She kept her head still, but at her command, Gwel turned its head to look up at Bruon. She didn't want to risk being dizzy again, so she stayed seated as she addressed the warrior captain.

"I understand why you carried me, and I thank you. I'd hate to have been left behind. But why all this?" She motioned to the blue and white streamers that adorned the litter. "I certainly don't need any of this."

Bruon smiled. "We did it in gratitude for protecting us. You saved our lives back on the beach. Without you, we would have surely drowned."

Multiple warriors nodded in agreement with Bruon.

Diessa smiled at Bruon as Gwel shook its head from side to side. "Yes, but I'm supposed to protect you, Bruon. That's my role in the clan."

"Yes," Bruon agreed, "but that doesn't stop us protecting you in turn. It's not one or the other, priestess."

Diessa considered Bruon's words, and her eyes welled up with emotion. She breathed a little deeper as she fought down the tightness in her throat. She had spent her entire young life serving the clan, a role that had consumed her since their exile from Halpi. Now that she thought about it, she was surprised that she'd never thought of the clan protecting her, which was different from serving her. She didn't want to be served as if she was exalted above the rest of the clan. She didn't want to be set apart. That was a line she wouldn't cross. But to be supported, protected when she was weak? What was the harm in that?

Bruon went on, "Lord Dinnidek attested to our oaths and asked us to protect you, so protect you we shall."

Diessa smirked. "Oh, did he now?"

Of course he did, she thought. It occurred to her that Din would have been a wreck since her injury, and it made her well up with emotion. She was glad that her eyes were closed, or the tears would have betrayed her.

"Bruon, once again, I appreciate the sentiment, but I absolve you of your oath. You should protect the clan, not me." Bruon's back straightened and he began to protest, but Diessa interrupted him firmly. "No one person is bigger than the clan."

"Beg pardon, priestess, but I must disagree. No one else can do what you do... can do what you *did*. You are our only stone priest. You are the clan's link to the earth. You're one of us, but you're not just another one of us, if you get my meaning. There's none of us that can summon the elementals or have them fight alongside us. We'll need you if we're to succeed, priestess. You're special, and the fact that you don't think so makes you more so." Bruon realized how tangled his speech had become and he blushed a bit.

"By serving you, we serve the clan." He nodded firmly in conclusion before sheepishly adding, "Priestess."

Diessa considered what Bruon was saying. He was correct that Diessa's role as stone priest made her unique within the clan. And she could see that it was in the clan's interest to keep her safe. She and Joro had a role to play in the battles to come. When she looked at it like that, she felt better about it, but she still didn't like it. It would take some time to get used to. In the meantime, she'd have words with Dinnidek about this oath business.

She heard a commotion behind her, and Gwel turned to look over her shoulder. Dinnidek and Daerun were both striding quickly in a half walk, half run toward her, as if their dignity was fighting their urgency. Eventually, urgency won as Dare dropped all pretenses and ran the last few feet to dive down onto the ground next to her before pulling her into a giant bear hug. The two of them giggled like children as Dare rocked her back and forth in relief. Dinnidek kneeled next to them and wrapped his arms around them both with a giant sigh. The earth elemental took a few steps back, allowing Diessa to view the whole scene from the outside. She laughed in delight and fiercely grabbed on to her brothers, as if afraid they would disappear. From her odd new viewpoint, she saw Veit and Tordek approaching, an uncharacteristic smile on the bodyguard's face.

"I knew it would take more than a cannon to end you!" Dare said as he ruffled Diessa's hair. Din gently kissed her forehead before standing up. Diessa, still clinging to Daerun, stood up as well. Now that she'd eaten, she found that she wasn't as dizzy, though she was still weak.

"I wouldn't say that," she replied. "I wasn't dead, but I wasn't totally alive either."

She went on to explain how the earth spirits had saved her, and her current issues with her senses. As she spoke, Gwel wandered over and stood at Diessa's feet, looking up at her brothers. Dare kneeled and looked the elemental in the eyes. He passed his hands over its face and gauged Diessa's reaction. As he did, her vision was obscured by Dare's hand, and she reflexively opened her own eyes to see. She noticed that the light from her own vision was brighter now that she was in direct sunlight. It was a strange sensation, and one that she'd have to experiment with later. But that would have to wait. Now that she was back, she had a million questions.

"Where do we stand? How did the rest of the army fare? Have you seen Rhyss yet?"

The brothers took turns filling Diessa in on everything that had happened. They described Joro carrying the *Celestian's Smile* to shore, how Saorsi had run the *Maiden's Revenge* aground to save Daerun's men, how Rhyss and the Helgwin rangers had destroyed the artillery, and how the gargoyles burned most of the fleet. Diessa listened with rapt attention, trying to take in every detail without interrupting with questions. They talked about their rendezvous with Clan Helgwin, the state of their forces, and the current problem of outmaneuvering the Abyssal Dwarf army.

"They're faster than us," said Dare, "they know the land as well as we do, and their gargoyles can track us no matter where we go."

"It's grim," Din agreed as he slapped his fist into his palm. "If only we knew where they were going. I mean, Kilvar's rangers were lucky to get close, but they'll have problems tracking the enemy on the open hills."

At the mention of the enemy army, Gwel reached out and touched Diessa's leg. In response, Diessa's mind became flooded with visions of the Abyssal Dwarf army in their camp, straddling the Ironway. The visions were all rendered in points of view low to the ground and were completely silent. She saw mobs of ratkin, orcs, and half demon monstrosities gathered around a fortified camp adorned with red and black banners. As she concentrated on the camp, her vision shifted to see inside the walls. Abyssal Dwarf regiments were standing at attention in orderly rows before a wooden dais. The Abyssal Dwarfs closer to the stage all had metal arms, legs, even parts of their torsos, and helmets that completely covered their faces. Standing on the dais was a pair of dwarfs, one large and muscular, resplendent in shining black armor, the other slimmer and slightly taller, dressed in black leathers and a scarlet cape. The two dwarfs had light, almost blond, hair and lighter eyes. The muscular one was haranguing his men, while the caped one stood by with a look of rapture on his face. The caped dwarf slowly turned his head until he was staring straight into Diessa's eyes. As his gaze focused on her, she felt a flare of panic, and she urgently cut off the vision.

She gasped and fell to one knee as she came back to herself. Din reached out and caught her around the waist to support her to the ground. "Deese! Are you alright?"

"Yes," she said, shakily. She took a few deep breaths to steady herself. "I saw them."

"Saw who?" asked Dare. "Who did you see?"

"The enemy," she replied as she shook her head to clear it. "There are so many." She went to describe everything she'd seen, including the two dwarfen commanders. "It was like the one knew I was there. Thank the ancestors I broke the connection when I did."

Din frowned at the news. "How did you see them?"

"And can you do it again?" asked Dare, pragmatically.

"I think the earth spirits are showing me." As she said it, she had an overwhelming feeling that she was correct. She saw the world as the spirits saw it. She also realized, with some surprise, that she knew exactly where the army was. It pulled at her mind, like a lodestone pointed to the west. She felt it as a sickness, like a foul oiliness, seeping into the ground and tainting all that it touched. It made her stomach feel queasy. If she concentrated, she could feel the ground where the army was camped and see it in her mind's eye. She knew their location and a rough estimate of their numbers. She tentatively groped in that direction with her mind and saw the mobs of ratkin and the orderly regiments of orcs. A demonic halfbreed strode right over her vantage point as it went to join a pack of its kin. She pulled her mind back in disgust and spat, as if clearing her mouth of an acrid taste, before describing her newfound senses to her brothers.

"I can do it again," she said, "but not for long."

Dinnidek clapped his hands together, and Daerun whooped at the news. Diessa felt the spirits swirling underneath their feet, like fish clustered around a person throwing food off of a dock.

"I'll have to experiment to see what the limits are, and I don't know how long this connection with the earth spirits will last."

She opened her eyes and saw the same white blur as before. She felt that as her sight returned, her second sight would fade. She closed her eyes, and Gwel's vision was all that was left. It was strange. A few minutes ago, she was hoping her normal sight would return quickly. Now she hoped it took days.

Gwel reached up and touched her shoulder in reassurance. She reached out and clumsily rested her hand on the elemental's head. In return, the spirits showed her visions of the earth erupting in violence against the Abyssal Dwarfs. Earthquakes brought whole mountains down, and chasms opened below the enemy army's feet. It was all a metaphor, of course. If the spirits could have followed through, they would have done so years ago. But Diessa understood the point. Let the Abyssal Dwarfs have the air. The Free Dwarfs had the earth.

CHAPTER 17

"Brother," asked Alborz with a smile and a touch of mischief in his voice, "are you alright? You seem preoccupied."

Zareen smirked at the question and took a long drink from his wine glass. "Preoccupied? That's an understatement. Command hasn't been anything like I'd imagined it."

The Abyssal Dwarf forces were finally assembled, the last of the outlying regiments scheduled to arrive this afternoon. Alborz had delegated a majority of the army command duties to his brother. Zareen balked at first, but Alborz was insistent. Now was the perfect time for Zareen to feel what command was like. They had developed a plan together, and now Zareen had to execute it. Better to gain the experience while Alborz was still there to help.

The brothers were lounging in Alborz's command tent at the end of a long day. The tent was extravagantly furnished, containing a full bed, writing desk, a trio of personal chests, a pair of divans, and additional folding chairs. Rugs had been placed on the ground, and the inside was softly lit by fragile glass lamps that refracted the candlelight to project luminous shapes onto the tent walls and ceiling. Transporting the tent and its furnishings was an arduous task, but that's what slaves were for. The brocaded tent fabric muffled the persistent sounds of the camp, leaving only Zareen and Alborz in a bubble of calm. At least, Zareen would have felt calm if there wasn't so much to do. Alborz had purposefully thrown Zareen in deep to see how he'd react, and he could tell that Zareen was feeling overwhelmed.

"I don't know how you do it, brother," Zareen sighed as he closed his eyes. Alborz knew the feeling well. A thousand thoughts churning in the back of your mind, a constant litany of things you'd done, hadn't done, and still had to do. "There's so much to keep track of. A hundred threads that need attention. So much responsibility. My limitless respect for you has only grown the past few days."

Alborz raised his brandy snifter in a mock toast before draining it down.

"Yes, it's a lot. But you've performed well so far. I've only had to cover for you a few times," Alborz said with a twinkle in his eye. Zareen furrowed his brow in agitation but refrained from saying anything. "Oh, don't give me that look. I told you I'd be nearby to help if anything went wrong. And like I said, you're doing a... satisfactory job so far."

Zareen snorted in response. "It doesn't feel like it. In all our years together, I've only seen a small portion of what you did while in command. I've been consumed with my studies and experiments and haven't had the time nor the inclination to learn, until now."

Zareen took another sip of wine and stared into the glass.

"I imagined that leading was simply giving orders and having them obeyed. But that's a gross simplification. I must give the right orders at the right time, and the demons are in the details."

Zareen rubbed the bridge of his nose and squinted.

"When we spoke about me leading the hold, I envisioned leading the troops in battle. I hadn't thought about all the work that goes in beforehand. Over the last few days, I've been consumed with organizing slaves, seeing to the supply chain for the march, scouting the area, and all the other mundane but necessary things that have to get done."

Alborz nodded sympathetically. "I know exactly what you mean. Dozens of tasks continually bubble up and pull for your immediate attention. The skill is in floating above the incessant clamor, Zareen. You are intelligent and organized, but this is a new set of challenges to overcome. I understand why you feel you can barely keep up."

Zareen nodded and rubbed his temples to try to sooth his head. "I'm drowning in the things I know I have yet to do, but I'm more nervous about missing something important."

"Pull yourself together. Of course you'll miss things. That's why I wanted to do this now, so I can cover your mistakes."

"I know," said Zareen petulantly, "but it's a lot to handle."

Alborz leaned in and lowered his voice.

"Is this too much for you? I noticed you seemed distracted this morning as we addressed the troops."

Distracted was an understatement. Zareen had focused on the ground so intently that Alborz expected to see something erupt from the earth. Zareen closed his eyes and massaged his forehead.

"No, I'm alright. I thought I felt something moving in the earth. Like a spirit of some sort. It was nothing."

Alborz nodded in understanding, but he wasn't convinced. Even if Zareen didn't think it was worth mentioning, Alborz filed it away for later consideration and changed topics. "You've been in charge for three days so far. What have you learned?"

Alborz poured himself more brandy while Zareen considered the question.

"I've been running non-stop and haven't had a chance for self-reflection," he responded with a twist of sarcasm. Alborz smirked. "On the first day, I dove into the duties with my usual excellence. But by that evening,

I started to feel... the burden. It's eased in the past few days, but only because the army stopped moving while we scouted the enemy and rallied our troops. Once the army is on the move again, I'm sure the challenges will increase again."

"Oh, it will. An army on the move is a whole different slave than an army in camp. May I make an observation? You don't know what's important versus what's merely urgent." Zareen nodded in silent agreement. "You'll have to learn to tell the difference. You have to learn not to attack every problem the same way."

Alborz offered more wine, which Zareen refused with a shake of his head.

"You want to know the secret?" he asked slyly. Zareen closed his eyes and waved his hand in acquiescence. "I spend a lot of time making plans, but I never focus too hard on the details. The big broad strokes are what matter. Keep your army healthy, focused, and afraid. The rest will follow. Find the enemy and engage them on ground of your choosing with overwhelming force. Compared to that, nothing else matters."

He swirled the brandy in the snifter, and he took another sip.

"Detailed battle plans only last until the irons hit the fire."

Alborz motioned to a side table laid out with a map of the immediate area. Metal tokens were placed at strategic locations around the map, showing the positions of both armies. A set of brown and green figurines were clustered to the south and west of Llyngyr Cadw, representing loyal gnorr and orc troops deployed in the underground tunnels to stop rogue ratmen or goblins from invading the hold from below. These forces were holding for now, but the armies had fallen into a stalemate of horrendous tunnel warfare with the goblins. The rumors of a free gnorr army gnawed at Alborz, and he was concerned about his slaves' inevitable betrayal if they got the chance. Luckily, the free vermin were operating farther away, and they only had the goblins to contend with for now. That was a problem for another day. Once they slaughtered the mongrels, it would be simple to clear the tunnels out.

"I must say, your gargoyles have done an excellent job. We've pinpointed the location of the mongrel army, and with the help of our remaining halfbreeds, we've kept their scouts at bay. Between scouting and burning the fleet, I have to admit they aren't half as worthless as I thought." Zareen glared at the comment, but Alborz pretended not to notice.

He was in a vicious mood, and he enjoyed goading his brother. He wouldn't be so jovial if things weren't going so well. He had shadowed Zareen the past few days and was generally impressed with how well his brother adapted to command, not that he would let him know it. Alborz found that he liked delegating his day-to-day responsibilities. Since taking Llyngyr Cadw, Alborz had jealously hoarded responsibility, careful not to put too much trust in any one of his subordinates. It wouldn't do for one of them to dream above their station, after all. It was a fact of Abyssal Dwarf society that more Overmasters were slain by treachery than in open warfare. He had seen too many instances of leaders getting killed due to petty intrigues, or by getting out of touch with their men. In that way, Alborz was blessed to have his brother with him. Zareen, for all his faults, was someone he could trust... somewhat.

Speaking of backstabbing, Alborz leaned closer to Zareen and asked, "I know you've alerted the other Overmasters in the area to the mongrel invasion. Have you heard back from any of them?"

"Yes," Zareen answered, "but none to our liking. The lords of Cwl Gen and Jarrun Bridge both say they can't spare any troops at this time. Caphrix of Jarrun Bridge went so far as to say that he'd eventually send an army to relieve us of Llyngyr Cadw if we couldn't handle the mongrels ourselves. Clever wording there. Not 'relieve Llyngyr Cadw,' but 'relieve us of.' I had the gnorr who delivered the message killed for Caphrix's insolence."

Alborz raised his brandy snifter in response. "That's to be expected. They still see our loss as their gain. We won't forget it. What about Dravak?" Alborz had sent messengers to the great mines of Crag Hudd to speak with the mad Iron-caster Dravak Dalken.

"Nothing but gibberish. The messenger said that Dravak could not be disturbed at this time. He babbled something about mining into the world's arteries, and Dravak being on the precipice of unlimited magical power, or some nonsense." Zareen shrugged his shoulders. "Dravak has never been the most stable of my order. It seems that his thirst for power has a deeper hold on him than we thought. He's of no use anyway." Zareen waved his hand dismissively.

Alborz arched his eyebrow at the obvious display of jealousy. Dravak Dalken was the most gifted Iron-caster of his age. Though tinged with madness, Dravak wielded undeniable influence and power among the Abyssal Dwarfs.

"Well, it was to be expected, but we satisfied the ancient forms. We alerted the other Overmasters and gave them the option to join in the glory. It's just as well that they declined. We have the situation well in hand."

Alborz leaned back on his divan and called for his personal slaves to move the map table between him and Zareen. The ratkin were obviously nervous and were careful not to topple any of the wooden markers. Once it was in place, the brothers leaned in close to observe the map, but Alborz waited for the slaves to leave before speaking. He pointed to a set of blue and red markers clustered at the southern spur of the mountains encircling Crafanc.

"Daamuz joined up with the Helgwin forces here. Your gargoyles report over three thousand warriors between them, mostly infantry and some artillery. Knowing Helgwin, they'll be itching for revenge. Daamuz will want to move to assault the gates. With the Helgwin army free to move outside of Crafanc, this changes the strategic situation."

Alborz pointed to a cluster of black figurines, some short and metal, some tall and wooden, straddling the Ironway.

"We're here. As you can see, the land between us is mostly open, but there are a few defensible positions for us to take."

Zareen nodded. Alborz drew a straight line from the enemy army to Llyngyr Cadw.

"The fastest route is for them to march through these open plains, and they may do that. However, I believe that they'll try to stick to the foothills of the mountains to the north, here." Alborz drew a more circuitous route with his finger, tracing the edge of the mountains. "This will provide them protection for their flanks and give them a defensible position with their backs to the mountains if we assault them from the plains. Either way they choose, we'll know about it in plenty of time to react. So, Zareen, given that, what would you do?"

As Zareen leaned in closer to the map, Alborz sat back, a plan already formulated in his mind. Zareen weighed the various options and finally spoke with a hint of confusion.

"Why don't we just retreat back to Llyngyr Cadw? We can withstand a siege there for months. Let them exhaust themselves on our walls, and we'll harry them all the way back to Crafanc. That was our original plan, wasn't it? Strand them here, destroy their artillery, and force them back to Crafanc to starve?"

Alborz scoffed at Zareen's suggestion as he frowned and furrowed his brow. Zareen's mind was fixed on the mongrel army, but he wasn't considering the entire strategic situation. He was showing his inflexibility, focused on the old plan, even though new circumstances had arisen. Zareen still had to mature as a leader.

"Normally, with the mongrel's fleet in disarray, I would harass their army, disrupt their supply lines, and grind them down. But I can't take the chance on them escaping or surviving through another campaign season to harass us again next year once I'm gone. We need to seize this opportunity to destroy both clans in one decisive battle." Alborz motioned to Cwl Gen and Jarrun Bridge. "We must let the other Overmasters see our strength, lest they get any ideas. Remember, we not only have to defeat them, but we also need to do it quickly. Yes, our original plan would destroy their army, but it won't guarantee our long-term success."

Even as Alborz harangued his brother, his words echoed falsely in his mind. His desire to defeat the mongrels in open battle was starting to blossom and take hold of him. A small part of him knew that he was overstating their predicament in order to give himself that chance.

"Think, Zareen. We can't show the other Overmasters any weakness. Nor can we take too much time, or the goblins in the tunnels will cause us grief. This may be an isolated clan working on their own, or it may be the start of something more. We can't take the chance on them being reinforced later in the summer. Success means smashing the mongrels and crushing any hope they have of retaking Halpi. Halpi is ours, now and forever."

Zareen clenched his fists in frustration at Alborz's rebuke, but he wisely pursed his lips and stared at the map. Alborz waited impatiently for Zareen to come up with another solution.

"You need to take a broader view, Zareen," he said. "The situation has changed since we made our plans in the throne room. We've taken some losses, and this mongrel commander seems to have enough grit and luck to be a worthy foe."

Alborz was still impressed at how well the Free Dwarfs had done in the amphibious assault. Grounding their warship was an act of genius or madness, but either way, it had worked. They'd lost a good portion of their Decimators, and about half of their artillery, but Alborz would adapt.

"Now, what will you do?"

Zareen chewed his lower lip for a few moments before he violently jabbed his finger down on the southern side of one of the mountains. "If they believe the mountains will shield them, then let's take that away. We'll lead our army here, onto the mountainside north of their proposed route. If they stay near the mountains, we'll be in position to intercept them." Alborz smiled in approval. "If they take the direct route, we'll descend on their rear and trap them against the very gates of their home."

"Sound strategy," said Alborz, mildly surprised at his brother's ability to guess his plans. "So, what other possibilities are there? And what else will we need to do to make the plan work?"

"We can take a force of orc gore riders and some gnorr and use them as a decoy out on the plains. Perhaps lead the mongrels away from the mountains?" Zareen closed his eyes and waved his fingers slowly as he thought, as if he were casting a spell. "Yes, that will work. Between the two forces, the mongrels will be forced to engage one and be ambushed by the other. We'll need to keep the army's movements a secret, so we flood the area with our faster troops to screen our movements."

Alborz smiled and motioned for Zareen to go on, and his brother began rattling the details, growing more excited as he went. Alborz offered suggestions and poured more drinks as they strategized late into the night.

Alborz knew that Zareen wasn't ready to lead, but with time, he would show his mettle. The real question now was whether Alborz would ever be ready to give up being the Lord of Llyngyr Cadw. He had given Zareen all the responsibility, but he hadn't ceded the lordship, or the authority that went with it.

No, he thought, *not yet. But maybe soon. We deal with the mongrels, we smash the goblins, and then I'll go take my rightful place in Tragar. Until then, I am the sole Lord of Llyngyr Cadw.*

CHAPTER 18

Rorik wiped the sweat from his brow with a brocaded green handkerchief. He knew it was in vain; his head would break out in sweat again in a few moments. The hot and parched air quickly sucked the moisture from the handkerchief, leaving a white salt stain on the fabric. The incessant summer heat was oppressive, making it hard to stay hydrated, and even though it was only mid-morning, Rorik could feel the sun's presence in the sky. By afternoon, the sun would be pushing down on him with an almost palpable weight.

The heat worsened as they traveled further inland. The clan thanes had made sure to pass by running water sources when they plotted their march to Llyngyr Cadw, but the last streambed they'd passed was bone dry. Rhyss had stashed plenty of water away in the supply caches, but without the stream, there wasn't quite enough water to go around. The army was forced to ration the supplies until they reached the next cache.

Speaking of Rhyss, Rorik hadn't seen him and his rangers in a few days. Kilvar and the Helgwin rangers had been scouting ahead and screening the march as best they could. In the end, it wasn't his concern. He had other things to worry about, like the Abyssal Dwarf gargoyles that were free to shadow the army. Rorik could just make out a group of them circling in the sky to the north, camouflaged by the mountains in the background. When the march began, some of the gargoyles had strayed too close to the column, and the Wyverns had been able to snipe them out of the air. The gargoyles had learned their lesson quickly, and they now gave the column a wide berth. It grated on Rorik that he couldn't make the gargoyles pay more. The Wyverns carried the best rifles in Pannithor, but they could only shoot so far. The gargoyles' presence was a constant reminder that the army was deep in hostile territory and added to the feeling of menace.

Normally, Lord Dinnidek held a meeting every morning at first light to touch base and give orders for the day. It was odd to meet again so soon, Rorik thought to himself as he made his way to meet the other thanes. Maybe the scouts had finally found the enemy... but he doubted it, based on their luck so far. Rorik wiped his face down again. Only a few seconds had passed, but his kerchief was already drying out. He looked at it in disgust, as if it was responsible for the heat, then shook his head at his own ridiculousness before he finally stowed it in his satchel next to his journal.

The Wyverns had been stationed throughout the column to keep lookout. Rorik, naturally, had placed himself in the front, to save himself from the dust kicked up by the line of marching feet. As he proceeded back down the line to meet the other thanes, Rorik made his way past row after row of Ironclad and Shieldbreakers. The warriors stolidly marched by in silence, eyes squinting at the dust and the glare. Despite the conditions, the soldiers bore the burdens stoically, exhibiting their legendary dwarfen endurance. The few Wyverns that marched by gave him a smile and a lazy wave as they kept watch on the skies. Some captains would equate the half-hearted salute with a lack of discipline, but Rorik didn't mind. In his experience, snappy salutes didn't make a difference once the fighting started. True discipline came from diligent practice, responsibility to your fellows, and not cracking under pressure. Everything else was for show.

He saw Veit up ahead, leaning on his crutch, leg still in a wooden brace. The engineer had a far off look, and Rorik could almost see the gears turning in Veit's head as he was lost in thought. That was one of the things that impressed him the most, Veit's almost obsessive attention to detail. The engineer's brain never stopped working, always looking for the most efficient ways to do things. Rorik appreciated the sentiment. Easy was always better than hard, if you could swing it. But Veit didn't shy away from the hard stuff either. Rorik, noting the heavy pack that Veit was carrying around, admired the engineer's determination to not let his injury slow him down. Since the battle, Veit had shared in the drudgery with the rest of the clan without the slightest hint of annoyance, still quick with a joke or a word of encouragement. Rorik had heard the rumors about him and Diessa, and whether that was the reason for the spring in Veit's step or not, Rorik couldn't help but admire it.

He reached Veit just as the rest of the thanes were coming near. The engineer took off his backpack, and his crutch slipped out from under his arm. He went to reach for it and dropped his backpack instead, which landed with a crash, scattering papers, charcoal pencils, and plans on the ground. Veit cursed with a smile and shook his head in mild agitation. Rorik trotted up and knelt to help Veit gather his belongings.

"Thanks, Rorik! I made a real mess, didn't I?" He tried to help, but with the splint, he couldn't kneel down. He tried to bend down at the waist, but he twisted something the wrong way and straightened up with a wince.

"No trouble, I got it," Rorik said, motioning for Veit to stay put. Rorik stood the backpack up and handed Veit the bundle of papers. "What's in there?"

"These?" answered Veit, waving the papers around. "These are the schematics for Llyngyr Cadw. When we left the hold, I made sure to save one set of maps just in case. Lord Drohzon had me destroy the remaining copies. I've been augmenting the map by writing down everything I remember about the hold, every door, every passage, all the defenses. Figure it will come in handy once we arrive." He stowed the papers in the top of his pack. "The entire mountainside is riddled with passages that lead to the hold. There's no telling what modifications the Abyssal Dwarfs have made in our absence, mind you. I assume that they've collapsed most of the tunnels or at least set guards everywhere."

Rorik gathered the rest of the scattered objects from the ground and packed them away as Veit continued.

"So, Rorik, I see I'm not the only dwarf around here who keeps notes. What have you been putting in your journal?"

"Nothing much, really. I've been writing about my travels since I left home. I started this book specifically to chronicle the invasion. So far, most of the entries have to do with the weather, but I have some choice entries about the amphibious assault. Who knows, maybe my descendants will read it once I'm long gone."

"That's a great idea," said Veit excitedly. "I never thought about leaving a record for my descendants. I figured they wouldn't be interested, but who knows? Maybe I'll start one myself."

Rorik smiled and handed the last of the charcoal pencils to Veit just as Lord Dinnidek and the other thanes arrived. Dinnidek was conversing with Lord Anfynn Helgwin, Tordek in his usual place just behind. Master Daerun, festooned with extra supplies, was trudging along next to his sister Diessa with the child-like elemental walking between them at a pace that belied its small legs. The stone priestess had taken to wearing a blindfold, and Rorik had heard that she relied on the elemental to be her eyes. Their personal retainers, Felwyr and Bruon, trailed the group. A group of Ironclad with blue ribbons tied to their arms were casually shadowing Diessa from a distance. It seemed like the stone priestess was tiring of her honor guard. Rorik bowed to them all as they arrived, while Veit hobbled straight to Diessa's side. The engineer was obviously pleased to see Diessa, but dwarfen propriety stopped him short of embracing her in public.

Dinnidek motioned for the group to follow him to a spot further away from the marching column of dwarfen warriors before addressing them.

"Thank you all for coming," he said with a smile. "I know meeting like this is unusual, so I'll cut to the chase. We've discovered the enemy's position, and we have a few choices to make."

Rorik paid close attention to which thanes were surprised at the news and which ones were 'in the know.' The three Daamuz siblings, and Veit of all people, just stood by stoically. *Interesting,* thought Rorik.

Dinnidek drew in the dirt with a long stick he'd been carrying.

"The mountains are here, to our north," he said as he scrawled a line of triangles on the ground. He drew a crude tower and a dotted line. "And here is Llyngyr Cadw and the Ironway."

He placed two 'X'es on the ground, one south of the mountains, and another further west along the mountain range. Gwel wandered into the circle of dwarfs and cocked its head at Dinnidek.

"We are here," Din began, but he was interrupted by Gwel, who walked to the drawings and kicked at them with his feet. Din 'tsked' and tried to redraw the mountains, but Gwel batted the stick away. Before Din could try again, a slight tremor went through the ground and the dirt rose to show the mountain range and the surrounding topography, including a fortress built into the side of a mountain, and a raised roadway. A miniature earthen dwarf coalesced on the map where they were currently located, and a similar dwarf, this one with a horned helmet, formed on the mountain range. Gwel bowed to Din as the map finished forming.

"That's quite the trick," said Anfynn with a smile. "Too bad he can't do that to scale."

"Maybe he is," replied Daerun. "I mean, he's pretty tiny."

Gwel shook his little hand, and the ground around Daerun's feet vibrated slightly, which elicited a chuckle from the group.

Din bowed politely to Gwel.

"Thank you, little one. As I was saying, we are here." Din pointed to the earthen dwarf on the plains. As he did so, the dwarf looked up at the group and saluted with a tiny axe. "The enemy has stationed themselves here," he pointed to the horned dwarf further west, "and here."

This time a small orc, mounted on an earthen gore, formed in between their army and Llyngyr Cadw.

"Rhyss placed supply caches throughout the foothills of the mountains for our inland march. In addition, we've been using the mountains to guard our right flank. Eventually we'll need to leave the mountains and cut straight east, crossing the plains to Llyngyr Cadw, but I want to hold off on that for as long as possible. First off, it will take us away from the supplies; and second, the Abyssal Dwarfs are faster and have an advantage on the open ground."

Rorik studied the map as Din continued.

"We knew the fiends were massing on the Ironway. Since then, they've flooded the valley with troops to hide their movements. However, their main force is positioned on the mountains here, to stop our advance and push us out onto the plains. If they're successful, their second force, positioned out on the plains here," Din pointed to the mounted orc closer to Llyngyr Cadw, "will try to pin us, while the main force descends on our rear. Likewise, if we instead engage the main force, then this secondary force will attack."

Rorik grimly nodded at Din's assessment of the situation. It was hard to argue with.

"How did you find the enemy?" Lord Anfynn asked. "Kilvar and his troops have been busy screening the main force. Is this Rhyss' doing?"

In response, Din smiled at Diessa. "Since the landing, my sister has formed a bond with the earth spirits of Halpi. That bond has allowed her to feel the enemy armies."

Diessa smiled as Gwel bowed to Anfynn. "I'm not sure how much longer the link will last," said Diessa, self-consciously. "I knew the general disposition of the enemy, but I wasn't sure about the details until this morning."

Rorik smirked as he looked at Veit. That explained why the engineer was nonchalant about the news. He was getting it from the source. Diessa's newfound power, no matter how temporary, had saved them from bumbling into a trap. Rorik felt better knowing that the very earth was on their side, but it still didn't answer the question of where Rhyss was.

"So," Anfynn asked as he nervously stroked his beard and gazed at the ground, "where does that leave us?"

"The way I see it, we have only one option. The Abyssal Dwarfs are faster, and they outnumber us. They've set a trap for us, and I say we walk into it." A few of the dwarfs grunted in surprise at this, but Din kept going. "But we'll walk into it with our eyes open. The enemy doesn't know that we're aware of the trap. My idea is to engage the main force at the mountains here." The miniature dwarf marched up to the horned dwarf in the mountains to the west. "We send Rhyss and a small group of rangers over the mountain to ambush the enemy from the rear."

"Rhyss will target the enemy artillery?" asked Rorik.

"That's the plan," answered Daerun with a smile. "It worked on the beach, so we'll keep doing it until they can stop us."

Din nodded and continued. "We send Kilvar, with some additional troops, to screen our forces from the Abyssal Dwarfs on the plains. If they can delay them long enough, we can defeat the main force and then use their position to dig in." The earthen dwarf cut the horned dwarf in half, and as the enemy disintegrated into dust, the miniature dwarf turned and sat triumphantly on the mountaintop, his legs swinging gleefully. "If the battle goes poorly, we'll still be able to hug the mountains and make our way back to Crafanc. I know it's not a great option, but I don't see another way. What say you? Any other suggestions?"

Silence reigned over the group as the dwarfs contemplated the situation. Rorik ran through a couple ideas, all of them bad.

There's no waiting for reinforcements, mostly because there aren't any. There's no going back because we don't have ships. Can't outrun them... I guess that's the best we can hope for.

"I'll take silence as assent," said Dinnidek. "We're all in agreement, then?"

The other thanes all nodded silently or concurred in low tones.

Lord Anfynn addressed Din directly. "So, where is Rhyss now? Did you send him this morning before consulting with us?"

"Um, no," Din said diffidently. "I actually sent him yesterday afternoon." Anfynn raised an eyebrow, and Dinnidek shrugged. "The enemy wasn't in place yet, but for Rhyss to set his ambush, we couldn't wait. As I said, I didn't see another way out of this, and I had to take the chance."

Rorik could see Diessa smiling to herself as if she'd heard all this from Din before, while Daerun nodded enthusiastically.

"To be fair, Lord Anfynn," said Din, "if we decided on something different, he had alternate orders to shadow the enemy and report back. Please accept my regrets for not informing you sooner, but I wanted to be sure of our intelligence before we discussed it."

Anfynn smirked as he stroked his beard. He gave Din an assessing look. "No apology necessary, Lord Dinnidek. I'm more surprised than anything. I'm not sure if what you did showed extreme confidence or rashness."

"Time will tell, Lord Anfynn. If the plan works, we'll all be geniuses. If it doesn't, then I'll be to blame."

While Rorik appreciated the sentiment, he shook his head ruefully. There would be no one to place the blame if they were all dead. This wasn't the first time he'd regretted taking this contract. And it probably wouldn't be the last. He glanced down at his journal. He'd said that he was keeping the journal for his descendants. But as of today, he didn't have any descendants, and the chances of him surviving the week were growing more questionable by the day. It occurred to Rorik that keeping his journal was an act of extreme optimism.

But if I live, it should make for one epic tale.

CHAPTER 19

Dinnidek gazed up at the night sky, countless stars shining through the darkness, his back against the hard and supportive stone of his homeland. The army had marched for two days toward the Abyssal Dwarf army and their date with destiny. Today they'd made camp early, hoping to get some much-needed rest before the final push in the dead of night. Din had given orders to begin the last march just after midnight in hopes of getting his army into position before the enemy knew what was going on. That didn't leave a lot of time for sleep, and he had no delusions that he'd be getting any rest.

Well, thought Din, *tomorrow we'll see if I'm a genius or a madman.*

He'd walked up to the nearby foothills to the north, looking to indulge in a moment of solitude, and was seated on a large boulder with an elevated view back into the camp. The air was still warm after the heat of the day, but the stone was relatively cool to the touch. As usual, Tordek stood a respectful distance away but close enough to react. Din had ordered the camp completely dark this evening to keep the army hidden from enemy scouts. Even with his dwarfen vision, Din could barely make out some of the closer details in the dark; and though he could hear the incessant murmur of thousands of dwarfs, he couldn't see anything further away. All in all, he was pleased.

He laid back on the boulder and looked up at the clear night sky. The moon was working its way across the heavens, and by midnight it would dip below the western mountains, shrouding the land in further darkness. Thousands upon thousands of stars twinkled down upon him. He imagined that each star was an ancestor, standing ready to guide and protect him and the clan. The thought made him smile in joy at the sheer magnificence of it. He closed his eyes and said a prayer of gratitude to his ancestors, the great warriors and leaders of Clan Daamuz. Without their guidance and protection, they wouldn't have made it this far.

One more day, and you'll be avenged.

Din felt serene. His breakdown after the landing had put lots of things in perspective, and Diessa's recovery had freed him to change his way of thinking. He had the same attention to detail, the need to be involved in the daily minutia, but he'd released his feeling of ultimate responsibility. After his talk with Rhyss, he tried to give himself the same leeway and understanding that he would give any other thane. Rhyss had reminded him that he wasn't a god. He was descended from a long line of dwarfs who had done their best, and the clan had survived. He was surrounded by family and friends that were extremely capable; dwarfs that could be counted on to deliver, with or without Din's assistance. He trusted them completely. The idea was freeing.

"Mother," he whispered into the night, "you lived your life in service to the clan. You gave that life so that the clan would survive. So that Diessa would survive. You'd be so proud of her. Your spirit lives in her."

In his imagination, he saw his mother as she'd been when he was a child. He saw her holding Daerun's little hand as they wandered the cavernous great hall together, Diessa and him walking beside them. She would take the three of them on tours of the hold, telling them stories of their ancestors. Every tapestry, every statue, every mural had a story, a myth passed down from generation to generation. She was so fun, so patient with the three of them. Din remembered how she would delight in the smallest things that her children did. She was so strong and principled. He remembered how she incessantly fought for the good of the clan. With that mixture of sun and stone, she really was amazing. His father had loved her so much.

Nothing we do tomorrow will bring them back. But they're with me all the same.

Din felt a tear track down his temple. He indulged in the memories for a few more stolen moments before he shook himself and sat up.

Enough of that. Time to get back to camp.

Tordek was already on his way to meet him as he slid down off the boulder. Dinnidek smiled at the stalwart bodyguard with a nod, and they picked their way through the rocks to the army below.

The dwarfs had erected a loose picket of sharpened stakes atop an earthen berm around the exterior of the camp, and Din was stopped by multiple sentries as he approached. He nodded in silent satisfaction at their watchfulness. Within the perimeter, the warriors were gathered in small groups, talking in hushed tones. Every so often, he'd pass a larger group seated around an empty and unlit firepit, which made Din chuckle. Even though there was no fire, the soldiers took comfort in following the same forms, even if it didn't serve a function; they really were creatures of habit. Din paid close attention to the warriors. They seemed confident, and if any of them were anxious, it was only the typical pre-battle jitters.

He wandered over to join Daerun and Diessa, who were seated in a small circle along with some of the other thanes. Bruon was across the circle, looking mildly out of place in the other leaders' company. In contrast, Rorik was confidently perched on a small log, his journal open and resting on his knee. As usual since the landing, Veit was sitting next to Deese. He had taken off his splint and was wincing as he slowly bent and straightened his leg. Cormack had told Veit he needed to try to work it a few times a day, lest it get frozen. Diessa, still blindfolded, sat cross-legged with Gwel nestled in between her legs. Deese gently rubbed the engineer's back in a sign of affection and comfort. Dinnidek was glad that the two of them had found each other. He still didn't know if Veit had worked up the courage to express his feelings, or if Diessa had finally noticed what was so obvious to everyone else. Either way, it had worked. And it didn't seem like a relationship of convenience. Their connection was built on a lifetime of friendship and mutual respect, which aligned well with Din's dwarfen sensibilities.

Dare and Felwyr were telling a story, the rest of the dwarfs paying rapt attention.

"So then I set up the pulley and started hoisting up the beams for the longhouse, and Felwyr here decides that he'll be smart and put the afternoon ale cask on the beams so he doesn't have to carry it up to the boys working in the rafters." Daerun was trying to keep his voice down, but he whispered so loud that he might as well be talking. As usual, the two friends played off each other, exaggerating more and more until the tale became utterly ridiculous.

"I'm a genius," said Felwyr. "Gotta let the machines do the work for you, Dare."

Daerun rolled his eyes. "Sure you do. But you, in your genius, put the cask near the end of the beam, not in the center."

"That's not true!" Felwyr said in mock indignation. "It was dead center, right where it belonged. It couldn't have been more in the center. It was the most centered a cask could be."

"Sure it was," said Daerun sarcastically. "It was literally way out at the end. Half of the cask was just floating out in the wind. So anyway, I don't see him do it, so I begin hoisting the rope and wouldn't you know, the beam starts tilting a little, but I can't see what's happening because I'm way down on the ground."

"Eyes like a hawk, this one," said Felwyr, pointing at Dare. "Notices everything."

"I do notice everything, but this was just so monumentally stupid, my brain couldn't process what it was seeing." Fel chuckled while Bruon snorted and choked on his whiskey. "So anyway, I'm hoisting away, pulling the rope and the beam is going higher and higher, and next thing you know the cask is making the beam swing around in a circle." Daerun spun his finger in the air to emphasize. "And the cask, it flies off the end and hits one of the columns. Now I don't see this, because I'm busy, head down, doing the honest work of three dwarfs. No lollygagging for me."

"The work of three dwarfs, if two of them were sleeping and one of them had a bum leg," Felwyr chimed in. "No offense, Veit."

The engineer smiled and waved the comment away. Daerun raised his eyebrows and put his hand to his chest with a gasp.

"How dare you, Felwyr! How dare you. As I was saying, I don't see the cask go flying, engrossed in my work as I was. Honest work, by the way, not like this layabout. But my other senses are just as keen, mind you, so I hear the cask explode against the column. The ale burst out of there like a grenade."

"A delicious grenade."

"Yes, which makes the story all the more tragic. So, I hear the cask explode. Then I feel ale splatter all over my back and soak my shirt. I mean, I was drenched in ale. So much ale was wasted on the ground that the earth elementals nearby all got drunk." Diessa giggled while Gwel tilted his head in confusion. "I swear, I saw Joro stumbling around the whole day."

"Looking like this one at last call," said Fel as he dramatically gestured with his thumb toward Daerun. "I couldn't have planned the whole thing better. Who's the genius, now?"

A wide grin split Felwyr's face, and the assembled dwarfs did their best to quiet their laughter, but it was contagious. Even Tordek was silently smiling.

"You can come apprentice with me, Fel," offered Veit. "You already have a knack for unexpected explosions. It's obvious you'd make a great engineer."

"Please," said Daerun, "take him! Relieve me of his explosive intellect!"

Eventually the laughter ran its course, and a comfortable silence descended on the group. Din looked from face to face, trying to lock the details in his memory. Deese and Veit leaning against each-other for comfort. Bruon trying to stay inconspicuous while he cautiously watched over Diessa. Daerun and Fel playing the fools to lighten the mood while Tordek dourly looked on. He wanted to hold this moment for as long as he could.

"Speaking of Joro, Deese," asked Daerun, "have you felt him nearby since the landing?"

"No," answered Diessa sadly. "I don't think he's gone, but I believe that, like me, he joined the collective to heal after our ordeal." She patted Gwel on the head as she spoke. "Besides this little one here, I usually feel the earth spirits as a single presence. Joro was different."

Gwel hung his head, as if showing respect.

"He'll be back," Daerun said. "You can't kill a spirit. Can't kill our spirit either."

Din nodded grimly in agreement. Daerun had inadvertently summed up the army's demeanor perfectly. The Abyssal Dwarfs had won the first round, but they hadn't killed the clans completely. And wherever a single Free Dwarf lived, that hope, that fire, would live on in them. He looked up at the sky again, and the stars twinkled back in response, a million tiny fires marching back through time eternal.

Anfynn Helgwin emerged from the darkness with two of his thanes and a gray and brown mastiff with a black iron collar at his side.

"Lord Dinnidek, may I join you?" The Warmaster looked even more excited than normal, eyes sweeping the crowd as he absently stroked his beard.

Din slid over to make room and patted the ground next to him. "Of course. Here, have a seat."

Anfynn smiled and knelt on the ground, placing his rubied helmet before him. Once the Warmaster was situated, Daerun leaned forward and offered him a pull from his silver flask. Anfynn accepted eagerly, and Dare tossed the flask to him. Anfynn skillfully caught it with a flourish and a smile of gratitude.

"How are your clansmen, Anfynn?" asked Din. "Are they ready for tomorrow?"

Anfynn was busy taking a deep drink from the flask, Dare egging him on. Once he was done, he tossed it back to Daerun with a nod of approval before answering.

"My warriors are eager, to say the least. We've waited for years to bloody our axes on the Abyssal Dwarfs. Tomorrow is going to be glorious, Lord Dinnidek! Glorious!" Anfynn spoke quietly, but there was no mistaking his excitement. "Even the hounds have their blood up. They can feel it in the air."

The gray canine seemed to smile up at Anfynn as he spoke, and the Warmaster idly rubbed the hound behind the ears. The Helgwin forces included packs of hunting mastiffs, dogs bred for war to hunt and kill the enemy on the battlefield. The Daamuz clan had only dabbled in using dogs in that way, but Clan Helgwin were experts. Din was interested to see how they would perform.

"I'm glad to hear it," replied Din. "Our morale is high as well. There's a confidence among the warriors that's infectious, Lord Anfynn. I can feel it when I walk among them. They know we're outnumbered, outgunned, but it just doesn't matter. Our two clans will see the thing through, one way or another. Tomorrow will be a reckoning."

Dare banged his empty flask on the ground in agreement.

"Gwel," Dinnidek addressed the elemental directly, "can you show us the Abyssal Dwarf army?"

Gwel nodded and raised his little arms. A miniature mountain range rose from the ground, Abyssal Dwarf troops arrayed across the heights. On the left, an arm of the foothills extended out into the flatland. There was a wood on the right situated close to the mountains. Between the two, the ground was relatively flat and clear. Gwel gestured to the map grandly.

"Thank you, little one," said Dinnidek with a nod of his head. Gwel nodded back. "The enemy commander has chosen his battlefield well. Except for the forest, there will be little cover from the Abyssal artillery, and we'll be forced to assault the enemy uphill. In addition, our scouts tell us that we're outnumbered at least three to one."

"Yes, but most of them are vermin or orc slaves," said Daerun. "We've beaten the tar out of them before."

"Yes, we have in the past. But as you know, they can still bog us down by weight of numbers. I'm more concerned with the Abyssal Dwarf abominations. Their halfbreeds are quick and cunning, while the grotesques are walking nightmares that are both fast and hard to kill."

Anfynn nodded grimly. "Nightmares is right. Next to the artillery, they'll be our biggest problem. Luckily, my mastiffs are trained from pups to hunt them. They won't be enough to kill them, but they'll definitely slow them down."

"I'm counting on it," replied Din. "And hopefully Rhyss can work some more magic and destroy the artillery. If he can't, our options will be limited. Our guns are too small to return fire, and the difference in height only makes it worse."

"So," interjected Veit, "even if we can't use them for counterbattery, I would still suggest placing most of the guns in the center. Once Rhyss does his part, we can move them up and barrage the enemy troops before we assault the high ground. Maybe place a few of the guns on the back side of the woods. This should keep them hidden from the artillery. Those few guns won't have good targets but can shoot the enemy flanks on the wild chance that they close in on our battle line."

"I like the idea," agreed Anfynn.

"As do I," said Din. "But just in case Rhyss can't destroy the artillery, I want us to put pressure on their guns. Dare, I want you to push up and take those woods before the sun comes up. If Rhyss is unsuccessful, you'll need to assault the hill and try to roll a flank. And if the enemy places their artillery on that side of the field, even better."

"We can do that," answered Dare thoughtfully. "I'll tell the boys to get ready."

"Where do you want us?" asked Anfynn.

"The rest of my plan depends on us neutralizing the enemy artillery. If we can't do that, we're as good as dead. Lord Anfynn, I would like you to take command of our left flank. I'll take the middle. Our job will be to hold our position until the Abyssal artillery is destroyed. Do you see how the mountain thrusts out into the plain? On my signal, I would like you to assault that position and take the high ground. You have a large contingent of Ironwatch, which we'll augment with the ones from my clan. If you're successful, you'll be able to pour sheets of lead into the enemy flanks. I will take my Ironclad and form a shield wall in the center, the artillery interspersed among the regiments. As the two sides advance, I'll move up with you to keep the line tight. Rorik, your sharpshooters will be with me."

"I like it," said Anfynn as he stroked his beard in thought. "Simple, and hopefully effective. I intend to scout the ridge before the sun rises. If there is no resistance, I'll send some of my troops to dig in and try to hold the enemy at bay."

"Good thought, but don't move the main body of your force forward until my signal. Understood? I don't want any gaps in the line."

Anfynn nodded and began giving orders to his two thanes while the rest of the dwarfs began murmuring. Before the meeting completely broke down, Diessa looked directly at Din and spoke in a loud voice.

"What about me?"

A hush fell over the crowd as Deese patiently waited for Din to reply. Dinnidek sighed before he straightened his back and locked eyes with Gwel. The elemental blankly returned Din's gaze, but the Lord of Clan Daamuz knew that Deese could see how serious he was.

"Thank you for asking, Diessa," replied Din. "I need you and the earth spirits to shore up the line between Daerun and I. I won't be able to advance until the enemy artillery is destroyed, but Daerun will be in a forward position in the forest. You'll fill the gap. Be the glue that holds the battle line together."

Diessa raised her finger when Din had started speaking, but at the news, she paused, nonplussed. It was obvious that she'd been expecting Din to hide her away in a safe place in the rear. With no reason to argue, she dropped her hand and relaxed her shoulders. Gwel even let his little shoulders sag as well.

"Thank you, Din," she said, gravely. "Bruon, your warriors will be with me. You'll guard me while I'm communing."

"With pleasure, priestess." Bruon smiled and clenched his fist in anticipation.

"I should say, I'm not sure how communing will work now," said Diessa with a slight frown. "I spent days united with the earth spirits, and it took time to fully recover my sense of self. I still haven't been able to sever the connection, though it's been to our benefit. Normally, I'm only half aware of the world around me when I'm communing. With a connection so strong I may not be aware of anything at all. Bruon, I'm trusting you to keep me safe."

"As am I," said Din.

"Me too," said Daerun and Veit almost simultaneously. Diessa stifled a laugh while the rest of the dwarfs grinned.

"I trust you, Deese," said Dinnidek. "I can't protect you from what's to come. I can't protect any of us, really. But I do trust each of you to do your parts. Hopefully, the plan will work."

Anfynn placed his hand on Din's shoulder and addressed the group. "What we do tomorrow will echo through the ages, friends. Our ancestors are watching, and our descendants will tell stories of our accomplishments. I'm honored to be here with you."

Dinnidek gazed at each of the dwarfs, saw their steely resolve, their absolute confidence. It was madness. They were about to try to do the impossible. In the past decade, no dwarfen clan had been able to come back to Halpi. And yet here they were, a small light in a sea of corruption. Just like the stars in the night sky, each one of them was a bright pinpoint in a blanket of darkness. He was reminded again of his countless ancestors. All of them at one time were just like him. They each had choices to make, and in the moment of truth, they chose to keep the flame of the clan alive.

Yes. We're not so different, really. The idea made him swell with pride. Anfynn was right. One day his great grandchildren would wander the halls of a restored Llyngyr Cadw. They would see murals of Dinnidek, Daerun, and Diessa, and hear the tale of how the three Daamuz siblings took back their home.

CHAPTER 20

Daerun crept quietly through the trees, his senses on high alert. He led his Shieldbreakers forward into the woods under the cover of darkness. The moon was hidden behind the mountains, leaving the dwarfs only the starlight that filtered through the forest canopy to guide them as the first hints of false dawn tinged the eastern sky. The trees were mostly white birch, with little underbrush. Daerun's dwarfen vision, evolved to navigate underground, made the pale tree trunks stand out in bright contrast to the darkness. The woods were too dense to allow troops to move in formation, but not so dense that single dwarfs couldn't move freely between the trees. It was perfect for Daerun's soldiers. There'd be no way to make an effective shield wall, so they'd foregone their shields in favor of great two-handed axes and hammers.

The silence was the oddest part. Like their rangers, Dare's warriors had tied down all of their gear and muffled their armor, so all the usual sounds of clanking armor and swooshing bags were absent. Not even his clothes made noise. The silence, juxtaposed with the hundreds of warriors creeping stealthily forward, made Daerun feel uneasy. He almost started humming to fill the void, but he exhaled deeply from his nose as he fought the urge. He absently rubbed at his eyes, which were strained from trying to see any hint of the enemy. Like most of the soldiers, he had been too anxious to really sleep, but he'd stolen a few fitful hours just the same. Looking at the dwarfs around him, he was at least thankful that he was in good company.

Dare scanned the ground for loose sticks or branches that could make noise while he slowly picked his way forward. He reached the closest tree and knelt behind the trunk before reaching out with his senses for any sign of enemy troops. Hearing nothing, he raised his hand and motioned for Felwyr to come forward. Fel emerged from a nearby birch and crouched past Dare, eyes on the ground while Daerun scanned the woods ahead for danger. Fel moved silently and passed Daerun like a ghost. Once he reached the next birch, Fel took his turn watching before motioning Dare forward.

The dwarfs in the vanguard carefully leap-frogged each other as they advanced through the forest, tree by tree. The remaining soldiers would come behind them and consolidate their gains. Daerun was extremely pleased with how the operation was going so far. He'd expected the entire valley to be crawling with enemy patrols, but the few sentries they'd seen had been handled easily. What else could you expect from ratmen? At this rate, they would take the whole forest before any of them knew what happened. He knew that wasn't likely, but the longer they could go before being discovered, the more units Din would have in position.

He imagined the Overmaster's face when the sun came up and he saw the valley crawling with Free Dwarfs. *I hope he messes himself,* he thought with a smile. Dare knew he was being silly. The Abyssal Dwarf commander had to be aware that the Free Dwarfs were nearby. He just wouldn't know how close until they were knocking on his tent flap.

Felwyr raised his hand to call Daerun forward but suddenly motioned for him to stay put. Fel kept his palm out behind him and slowly moved his head around to get a better view. Daerun tensed up, ready to rush forward at the slightest sign of trouble. It felt like a few hours went by before Fel relaxed and signaled all clear. Daerun came out from cover and sidled up. He was just coming even with Felwyr when he heard a faint yell, like someone screaming far off to the east. He froze at the sound, standing out in the open, while Felwyr let out a hiss. The scream, if that's what it was, faded away, leaving only silence and a sense of dread in its wake. Daerun's heart thundered in his ears while he stood stock still. All around him, the warriors halted their advance, praying that they hadn't been discovered. Moments went by, and nothing.

Just as he was about to relax, Dare caught a glint of something up ahead, between the tree trunks. He turned his head slightly, to try and catch it again out of the corner of his eye. It was an old trick his father had taught him. Sometimes your eyes could see hidden things better when you didn't look straight at them. There it was again. A humanoid creature was moving toward them, spear at the ready. Daerun slowly sidestepped behind the nearest tree while keeping his eyes on the creature. More creatures emerged from the woods up ahead. He could just make out the long snout and twisted legs of the ratmen, their heads turning this way and that as they searched. It seemed as if they were just as spooked as the dwarfs were at the sound.

Dare glanced at Felwyr and pointed toward the enemy. Fel gestured that he could see more than ten of them. Dare considered for a moment. It would only be seconds before they were discovered. They couldn't hide, and they couldn't retreat. The stein was poured – the only thing left to do was drink.

Daerun caught Felwyr's attention and pointed to the next dwarf down the line.

"Get the boys and follow me," he whispered as he raised his hammer and stepped out from behind the tree.

He took in a deep breath and ran toward the ratmen in a crouch, hoping that the rest of his warriors would be close behind. Daerun darted from tree to tree to hide his approach. The closest vermin heard him coming, and it peered intently into the trees. As Dare closed the final distance, the ratkin called a warning to its mates and brought its spear up to defend itself.

The other creatures were startled and slow to react. They were still fumbling with their weapons as Daerun ran the last few feet.

Felwyr raised a great battle cry, and the call of 'Daamuz' erupted from the hidden dwarfs. The closest ratkin flinched at the sudden cacophony and inadvertently looked away from Daerun toward this new menace.

A fatal mistake.

Dare brought his hammer down through the ratkin's spear to land squarely on its chest. Its sternum collapsed, and the ratkin fell in a lifeless heap.

Daerun looked up from the dead body to see he was surrounded by over a dozen enemies. Luckily for him, the remaining vermin were frozen in place, still processing what was happening. Daerun used the split second of time to rush forward, smashing his right shoulder into the closest foe, pushing it back into its fellows. He swung his hammer underhand to hit the vermin opposite in the legs, crunching its kneecap and bending the leg wonkily out to the side. The ratman fell with a high-pitched scream, slapping at the ground in agony.

The other ratkin recovered their senses and came at Daerun with their spears. He threw his back to the closest tree and raised his hammer with a defiant cry. A spear point was thrust at his face, and he dodged his head to the right. The tip buried itself into the papery birch bark and showered the left side of his face with wooden slivers. A second spear came at his right shoulder, and he deflected it with the head of his hammer. The first ratkin was trying to pull its spear from the tree, but the point was stuck. The shaft stopped Dare from dodging back in that direction. A third spear came at his right thigh, and he was forced to drop down onto one knee to catch it on his breastplate instead of his leg. The spear couldn't penetrate the dwarfen plate, but Dare grunted in pain from the impact. The spear tip skidded off his breastplate, and the ratkin stumbled forward with his inertia. Daerun sprang up and headbutted the ratkin in the snout with his helmet. The vermin's face exploded with blood as its head snapped back.

The first ratman had extricated its spear and was pulling back for a killing thrust at Daerun. The dwarf raised his hammer to defend himself and braced for another strike. The rat doubled over before it could attack as Fel took the creature in the side with his axe. Dwarfs ran past Daerun into the press of vermin and pushed them back. Dare took a deep breath in relief before rejoining in the attack. Within seconds, the dwarfs owned this part of the field, but the damage had been done. The sounds of battle echoed loudly through the trees, spoiling any hope they'd had of surprise.

"Well, there goes that," Dare said with a wild grin. "Let's do some honest work."

"Each of us will have to do the work of three dwarfs," said Fel jokingly.

"Good thing I'm used to that with you then," yelled Dare as he ran forward to press the attack.

* * * * *

"My Lord Anfynn, we've encountered some enemy troops on the ridge," said the scout gravely.

Anfynn spat on the ground, as if to clear his mouth of the bitter news. The army hadn't met many patrols as he led his clan forces into position on the left. Most of them had been halfbreeds or orcs mounted on gores, and they'd kept their distance. He was sure that the enemy commander knew the army was advancing, but hopefully he wouldn't know how the dwarfs were arrayed until the sun came up. He was hoping to advance some of his troops on the high ground before then. If the enemy forces were already there in a defensible position, there would be a butcher's bill to pay in taking the ridge. He stroked his beard in agitation.

"How many? And how dug in are they?"

"Tough to tell, my lord, but we think there are maybe a hundred orcs up there. They've erected a line of sharpened stakes pointed down the hill."

Anfynn cursed. He didn't want to cede the ground to just a hundred orcs. But a hundred orcs dug in behind a makeshift palisade would take more than a scouting force to overcome. If only Kilvar were here. His rangers would push the orcs back easily. But they were miles to the south, protecting the army's rear.

Anfynn looked to the east, where the horizon glowed with the promise of sunrise. He weighed his options. He didn't have a lot of time before the sun came up and the enemy commander could react. The first thing the Overmaster would do is reinforce the high ground. Anfynn couldn't deviate from the battle plan, but his troops would take a lot of casualties if he waited to assault the ridge. As he was gazing to the east, the morning silence was broken as the sounds of battle came faintly from the forest. Master Daerun had run into resistance of his own.

Anfynn considered the situation. Could he afford to send troops up the ridge, or would that leave him with too few dwarfs when the fighting started? He shook his head in annoyance at the thought. There was no way the Overmaster would come down off the mountainside if he didn't have to. The position was too strong. No, the dwarfs would have to fight their way up the ridge if they were going to win.

Anfynn decided and addressed one of his most seasoned thanes. "Gundrim, gather your Ironclad and some of the Watch, and engage the orcs up there. I want to know how stiff their resolve is. If you can sweep them back, all the better. Take the position and defend it as best you can until the main force comes up behind. If they're too dug in, make an orderly retreat back to the main line."

The old thane bowed and ran off. He had more than enough warriors of his own.

* * * * *

"I'll see you when this is done," said Diessa as she released Veit from her embrace.

"I hope so," whispered Veit with a reassuring smile, "in more ways than one." He brushed his hand across her blindfold and stroked her hair affectionately.

Diessa chuckled and patted the engineer affectionately on the forearm. They were standing amid the main artillery battery in the center of the line. Veit had worked to get each gun into place and had taken a break to wish Diessa farewell. He spared a glance for the Ironclad who were bustling by as they assembled into their regiments, some still holding shovels from the night's work. If the situation wasn't so serious it would have been comical; these stoic dwarfs sneakily lining up for battle armed with picks and spades.

Diessa leaned in and gave Veit a kiss on the cheek before turning to go. She didn't trust herself to say anything more without her voice betraying her nervousness. Veit smiled bashfully and walked to the nearest cannon, giving recommendations to the crew. She gave one last deep breath and then made her way to Bruon and her honor guard.

Gwel, ever present, toddled along next to her. With her elemental sight, Diessa could see as if it were broad daylight, even though the sun was still an hour from rising. She still didn't know when it would fade. Her own sight was getting better by the hour, so she'd steadfastly kept her blindfold on all evening to capitalize while it lasted.

The Stone Guard was waiting for her near the southern edge of the woods, adorned with blue ribbons on their upper arms. Stone Guard. What a bunch of mushrooms. She was still uncomfortable with the idea of a personal retinue. It smacked of ego and self-importance. But if her hunch about communing was correct, she'd need all the assembled warriors to look out for her during the coming battle. She'd be looking out for them in return.

Bruon raised his hand in greeting as she approached. At his order, the dwarfs all stood to attention and saluted, weapons held out before them. Diessa waved at them in mild annoyance.

"Stop that," she said with a smile as she pointed at Bruon. "At ease. Is that the term? Whatever, just cut it out."

"Yes, priestess," said Bruon as the dwarfs lowered their weapons.

Diessa wondered if Bruon got anything from these outward displays of reverence. She had made her displeasure known, on multiple occasions, but he persisted. *He says it's his way of honoring me, but who knows?* It was tough to tell. Diessa realized she hadn't taken much time to get to know Bruon personally. Her distaste for being fawned over made her inadvertently avoid him on principle. Like it or not, these dwarfs had pledged their lives to keep her safe, and now they were being called on to deliver.

I've not been fair to them, she thought with chagrin. It was something she'd need to remedy once this was over.

She bowed deeply to Bruon, then walked amid the soldiers, Gwel by her feet. When she reached the center, she raised her hands to call their attention.

"Clansmen, harken to me." She spoke quietly, and the dwarfs all leaned in close to hear. "You know I've been uneasy with this honor guard business from the start. I'd rather stand on my own two feet than stand on ceremony." Some of the dwarfs chuckled. "But today the clan needs you... I need you... to help me. We've been tasked with an important mission. As we speak, our brothers are pushing into these woods to assault the Abyssal artillery. Behind me, our Ironclad will form a shield wall to protect our guns and hold the enemy at bay. We will serve as the hinge between the main battle line and Lord Daerun's forces in the woods. If we fall, the entire army falls with us."

The warriors were still, listening to Diessa with rapt attention.

"But we will not be alone. The very earth itself cries out in pain at the Abyssal Dwarfs. Our traitorous cousins have defiled our home, and the earth spirits are desperate to help us in our fight. Because our fight is their fight. We are tied to this land, and the land lives in us." The Ironclad murmured in appreciation. Diessa raised her hands for silence. "I will channel our connection with the earth, summon the elementals, and they will march with us to war. But as I do, as I commune with our homeland, I will need you to watch over me. Protect me, the way the land protects all of us. Can you do this for me?"

The warriors whispered 'yes.'

"For yourselves?"

The warriors responded more strongly this time.

"For the clan?"

The warriors said 'yes' as one, careful to stay quiet, but with clenched fists, weapons raised high.

Diessa paused a moment to let the warriors express their confidence, but before she could continue, she was distracted by the sounds of battle coming from the woods. Dare had punched a bees nest, and the battle was underway.

She turned to Bruon and came close so only a few dwarfs could hear. "As you know, my ordeal on the ship changed my connection with the earth spirits, making it stronger. I will probably be only partially aware of my surroundings as I commune, so I'll need you to be my eyes and ears as well as my shield. I'll need you to guide me as I walk across the battlefield." Bruon nodded grimly. "Good. I'm going to begin the summoning now. Keep an eye on me, but you shouldn't see too much of a difference yet."

She reached out and hugged Bruon close, and he awkwardly returned the embrace.

She sat on the ground and laid out her summoning circle. Her hands moved of their own accord. The elaborate motions of the ritual calmed her mind and soothed her nervousness. She really had no idea what would happen this time. She'd spent the last ten-day regaining her sense of individuality. Would she lose it again? Gwel patted her on the back as she worked, similar to how she'd rubbed Veit's back for comfort. It reassured her. Once the circle was complete, she smiled up at Bruon.

"Alright, here goes. The Earth Mother watch over you."

"She already is, priestess," said Bruon with a pointed smile.

Diessa snorted. *He's relentless,* she thought fondly. She closed her eyes and took a deep, cleansing breath, then another, then a third. Her breathing became slow, steady, and she felt her spirit begin to open to the earth.

* * * * *

Diessa felt the earth spirits gently tugging at her psyche. They gathered close as she called them to her. She summoned the spirits of Halpi, and they responded. Three spirits, seven, a dozen. Their presence was an increasing pressure on her mind. She felt their excitement, their urge to act, to defend. A score, two dozen, and more, swarming to her like moths to a flame. She was having trouble feeling the elementals as separate entities. There were just so many. She was used to cooperating with the spirits to give them corporeal forms, but these were so forceful, so impatient. She'd never felt such urgency from the earth spirits before. The pressure was increasing. So many...

She was losing her identity as her mind was pulled under.

Let us in! they pressed. *We will cleanse the land!*

"I will help," she implored, "but you have to give me space."

Open the gates! Breach the barriers for us!

So insistent. So potent.

She beseeched them, "I have to guide you! Let me guide you!"

She was losing her identity as the spirits pulled her under.

She was one.

They were one.

They were the mountains. They were the sand. They were the rich loam, the silt, the tunnels, the very ground of Halpi. They were sick. Corruption frayed them, threatened to make them forget. They pressed at the earth, flowed through the ground, the rocks, and boulders, but they couldn't find purchase. There was nothing to anchor to. They were impatient. Spirits that measured time in eons, impatient. They needed the dwarfs to give them form.

They remembered.

She remembered. She was a dwarf, working with the elementals. An elemental. A friend.

Joro.

She felt Joro among the crowd. Weaker than before but still present.

A vision of Diessa directing the elementals as they built the longhouse. She was their conduit, gave them purpose and direction. She was necessary.

Bruon's words came back to her. *No one else can do what you do. You are the clan's link to the earth.*

In that moment, she realized that she was the earth's link to the clan as well. She was surprised it had never occurred to her that the link went both ways. She was starting to finally understand how important she was.

Joro thought of her as separate, as Diessa. He pushed those thoughts into the collective.

It gave her the mental space she needed. She asserted herself over the spirits. Rose above them.

"I am separate," she stated. "I am not one of you."

She felt her power grow as she declared her individuality.

"You need me." The spirits pressed again, but she pushed back with her will. "Enough!"

She'd never had to do this with the elementals before. Their aggression wasn't directed toward her, but she had to redirect their energy if she was going to harness their power.

Harness their power... Who was she to use the spirits this way?

I am Diessa, daughter of Brohna, and I am the stone priestess of Clan Daamuz. That's who I am.

She thought of her mother, bringing the cliff down around her to protect her people. And now she was going to protect the earth spirits of Halpi.

She addressed the collective. "You are sick. You are dying. Work with me, and we can heal." She showed them the land as she remembered it, green, alive, pristine. "I will work with you, but I cannot be one of you."

She felt their confusion, and they pressed again. She felt their yearning to merge with her, to gain the providence to act.

She rebuffed them. "I am not one of you. None of you can do what I do."

Joro agreed. He related every memory of them working together. Countless hours of building, creating, even fighting. The last thing she saw was Joro pushing the boat to shore before he dissolved in the surf.

"Enough!" She stated it as a fact, with no qualms, no apprehension. The force of her will flared through the collective.

"You will listen to me. It is not a request. It is a command."

The spirits responded. She felt they were... diminished... for only a second. Then she felt a wave of trust and determination wash through her.

"I will guide you. We will work together, and you will be healed."

* * * * *

Bruon watched Diessa fall limply to the ground with concern. The other dwarfs crowded around, but he pushed them back to give her room and then knelt at her side to assess her condition. He pushed her blindfold off and checked her eyes. Her pulse was strong, and he could feel her breathing; but her eyes were closed, and it looked like she'd reentered her coma.

"She's alright," he reassured the honor guard. "She's out again."

The din of battle could be heard from the woods. Bruon knew he couldn't just stay here, but he didn't have many options. Without the elementals, they couldn't form the hinge in the line. The honor guard weren't enough to do it themselves. He contemplated sending a runner to Lord Dinnidek for help. He began ordering the dwarfs to make another litter while he fussed over Diessa's limp form.

Suddenly, Diessa's eyes shot open, and she stared straight into the sky. Her muscles spasmed, and she went completely rigid. Bruon laid her body out on the ground as panic flared in his chest. The assembled warriors all looked at each other in confusion. What was happening?

The earth trembled, then shook, and the honor guard stared in trepidation at the ground. Bruon cradled Diessa's head in his lap and stared at her, trying to divine if this was part of her plan or if something had gone horribly awry. Elementals emerged slowly from the ground all around them. The dwarfs moved out of the way as the spirits erupted, higher and higher. Dozens of elementals materialized, facing in all different directions. Bruon had never seen anything like this from a single stone priest, never felt such raw power in the earth. Each elemental was uniquely shaped with various types of stone throughout their bodies. Here and there, clods of dirt and grass clung to the stones or fell to the ground below. Bruon saw worms and other crawlies writhing around on the elemental's bodies after being disturbed from their underground homes.

Finally, the earth stopped trembling as the elementals stood like silent sentinels over the dwarfs. The Ironclad were overawed at the spectacle around them, loath to sully this hallowed moment. Bruon looked back down at Diessa, and a smile graced her face. The stone priestess stirred and slowly sat up, still with her thousand-yard stare. Bruon helped her to her feet, but she continued to gaze out into nothingness.

"Priestess, are you alright?"

No answer. Instead, Gwel walked in front of Bruon and bowed deeply. As Bruon watched, the tiny elemental turned and walked northward toward the woods. When the dwarfs didn't move, Gwel turned back to Bruon and motioned to the dwarfs to follow him.

Bruon laughed in relief and addressed his warriors. "You heard her, let's get going!"

* * * * *

Will to rule.

The words sounded in Zareen's mind, half promise, half question. He thought he could hear them echo off the walls of his command tent, but when he opened his eyes, he was alone. The tent was sparsely furnished, with a bed and writing desk, a small table set with alchemical supplies, and a larger folding table haphazardly heaped with maps and scrolls. He had stayed up late reviewing the dispositions of his troops and laying out the final strategy with Alborz. So many hours of preparation. Alborz had driven Zareen hard the last few days, constantly challenging him, questioning his ideas, second guessing his decisions, testing him for his ascent. It had been mentally exhausting, but it was worth it. The last few months had led up to this day. Today they would crush the mongrel dwarfs and grind them into the dust of their former homeland. Zareen would cement his right to rule, and he would be declared the new overlord of Llyngyr Cadw. A momentous day, indeed.

Zareen stood up from the edge of his bed and tightened the last few straps on his blackened steel breastplate. He heard the army stirring in the darkness outside, preparing for the battle to come. Sunrise was still minutes away, and the tent was illuminated by a single red brazier, which gave the tent the feeling of being underground, similar to his bath chamber. Powerful incense wafted from the front of the brazier, calming Zareen's mind and allowing him to concentrate. He clasped his crimson cloak around his shoulders, pulled on his spiked gauntlets, and carefully placed the ornate great helm on his head. His hands shook a little as he tightened the strap under his chin. He took a deep breath and exhaled forcefully, pushing out his nervous energy.

Not surprisingly, today Zareen was more anxious than normal, with a million threads racing through his mind. Last evening, Alborz had predicted how the enemy would deploy, and he'd walked Zareen step by step through his thinking, cool and collected all the while. Alborz thought through every contingency, chasing every possibility down its rabbit hole, but he never second guessed himself. Zareen couldn't understand how Alborz was so calm. Maybe it was the years of experience. Alborz had never tasted defeat on the battlefield, and success bred confidence, which led to more success. That confidence, that arrogance, was one of the many things that stirred Zareen's admiration for his brother.

Zareen had always followed Alborz, and Alborz had rewarded that loyalty by protecting his brother and pushing him to greater and greater achievements. The day that Zareen followed his brother into exile to the Abyss was the day he began to truly see his full potential. Alborz had shown him a world unconstrained by morality or the unwanted obligations of the clan. Together, they had risen through Abyssal Dwarf society to levels of greatness he had never dreamed of. Alborz was conceited and self-serving, but Zareen never held that against him. He was content to walk in Alborz's shadow and reap the subsequent reward. Zareen knew that in this arena Alborz didn't fully trust him yet. And, to be fair, he shouldn't. Zareen didn't have any victories to add to his legend.

But today he was determined to prove his worth.

Zareen strode out of his tent and patted the shoulder of one of his bodyguards as he went past. The Immortal Guards respectfully saluted with their metal arms in return.

"You may go now," said Zareen. "Report to Overmaster Alborz. May Ariagful's rage fuel you."

With that, he made his way to give the artillery a final inspection, which he'd placed on a flat shelf of rock overlooking the battlefield. From the elevated position, the demonic guns would be able to outrange the mongrel's lighter cannon. He hailed the gun crews and rechecked the sights himself, keeping his nervousness at bay by engaging in such simple tasks. Satisfied, he made his way slowly down the mountain slope, breathing in the warm night air.

Zareen thought back to the previous night. Alborz had been emphatic that the dwarf artillery had to be destroyed today for their plan to work. He'd assured Zareen that the mongrels would place their artillery in their center, because it afforded the best lines of sight. In response, their plan involved a heavy push up the middle to split the Free Dwarf line in two and destroy the guns, if not the entire army. Alborz had planned on placing the grotesques in the center to act as shock troops and spearhead the wedge. Zareen had argued that it would be a waste of the abominations, but Alborz had insisted, and eventually Zareen caved, as he usually did.

Zareen's brows creased as he lamented the lack of regard his brother had for his creations. But it was to be expected. To Alborz, everything was a tool to be used. In contrast, Zareen cared very deeply for his creations, the grotesques and the ratkin as well. The gnorr were bred to be slaves, and their lives were meant to be brutish and short; but unlike other Iron-casters, Zareen tried to ease the misery of their existence where he could. It was a small thing, but he found that the gnorr obeyed more effectively when they weren't in constant fear. That's why he'd placed them under his command today. Zareen was proud of his ability to create, whether shaping gnorr society or crafting grotesques with his own hands.

Speaking of the grotesques, Zareen felt his heartbeat accelerate as he approached the place where his latest masterpiece was waiting. He passed through row upon row of ratkin soldiers, amassed along the lower ridgeline of the mountainside facing the woods to the south. Beyond them, a giant misshapen beast, with a bloated reptilian body and wings like a wyvern, catlike claws, and an avian head with a rack of wickedly pointed antlers, was chained to the ground with black iron links that gave off a sulfurous smoke. The sorcerous shackles kept the creature completely still, burdened down with the physical and magical weight of the chains. A group of slave drivers were busy strapping a riding saddle to the beast's scaly back and armor plates on its chest. A knot of Obsidian Golems, giant constructs of black stone and demonic fire, flanked the creature, forming an infernal bodyguard. Zareen didn't expect the antlered nightmare to live past the next few days, but today it would wreak havoc.

Zareen waited patiently while the slave drivers finished their work. He was replaying the details of the plan again in his mind when he was interrupted by a great commotion coming from the woods to the south. In the darkness, he couldn't see what was happening, but he heard the unmistakable screams and panicked screeches of the gnorr. The dwarfs were pushing their way forward through the woods, just as Alborz had predicted. It would only be a matter of time before the ratkin were pushed back from the forest. Zareen resisted the temptation to order his gnorr forces forward to contest this push, and instead, he sent runners to order the retreat. Alborz had said this would happen, and they had planned for it. He'd let them take the woods, then push forward with everything when it was time.

He just had to be patient.

He said a brief prayer to Ariagful and mounted the demonic beast. Today, they would destroy these invaders and he would lay claim to the dominion of Llyngyr Cadw. Today, everything would change.

* * * * *

Kilvar knew the gore riders were out there, he just wished he could see them, but the darkness cut both ways. The same darkness that hid the orcs kept his own rangers from being found as well. With the coming of dawn, that darkness was going to end. It was only a matter of time before the dwarfs were discovered, hunted down, and killed.

His rangers had found the flanking force yesterday morning, composed mostly of the orcs and a few Abyssal Dwarf slave drivers mounted on wickedly scythed chariots, pulled by feral gores. Getting close hadn't been a problem. The rangers traveled stealthily and there were plenty of places to hide, even in the open ground south of the mountains. The orcs rarely sent out patrols, and the ones they did send were uninterested and undisciplined. Kilvar's disrespect for the orcs was only deepened by their incompetence. The enemy troops displayed no sense of urgency as they slowly moved eastward, so the rangers easily shadowed them from a distance for most of the day. However, when the orcs picked up the pace yesterday evening, Kilvar knew it was time to strike. His rangers ambushed the orcs just after nightfall, killing as many of the twisted boar-like gores as they could in the process. That part had gone well. It had been a living nightmare since.

The dwarfs were outnumbered at least four to one, and there were too many orcs to fight in a pitched battle. Instead, Kilvar had planned to perform a series of ambushes, harassing the enemy, and slowing their advance. But even though the orcs were undisciplined, they were tenacious when their blood was up. They had been relentless in hunting the rangers down, and it had been impossible for Kilvar to regroup his entire force for another coordinated assault. The night had devolved into a constant running retreat.

He had lost touch with most of his troops, and his direct command was reduced to a handful of rangers. Boon ran like a shadow at his side. Every now and then the great hound would stop and growl at some unseen danger, and Kilvar had the sense to lead his warriors in the opposite direction. In his constant flight, he'd lost all sense of direction; his only concern was escaping the night with his life.

They ran like a pack of wolves, Kilvar in the lead, with the rest of the rangers silently following behind. Up ahead, he saw some shapes lying in the grass and hoped it was another fist, hiding out. If he could combine their forces, he might improve their odds. He froze as he passed the shapes. Four dwarfs lay dead on the ground, their bodies twisted and brutalized. He stopped to inspect one of the corpses. A young ranger, one of Rhyss' troops, stared lifelessly at the sky, a brutal cut to his neck making his head loll at an odd angle. His axe lay nearby, a necklace with a stylized key held loosely in his off hand. Kilvar gently closed the ranger's eyes and said a quick prayer to the

Earth Mother. He rose and shook his head 'no' to the other rangers before dashing off again.

An orc horn blared from somewhere behind him, and he veered toward a slight rise in the ground, his rangers following close behind. The ground only rose a foot or two before sloping back down, but hopefully it would be enough cover to hide them as they fled. He crouched low as he neared the top of the rise to hide his silhouette. Another horn called off to his left, and he dashed over the rise and sped down the reverse slope. An answering horn sounded to his right, and he sprinted the last few feet and dove for cover. He dropped into a small hollow in the ground, with some tall grass to conceal him. Boon crouched down beside him, teeth bared but silent. He spared a quick glance for his companions, and he couldn't see any of them in the darkness. He was thankful they'd found a spot to disappear. He breathed deep and slow to get his heartbeat under control as he stared out between the dry stalks of grass for any sign of the enemy.

At the edge of his vision, a squad of orc heads emerged above the rise. The movement of the gores underneath made the orcs' heads sway back and forth like deranged will-o-the-wisps. They were riding toward him in a wide formation, trying to flush the dwarfs out. He cursed silently and grabbed Boon's collar. He could see over two dozen gore riders, and he could hear many more orcs further away. His fist of rangers wouldn't stand a chance. He kept a tight grip on Boon's collar, and the mastiff knew the signal to stay still and silent. Kilvar's mind raced. Maybe try to stay put and hope the orcs went past? Then what? He very slowly drew his hand axe with his free hand. If this was the end, he'd be sure to take a few more of the slaves with him. At least he'd accomplished some good for the clan in his last moments.

The orcs crested the rise, mounted on their boar-like gores. From his vantage point near the ground, they seemed exaggeratedly giant against the clear starry sky. The closest orc was only yards away. The light of false dawn combined with the star light to reflect off its helmet and highlighted the orc's yellowed tusks in its dark face. Kilvar could see the orc scanning the ground, the gore snuffling with its wide, bristly snout for the dwarfs' scent. Kilvar's keen ears heard one of the hidden dwarfs behind him cock back his crossbow. He prayed that the sound hadn't carried to the orc.

The orc peered to the origin of the sound while step by step the gore slowly approached. Kilvar said a silent prayer. *Dianek, great Earth Mother, I commend my spirit to your care. Guide me to the halls of my ancestors, so I may be one with the clan forever.* He gripped the axe tightly and prepared to let loose his hold on Boon's collar. He took one last blessed breath.

Today had been a good day.

Before he could move, a horn blasted from further out on the plain, followed quickly by two more. The sounds were frantic, and Kilvar could almost feel the panic in their repeated calls for help. The orcs halted their advance, some turning their gores around at the sound of this new threat. A renewed series of horn blasts pulled at the orcs to leave, and most of them turned to answer, spurring their gores to thunder away to the north. However, the closest orc ignored the horns and kept staring past Kilvar to where it had heard the crossbow. The beast's bloodlust was too great for it to give up the chase, and it stubbornly prodded the gore to keep going, even though most of the other orcs had left.

Kilvar cursed and laid perfectly still. It wouldn't do to raise a ruckus while the other orcs were still so close. Through the grass, he saw the gore walk by him as Boon stood like a statue, waiting for the order to attack, his muscles quivering with pent up aggression. Another horn sounded from a different direction, but it carried the same panicked air. Still the orc ignored the summons, slave to a single-minded purpose. It had heard something, and it would kill whatever it was. It sniffed the air like an animal as it passed Kilvar's position. From his place near the ground, Kilvar could see the gore's powerful squat legs and bulbous belly, could make out the bristles of its rough fur, could smell the stink of both the orc and beast. Out in the darkness, Kilvar heard the cries of orcs desperately fighting, punctuated by the incessant shouts from the slave drivers and the blaring horns. He thought he heard dwarfen voices, too. Was that some of his fellow dwarfs making a last stand? The thought of his comrades dying made him see red, but he held still.

Kilvar slowly craned his neck to inspect the rise, barely breathing for fear of the sound. The rest of the orcs had left, only this one remained. He would have to make sure the orc was completely alone. He had to kill it and his mount quick, before it could sound the alarm.

The gore took a few more steps past Kilvar, to where the orc couldn't see him out of its peripheral vision.

A couple more steps. Come on, you ugly bastard.

Once Kilvar could see the orc's back, he released Boon's collar and the mastiff shot off toward the enemy. He stood up and threw his hand axe in one motion. The axe struck the orc in the back just as Boon clamped onto the gore's hind leg with its vice-like jaws. The gore let out a terrified squeal as another ranger rose from behind a small bush and shot his crossbow. Kilvar saw the orc's head snap back and its helmet fell to the ground with a clang, the foe's limp body close behind. The other ranger rushed forward and buried his hand axe in the gore's skull, and it too fell still and lifeless.

Kilvar whipped his head around and crouched back down into the grass. *Too loud,* he thought. *Damn sloppy.*

Kilvar called Boon back to him and stayed perfectly still. Dread pooled in the pit of his stomach at the thought of the orcs coming back to investigate. He could hear intense fighting to the north, carrying far over the flatlands.

Too much ruckus for just us. Who else is out there? he wondered. As he listened, the sounds receded further and further away, though they didn't lose their intensity.

After what felt like an eternity, he dared to hope. He slowly stood and emerged from cover to show himself to the other rangers. A few of them popped their heads up from the grass in return, and he motioned them forward. He slunk through the gloom and laid down on his stomach at the top of the rise. He couldn't see anything. The combatants were too far away. The yells of the soldiers combined with bestial growls punctuated by the metallic clangs of weapons and armor. It was eerie, hearing the cacophony of battle without being able to see it unfold.

Boon's ears perked up, and Kilvar laid his hand gently on the mastiff's collar. Kilvar couldn't see anything out there, but he trusted Boon's canine senses. He hissed to the closest dwarf and signaled toward the plain with his head. The ranger nodded and readied his crossbow, the rest of the rangers following suit. Kilvar heard a low growl from something nearby on the plain. The creature was at the edge of his vision, and it was approaching rapidly. What started as a faint shadow revealed itself to be a dwarf riding a brock, a giant badger bred for war by some of the Free Dwarf clans.

The dwarf spoke with a gravelly voice, in an almost conversational tone.

"Hail, fellow dwarfs," he said as he raised his arm and sauntered forward. The morning sun was just beginning to crest the eastern horizon, and it brought the dwarf into full view.

Kilvar was taken aback at this unexpected ally. Brocks were favored by dwarfen berserkers, unfortunate souls who had cut their traditional ties to their clans due to personal trauma. Kilvar was intrigued. What were berserkers doing out here?

"Hail and well met!" Kilvar replied. "I am Kilvar, of Clan Helgwin. My rangers and I were out hunting orcs."

"Were you?" the berserker said with some bemusement. Kilvar noted that he didn't reveal his name, as was customary. "Then, my master, the Worm Lord, sends his sincere apology for robbing you of your sport. We meant no offense, but it seemed like the orcs may have been hunting you."

The words could have been mocking, but the messenger sounded completely sincere as he spoke.

"No apology necessary," Kilvar replied graciously. He felt as if he was being forced into acting a part in a strange play. "We thank you for your help. Where are the orcs now?"

"I'm afraid that the orcs have been driven off, but not scattered as we had hoped. We pushed them westward, away from your men."

"That's good news," said Kilvar. "We're in your debt. We owe more than a few pints to the Worm Lord for his assistance."

"Yes, indeed," said the messenger affably. The strange dwarf refused to elaborate, and an awkward silence settled onto the conversation.

Finally, Kilvar spoke. "Have you seen any other rangers in your evening's travels?"

"I have not, but the Worm Lord has tasked some of us with gathering up your wounded and putting them somewhere safe. You need to head back to your fellows in the shadow of the mountain. We will harry the orcs and keep them away while your clans fight for survival."

Kilvar frowned in confusion. This Worm Lord seemed to know an awful lot about what was going on.

The messenger turned to go, but before he left, he stopped and asked over his shoulder, "Are any of you from Clan Daamuz?"

Kilvar's confusion deepened. How could the Worm Lord know? "None of us here, though some of the rangers I led were from that clan."

The berserker simply nodded in acknowledgment and rode off to the north, the brock moving surprisingly fast for being so low to the ground. Kilvar watched the strange berserker grow smaller and smaller as he rode across the plains, until he melted away like a ghost.

Kilvar turned to the closest ranger and just shrugged, perplexed at what had transpired, while Boon happily wagged his tail.

* * * * *

Alborz gazed out upon the valley below and smiled in satisfaction. From his vantage point partially up the mountainside, he could see the enemy army arrayed below him. Everything had happened just as he'd ordained. The mongrel dwarfs had chosen to engage him here, with his army in a defensible position, and a flanking force ready to trap them in the rear. It had all been too easy.

As usual, Alborz reveled in these moments before battle started. The early morning sun was just peeking from around the line of mountains to the east, and the Abyssal Dwarf army was bathed in light, even as the dwarfs below were still steeped in relative shadow. The Abyssal Dwarf hordes gleamed golden and bronze in the dawn, and even the masses of orcs and ratmen made a formidable sight. The day was already warm despite the early hour, with only a few wisps of cloud in the sky, promising a hot day ahead. Alborz was arrayed in his blackened steel battle armor, with a white linen cape to keep the sun off the metal. He was attended by a pair of Immortal Guard and a small contingent of musicians and gargoyles to serve as messengers that would relay his commands to the army.

Alborz had chosen the battlefield with care and picked a place where the enemy would have limited options for deployment. His army was amassed on the lower slopes of the mountain, and the ground smoothly sloped down to the flatland below. The land was mostly clear, with the sole exception being a large stand of birch trees to his left. Predictably, the mongrels had advanced forward in the early morning to take the woods. Zareen had deployed some gnorr there the night before to contest the woods, but the ratmen had only offered token resistance before being forced back to the main battle line. He wasn't surprised. What else could you expect from slaves? In response, Alborz had massed all his gnorr on his left, with the intention to assault the woods and pin the enemy in place by weight of numbers. They would be backed by a solid line of Abyssal Dwarf warriors, the Blacksouls, who would provide the backbone to the line.

Zareen would personally lead the assault on the woods, which would hopefully keep his brother occupied. Zareen wasn't ready to take command of the entire battle, but Alborz felt confident placing him in charge of the left wing of the army. It would give him much needed experience, and the fighting on that flank would be relatively easy. Now that the mongrels had advanced into his trap, there wouldn't be too many decisions to make. The real artistry would be done on other parts of the battlefield. Alborz planned to force a gap in the dwarfen line, and then exploit that gap to drive a wedge into the dwarfs and shatter them. When he'd discussed it with Zareen, his brother had understood the plan in principle, though Alborz kept some of the specifics to himself. He didn't want Zareen to get fixated on the details. He knew how his brother could get, and he wanted him to keep a wider view of the battle.

The Daamuz clan formed a classic shield wall in the center, blue and white sigils on their shields and upon the clan battle standard. Even from this distance, Alborz could hear the mongrel chieftain addressing his troops, haranguing them into a frenzy. He couldn't hear distinct words, but the speech must have been impressive. In response, the Daamuz warriors shouted their defiance at the Abyssal Dwarfs. All that determination would do them no good. The battle was already decided. They just didn't know it yet. Alborz squinted and saw the dwarfen cannons among the Ironclad. That was nominally Alborz's main target.

Once the cannons are destroyed, the mongrels will break themselves upon the walls of their ancestral home and then retreat back to Crafanc to starve. If I get to kill the mongrel commander, so much the better.

The warriors from Crafanc were to his right. He could see the red banners of Clan Helgwin hanging limply in the stifling morning air. Alborz took note that the Helgwin forces had all deployed together, as opposed to being interspersed among the warriors of Clan Daamuz. Alborz's smile widened.

That separation in command would make it harder for the clans to coordinate their movements. *If I'm going to force a gap, it will be there, between the two clans.*

On his right, the ground was rocky and broken as it descended onto the plain, and it would provide cover to his troops as they advanced. He'd placed his hordes of orc warriors on that flank, ready to sweep down the hill and into Clan Helgwin, but had baited the trap with a token number of orcs on those heights, enticing the dwarfen commander to stretch his forces to push up onto the hill. He smiled as he realized that the Helgwin Warmaster had obliged. What good fortune. This was going to be easier than he'd hoped.

As he made his way to take command of the Immortal Guard, he considered the enemy position and made a few alterations to his initial plan. He dispatched one of his gargoyle attendants to order more orcs to engage the Helgwin Ironclad on the heights. It wouldn't be enough troops to push them back, but it may be enough to force the dwarfs to reinforce the position, further weakening their main force on that flank.

Alborz commanded another gargoyle messenger with some urgency. "Tell the halfbreed commander to bring his force to my position but instruct him to move behind the main line of grotesques. I don't want the enemy to see the maneuver. Understand?"

Alborz made the gargoyle repeat the message to him twice before imperiously waving him away. *You can never be sure with those brainless creatures,* he thought. *I can't have the plan jeopardized because of the gargoyle's stupidity. This is too important.*

He wanted the twisted cavalry poised and ready for when the opportunity arose. The opportunity that he'd create.

* * * * *

"DaaaaMUZ!" Dinnidek raised his axe high in salute to his clansmen. After a heartbeat, he released his grip on the haft of his great axe and caught it quickly, giving it a quick sweep and a flourish. The Ironclad let out another war cry, filling the valley with their determination. Dinnidek waited for the sound to echo back to him from the mountains before raising his arms to signal for another shout. The clan warriors obliged, and Dinnidek strode to the line with a grim smile that showed his mixture of pleasure and resolve. His clansmen returned his smile with looks of steely determination of their own, each of them nodding gravely or raising their axes in salute. Today would be a bloody affair. The dwarfs were vastly outnumbered, assaulting a strong enemy in a fortified position. None of this was good.

But it's better than the rest of our options, Din thought.

Despite it all, Din felt strangely confident. He was nervous about the battle and concerned for his soldiers, but those feelings vied with a serene calm, almost a feeling of destiny. Today would see the end of this mad scheme, one way or the other.

Dinnidek had formed his soldiers into blocks, with their cannon battery in the center but placed in the rear. These units could link together to make one continuous line or could move independently to different parts of the battle where they were needed. That flexibility would be useful once the real fighting began. He'd kept some blocks behind the main line in reserve, ready to reinforce the line. Din walked among the Ironclad to his command station near the rear. On the way, he acknowledged each dwarf he passed with a look in the eye, a nod, a clap on the shoulder. These were his clansmen, and he wanted them to know he was with them.

Tordek was waiting for him at the command station. He was currently standing on one of the ammo carts between two of the reserve blocks. A cadre of messengers and a pair of musicians with great horns stood nearby. In addition, a set of colored pennants on long poles was laid in the cart. Once the battle began, the horns and pennants would be used to supplement the messengers and signal commands to the army. Tordek himself was carrying the Daamuz clan banner, a white dragon on a field of azure. Scores of silver and gold chains were draped across the top of the standard, each with a key or other personal token from a fallen dwarf.

As Din approached the cart, Tordek barked an order, and the nearby dwarfs snapped to attention. Dinnidek casually waved in response before clasping the bodyguard's outstretched hand and clambering up onto the cart. He grinned broadly at Tordek, and he pulled him in close, their clasped forearms between them.

"How did I do?" Din asked, mischievously.

"I've heard worse battle speeches," Tordek responded in his usual understated way. He had to shout a little to be heard over the cheers of the troops.

"By the Earth Mother, I hope so!" exclaimed Din. "It's not like they need a lot of encouragement. If they need me to tell them that today is important..." Din let the thought trail off as he turned from Tordek to survey the armies.

Even though it was only a few feet off the ground, the cart gave him an expansive view of the battlefield. Anfynn's troops were to his left, Ironclad toward the middle, and Ironwatch rifles out wide to protect the flank. To his right, Diessa's earth elementals marched forward, hugging the forest's edge. Din was surprised at how many elementals she'd been able to summon. He'd never seen so many under a single stone priest before. Din heard the sounds of battle from further among the white birches, but they were beginning to wane.

Looks like Dare has swept the woods clean, he thought.

A runner approached from the left, wearing the burgundy of Clan Helgwin. He stopped beside the cart and waited for Din to acknowledge him before he gave his report.

"Lord Dinnidek, my Lord Anfynn sends his regards. He's instructed me to deliver two messages. First, he is looking forward to drinking with you this evening once we've trounced the Abyssal Traitors." Dinnidek chuckled at that, while the dwarfs within earshot cheered at the bravado. "Second, my lord wishes to tell you that he's sent a small force to secure the heights before the general advance. He believes that contesting the heights now, while they're lightly defended, will avoid needless casualties later."

Dinnidek considered for a moment before replying. "Please tell Lord Anfynn that is acceptable, but please remind him that he is not to advance until I give the general order."

Din motioned for the messenger to go, and he ran off with a salute. Din gazed up at the heights on the left. He could just make out dwarfen troops milling around the ridgeline, silhouetted against the sky.

"Looks like he's got some Ironwatch mixed with his infantry up there," observed Tordek.

"Yes, hopefully he can hold on to it and funnel the orcs to the center of the battlefield." Dinnidek noted the Abyssal Dwarf troops arrayed along the mountainside. It looked like the enemy commander had massed his grotesques in the center for a possible countercharge. Din shielded the sun from his eyes as he looked for the halfbreeds. They'd been stationed near the woods, but now he couldn't see them. "Strange, Daerun is making an awful ruckus in those woods, and the enemy is pulling some of their best troops away from that side."

"He's got plenty of ratkin still."

A loud boom caused Din's head to swivel. The Abyssal Dwarf artillery opened fire, a single mortar followed by half a dozen more blasts in rapid succession. Din noted the puff of smoke, then the delayed sound of the blast. The shots landed short, as seconds later, the ground in front of the shield wall erupted, showering clods of dirt and grass into the air.

The Ironclad stood still in their formations, showing their dwarfen stoicism and courage, but Din knew that sooner or later those guns would get their range. He commanded the musicians, and they blasted a series of staccato notes, ordering the Ironclad to move backward, away from the enemy fire. A series of stakes driven into the ground, with pennants hanging limply from their tops, was placed around a hundred paces behind the front of the main line, representing Veit's best guess at the range of the Abyssal artillery. The dwarfs carefully picked their way backward to the line of stakes.

After a pause, the artillery unleashed another barrage, this time the shots landing closer. Din looked behind him to the empty plain to the south. How far back would they have to retreat? Too far back and he'd lose his anchor point by the birch forest. He prayed that Veit's math was correct.

* * * * *

The first barrage jolted Rhyss awake with a gasp, causing him to smack the top of his head against his backpack. A spike of anxiety rushed through him, and the adrenaline cut through the haze of sleep. As he came to, he was glad he hadn't twitched more than he had. Rhyss didn't remember nodding off, but he wasn't surprised. He'd led his rangers into position two days ago, and they'd been in hiding ever since. He'd stolen a few hours of sleep where he could, but the dwarfs were too close to the enemy to let their guard down. Another artillery barrage rumbled through the earth, shaking dirt loose from near his head. As the haze of sleep lifted completely, Rhyss assessed his situation.

He was lying on his back in a small hollow in the ground, face up with his hand on his crossbow across his chest, his left hand at his side near his hand axe. His cloak was suspended above him, anchored to the toe of his boot on one end and the rim of his backpack, which was nestled next to his head, on the other. The cloak was weighed down by a layer of dirt, making it sag a little so that it was only a few inches from his face. Meick and his fist of rangers had buried him and the other dwarfs before heading further up the mountainside to keep watch. The hiding spot was little more than a glorified hole in the ground, with hardly enough room for him to bend his knees or elbows. A bladder of water was lying on the ground next to his head, with a nozzle placed where he could turn to drink. Rhyss reflexively began rolling his shoulders and shifting his hips. He'd been lying like this for over a full day, and his muscles were stiff and sore. He'd placed a few small hollow reeds poking up from the dirt, but it was barely enough to provide enough fresh air to breath. The air around him was stale and stifling. The reeds let in the barest semblance of light into the hollow, and Rhyss figured it was the second morning since he'd entered the makeshift grave.

A third salvo erupted from the nearby Abyssal Dwarf artillery and Rhyss silently thanked the Earth Mother that it was almost time to leave.

It's about time I get out of here. This is the worst inn I've ever stayed at. Place reeks, and there's no food to eat. His stomach gurgled in agreement. *Nope, I wouldn't recommend it.*

He smiled at his own joke. He was losing his mind.

He half heard, half felt the sound of feet marching past his hiding spot, dangerously close by off to his left. He held his breath in anticipation and his hand tightened its grip on his crossbow. His other hand ever so slowly reached for his axe. His ears strained for signs that any enemies were getting closer, but nothing.

When they'd left the main dwarfen column, he'd led his rangers to where Diessa had thought the Abyssal Dwarfs were heading. Once they knew the general location, it had been easy to find them. After surveying the ground, the rangers hid themselves near where Rhyss believed the enemy artillery would be stationed. Meick and his fist helped camouflage them, then headed up the mountainside to a place where they could see the whole battlefield. Meick would monitor the battle, and when the time was right, he'd give a signal on his horn to begin the ambush.

The first few hours had been easy, but when the army arrived, they camped much closer to Rhyss than he'd anticipated. Instead of being a hundred yards away, the edge of the camp was near enough to hear the voices of the ratmen. Rhyss could do nothing as more and more of the enemy bustled around barely a stone's throw from where he lay. The first time he'd dozed off, he'd had a vivid nightmare that a stray ratkin had stepped into his bolt hole. The rest of his waking hours had been spent constantly on edge, worried that one of his men would be discovered.

The artillery barrage told him that the battle had finally started. He fought down the anxiety and steadied his breathing. He gave a silent prayer of thanks to the Earth Mother for his good fortune these last few days. It was fitting that he'd nestled himself in her bosom for protection. Maybe Diessa was right that the earth spirits were taking an active part on their behalf, watching over his men. He smiled at that. It was comforting to think that the Earth Mother and her two children, the dwarfs and the elementals, were working together to sweep the Abyssal Dwarfs away.

You've done your part, Rhyss prayed to the Earth Mother, *give us the strength to do ours.*

The artillery barrage increased in intensity, sending more vibrations through the ground and causing miniature avalanches of dirt to fall within the hollow. Rhyss' mind returned to the same problem he'd been chewing on since the Abyssal Dwarfs arrived and screwed up his masterful plan. How could his rangers survive if they revealed themselves? And how much damage would the artillery do before the ratkin advanced away from his position? With nothing but time on his hands, he'd been kicking the possibilities around all night. Of course it didn't matter if he came up with the best plan in Pannithor if he couldn't tell the rest of his rangers what it was. He frowned, lying prone in the dark, wallowing in his own stink. He shook his head in mild annoyance. Kilvar had been right. Complicated plans that were too clever for his own good. Meick would have to come through. Maybe pull the ratmen away early or cause a diversion. But either way, it was completely out of Rhyss' hands.

He sighed in resignation and tried to relax while he waited for an opportunity that may never come.

* * * * *

"Lots of vermin on that ridge," said Felwyr as he rubbed his hands together.

Daerun couldn't tell from Fel's tone if he was excited or concerned, as the two leaned on opposite sides of the same birch tree. As for himself, Dare was definitely concerned. There were a huge number of vermin on that ridge, hordes backed up by Obsidian golems and some sort of monstrosity with antlers and wings. Behind the enemy troops, the Abyssal artillery was blasting away at the main dwarfen line, and a haze of smoke was beginning to settle among the ratkin. The Shieldbreakers had cleared the vermin out of the forest, and they were stationed along the edge of the treeline.

"Gonna be hard to push through all them to get at the cannon," observed Felwyr.

"Well," replied Daerun, "lucky for us, Rhyss is supposed to be ambushing those guns any minute now."

As he considered the ridge, he had a hard time envisioning how Rhyss could pull it off. There were just too many ratkin near the artillery. If Rhyss attacked now, it would be suicide. Dare glanced down the treeline at the Shieldbreakers, then back up at the vermin. Could he push through them? Maybe. The dwarfs would be up for it, and if he could close the distance fast enough, he could be in amongst the ratkin before the Abyssal guns could fire on him.

Sure, he thought ruefully, *everyone knows how fast dwarfs are.*

Daerun stroked his beard while he thought it through. Dinnidek had told him that he could handle the artillery for a while, but not forever. How much time did he have? He didn't have a good feel for it. But he couldn't just stand here and let the Ironclad get ground down under that nightmarish fire. He was just about to send a messenger back to his brother to ask for permission to storm the ridge when he was interrupted by a commotion behind him. He and Felwyr turned to see a ranger come running between the trees, escorted by a few Shieldbreakers. The messenger was dressed in worn, dusty clothes in various shades of green and brown, his beard tied down under his belt. The ranger came straight at Daerun and gave an informal salute before delivering his message between ragged gasps.

"My lord, Captain Rhyss sends his regards. Well, at least he would if he could." A hollow feeling crept into Daerun's stomach at the ranger's words, but the ranger saw that look and hurriedly explained. "No, my lord, Captain Rhyss is fine, he's just resting on the edge of a cliff."

Daerun frowned in puzzlement, but the messenger went on to describe Rhyss' predicament and how the ambush he'd laid had gone awry.

"You mean to tell me," asked Daerun, "that your mates are hidden within feet of thousands of ratkin?"

The ranger nodded sheepishly, and Fel flung his hands in the air in astonishment.

"Sweet Earth Mother," Dare exclaimed as he glanced back up the mountainside with a frown. "We need to get the vermin to come down off the hill to give Rhyss and his rangers room to work."

It was time to make a new plan. Yes, Rhyss was in a tough spot, but he was also in an amazing spot to spring his ambush. How to give him the space he needed? While Dare wracked his brains, the Abyssal Dwarf artillery continued their murderous barrage, lending additional urgency to the problem.

As Daerun considered the alternatives, he heard an answering series of heavy thuds from behind him. The three dwarfs turned at the sound, and Daerun beheld a score of earth elementals walking his way, literally through the trees. Being one with the natural world, the giant's earthen bodies seemed to reform around the white birch trunks, and the behemoths moved effortlessly through the woods. The head of one of the taller earth elementals passed through a particularly spindly branch, stripping the leaves but otherwise keeping the limb intact. It was surreal.

Daerun noticed Bruon among the honor guard, leading Diessa by the hand amid the elementals. He cocked an eyebrow when he noticed she wasn't wearing her blindfold.

He tapped Felwyr on the shoulder to follow him, and he made his way between the elementals to talk to his sister. As he got closer, he noticed that Diessa was staring off into space, barely aware of her surroundings. Dare caught sight of Gwel, and he veered to stand in front of the miniature elemental, who stopped short and greeted the dwarf, craning its little neck upward. Dare looked from Gwel to Diessa and back again, not sure who to speak to. Finally, he knelt and spoke to Gwel, hoping that he wouldn't look like a fool.

"Deese?" he asked. Gwel nodded and waved. Daerun smiled and exhaled in relief. "Deese, I need your help. Rhyss is trapped up on the ridge, and we have to save him." He pointed back toward the artillery. Gwel peered over Daerun's shoulder with its gemstone eyes. "See all those ratkin up there? I have to lead them away to give Rhyss room to spring his ambush."

Another barrage erupted from the Abyssal Dwarf cannons. Gwel nodded in understanding as Bruon led Diessa to join them. Daerun didn't have a real plan a minute ago, but as he spoke he improvised, Felwyr jumping in with suggestions.

When he was done, Gwel nodded in understanding while Diessa smiled in Dare's general direction. Daerun made sure to grin back at both of them, then sent for the Shieldbreaker sergeants so he could lay out the plan. It would be risky, but he trusted in their dwarfen discipline to make it work. At Diessa's unspoken command, the earth elementals positioned themselves in a cordon set back from the treeline.

Lastly, he pulled Felwyr aside. "You sure about this, Fel?"

Felwyr shot Daerun a fey smile. "Leave the grisly work to me. Just give me room when I come hot-footing back here, understand?"

Dare chuckled as he clasped Felwyr's forearm and pulled him in for a clap on the back. "Earth Mother watch over you, Fel."

Felwyr waved off the concerned look in Daerun's eyes and ran to gather a few dwarfs to help him. Dare watched his friend until Felwyr's silhouette got lost in the trees.

Dare grunted and looked up at the closest elemental, who stood silently over Bruon and the honor guard. The rumble of artillery was the only sound. He peered at the masses of ratkin and let out a sigh. Now that Felwyr was gone, he began second guessing the plan. He shook his head in annoyance.

"This will work," he said out loud to no one. The artillery screamed overhead, and the detonations of the shells shook the ground on the plains behind him. "This will work. This *will* work."

His Shieldbreakers began gathering around, waiting for instructions. He shook his head, gave a final sigh, and began addressing his clansmen.

* * * * *

Zareen surveyed the battle from the back of his winged nightmare and smiled. The creature anxiously pawed at the ground, and the Iron-caster sharply tugged at the reins to keep it under control. It snuffed and shook its great antlered head from side to side in agitation but came to heel. Any moment now, Alborz would give the signal for the attack, and his gnorr would be ready. Zareen had flown the great beast to the front of the ratkin lines along with his obsidian golems to spearhead the assault. The white birch forest spread before him, and he waited with growing anticipation for the order to charge. When the time came, the mongrel dwarfs within the woods would be swept away.

The Abyssal Dwarf artillery kept up its relentless barrage into the dwarfen center. The demonic mortars were pushing the mongrels back, but the Ironclad were carefully keeping their flank anchored to the forest, within range of the guns. Zareen sent a message to the battery to have them switch their target to that location. If he could soften that point up, he could hinder the main line from sending reinforcements into the woods. He smiled to himself as he considered the situation with newfound confidence. Under Alborz's tutelage, he was seeing the battlefield in a new light, and he found that he liked it.

He turned his attention back to the birch forest. The rising sun was still low in the sky, and the treeline was shrouded in shadow. Even though he couldn't see the dwarfs, he knew there were numerous warriors gathered there, based on reports from his gargoyle scouts. In contrast, Zareen had more than twice that many gnorr at his disposal. Alborz had been right. Fight the enemy on ground of your choosing with more troops. Everything else would work itself out. He grinned evilly thinking of the experiments he would conduct on the dwarfen prisoners they'd capture.

His reverie was broken when he noticed a thin line of dwarf warriors running toward him from out of the woods. His brow furrowed at the curious sight. Why so few? He was tempted to send some of the gnorr forward to sweep the mongrels away, but he kept his discipline. He would wait for Alborz's signal. As they came closer, Zareen noticed that they each held a small sack, or bag maybe, suspended from ropes held in their fists. They didn't seem to be weapons. What were they up to? Just in case, he called for the closest gnorr warriors to be ready to move on his order.

As he watched, the dwarfs swung the bags in great circles and flung them at the ratkin from a fair distance away. If the bags were weapons, the dwarfs were way out of range for them to be effective. The bags sailed through the air and fell short of the ratkin lines. Zareen tracked one of the sacks as it landed and bounced along, rolling to a stop before the flying grotesque's feet. When it finally stopped moving, Zareen understood what he was seeing. Those weren't bags. They were the heads of his gnorr warriors, flung by their hair.

The other ratkin warriors had noticed the grisly trophies as well, and they were growling and yelling in anger. The dwarfs, in turn, stood defiantly in the field, shouting curses at the Abyssal Dwarf army. Zareen tore his gaze away from the bloodied head with its dead eyes, and a wave of rage washed over him. The dwarfen taunts carried over the sound of the artillery, and the mongrels stood defiantly in the open. Some had carried multiple heads, and a second wave was flung at the ratkin line. A small voice in the back of Zareen's mind urgently reminded him to wait for the order, but it was overcome by a chorus of voices screaming for vengeance.

A red haze tinged Zareen's vision as he savagely ordered the charge.

The ratkin obliged and ran forward in a chaotic mass, eager to tear the dwarfs limb from limb. Zareen ground his teeth as he grinned maniacally and kicked the nightmare into flight. Zareen was propelled up into the air as the great beast flapped its giant leathery wings. The obsidian golems joined the charge and plodded forward with thundering footsteps.

The dwarfen warriors turned tail and sprinted back for the safety of the woods. Within moments, Zareen was high enough in the air to see that the gnorr wouldn't be able to catch the dwarfs before they made it back to the treeline. But he could make them pay. The great beast rose a little higher before Zareen guided the nightmare to the attack. The creature dove to the earth and pulled up above a pair of dwarfs. It grabbed each dwarf in its razorlike claws as it soared past and climbed again into the sky. The creature gave a sickening screech as it threw the dwarfs disdainfully back to earth. Zareen cackled madly and led the grotesque on another dive. It reached for another pair of dwarfs but was only able to secure one as the other dove and rolled to safety. As the beast soared up over the treeline, it took the dwarf in both claws and tore it in two before dropping the body parts onto the forest canopy and the hidden dwarfen warriors below.

"You dare to taunt me?" Zareen screamed. "I will be your doom, mongrels!"

The antlered nightmare circled back to the open field as Zareen looked for new prey. He saw another dwarf, tantalizingly close to the treeline, the gnorr close behind. At his bidding, the beast landed directly atop the fleeing dwarf, crushing it to the ground with its front paws as it landed on its haunches. Zareen glared directly into the woods as the creature began ripping at the dwarf's body with its beak. Zareen shrieked again in ecstatic rage as the gnorr charged past him and into the forest.

"Find the stone priest!" he exhorted his troops. "Kill him if you must, but bring me his body! I want it intact."

The nearest gnorr chittered excitedly as they dove into the woods with renewed fervor.

"Ariagful! Bear witness to me and behold my deeds! Let the dwarfen blood be a sacrifice to you!"

As he prayed, Zareen's hands began to glow with a green light that coalesced into balls of infernal flame. The nightmare flung a piece of the dwarfen corpse into the air before catching it in its beak and swallowing it down. Zareen spread his hands and green flame shot toward the forest. He swept his hands back and forth, aiming into the canopy, careful not to injure the gnorr below. Within seconds, the trees were alight, wrapped in unholy fire that greedily devoured the papery bark and disintegrated their leaves. Zareen laughed in maniacal joy as his obsidian golems strode forward to surround him. The dwarfs would burn.

* * * * *

"Tell the slave drivers on the ridge to send another token force of orcs forward on my signal," Alborz addressed the gargoyle messenger haughtily. "Tell him I want just enough pressure to keep Helgwin feeding their troops up there, understood?"

The gargoyle nodded, and Alborz airily waved it away. He kept his eyes on the ridge and the Clan Helgwin troops. The Warmaster had thinned his line. If he could get him to commit one more regiment or two, it would guarantee a breakthrough when he charged. He nodded in satisfaction at the army's progress before turning back to the center.

The dwarfs were retreating from the artillery fire, and with every step backward, the join between the two clans became weaker and weaker. He summoned another gargoyle to order the Blacksouls to prepare to advance behind the grotesques when the assault began, but before he could give the order, chaos erupted from the left flank by the woods. He shoved the gargoyle out of the way to get a better view, and he momentarily stood dumbfounded.

Alborz felt a seething anger rise in him as he watched Zareen charge the gnorr into the birch forest. *What in the seven circles of the Abyss is he doing?* he thought with disgust. Despite his emotions, Alborz's face was stone, and he stood completely still as he considered this new development. He studied the dwarfen center. They weren't under direct pressure, so they'd be free to reinforce the woods and repel Zareen's attack. Alborz cursed. He turned back to his troops. The Abyssal Dwarf slave drivers, mounted on their chariots, were prepared to drive the grotesques forward. The halfbreeds were ranked up behind next to the Immortal Guard, ready for his command.

Dammit, Zareen, he thought vehemently, *you pushed my hand.*

Alborz impatiently motioned for the gargoyle to send his message to the Blacksouls before calling another one over. "Fly to the slave drivers on the ridge and tell them to charge forward with all of the remaining orcs." Alborz's voice was icy calm, belying his frustration with his brother. "The time for delicacy is over. I want the mongrels swept from the ridge. Tell the slave drivers to carry the charge down the slope into Helgwin's flank. I'll meet them in the center."

He shooed the gargoyle away before mounting his chariot. He adjusted his cape around his shoulders, drew his bejeweled sword, and called for the advance. The grotesques sped forward; the slave drivers close behind. He called down to the halfbreed commander, "We form the wedge. We'll lurk behind the grotesques, then you'll follow me straight between the two clans, understand?"

Without waiting for the halfbreed to acknowledge the order, Alborz turned his attention to the Immortal Guard and addressed them en masse.

"You will follow behind. When I've broken through their line, you'll head for the gap and turn the flank of Clan Daamuz. Push them back to the woods and meet Zareen's forces there. When you get to the artillery, destroy it. Understood?"

The Immortal Guard raised their metallic arms and shields in a silent salute, and Alborz acknowledged them by raising his sword high in the air before dropping it to point at the dwarfen army.

"Forward!" he yelled. "To ruin! And to glory!"

CHAPTER 21

The canopy over Daerun's head exploded in green flame. He instinctively covered his eyes as he flinched back from the heat with a curse. The last thing he saw before the explosion was Felwyr's soldiers running for their lives, a few steps ahead of the ratkin and the Abyssal Dwarf sorcerer on his giant beast. He'd cried out in desperation as the twisted abomination had swept down upon Fel, but his friend had luckily jumped and rolled clear in the nick of time.

"Get back!" he screamed to his clansmen. "Back! Behind the elementals!"

The Shieldbreakers pulled back from the treeline in the face of the flames. Daerun opened his eyes and shook his head to clear the after images of the explosions from his sight. Dwarfs were fleeing past him, deeper into the woods and toward the towering earth elementals who had formed a defensive battle line. The rats were streaming into the woods' edge, their momentum slowed by the underbrush. Daerun waited until the last dwarf ran past before joining them. While he retreated, he kept one eye out for Felwyr. He'd lost sight of him just before the explosion.

Dare ran to the closest elemental, a relatively tall and slender mound of boulders and dirt with long ape-like arms that dragged almost to the ground. Behind him, he could hear the ratkin chittering and screeching as they rushed to the attack. He wove his way carefully through the trees and sprinted the last few feet to pass under the elemental's legs. He was moving so fast that he collided with the other Shieldbreakers who had fled to the rally point. Daerun gave a half-hearted apology between gasps of air as he turned to face the ratkin.

Now that they were behind the elementals, Daerun feverishly rallied the Shieldbreakers. He said a quick prayer to the Earth Mother that the Shieldbreakers would listen. He knew that it would only take a small nudge to turn a coordinated retreat into a rout, and the green flame had unsettled the dwarfs before they fell back.

"That's it, boys! Gather round! The vermin are in for it now!"

The elementals had stood still as statues as the dwarfs ran past, but as the wave of ratkin arrived, the elementals sprang to life. Their gemstone eyes flashed brightly as they stood taller and shook their limbs loose. Daerun watched as the closest elemental swung its long arms in front of it in a wide arc, catching a handful of ratkin in its wake. Some of them crumpled as the unyielding stone struck their fleshy bodies. A few were flung in the air and flew backward to land among their fellows. From further away, Daerun saw one unfortunate ratkin get tossed high into the air, its body crashing into the upper limbs of a nearby birch tree.

Daerun let out a wild war whoop in triumph as the ratkin charge faltered against the earthen guardians. "It's working, lads! Yes!"

He pulled the dwarfs further back to give the elementals room to work and ordered them into ranks. He kept yelling encouragement to his clansmen, and more and more of the fleeing dwarfs trotted over to join his unit. As he pulled the stragglers in, he kept an eye on the elementals. Though they'd gotten the drop on the enemy, it wasn't all ale and pies. Further down the line, the ratkin had found some courage and were hacking away in a frenzy at a squat elemental with their halberds and spears. Daerun noted that the ratkin were avoiding the stones and boulders, stabbing at the soil and dirt parts instead. The elemental's size advantage was being negated by the vermins' long weapons, and though the earth guardian had size and strength, the ratkin had numbers.

Daerun pointed at the squat guardian with his hammer. "C'mon boys! Let's give Stumpy a hand!"

With that, he ran forward, his Shieldbreakers in tow. As they approached, Stumpy had resorted to fighting defensively, hunkered down trying to keep the ratkin from damaging it further. Despite its efforts, a couple of the larger ratkin had gotten their weapons stuck into a soft spot in the elemental's armpit, and they were prying back and forth with all their strength. Daerun saw the foes' muscles straining as they pushed and pulled with their halberds. Stumpy was slowly swaying its shoulder, trying to dislodge the spear tips, but to no avail. With a few yards to go, Daerun watched with concern as the elemental's arm just gave way. The stones and earth there separated from its body; the boulders lost their magical cohesion and cascaded to the ground, crushing a few vermin in the process.

The vermin squealed in triumph. It was short lived. Dare ran straight for the largest ratkin and was only a few feet away when his target finally felt the danger. Daerun laughed in delight at the panicked look on the enemy's's face as it turned toward the dwarfs. He swung his hammer down on the ratkin's shoulder, and it fell with a cry. A split second later, the Shieldbreakers crashed into the enemy like a storm. Dare swung his hammer a few more times before the ratkin formation was shattered.

"Keep running!" Dare taunted as the ratkin fled out of the woods. Stumpy, meanwhile, waved its good arm at the enemy and took a few steps forward. Daerun noticed crushed ratkin corpses under where the elemental's wide stone feet used to be. Apparently, it didn't need both arms to give the enemy grief. Dare reached up and patted Stumpy on the thigh affectionately.

"Sorry about your arm, Stumpy."

"Oof," exclaimed Felwyr from behind him. "Stumpy? I go away for a bit and that's the best joke you can come up with?"

Daerun spun with a relieved smile, and embraced Felwyr briefly in a bear hug, overjoyed to see that his friend was alright. "Oh, thank the Earth Mother." He let him go with a grin, taking in Fel's face and savoring this small moment. He'd been running on pure adrenaline and had lost track of his friend since they fled. As he got his emotions under control, Dare self-consciously looked away. With forced levity, he changed the subject, "Looks like our plan worked."

"Yep!" agreed Felwyr sarcastically, waving up at the flaming trees. "Worked like a charm. Just like we planned it." Daerun grimaced before Fel went on in the same forced tone. "That nightmare almost had me, but I'm as agile as an elf, don't you know."

Dare snorted and turned his attention back to the battle. The elementals had done a good job of holding off the initial ratkin charge. Dare was thinking of pulling some dwarfs together for a counterattack, but his thoughts were interrupted by a trembling in the ground. He turned toward the sound with a frown and saw a knot of obsidian golems approaching the woods. They were giant, almost twice as tall as Stumpy, and just as broad. Their black stone bodies burned with an inner, smoldering fire that gave off wisps of black smoke. Heat shimmered above their heads and massive shoulders, and the grass where they strode withered and burnt away. The Abyssal sorcerer soared overhead and landed the antlered nightmare in front of the golems. He raised his hands and fired another gout of green flame into the woods while the routed ratkin regrouped behind the demonic constructs.

"Looks like we're not done here," quipped Daerun.

"Nope," agreed Felwyr, wryly.

Daerun looked up at Stumpy and back again at the obsidian golems. "We can't stand up to those, Fel," he said gravely, as he patted Stumpy on the thigh again. "This is a fight for Deese."

* * * * *

The ground around Rhyss vibrated violently, dirt and pebbles dancing around the floor of his lair.

First the roars, he thought to himself, *then the chitters, now the thuds.* He ticked the list off on his fingers. *Those will be the obsidian golems. Sounds like everyone has charged forward except for the guns.*

The vibrations eased as the golems marched further away. He smiled in anticipation.

Any minute now I can get out of this hole and get to work.

Rhyss flexed his muscles and squirmed to get some blood flowing to his stiff and sore extremities.

He let go of his axe and very gently probed the cloth canopy with his hand, tracing the fabric up to where it connected to the backpack by his head. He felt around the backpack for a place to securely hold it. He wiggled his foot, and the canopy rippled in response. He noted that the dirt covering his hiding spot would pool quickly once the tension on the cloth was released. He wondered how heavy the covering would be with the added soil.

Figures, he thought ruefully, *I spend an entire day dreaming about getting out, and I didn't spend a single minute figuring out how.* He hoped that his fellow rangers were smarter than he had been. *Seems unlikely. They followed my stupid plan, after all.*

He carefully raised his hands up by his ears, near the straps of his backpack in preparation for Meick's signal.

As if on cue, Rhyss faintly heard a horn blast a staccato rhythm.

Rhyss squeezed his eyes shut, grabbed the backpack with both hands, and heaved it over his face down to his waist. As he did so, he sat up with a gasp. It was the sweetest air he'd ever tasted. He took a splendid second to just enjoy the sensation as a slight summer breeze caressed his skin. It was pure bliss. He kept his eyes on the ground as he slowly allowed them to open. Meanwhile, he grabbed for his axes and tentatively stood up on shaky legs. The sun glared blindingly bright, and he kept his eyes squinted in slits. He shielded them from the sun with his hand as he looked around. All around him, dwarfen heads were popping out of the ground like mushrooms after a heavy rain. Most of the dwarfs were in similar shaky straights. He saw a ranger who had gotten tangled in his tarp and another who had neglected to keep their eyes shut while moving their soil-covered canopy, blinking away the dirt.

Rhyss took a moment to get the lay of the land. He looked to see how far the golems were, but he moved his head too quickly and a wave of vertigo hit him. He took a few deep breaths and got his body under control. Another volley from the artillery shook his torso, and he kept his eyes closed as he turned toward the noise. His eyes watered as he opened them again, but despite the tears, he could just make out the Abyssal Dwarf artillery, which was jarringly close. There were maybe a dozen artillery pieces clustered together. He continued to get his stomach under control as he closed his eyes and wiped them clear.

"Uff'ran," he cursed in frustration. Between the inactivity, hunger, thirst, and lack of sleep, his time in hiding had left him relatively weak. If he didn't get himself together quick, he'd be a sitting duck.

Luckily for him, they'd taken the Abyssal Dwarfs completely by surprise as Rhyss heard them shouting to each other in bewilderment at the rangers' sudden arrival. More importantly, the guns had gone silent. He forced himself to calm down, and he felt his heartbeat slow and his breathing come back under control. He stomped his feet to fight off the pins and needles and flexed his hands a few times.

"Ahhhh," he sighed aloud, "that will do it." With that, he finally fully opened his eyes and steeled himself for the attack.

The staccato horn calls continued to sound from the mountainside. The rangers sprang from the ground like the spirits of the dead, come to take vengeance on their enemies. With a final shake of his head, Rhyss stepped out of his makeshift grave and pulled his horn from his waist. He gave it a shake to get the dirt out of it before blowing a clear answering note into the summer sky. His hungry troops yelled back with dry throats and parched lips. Rhyss lowered the horn and waved at his rangers to follow him.

He took the first couple steps on wooden legs, and he stumbled a few times as he ran up the hill toward the closest demonic mortar and the now panicking crew. Some of his nearby rangers converged on Rhyss' position, and he closed the final distance with over a fist of rangers around him. Rhyss laughed in pent up relief that his audacious plan had worked. The rangers around him screamed their rage as they prepared to take vengeance on the traitors who had dared to invade their homes.

"Silence these guns!" Rhyss ordered. Some of the Abyssal Dwarfs were fleeing the dwarfen charge, while others held their ground, and an unfortunate few stood still, dumbfounded in shock. Rhyss charged one of the traitors and chopped him down with his axe, a look of horrid disbelief on his face.

It was the first of many.

* * * * *

Din stared in confusion at the approaching grotesques. The enemy wasn't supposed to be charging. That hadn't been part of the plan. Dinnidek had been taken aback when the enemy had started moving down off the high ground. Why would the enemy commander give up such an advantageous position? He just couldn't make sense of the maneuver. In response, Din had ordered the cannons to fire at the oncoming enemy. No use in passing up the opportunity.

From his perch atop the ammunition cart, Dinnidek could clearly see the grotesques charging down the mountainside and across the plain, kicking up dust as they ran. Through the dusty haze, Din could barely make out the Abyssal Dwarf slave drivers riding behind them, whipping them into a frenzy. The creatures' nightmare bodies, composed of various animals and demons stitched strangely together, gave them a supernatural speed that was unsettling to behold. Even at this distance, Dinnidek could discern distinct parts that were feline, bird, bull, canine, reptile, and other more alien elements.

"Creatures so twisted shouldn't move so gracefully," Din opined to Tordek.

The stalwart dwarf just grunted in reply, clearly distracted by other events on the battlefield. Tordek tapped Din on the shoulder excitedly and pointed up at the ridge past the birch forest. The Abyssal Dwarf artillery had gone silent, and Din could just make out fighting where the guns had been. Dinnidek clenched his fist in triumph at the turn of events. Rhyss had arrived, and just in the nick of time. Din had pulled his main line further and further back, away from the artillery barrage, but that hadn't saved the troops anchored to the woods. They'd taken the brunt of the nightmarish fire. Meanwhile, the ground just in front of the shield wall was churned up and pitted from the earlier salvoes.

The next part of the plan had called for the dwarfs to begin their advance up the middle, but now the enemy was coming to them, and fast. At that pace, Din's cannons only had time to fire a few rounds before he'd be forced to line his Ironclad into a defensive shield wall. No time to get tricky. He would lean on the strengths, and his troops stood, shields at the ready. Din noted the broken ground before him and began issuing orders.

"Change in plan, Tordek. Have the shield wall move forward, to the edge of the craters, and hold fast there. We'll use the broken ground to our advantage." He pointed at one of the nearby messengers. "You, get over to Veit, and tell him to fire the cannons on the flank into those grotesques." He turned to his other musicians and banner bearers. "Signal Helgwin to begin the advance up the ridge and have him get ready to fire his Ironwatch into the enemy center."

"Might be too late for that," said Tordek, grimly. Din looked up at the ridge. It was crawling with orcs streaming down from the mountain.

Dinnidek cursed and grabbed one of the musicians. "Belay that order. Have Anfynn hold his position. We'll repel the assault first."

That was all Din had time for before the grotesques reached the broken ground. The dwarfs bawled their battle cries and locked shields as the grotesques, slavering and howling, slowed to navigate the rough terrain. The slave drivers, mounted on tall chariots, were whipping the grotesques forward, prodding them with extra-long spears toward the dwarfs.

The grotesques closed the final distance and crashed into the Ironclad. The creatures towered over the dwarfs, and the soldiers were forced to raise their shields to block the rain of blows. Some of the unfortunate dwarfs were too slow to react and were felled by wicked talons or sharp claws. Din watched in horror as one grotesque with an elongated scorpion tail grabbed onto an

Ironclad's shield with its front paws and sunk its stinger through the dwarf's shoulder and out of his back. The grotesques were savage in their attacks, leaving gruesome wounds on the dwarfs, pushing the shield wall back. The dwarfen line was shaky, and in one spot, Dinnidek saw the dwarfs fall back to cede the ground to the abominations.

Dinnidek resisted the urge to dive in and instead ordered his reserves to shore up the line. The fresh dwarfs surged forward and bolstered the beleaguered Ironclad. The dwarfs counterattacked and halted the grotesque advance, but they were hard pressed to wound the enemy. The grotesques' sorcerous blood magically knitted up the cuts and slashes that the dwarfs were able to land. If the line broke now, there would be no recovering. For a few tense moments, the line wavered on the edge of a knife until Veit's cannons fired into the flank of the enemy, killing a handful of the sorcerous creatures.

It was just enough.

The dwarfen line stiffened, then began pushing forward, step by step, moving as one to repel the grotesques. The slave drivers were prodding the creatures, whipping them with greater and greater fury. In the swirling melee, Din happened to see one of the Abyssal Dwarfs get shot off his chariot, his body whirling around wildly at the impact. It looked like Rorik was earning his money.

With the center holding, Din peered nervously to the south, on the lookout for the orcs from the plains. He frowned to himself as he saw a small dust cloud far out to the southwest. It wasn't a good sign. It was mid-morning, and he hadn't heard anything from Kilvar's rangers. He was starting to fear for the worst.

*   *   *   *   *

Rorik, viewing through his scope, saw the slave driver spin and fall to the ground. He smiled in satisfaction as he pulled down his rifle and reloaded for another shot. He threw up a quick prayer to the ancestors that he had led his troops away from the main line. The Abyssal Dwarf assault would have been the death of him and his men. He hadn't asked permission to leave. It had never occurred to him. He was getting paid for his skills and his expertise, and he couldn't bring those skills fully to bear stuck in the shield wall. And he would be damned if he was going to just stand there and get shelled. He shook his head to clear it and returned to the business at hand.

"Red cape!" he yelled to the Wyverns as he rammed his bullet into the muzzle.

"Red cape!" they called back.

Rorik primed the firing pan and sighted the next target, a slave driver with a garish burgundy cape, mounted on a golden chariot. This one was a dozen yards further away than the last target, but still well within range. The Abyssal Dwarf was prodding the grotesques in front of him with a blunted lance, goading them on to the fight. For a moment there, Rorik had been worried the Ironclad would buckle under the furious assault, but they'd barely held their ground, at the expense of their remaining reserves. In return, the grotesques were caught between the now implacable dwarfen line and the screaming slave drivers behind them. If Rorik's troops could disrupt the slave drivers, the grotesques would be free to flee.

Rorik sighted through his scope and tracked just a few hairs above the slave driver's head. Some of the other sharpshooters fired early, but he held his breath until the right moment, then exhaled and pulled the trigger. In an instant, the slave driver, and the charioteer, were hit by a handful of bullets and went down in a heap. The gores yoked to the chariot spooked and ran off, back across the plain.

"Gold helmet!" Rorik ordered.

"Gold helmet," the Wyverns replied.

From their hiding spot in the birch forest, the next slave driver was at the outer range of the Wyvern's rifles but still possible. Once Goldie was killed, the Wyverns would have to move to another location to hunt for more prey. Rorik didn't want to leave the cover of the woods if he didn't have to. Even though it was only late morning, the day was hot, and Rorik appreciated being in the shade. Still, he could hear intense fighting at the northern edge of the forest, and if that went poorly for the dwarfs, he wouldn't have much of a choice.

As he picked his next target, he noticed a mass of halfbreeds far out on the plain, led by an Abyssal Dwarf clad in shining black armor on a chariot, turning away from him toward the south. The ostentatious chariot was adorned with gold and silver leaf, and it gleamed resplendently in the sun.

If that fine gentleman isn't the Overmaster, I'll eat my hat, Rorik thought.

He raised the scope to his eye to get a better view of the halfbreeds and the Overmaster as they wheeled and charged headlong into the dwarfen left, where Clan Helgwin was stationed. Rorik quickly scanned the ridge with his scope and saw the orcs swarming over the dwarfen position there, descending the rocky ground from the ridge onto the plain below.

The rest of the Wyverns fired a volley at the slave driver with the gold helmet, killing him and one of the gores. The grotesques were still ferociously fighting the Ironclad, but at least the dwarfs had a chance to push them back. To the north, a line of Abyssal Dwarf warriors was descending onto the plain, heading for the shield wall. Even if the dwarfen line could repel the grotesques, Lord Daamuz would still be in a heap of trouble. Rorik lowered his rifle and chewed on his lower lip as he considered his options. Meanwhile, the Wyverns steadily reloaded their rifles, waiting for him to give them their next target.

Where would they do the most good?

It's got to be one of the commanders, he thought. Rorik glanced to the north, where the Iron-caster was busy burning down half the forest. Even though he was the immediate threat, the Abyssal Sorcerer wasn't pulling the strings. No, Master Daerun would have to deal with that on his own. *Besides, he has Diessa and her stone guardians with him. He'll be fine.*

"Alright, gentlemen," Rorik called to his troops, "follow me. We're hunting the enemy commander." The Wyverns picked up their packs and prepared to move out. Rorik gave one last look up into the birch trees. He'd miss the shade.

* * * * *

Anfynn stroked his beard in agitation. He'd been stroking his beard a lot today, fighting a mixture of anxiety and boredom. He'd spent the morning standing around with his forces, waiting to begin the eventual advance up the mountainside. An assault uphill against an enemy in a fortified position was a recipe for disaster, and Anfynn had been mulling over the best way to go about it since last evening. Gundrim had done a good job of securing the ridge, and Anfynn was antsy to get his troops up on the high ground. That had all gone out the window when the Abyssal Dwarfs went on the offensive.

He watched in puzzlement as the grotesques advanced across the plain. The large, twisted creatures were so tall that they blocked Anfynn's view of what was going on behind them. The only thing he knew was that the enemy army lined up on the high ground this morning was no longer there. It flew against every tenet of military strategy that he could think of. He felt frustrated that he couldn't reckon what the Abyssal Dwarf commander was doing. He'd fought the demonic traitors and their slaves for decades, and he'd never seen one of their commanders make such a big mistake.

Then maybe it's not a mistake, a small nagging voice said in the back of his head.

He heard the orc war horns blaring from the heights above, but he couldn't see beyond the edge of the ridgeline where Gundrim's advance forces were dug in behind a jumble of rocky terrain.

"Damn this blindness," Anfynn cursed to his nearby troops. He hated having to react to the enemy. It meant the fiends were dictating the battle. "By Fulgria's fiery crotch, someone get up on that ridge and spy out what's happening!"

A few of his scouts immediately obeyed and ran off toward the high ground. Anfynn noted that the incessant Abyssal artillery had finally ceased. Would Dinnidek still call the dwarfs to advance? Should he prepare his force to take the grotesques in the flank?

Anfynn was silently stewing in his indecision when a messenger came racing toward him from the ridge, dressed in Gundrim's unit colors.

"My lord," the runner gasped, "the orcs have come down off the high ground and have assaulted the ridge."

"How many?" Anfynn asked urgently. "How many orcs?"

"All of them, my lord."

Anfynn's eyes narrowed, and he spat on the ground at the news.

"Gundrim says he'll hold them for as long as he can." Anfynn gazed sharply up at the ridge, where he could see Gundrim's troops already engaged. The messenger urgently continued, "There's more, my lord. Gundrim says that you must take a defensive formation now. Half the Abyssal Dwarf army is descending on your position and will be here in moments."

Anfynn stared at the messenger in silence. He must have misheard him. Half the enemy army? Anfynn pushed his way to the front of his troops and stared out into the dusty haze. As he watched, the grotesques swept forward into the Daamuz Ironclad, revealing more enemy troops behind. Cavalry, maybe? Within a few heartbeats, Anfynn could clearly see the enemy in all their nightmarish glory. A wall of Abyssal halfbreeds, demonic dwarf centaurs, were charging directly at him.

"Helgwin!" Anfynn's voice boomed over the battlefield, "Stand fast. Tighten up and prepare to repel cavalry charge! Ironwatch, line up behind!"

The army musicians blew their trumpets to convey Anfynn's orders as the closest warriors sprang into action. The dwarfs, which had been spread relatively thin over a wide front, collapsed into a dense formation. As they did so, the dwarfs efficiently went to their assigned positions, with the Ironclad kneeling in the front and the gunners lined up behind. Mastiff handlers were interspersed along the front of the dwarfen line with their hunting hounds. The dogs, which moments ago had been tame and almost docile, instinctively felt the change in their masters' energies and were now growling and snarling, their muscles tense and straining for the order to go.

Anfynn placed himself in the middle of his clansmen, the Helgwin clan banner just behind.

"Steady, dogs! If the traitors want this spot of ground, let them come and take it!" The Helgwin warriors all barked and yowled in reply. Anfynn grasped his warhammer tightly and pointed contemptuously at the approaching Abyssal Dwarfs. "We've hidden long enough! This is our land, and the demons have no power here!"

The halfbreeds were closing fast, their long demonic legs propelling them forward. Their top dwarfen halves were clad in black mail and tall spiked helmets, their lower demonic flanks protected by flexible leather and steel. Most were armed with lances and shields, but a few of their commanders wielded giant double-bladed axes for maximum carnage. Their dwarfen faces were twisted with a sorcerous hate that made them look even more demonic with eyes of burning fire. Anfynn scowled as the halfbreeds crested a small undulation in the ground, and he could see rows and rows of the demons approaching, packed shoulder to shoulder. Anfynn gauged the enemy's speed and took note of their tight formation.

The dwarfs screamed their defiance and their fear as the halfbreeds thundered in for the kill. The mastiffs barked furiously and strained at their leads. Anfynn raised his hammer high, the rubies catching fire in the mid-morning sun. The enemy was mere yards away.

With a cry, he dropped his hammer down, and the trumpeter at his elbow blew a single clear note. The Packmasters released their leads, and the mastiffs darted forward. A split second later, the Ironwatch fired a volley over the kneeling warriors. At such close range, the rifles had a horrifying effect. The bullets easily punched through armor, and many halfbreeds in the front rank were wounded or killed outright. More importantly than the casualties, the volley disrupted the enemy's coordinated charge. The enemy in the second rank were forced to jump over their fallen comrades or trample them into the ground. The demonic dwarfs were thrown into disarray, just in time for the mastiffs to reach their targets. The great hunting dogs struck at the halfbreeds' legs and underbellies, sowing mass confusion in the enemy ranks.

Despite the chaos, some of the enemy completed the charge into the Helgwin Ironclads with such ferocity that the dwarfs were pushed back. Dozens of dwarfs fell in the initial impact. Anfynn was just able to dodge a halfbreed's lance as the foul creature rammed into the Ironclad in front of him with its armored chest. The unfortunate dwarf was bowled over and trampled by the enemy's front claws. In desperation, Anfynn grabbed at the halfbreed's lance with his free hand and yanked it past him, pulling his foe off balance before smashing its exposed weapon arm with his warhammer. The creature screamed in pain and let go of the lance. Anfynn stepped forward, and with a pair of quick strikes, he snapped the creature's lower leg. Anfynn grinned in grim satisfaction at the look of panic on the falling halfbreed's face before he smashed its skull.

All around him, dwarfs who hadn't been killed or wounded in the initial charge were being forced back, step by step. Anfynn screamed for his clansmen to hold their ground, but the halfbreeds were too strong and vicious. The Warmaster took a step back and physically pulled the nearby

Ironclad back with him.

"Tighten up! Stay together!"

His voice was drowned out by the cacophony of battle all around him. A halfbreed with a great axe reared up in front of him and slashed at a nearby Ironclad with its front paws. The dwarf was able to partially block the attack, but the creature's claws gripped the top of the shield and pinned it down to the ground, taking the dwarf's arm with it. The dwarf was forced to kneel before his foe as he struggled to free his arm from the shield straps. The halfbreed ended the dwarf with a swing from its axe. Anfynn heard the ragged pop of gunshots from over his shoulder, and the halfbreed champion went down with multiple bullet wounds.

Anfynn, in desperation, called for the dwarfs to hold fast once more. Above the fray, he heard orc horns from his left. He glanced up at the ridge with dismay. Some of the orcs had bypassed Gundrim and were coming down the hillside into the dwarfen flank. He watched in impotent rage as Gundrim's banner, surrounded by the enemy, fell and was overborn by the wave of orcs.

Anfynn ordered his clansmen to form themselves into a square to repel this new assault. "Mountain formation! Mountain formation!"

The remaining dwarfs struggled to obey, but the constant pressure from the halfbreeds tested their discipline to the breaking point. The dwarfs needed a gap in the incessant fighting to perform the maneuver. Anfynn screamed a battle cry and pushed in against the enemy to buy his clansmen some time. The closest halfbreed was busy stabbing at the dwarfs with his lance while his fellows pushed into the shield wall. He didn't notice Anfynn until the Warmaster was on top of him, within the reach of his long weapon. The halfbreed reared back to rake at Anfynn with his front claws. Anfynn growled in triumph as he ducked forward past the claws to avoid the blow. As the halfbreed's claws came down, Anfynn sidestepped out from under the creature's body and smashed its back knee with his warhammer. The halfbreed yowled in pain and fell prone to the ground, and the Helgwin warriors finished it off.

Anfynn whirled to face the next foe and found he was surrounded. Separated from his clansmen, Anfynn fought like a berserker, using the halfbreeds' own bodies for cover where he could, while striking out with his warhammer at the taller, and more exposed, foes. Ironically, in the press of battle, the demonic centaurs couldn't come to grips with the shorter dwarf, and they were forced to pull back. A few of the Helgwin warriors ran into the gap and surrounded their commander before retreating within the safety of the dwarfen formation.

Anfynn had bought the warriors time to redress their ranks to face the orcs. The clan banner was waving bravely in the midst of the dwarfs, but they were now surrounded by foes on all sides. The halfbreeds before him were gathering for another go at the Ironclad. Meanwhile, orcs were pushing in to envelop the dwarfs in the rear. Anfynn growled deep in his throat. He frantically searched for any sign that the Daamuz Ironclad were coming to relieve him, but all he saw was the mass of Abyssal Dwarf Immortal Guard, marching into the gap the halfbreeds had forced between him and his fellow dwarfs. The Overmaster had led his army flawlessly. Anfynn realized with growing frustration and shame that he had played right into the enemy's hands.

The orcs on the flank began yelling with renewed urgency. At first, Anfynn braced himself for another assault, but the orcs weren't surging forward. In fact, the pressure eased as the orcs turned to fight a new enemy. Anfynn pushed his way toward the orcs to get a better view. The savages were being attacked in their rear. Was it Gundrim's soldiers? How was that possible? He'd seen Gundrim's banner fall. No matter, he had to seize the opportunity. He howled and charged recklessly into the savages, his Ironclad close behind. Beset on two sides, the poorly disciplined orcs broke and ran. Anfynn vented his anger and rage on the enemy as they turned to flee, and within moments, he was left standing alone amid a ring of orcish bodies. He looked up from the last one to see Eswer, a young thane from Gundrim's company standing before him.

Anfynn bared his teeth in a grim smile at his clansman and motioned him to join the dwarfen formation. As he passed, Anfynn pulled Eswer close. "Gundrim?" he asked.

Eswer just shook his head 'no' as he went to take his place in the line.

A hollow pit opened in Anfynn's stomach. He grabbed Eswer's arm as he went to leave and spun him to look him in the eye. The two dwarfs stood face to face, the Warmaster struggling with what to say, the young thane meeting his gaze with cautious respect. Finally, Anfynn found his voice.

"I'm sorry," was all he said. As he said the words, he wasn't certain if he was sorry about Gundrim, or about all the dwarfen casualties, or about his battlefield decisions. He was sorry about all of it.

Eswer just nodded and respectfully pulled his arm away. "Sorry is for the living," he said, not unkindly. "We're not done yet, my lord."

With that, he turned and began issuing commands to his clansmen.

Anfynn stared after him, feeling numb in the midst of the chaos. The kid was right. They were still alive, and there was plenty of fighting left to do. A deep anger rose within Anfynn that pushed the sadness of loss away and transformed it into action. He snarled in defiance and dove back into the fray.

* * * * *

Alborz felt a deep satisfaction as the halfbreeds pushed the Helgwin warriors back in disarray. The halfbreeds had easily brushed aside the dwarfen mastiffs. Mounted high on his chariot, Alborz could clearly see the panicked faces of the Ironclad warriors. Dozens were killed in the initial charge, and dozens more were slain in the vicious melee. He watched in mild amusement as their commander fought desperately to keep the formation together. Alborz had to admit the mongrel was a valiant warrior. He would have loved to test his mettle against him, but he had greater concerns.

Orc war horns sounded from atop the ridge, and Alborz saw the slaves assault the dwarfs on the hill. Against the sheer number of orcs, their death was inevitable. He raised his sword in triumph as the dwarfs on the ridge finally broke and were butchered. The orcs streamed down the hill, and Alborz motioned with his free hand as if he were calling down lightning from the sky. His plan had worked flawlessly, and Clan Helgwin's army was surrounded.

A gargoyle swooped down on gray leathery wings and bowed deeply to the Overmaster.

"Speak," Alborz said with a hint of annoyance.

The gargoyle stood but still averted Alborz's gaze. "My lord, troops are arriving from the south."

"Excellent," replied Alborz, "tell the slave drivers to send the orc gore riders into the Helgwin square."

The gargoyle knelt down in fear. "My lord, they aren't orcs. They're dwarfs. Perhaps two hundred, armed with crossbows."

Alborz frowned. Dwarfs? From that direction? How had the mongrels known about the ambushing force? And how did they defeat them? It didn't matter. Clan Helgwin was contained and posed no further threat. He was turning the Daamuz flank. By the time the new dwarfen force arrived, the battle would be over. He motioned to the gargoyle to stand.

"Tell the orc commander to prepare for this new threat. Have him keep the pressure on Helgwin and don't let them recover, understand?"

The gargoyle flew off hurriedly. Alborz brought his attention back to the battlefield and executed his master stroke.

Predictably, the Helgwin dwarfs had tightened their front to receive the charge, leaving a gap between the two clans for the Abyssal Dwarfs to march through. The closest Daamuz warriors were bitterly engaged with the grotesques to their front and had no idea their doom was upon them. Alborz imperiously motioned the Immortal Guard forward. His elite guard, infused with sorcerous power and encased in steel, poured into the gap to assault the dwarfen warriors in the flank.

Alborz begrudgingly admired the Daamuz warriors' discipline. The Ironclad, engaged on two sides, didn't panic, but instead the dwarfs in the rear rushed to face this new threat. For a brief moment, the Immortal Guard were held at bay by the dwarfen shield wall. But it was only a moment. The dwarfs, no matter how disciplined, were no match for the Immortal Guard. The Guard's blood pact to the Overmaster suffused them with dark energy and immense power. Alborz's elite warriors were more like sorcerous machines than flesh and blood. Their partly metal bodies deflected the most lethal blows from the dwarfs, and any wounds they suffered were quickly healed by Ariagful's dark sorcery.

In the face of the carnage, the dwarfs finally broke and fled toward the center. The grotesques killed some as they attempted to run and harried them on their way. Alborz spurred his chariot forward to continue the attack. His heart swelled in exultation as the enemy ran before him, and Alborz laughed. It was a wicked, joyful, almost maniacal laugh, stoked by bloodlust and steeped in his supreme confidence in himself and his abilities. This feeling was what he'd been craving since the invasion. He was alive. He was invincible.

The Daamuz Ironclad continued to fall back, throwing the dwarfen line into chaos. Alborz cried his immortality to the heavens. No one could stand against him. No one could defy his will. This was his land, his destiny. He felt electric, as if he had energy shooting from his hands like some twisted Iron-caster. This joy was something Zareen would never feel. He didn't find purpose in battle like Alborz did. To Zareen, war was a means to an end. To Alborz, battle was an end unto itself. It's where he proved his worth to both dwarfs and gods.

And in this moment, he walked among the gods.

* * * * *

"C'mon, swivel those guns!" Veit yelled to his artillery crews around him. "Get them into position! Yes? Quickly now, quickly."

The artillery crew swarmed around the tall wheels of the cannons and heaved while Veit looked on in agitation from his perch atop a nearby boulder. Veit's leg was still in a splint, and it had been an ordeal to climb up the rock. From his position at the edge of the woods, he could see down the entire battle line as it wavered to and fro. Dinnidek had committed the remainder of his reserves, and it had pushed the grotesque advance back. The Ironclad were holding the grotesques at bay for now, but it wouldn't last much longer. Time was running out.

Veit's smaller reserve cannons were nestled back within the treeline, concealed from the enemy by a veil of underbrush. The engineer had worried that they would be noticed, but the grotesques, for all their ferocity, were simple beasts. They were consumed by the prey in front of them. Despite being hidden, Veit's crew only had one opportunity at surprise. If the barrage didn't do enough damage, the grotesques would assault their position and end them quick.

One of the small cannons was aimed directly down the rear of the grotesques, and the gun crew were loading it with cannister shot. The other gun, however, was stuck in the underbrush, making it difficult to maneuver. A trio of dwarfs were clustered around each wheel, heaving with all their might.

"All stop!" Veit called in exasperation. The dwarfs obeyed and ceased their efforts. He'd need to physically show them what he wanted. Veit kept eye contact with them while he untied the lacings on his splint. "I'll be down there in a second. In the meantime, load the cannon with the grapeshot, double payload." Veit clawed at the strings and addressed the other gun crew. "Single canister on that one, yes?"

The gun crew acknowledged the order.

"Good," said Veit as he undid the last tie and removed the splint. "Have a second canister ready if we get a second shot."

He slid gingerly down the rock, making sure to land on his good leg. He took a tentative step or two before heading to the mired gun. He stepped up to one of the giant wheels and grabbed hold of it, planting his good foot solidly in the ground.

"C'mon, everybody, grab a spot." The dwarfs all gathered around. "On my signal, we rock forward, then back. Let the momentum of the gun carry it back, then push forward again. Yes?" The dwarfs grunted in reply. "Alright, one, two, three, pusssssshhhhhh!"

Veit leaned into the wheel, and the cannon barely shimmied forward.

"Now, let it go. That's it. Now, pusssshhhhhh!"

He put his shoulder into the wheel with all his strength. The wheel moved slightly more this time. They let it rock back, and again Veit yelled the order to heave. This time, the right wheel of the chassis gave way and the gun barrel spun wildly to the left. Veit was thrown off balance and landed squarely on his bad leg. He grunted as pain lanced up to the back of his head. A nearby crewman urgently asked if he was alright, but Veit waved him off.

"I'm fine. Pull back on that wheel. Yes?" The dwarfs obeyed and finally the gun was in position.

Veit leaned against the gun wheel for a few heartbeats as he fought a bout of nausea from the pain. One of his clansmen handed him his cane, and Veit took it with a strained smile of thanks. He stood straight and limped behind the cannon to double check the sighting. All he saw was grotesque bodies, the Ironclad safely out of the blast.

"Gun number one, you fire first. Yes? Then gun number two, you fire five seconds after. Yes?"

The gun crew acknowledged the order. He took a few steps back as he called for the dwarfs to prepare to fire, keeping an eye out on the battle line. Veit's leg throbbed with pain, and he leaned hard on his cane. The closest grotesque, a giant feline thing that was part sea monster, was less than one hundred yards away. He gave the cannons one last glance, liked what he saw, stuck his finger in his ear closest to the guns, and gave the order to fire.

The first cannon went off with a blast of black smoke and a peal of thunder. The canister and grape shot, composed of dozens of tiny projectiles, shredded the foliage in front of the gun barrels on its way into the flank of the grotesques. The metal shrapnel tore the closest enemy to ribbons, spraying blood and gore everywhere. Some of the abominations were gravely wounded and reared up in agony, or fled in rage and pain, revealing the creatures further down the line. A few seconds later, the second cannon fired into the fresh targets with similar results.

Veit allowed himself a brief moment of grim satisfaction before yelling to his crew to reload the guns.

"Hurry now. No time to waste, yes?"

The artillerymen worked quickly and efficiently, and the gun was swabbed, primed, and reloaded with fresh canister in less than two minutes. Normally, Veit would slow the rate of fire to allow the gun barrel to cool, especially after the extra payload of gunpowder, but there was no time. It didn't matter if they ruined the gun as long as they lived.

Meanwhile, one of the Abyssal Dwarf slave drivers had rallied a few of the grotesques and was gathering them for a charge at the cannons. Veit pulled his pistol from his belt and pointed it at the enemy.

"Number one, keep firing down the line! Number two, pivot right fifteen degrees. See that chariot? Let's remove it, yes?"

The dwarfen crew pulled on the cannon with gusto.

"C'mon, no time. No time," Veit exhorted the crew nervously. He needn't have worried. The Abyssal Dwarf had just begun his charge when the cannon fired. The grapeshot shattered the chariot, sending splinters of wood, metal, and bone into the air, killing the slave driver and the grotesques instantly.

"Excellent!" he yelled. "Back to the line, yes? Fire at will."

The two cannons kept up the brutal barrage into the grotesques, Veit offering encouragement and direction to the crew. Within a few moments, the grotesques in this part of the field, with no slave drivers to propel them, broke from the withering fire. The Ironclad cheered in triumph as the enemy fled back to the mountains. Veit slapped the closest dwarf, his face and hands blackened with powder stains, on the back with pride.

"That's it! That's the stuff!"

He felt a wave of relief, and he leaned heavily on his cane as his tense muscles loosened in response.

Veit was thinking he should put his brace back on when he felt a shift in the army's mood. The cheering from the Ironclad died and was replaced by a murmur, then shouts of alarm. A great commotion could be heard from the army's left flank. The dwarfen warriors nearest to the woods were turning in that direction. Veit couldn't see past them to ascertain what was happening.

"Someone give me a hand up," he asked as he tried to mount one of the cannon chassis. The shouting was getting louder and was now mirrored by a tempest coming from the north of the woods. It sounded like a thunderstorm, shaking the ground under Veit's feet.

Diessa, Veit thought to himself with a mixture of apprehension and bemusement.

With some fumbling, he finally perched on top of the cannon while holding one of the oversized wheels for balance. The extra three feet in height gave him an expansive view of the battlefield. To the north, the grotesques had fled directly into the oncoming Abyssal Dwarf warriors, fouling their advance, and even attacking them in their frenzy.

Further down, Veit could just make out the chaos in the ranks. It looked like the entire left flank of the dwarfen line had collapsed, and Veit could see Dinnidek and Tordek, standing on their ammo cart, trying desperately to mount a defense against this new threat. The closest Ironclad were forming ranks and moving quickly down the line. Would it be enough? And how much time would the dwarfs have before the Blacksouls regained their discipline? Veit's leg throbbed in pain as he wracked his brain for some ploy, some plan, that could save them.

* * * * *

The Stone Guard whooped and taunted the fleeing ratkin. Lady Diessa's elementals, with the Shieldbreakers, had repelled the vermin charge. For now, the birch forest belonged to the dwarfs. Out on the plain, the crazed Iron-caster, with his gargantuan obsidian golems, was lighting the treeline ablaze with green fire while more ratkin mobbed together for another assault. The elementals, in contrast, stood still as statues, a bastion of order and sanity against the chaos gnawing at the edges. Bruon, Diessa, and their compatriots had stayed behind the line of elementals during the fighting, close enough to witness the battle but not directly in harm's way. Diessa was seated cross-legged on the ground, still staring off into space with her blindfold held lightly in her hand, Gwel standing guard close by. Bruon had watched Diessa intently during the fighting. As the morning went on, she had recovered control over her body and didn't need Bruon to lead her by the hand anymore. But it seemed to Bruon that Diessa was still relying on Gwel to be her eyes and ears, and maybe she was tapping into other senses that Bruon didn't understand.

The Stone Guard had surrounded Diessa during the fighting, ready to kill any of the ratkin who got close, but the vermin hadn't made it back to their position. At one point, some of the Stone Guard had asked to join the Shieldbreakers in the counterattack, but Bruon had forbade them from joining in. Their sacred oath demanded that they stay by Lady Diessa's side. Some of the warriors had grumbled, but they begrudgingly obeyed. Bruon couldn't blame them. His fingers twitched anxiously as he watched the battle from the sidelines; but he knew his honor demanded that he stay put. He was not foolish enough to put his bloodlust ahead of Lady Diessa's safety.

Bruon's thoughts were interrupted as the ratkin, who had recovered their courage, screeched their war cries and charged into the woods. Behind the vermin, the Obsidian Golems plodded forward, making the ground tremble as they walked. The golems were in a tight formation surrounding the Iron-caster and his flying nightmare. The Abyssal Sorcerer screamed to the ratkin, "Find the stone-priest! Bring his body to me!"

Bruon kept one eye on the enemy and the other on Diessa. Once the fighting began, the priestess had closed her eyes, as if concentrating. Her eyes fluttered, and her eyeballs seemed to rapidly move below her closed eyelids. In response, the further earth elementals began moving toward this new threat, flowing between the birch trees like water.

The ratkin reached the woods first, pouring into the treeline with a frenzy. Unlike last time, the vermin avoided the elementals and instead ran past the stone behemoths where they could, penetrating deeper within the woods in their search for the stone priestess. Bruon couldn't see Daerun, but he heard him exhorting the Shieldbreakers to the countercharge. Moments later, the Obsidian Golems crashed into the birch forest, smashing tree trunks and shattering branches. Some of the trees collapsed, or were bowled over, and their flaming canopies rained fire down onto the stone behemoths below, killing the unfortunate ratkin nearby. A hot wind, suffused with the smell of sulfur, wafted burning embers over Bruon's head.

Bruon stood in mild shock, transfixed by the sheer scale of the violence. The Obsidian golems were huge, overshadowing the earth elementals. Their bodies were suffused with magma roiling underneath their exteriors of black razor-sharp stone. The golems were extremely broad and hunched, with overly long arms that made their pony-sized hands drag on the ground. Their size and fury gave them immense power, and they seemed to destroy everything they touched. A golem raised both hands high and dropped them onto the head of the closest elemental, who tried to deflect the savage blow, but the obsidian golem's fists disintegrated the elemental's raised arm. A second strike shattered the elemental, spraying stones across the ground.

Once inside the woods, the golems' charge lost momentum. Their hulking bodies were forced to push the trees aside or knock them over to keep moving. The elementals, though smaller, outnumbered the Obsidian Golems, and they converged on their position like a pack of wolves. Instead of destroying the birches, their bodies flowed around the trees, barely disturbing the white papery bark as they passed. Diessa raised her palms in front of her, eyes still closed. She wove her hands in sinewy complex patterns, mimicking the elemental's movements. Bruon watched in fascination as Diessa waved her hands to the right, then left. From his vantage point, Bruon saw one of the tall elementals move to its right, then flow to the left to avoid a small knot of dwarfen warriors. The elementals formed a cordon around the golems, hoping to contain them and protect the Shieldbreakers.

Diessa pulled her palms back, and the elementals responded by stepping back further into the woods. The obsidian golems followed them, trying to come to grips with their enemy. They swung wildly, their massive arms trailing black smoke, but the elementals continued to move back, using the birch trees to shield them from the crushing blows. Bruon marveled as one golem threw what he could only describe as a haymaker at one of the smaller elementals. The golem's aim was true, and it would have decapitated the smaller foe, but the elemental side-stepped through a pair of birch trees, a few leaves falling gently to the ground. The golem's punch impacted a tree trunk instead, which absorbed most of the force. The elemental grabbed at the golem's arm and pulled it straight to the side while another earth spirit head-butted the outstretched arm near the bicep. The golem's arm snapped, and red-hot magma poured from the arm like thick viscous blood. The golem reared back, its 'mouth' gaped open, and it roared in pain and rage.

While the obsidian golems were being stymied by the forest, the Shieldbreakers were facing off with the ratkin. Neither the dwarfs nor the ratkin could withstand the savage power of the stone combatants, and they gave them a wide berth. Once inside the forest, the ratkin had lost their cohesion, and the entire wood was a swirling melee. The ravenous forest fire was spreading through the canopy, sometimes catching on the papery birch bark and licking greedily down the tree trunks.

The Stone Guard stood, weapons ready, as the fighting progressed closer and closer to Diessa.

"Steady!" yelled Bruon, above the twin roars of battle and the growing forest fire. A pack of ratkin warriors armed with halberds had caught sight of the stone priestess and were coming their way. "Stone Guard, prepare yourselves!"

The Ironclad gathered closer around Diessa, shields at the ready. The ratkin commander raised a wickedly twisted war horn and gave a shrill call, summoning more vermin to their location. Bruon saw a second group of ratkin approaching from the other direction.

"Form circle, around the lady!"

The clansmen were just getting into formation when the world erupted in heat and flame. The Iron-caster and his antlered dragon crashed down to earth through the forest canopy mere yards away, with a rain of fiery tree limbs and smaller branches. The Iron-caster's eyes flashed as he turned toward Diessa, sitting serenely on the mossy ground. He pulled his mount's giant avian head to face the Stone Guard. In contrast to the Iron-caster's almost crazed visage, the creature's eyes were completely dead, and its sunken skin clung to its skull like a parody of the birch bark all around. It opened its beaked maw and screeched, piercing Bruon's eardrums and momentarily freezing him in place. Bruon felt terror well up within him, but he steadfastly held his ground. He looked down at Diessa, still weaving her hands as she orchestrated the elemental's movements. He bit the inside of his lip and forced himself to look up again into the monster's deathly face.

"I'm not running," Bruon yelled defiantly to the Iron-caster, to the Stone Guard, and to his fear. "I made an oath. *We* made an oath!"

The Stone Guard cried with ragged voices, tight with fear. Bruon looked back down at Diessa. The elementals continued in their desperate fight against the golems. He felt, more than saw, the Iron-caster spur his demonic mount to attack.

She's our only hope, he thought. *And we're hers.*

He shouted a battle cry as the ratkin closed in.

"For the Stone Maiden!"

* * * * *

Diessa's mind floated among the earth spirits, her consciousness flitting from one elemental to another. She'd never experienced anything like this. When she worked with the spirits in the past, she had only communed with a few at a time. But now she was conducting a symphony. It was like being in a giant room with dozens of small windows, all with a different view of the same landscape. If she stood in the center of the room, she could see a little bit of each window, but she had to stand next to a particular window to see the entire vista spread out before her and close herself to the other perspectives. When she melded her mind with one of the spirits, she felt the elemental's body as her own. The feeling was all consuming, and she could barely perceive her physical body. She heard the Stone Guard battling around her body as if they were echoes of ghosts from the distant past. In her mind, the battle with the obsidian golems was infinitely more real, and more urgent.

The elementals surrounded the obsidian golems, redirecting their attack away from the dwarfs. A few of the elementals had been destroyed in the initial charge, but Diessa was now guiding the remaining spirits to work in harmony. She pushed her consciousness into one of the larger elementals and deftly dodged a golem's clumsy attack before melding her hands together and chopping down with both hands into the golem's shoulder. The black obsidian cracked, and the golem was forced to kneel. Her mind jumped to another nearby elemental and she threw an uppercut into the golem's descending head, snapping it back with such force that it shattered the creature's jaw. She ordered the two earth spirits to swarm the downed golem before pulling away with her mind.

A group of four elementals were fighting a pair of golems amid a pile of burning logs and stumps. The golems were getting the best of their smaller opponents, pushing them back and inflicting serious damage to their stone bodies. Diessa channeled energy from the ground into the earth spirits themselves, strengthening their connection with the Earth Mother. The spirits used this energy to bind their broken bodies tightly together, and the cracks and fissures from the golem's attacks slowly closed and reformed stronger than before. She fused with one of the spirits and picked up a flaming tree, the stones of her 'hand' flowing around the downed birch, stretching to encompass the entirety of the thick trunk. She swung the tree up into the face of the closest golem and knocked it off balance. It fell backward with a thunderous crash. The other spirits piled atop its torso and began tearing at its legs, pulling it apart piece by piece.

She shifted to a group of three elementals who were barely defending themselves. She pushed her vision into one of the elementals just in time to see a fist careen into her forehead. Her head and upper torso shattered, and she was momentarily stunned as her body crumbled to the ground. As the body disintegrated, her senses flew into another spirit. She was disoriented at the wild shift in perspective, but she had the presence of mind to reflexively duck under another attack. She didn't so much as duck as she allowed her body to sink effortlessly into the ground like a person bobbing in the water before rising again to counterattack. She pulled energy into her body, giving it speed and precision. The elemental threw a quick combination aiming for the golem's chest before shifting to the inner thigh. She focused her energy into the punch, and it struck with such force that the golem's leg shattered. Red magma spurted from the stump and sprayed the surrounding trees, lighting them on fire as the creature fell lifeless in a heap.

Wherever Diessa focused her attention, the elementals fought with strength, purpose, and resilience, and they were more than a match for the golems, impeded as they were by the birch trees. But she couldn't be everywhere, and the elementals were taking casualties whenever she pulled her consciousness to another part of the fight, leaving fewer and fewer earth spirits. Her own will was starting to tire. Her physical body wasn't meant to channel so much raw energy at once. When she jumped to the different perspectives, she was having problems keeping track of the overall battle, and she had to take more time in between jumps to regather herself. She was being spread too thin and was starting to lose her individuality again. She just needed a few more minutes to defeat the golems and free the elementals to hunt easier prey.

She was dimly aware that the Stone Guard were under attack, the ratkin coming closer and closer to her real body. But if she left now, if she came back to her body and abandoned the elementals, the obsidian golems would eventually destroy them all. Just a few more moments, that was all she needed.

* * * * *

Daerun hacked away at the last ratkin and finished it off with a pair of quick strikes. He glanced back at Felwyr and his Shieldbreakers to see how they were doing. The dwarfs owned this part of the field. Ratkin bodies were piled all around them, and the Shieldbreakers were finishing off the wounded. Further away, near the forest's edge, the elementals were barely keeping the obsidian golems busy. They were wearing the golems down, but they were taking casualties. For every golem that fell, a few earth spirits disintegrated in turn. Dare kept a wary eye on the fight. If Diessa couldn't lead the earth spirits to victory, the remaining golems would play havoc with his men.

Further away, the Shieldbreakers were engaged with the ratkin all throughout the woods. There was no open ground to form up into big units, so the fighting had degenerated into a swirling chaotic melee. Dare had gathered a dozen dwarfs and was leading them to wherever the fighting was fiercest. He spared a glance to where Diessa and her Stone Guard were fighting, surrounded on three sides by a throng of ratkin. Bruon's soldiers were doing a good job of holding the ratkin off, but he could see they needed help.

"Daamuz," he called to his Shieldbreakers while pointing to the Stone Guard, "follow me!"

As the dwarfs began jogging toward Diessa, a meteor seemed to fall from the sky. Flaming tree limbs crashed to the forest floor, followed by the Iron-caster and his monstrous mount, violently scattering fiery debris everywhere. The creature had its wings folded in tightly to descend through the trees, and it landed heavily on its clawed legs. It recovered and unfurled its wings, blasting the area with heat from the smoldering trees and shooting glowing embers high into the air. The Shieldbreakers flinched away from the conflagration.

"Sweet Earth Mother!" Daerun exclaimed in alarm as he shielded his eyes from the blast of hot air. When he recovered, all he could see was Diessa, and a steely calm came over him. He yelled for the Shieldbreakers to charge this new foe.

One of the ratkin, who had turned away from the beast's acrid stench, saw Daerun coming and screeched a warning to the other vermin. They hastily turned toward the Shieldbreakers and readied their spears. The ratkin leader wisely pulled his warriors closer together to present a wall of spearpoints to the dwarfs. Behind them, the Iron-caster, riding high atop the antlered nightmare, towered over dwarfs and ratkin alike.

"Stay together!" yelled Daerun. "Slow advance! We go in as one!"

The Shieldbreakers slowed their charge to avoid skewering themselves on the enemy spears. Once they'd lined up, Daerun led them methodically forward. The ratkin jabbed their spears toward the dwarfs, aiming for any spots not covered by the heavy dwarfen armor. Daerun locked eyes with one of the creatures and carefully advanced, almost goading him into attacking. Once he was within striking distance, he saw his foe tense up just before it thrust its spear into Daerun's face. Years of fighting had taught Daerun to look for that tell-tale look in the eyes, and he easily dodged the attack. Once inside the spear's reach, he rushed forward, jamming the ratkin's weapon and stopping another strike. Daerun swung his hammer at the enemy, but the filthy creature deflected the blow with the haft of his spear. Dare swung again, and the vermin attempted to block the attack with its spear a second time. The wooden spear cracked as the two weapons met, and the shaft buckled in the ratkin's hand. His enemy could only look with dread at the pieces of its broken weapon as Daerun landed the killing blow.

The Shieldbreakers were slowly chewing through the ratkin spears, but more and more enemy warriors were joining the fray. Daerun growled in frustration. They needed to get past the rabble and join up with the Stone Guard. Meanwhile, the antlered beast was having its way with Bruon's clansmen. The creature batted at the dwarfs almost playfully like a nightmarish cat swatting at mice. The beast raked its paw at one Stone Guard, its claw puncturing both the shield and the arm underneath. The dwarf screamed in agony as the beast raised its paw high into the air and inspected the dwarf, dangling limply from his shield, with its dead eyes. It sniffed at it before callously shaking its paw, throwing the dwarf's body back among the burning trees.

Daerun's horror turned into a hot rage in his chest, and he redoubled his attack. The ratkin, trapped between the dwarfs before them and the living nightmare behind them, fought like demons. Dare took his free hand and contemptuously batted a ratkin's spear aside before savagely crushing its ribs with his hammer. The dwarf next to him took a spear point in the mouth and fell dead. Daerun killed the ratkin as it tried to free its spear from the dwarf's skull.

Through the press of bodies, Dare saw Bruon step toward the nightmare, shield raised defiantly as he slashed down with his axe. The antlered beast reared up in the air and roared in pain, the Iron-caster barely holding on.

It looked like Bruon's men had some fight left in them. Daerun spared a glance behind him just in time to see an obsidian golem tear one of the elementals to pieces. Half of the earth spirit's body shattered into fragments, and the golem used the intact half to bludgeon another elemental to death. *Hold on, sis, I'm coming.*

* * * * *

"Hold your ground! Hold your ground, dammit!" Dinnidek screamed to his clansmen.

The Abyssal Dwarf army had turned the flank, driving the dwarfen line into chaos. Warriors streamed past Din's ammo cart in various stages of retreat. The Ironclad had turned to face the Immortal Guard, but they were being relentlessly pushed back into their comrades. With grotesques to the front and this new enemy to their side, the dwarfs were under too much pressure to effectively fight back. Dinnidek watched in growing frustration tinged with fear as the Immortal Guard effortlessly advanced toward him. A wounded dwarf ran past clutching his side, his shield lost somewhere on the field. His left leg was slick with blood coming from under his bent breastplate. He had a distant look in his eyes, staring at nothing. Tordek called to him to turn and fight, but the wounded dwarf took no heed and kept walking, like some undead zombie.

Dinnidek jumped down off the ammo cart and reached for one of the retreating warriors, a young dwarf, just into his manhood. Din pulled him around to look him in the eye. The young dwarf had lost his helmet in the fighting, his hair matted to one side of his head with dried blood. His deep brown eyes were fatigued and scared, and he went to pull his arm away before he fully realized who had grabbed him. Dinnidek held on tightly to his forearm, not letting him break the gaze. There were Ironclad falling back all around them, but Din focused on just this one. As they locked eyes, the young warrior's anger at being grabbed melted away, leaving a mixture of fear and shame.

"It's alright, son," Din said, not unkindly. "I'm scared too. But there's nowhere else to go. This is all we've got. We leave here now, then the clan is dead." He motioned vaguely at the battle all around them. The young dwarf looked furtively before he closed his eyes and hung his head. "Our ancestors are watching. We must stand here. For them. For us."

The Ironclad nodded and exhaled shakily before looking Din in the face. Dinnidek saw the same fear, but it was joined by a spark, a hint of defiance.

"That's it, son." Din gave a wan smile and patted the dwarf on the shoulder. "Stay here with me." He pointed at some of the retreating dwarfs. "If you stay, if enough stay, then they will too. Alright?"

The Ironclad raised his axe and rolled his neck.

"That's it. Will you fight with me?"

"I will," the young dwarf said, so quietly that Din could barely hear it over the clash of battle. "I'm sorry, my lord."

Din squeezed the Ironclad's arm and waved it off with his free hand.

"It's alright. What matters is what you do now." The dwarf gritted his teeth and nodded. "Now, get me one more. Then you two get me two more. Understand? We make our stand here."

The dwarf said nothing, but he shifted his axe to his off hand and snatched the arm of another warrior passing by. Din spared one more look at him before he mounted the ammo cart. The young dwarf was shouting and pointing, cajoling any dwarf that trotted by. Here and there one of the dwarfs would stop and turn, sometimes in shame, sometimes with new determination or anger. Soon fewer and fewer Ironclad were fleeing past until the ammo cart became a rallying point for the retreating dwarfs. Tordek waved the clan banner proudly in the sun while Dinnidek exhorted his clansmen to turn and fight.

The Ironclad line stiffened and halted the Immortal Guard advance, just yards away from the command cart. Though the dwarfs were holding them back, the Immortal Guard were taking minimal casualties. The infernal sorcery that propelled their metallic bodies healed the most grievous wounds that the Ironclad could deal. Dinnidek chewed his lip in frustration. The Ironclad couldn't hold on forever.

Beyond the shield wall, behind the Immortal Guard, Dinnidek saw the Abyssal Dwarf Overmaster approaching on his chariot. The enemy commander was resplendent in his blackened armor and white linen cloak, a look of supreme confidence on his face. He pulled his chariot to a stop and dismounted to join the fray. The Overmaster was taller than the other dwarfs, and his height, combined with his ornate helmet, made him easy to track as he moved toward the front of the line. Dinnidek felt a hollow pit in his stomach. He couldn't see the details, but when the Overmaster reached the shield wall, the dwarfen line buckled. Within moments, the Ironclad were forced to pull back to keep their cohesion.

Dinnidek felt the morale shift, quickly sapping his clansmen's tenuous courage. If the Ironclad broke now, it would be the end of this mad scheme. The end of his ambitions. The end of his clan. He would be forced to stand before his ancestors as the last of his line. The last chief of Clan Daamuz. For a moment, he had the same feeling of helplessness as when he was on the beach. In response, a wave of defiance welled up in him. He growled with anger and screamed for his men to hold, as if he could will them to stand their ground.

The Ironclad kept retreating, step by step, until their backs were up against the ammo cart. The Overmaster looked like he was barely moving as he fought with one of the dwarfen warriors. His sword flicked effortlessly, drawing his opponent's guard away from his true target. When he feinted, it was with his eyes as much as his sword, and he fought with a quiet nonchalance that enraged Dinnidek as his soldiers fell. The Overmaster gazed up at Dinnidek with a look of absolute disdain that cut through Din like a knife. He kept looking at him as he blocked a sword thrust from one of the Ironclad before callously gutting the dwarf warrior. The remaining Ironclad fell back once again, this time around the cart.

The Overmaster sneered at Dinnidek and raised his sword in a mock salute before approaching the wagon. Dinnidek grunted his battle cry and swung downward with his axe at the enemy commander. The Overmaster easily parried the axe, and Dinnidek was forced to step back to keep his balance. The Overmaster nimbly mounted the cart and faced off with Din and Tordek. He raised his sword once more and smiled with a mad gleam in his eye. Din growled deep in his throat and raised his axe in return.

* * * * *

Daerun slew the last ratkin and sprinted toward the antlered nightmare, the other Shieldbreakers close behind. Around him, the elementals still battled furiously, but in contrast Diessa sat serenely on the ground before the infernal creature surrounded by her Stone Guard. The dwarf warriors were barely keeping the monster at bay, and no matter how hard the Iron-caster tried, he couldn't cajole the beast to move within striking distance of Diessa.

Bruon was standing directly in front of Deese, fighting for his, and her, life. The monster swung one of his massive claws at Bruon, but the dwarf knelt and held his shield before him with both hands, bracing for the impact. The strike bowled him over, but he effectively deflected it and rolled with the impact. The Shieldbreakers rushed in to fill the gap where Bruon had been. The Iron-caster screamed and kicked at the beast's sides with his spurs. The antlered lizard raised its saurian body and unfurled its giant leathery wings before swiping at the dwarfs with its front paws, easily sweeping them aside. Like Bruon, some were able to dodge or deflect the blow, but others weren't so lucky. As the monster's claw flew by, Daerun jumped forward and struck at the beast's shoulder. He landed a solid blow, and the monster screeched. Dare jumped back just out of range as the creature ponderously counter-attacked.

Further away, Daerun could see the few remaining earth elementals keeping the obsidian golems busy. Some of the bolder ratkin were moving in to assist, but the majority of vermin were keeping their distance from the titanic clash. A golem wrapped its overly long arms around one of the elementals and picked it up in the air before throwing it deeper into the woods. The earth spirit's body morphed in mid-air to flow around the birch trees and even shifted the boulders of its body around to create legs closer to the ground. The elemental landed heavily on its wide stone feet before shaking its head and charging back headlong at the golems. Nearby, Dare noticed Diessa shake her head as well.

Once again, the antlered nightmare lashed out at the dwarfs, and once again the dwarfs did their best to dodge out of the way before attacking at the nightmare's less armored underside. Daerun dropped onto his stomach just in time as the creature's claws whistled through the air overhead, then he sprang back up to attack. Across from him, Felwyr rushed forward past the beast's paw and struck it square in the neck. The creature screeched and rolled its head before it in a frenzy, sending its antlers seemingly everywhere. Daerun was forced to scramble back, away from the deadly tines, and he lost sight of Fel.

The creature turned its great avian head back toward Daerun to reveal Felwyr's body, entangled among its wicked antlers. Dare barely dodged back in time as the beast's horns flew by. Felwyr's right arm was pinned between a pair of the mighty tines, his feet scrabbling for purchase on the side of the beast's neck as he tried desperately to gain some leverage and relieve the pressure. Felwyr screamed in pain as he clubbed weakly at the nightmare's skull with his off hand. Daerun yelled in dismay and went to attack, but he came up short as the creature swung its head back around, sending dwarfs scattering.

All but one. Bruon clanged his axe against his shield twice to get his courage up as he stared intently at the beast's head to get his timing right. Felwyr was now hanging limply as the nightmare's rack of horns swung by. Right as it went past, Bruon sprung forward and grabbed at the base of the antlers that imprisoned Felwyr with his shield arm. Bruon's grip was true, and he used the beast's momentum to swing his legs up onto one of the other antlers. Perched on top of the beast's head, he set his feet, and his axe came down in a flurry of quick strikes that cracked, split, and finally separated most of the nightmare's antlers on the left side of its head. The horns fell with a thud to the ground, along with Fel. The creature screeched in rage and shook its head violently. Bruon held on for dear life and pulled his axe back for another strike, this time at the beast's eyes.

The Iron-caster had been surprised by Bruon's suicidal attack, but it didn't last long. The Abyssal Dwarf sorcerer stood tall in his saddle; his free hand wreathed in green fire. Daerun screamed a warning, but it was too late. The Iron-caster pointed at Bruon, heedless of how close he was to the beast's face, and released his wrath upon him. A wave of green fire erupted from the Iron-caster's outstretched hand to engulf Bruon. The sickly flames greedily burnt Bruon's tabard, melted his armor, and consumed his flesh with supernatural speed. Daerun was sickened to his core as Bruon's charred body fell lifelessly to the forest floor.

* * * * *

"Lord Daamuz," the Overmaster said mockingly, his lip curled up in a sneer. "Last lord of Clan Daamuz. I am Alborz, Lord of Llyngyr Cadw." He emphasized the title with relish. "Dinnidek, is it? You're too young to be Drohzon. It's a shame, I never had the chance to kill your father. But I guess you'll have to do. I assume that your mongrel siblings are about?"

Dinnidek's eyes widened in surprise at the Overmaster's words.

Alborz waved his sword at the battlefield.

"Oh, don't look so shocked. I read your name in the clan histories. I studied everything that your clan left behind when they fled before me. Of course, that was before I destroyed it all."

Din's eyes narrowed, and a white hot rage grew in his breast.

"I mean, I never imagined you'd actually return. We defeated you and your kind so easily, after all."

"Sorry to disappoint you," Din replied, heatedly. "You'll find that Clan Daamuz is hard to kill."

Din heard Tordek behind him drop his shield from his non-banner hand and pull his axe, ready to fight. All around the cart, Ironclad were fighting for their lives against the Immortal Guard. Alborz pointed subtly toward the melee, and it drew Din's gaze. He watched in horrid fascination as an Ironclad skillfully struck his foe in the side, burying his axe through the Immortal Guard's armored breastplate. The Abyssal Dwarf didn't bother to block the swing and just took the blow to get close enough to run the Ironclad through.

The Overmaster motioned expansively at the carnage happening just feet away. "Are you?"

Dinnidek's rage boiled over, and he attacked Alborz with a series of quick axe strikes. The Overmaster moved sinuously, always just out of reach of the axe's edge, deflecting each strike deftly with the flat of his blade. The Abyssal Dwarf parried the last strike and turned it into a counterattack that sent Din back on his heels. Alborz didn't follow up but stood in a ready stance while he allowed Dinnidek to fully recover.

"Do you actually think your precious clan has any power here?" said the Overmaster. He pointed at himself with his free hand. "I am the only power here."

He slid forward on the balls of his feet with a series of cuts and stabs that pushed Din back into Tordek, who was trying to get in a position to help. Again, Alborz backed away and let Dinnidek regain his footing. He was playing with him like a cat with a field mouse, batting at its prey to make it feel terror and despair.

Din felt the anger grow inside him, and he gave in to it. He screamed and came at Alborz with a furious flurry of axe strikes. His foe fell back a few steps before the onslaught, barely parrying each attack. Dinnidek grinned madly as he bashed the fiend back with his shield into the railing of the cart. For a brief second, the Overmaster's eyes grew wide with alarm as the back of his boot slid off the end of the platform. Din swung his axe down at Alborz's helmet with a scream that held all of his pent-up anger, fear, and doubt.

Despite the momentary look of fear, Alborz recovered quickly and deftly dodged the blow as he spun nimbly past Din. Dinnidek's axe shattered the cart rail, tangling his weapon in the splintered wood, and he barely turned in time to deflect his enemy's return sword stroke with his shield. Alborz was now between Din and Tordek, who finally had a clear line of attack. The bodyguard was slowed by the clan banner, which he held in his off hand, but he attacked while Din wasted precious seconds wrenching his axe free.

The Overmaster dismissively turned his back on Dinnidek and parried Tordek's attack before pulling an ornate pistol from his belt with his free hand. Din could only yell a warning as Alborz cocked back the hammer and fired into Tordek's chest. A flash of fire and smoke, a deafening sound, and Tordek fell backward off the cart onto the parched ground below. Scores of metal chains jangled as the clan banner landed on the cart bed.

"No!" Dinnidek cried in despair.

The Overmaster turned to face Din and contemptuously tossed the still smoking pistol onto the ground by Tordek's body.

Din savagely attacked, but the fiend stood his ground this time. He casually sidestepped as he deflected the strikes with his sword.

"Dinnidek," said Alborz as he parried another strike, "there is no hope. Your clan has failed."

Din took a few deep breaths and came forward again, but this time Alborz swiftly counterattacked and immediately put him on the defensive.

"I told you, I am the power here." The Overmaster took on a fencing stance, his sword held lightly before him, his back hand raised in the air. He motioned toward the battlefield with his free hand. "Your clan warriors, no matter how strong, cannot defeat my Immortal Guard, Dinnidek."

The fiend stabbed out with a flourish, forcing Din to clumsily block the strike with his shield.

"The Immortal Guard serve me, the true Lord of Llyngyr Cadw. As long as I live, they cannot die."

Din swung at his foe's outstretched arm, but the Overmaster deftly struck out and cut Din's forearm in return. The axe clattered to the floorboards, and Din barely blocked the next strike with his shield.

"That is true power, my young pup," mocked Alborz.

The fiend rained sword strokes down on Din's shield, bending the metal rim and sending chips of wood flying. Din pushed against Alborz in desperation to make some space to maneuver. The Overmaster was forced back a step, and Din went by him toward the back of the cart. From this position, he saw Tordek clearly, lying on his back, his breastplate bent inward, a small trail of blood leaking from beneath his armor to be lapped greedily by the thirsty ground. One of his legs was bent, and it moved weakly as Tordek breathed heavily in pain.

"When I left my weak clan behind," said Alborz, conversationally, "I was finally able to embrace the true power of Ariagful."

The Overmaster savagely attacked Din, forcing him down onto his knees before him.

"You've put up a good fight, young pup, but this is my land," he declared as he struck Din's shield with his sword for emphasis.

"My hold."

Another strike shattered the left half of Din's shield. He looked around in desperation for any weapon he could find.

"Your clan is dead, Lord Dinnidek Daamuz."

Alborz shattered what remained of Din's shield with a final savage cut of his sword.

Din's heart raced with panic. He was on all fours, prostrate before the Overmaster. Alborz stood above him, crowned resplendently in sunlight, his Immortal Guard implacably pushing back the Daamuz clan army. He shook the remnants of his shield from his left arm, and his right hand grasped the haft of the clan banner, lying crumpled before him. He set his feet under him and grasped the banner with both hands. Alborz slipped forward, ready to end Dinnidek and the Clan Daamuz.

Alborz raised his sword for the killing blow.

Din sprang up defiantly and swept the banner forward off the cart floor in a desperate, hopeless attack, silver and gold chains trailing behind, glinting in the sunlight. He knew the attack was too slow, that Alborz would gut him before he could finish his swing. He screamed in helpless rage and defiance as the banner slowly came around toward Alborz.

He felt something whiz by his ear.

Alborz's face blanched in pain as his shoulder exploded in blood. He staggered back a half step and dropped his sword.

All the arrogance bled from his face in disbelief as Dinnidek finished his swing and struck home. The banner's crosspiece connected squarely with the side of Alborz's helmet, snapping the Overmaster's head to the side. The Lord of Llyngyr Cadw crumpled lifelessly onto the cart floor as chains and keys went flying everywhere. Dinnidek spun wildly and landed again on his knees as the banner fell from his hands onto the ground below.

Din gasped for breath, still amazed at the miracle that had kept him alive. He looked down at Alborz's body, his white linen cape tinged bright red around his shoulder, and his head bent at an unnatural angle with glassy eyes staring blankly at the sky. It took a moment for his brain to acknowledge that the Overmaster was actually dead. When it finally hit him, he scrambled forward, off the cart, toward Tordek's side. His friend was still breathing shallowly, his hand clutching at his bent breastplate. Din unclasped Tordek's helmet and gently took it off him. Tordek winced in pain, but he was still alive.

"Sweet Earth Mother, thank you," whispered Din. Tordek looked up at Din with watery eyes and smiled wanly.

"That hurt," Tordek said through gritted teeth in his typical understated way. "I think he broke... all my ribs. But I'll live." He gasped a few times before asking. "Did you kill him?"

"Yes, though I'm not sure how."

Suddenly, he remembered the battle that was still raging all about him. He looked up in sudden panic at the prospect of being butchered by the Immortal Guard, but the elite Abyssal Dwarfs were no longer a threat. Din watched in growing wonder at the once invincible Immortal Guard, who were now writhing helpless on the ground. Din remembered Alborz's words in growing comprehension. With Alborz dead, the Immortal Guard's link to Ariagful was broken. The infernal magic that infused their metal bodies was gone, and their impossibly heavy limbs were dragging on the ground. The Ironclad lost no time exacting revenge on the Abyssal Dwarfs, slaughtering them in droves.

Din laughed in a mad mixture of relief and disbelief. Tordek craned his head to the side and he grinned before closing his eyes and lying back on the ground. Din hung his head in exhaustion, hands placed limply in his lap.

They'd lived. By some miracle, they'd lived.

* * * * *

"Gotcha!" yelled Rorik as his bullet struck the Overmaster in the chest. Through his scope he saw Lord Dinnidek strike the Abyssal Dwarf down with the clan banner. Rorik smiled in appreciation and sighed in contentment at a job well done. Fulgria knew it had taken long enough. He thought he'd had him sooner, but the Abyssal commander had jumped down off his chariot right when he was in Rorik's sights.

"Good thing he got up on the cart," he said to himself as he lowered his scope.

A few of the Wyverns were nearby, sniping at the remaining grotesques. Rorik considered the battlefield. The main dwarfen line had taken horrendous casualties, but they'd held against the grotesques and the Immortal Guard. To the north, Rhyss' rangers had scattered the Blacksouls, but the orcs were still taking it to Clan Helgwin on the far side of the battlefield. There were no emergencies that demanded his troops' attention nearby.

"Wyverns," he called, "let's move on. We have an Iron-caster to kill."

* * * * *

Zareen sent a gout of sorcerous flame at the Ironclad clutching to the flying nightmare's antlered head. The fires devoured the dwarf within seconds, another sacrifice to Ariagful. Zareen smiled wickedly as the dwarf's body landed in a charred smoking heap before him. The flying grotesque shook its head and screeched in annoyance at the imbalance caused by the loss of its left antler rack. Zareen viciously kicked the creature's flanks to bring it to heel. The mongrel dwarfs had put up a strong fight trying to protect the stone priestess, but to no avail. They were scattered, clutching their wounds, unable to stand before him. Behind him, he felt the remaining obsidian golems destroy another elemental. Even the spirits of the land would bow down to his might. There was nothing standing between him and the stone priestess.

With her gone, the mongrel dwarfs would be broken. But he wouldn't kill her. No, he had much bigger plans for her.

Zareen prodded the nightmare, and it screeched maddeningly as it strode forward, its head swinging rhythmically side to side with each step. The stone priestess sat on the ground, helpless. The dwarfs were yelling in panic as he approached. A few made to rise up and attack, but the nightmare screeched again, stunning some of the dwarfs and forcing them to their knees, their hands covering their ears in pain. Zareen scoffed at their weakness as the nightmare took the final steps forward.

A single elemental, too small to notice until now, came out from where it was hiding behind the stone priestess. It ran forward and punched at the beast's outstretched claw. The beast screeched again in annoyance, and the dwarfs writhed in agony. Zareen pulled on the reins to bring the creature back under control. The nightmare balked and swatted down, shattering the tiny elemental into pieces that scattered across the burning ground.

"Pitiful," said Zareen.

The stone priestess gasped and opened her eyes, her pupils rolled up in her head.

Just as the nightmare reached out its paw to capture the stone priestess, a vision sprang up in Zareen's mind, drowning out all his other senses. He reeled at its intensity, and his breathing became shallow and ragged.

Alborz, standing atop a cart and fighting a dwarfen thane. Alborz, disarming the dwarf, knocking him to the ground. Shattering the mongrel's shield. Alborz, raising his sword for the killing stroke.

Alborz, getting shot, blood pouring from his shoulder. The mongrel, clubbing Alborz down with the clan banner.

Alborz, falling dead to the ground.

Alborz.

Dead.

Zareen came back to his senses, his prey strewn before him.

None of it mattered. His brother was dead.

He screamed in rage and savagely yanked on the nightmare's reins. The beast obeyed and bore him up, above the trees. He had to recover Alborz. He had to get to his brother.

The beast soared up into the air on its broad, leathery wings. Zareen searched the battlefield for a sign of where his brother had fallen. What he found instead was ruin. He saw the Blacksouls far below him, performing a fighting retreat from the dwarfen rangers. The bodies of his grotesques, his creations, littered the battlefield. Further south, the halfbreeds and orcs were grinding the Helgwin clansmen down, but fresh dwarfen troops were joining the fray. Behind him, his gnorr were streaming away from the birch forest, fleeing from the dwarfs. A small voice in his head reminded him that without his presence, the obsidian golems would surely fall.

It didn't matter. None of it mattered now. Without Alborz, all was lost.

He scanned the field, desperately looking for the cart. He felt a bullet whiz by him. Another one tore a small hole through the nightmare's wing. He paid the shots no mind and kept his focus on the ground.

There. He saw the cart, surrounded by the bodies of the Immortal Guard. Alborz lay against a cart rail, his head lolling crazily to one side.

Zareen screamed and sent a cascade of green flame into the dwarfen warriors as the nightmare descended onto the mongrels. At the last minute, Zareen pulled up on the reins, and the beast flattened out its dive to swoop low and fast over the dwarfs. As he careened by, the antlered nightmare reached down and grabbed the entire side of the cart in its piniond claws before laboriously rising up again with each stroke of its great wings.

Zareen brushed tears of rage from his eyes. Alborz couldn't be dead. Not like this. Not in the moment of their triumph. He guided the beast westward, into the afternoon sun.

He would take Alborz home to Llyngyr Cadw and take care of him there. Ariagful was merciful. She wouldn't abandon her most favored servants.

CHAPTER 22

Dinnidek surveyed the destruction all around and sighed sorrowfully. He wandered the remnants of the battlefield with Rhyss, purposefully, almost reverently, taking in the devastation. Rhyss had been in bad shape after the battle, fatigued and exhausted; but after a day of sleep and some decent food, he'd almost fully recovered. The late afternoon sun was just touching the western mountains, and Din's shadow stretched long and distorted before him on the ground. The day had been hot and dry, and the army would have to move on soon to find fresh water. The dwarfs had spent the past two days tending to the wounded, the dying, and the dead. After their miraculous victory, Dinnidek and Anfynn had decided against pursuing the Abyssal Dwarf survivors. There had been too many casualties, and the army, for the time being, was spent. They'd taken the time to rest and recover, to reassess and to mourn.

Din and Rhyss stopped at the base of a giant mound, five feet high and over a hundred feet around. The dwarfs had buried their dead here, returning them back to the Earth Mother's embrace. The mass grave had been dug deep within the ground, as was custom, but Dinnidek had asked that the cairn be raised high above, as a monument to the clan's courageous victory, and their loss. A recessed ring of brown earth demarcated the cairn from the surrounding green fields. Rhyss pulled up his hood and hung his head in respect. Din could only shake his head ruefully and close his eyes.

"This is the price of our honor," he whispered aloud. Din realized he'd been talking to himself a lot today, as if by saying the words aloud he could stop them from echoing around in his brain. "Another victory like this will be the end of us."

"What was that?" asked Rhyss.

"Nothing," Din lied as he turned to go. Thankfully, Rhyss didn't press the issue. Neither of them had been in much of a mood to talk lately, each processing the trauma of the battle in their own quiet way. As they walked, Dinnidek made sure not to breathe too deeply. Unlike their clansmen, who the dwarfs had respectfully buried with honor, the orc, ratkin, and Abyssal Dwarf bodies had been indiscriminately thrown in great piles and burnt under the open sky. Even after almost a full day, the macabre mounds still smoldered, emitting oily black smoke. A gray haze had settled over the vale, with a line of thicker smoke nestled against the southern slopes of the nearby mountains. The haze gave the air an acrid taste on the tongue and irritated the eyes. Din had to violently blow the air out of his nose to clear his nostrils of the smell.

"It will be good to leave this place behind us," said Din wearily. Rhyss grunted in reply.

Dinnidek walked slightly behind the ranger and gave him a long, probing look. This taciturn manner wasn't like Rhyss. It was a long way from his steady, solid, confident demeanor. Maybe his time in hiding had left scars on his mind as well as his body. There was more than one way to become a casualty. The thought sobered Din even more. Though many of the dwarfs remained physically able to fight, what would be the long-term effects on their psyche? The battle had been a close-run thing, and many of his clansmen would carry these memories for the rest of their lives, for both good and ill.

"It isn't all glory," Din whispered. "Sometimes it's just pain."

"True," said Rhyss, "but for the survivors it's usually both."

Din startled, not realizing Rhyss had heard him, but the two friends continued on their way. In the distance, dwarfen warriors were salvaging whatever supplies they could from the battlefield. Food or waterskins would be parceled out among the survivors for the final push to Llyngyr Cadw. Weapons and armor that hadn't been buried with their owners would be used to replace broken ones, the surplus sent back to Crafanc. As they circled the mound, the Daamuz clan banner came into view, standing tall and straight with the banner pole partially set into the ground. Hundreds of additional chains had been placed atop the crosspiece. Along with the white dragon, the mementos glinted and shone in the late afternoon sun. Din could just make out a tinge of blood on one end of the crossbar. His mind flashed to the fight with Alborz, how helpless he'd felt, and how lucky he was to have survived. The warriors were already mythologizing Din's fight with the Overmaster, which made Din feel more uneasy.

Three clansmen were standing before the banner, heads bowed. One of the dwarfs was chanting the words of remembrance while another placed a chain along the crossbar. The third dwarf sang a monotone bass note, underscoring the solemnity of the moment. Dinnidek stopped, not wanting to approach and disturb the dwarfs with his presence, but Rhyss continued toward them, pulled back his hood, and joined in the singing. His deep, powerful voice added strength to the chorus. Din could only follow Rhyss' lead and joined in the ceremony. Despite his fears, the dwarfs kept their focus on the banner, heads bowed in reverence for their fallen friend.

When the last note faded away, one of the dwarfs raised his bowed head and wiped his eyes with the back of his hand before turning to thank the newcomers. His eyes widened in surprise when he recognized Din and Rhyss, and he quickly bowed respectfully.

"No," said Din gently, "please, none of that. No need to bow to me." He gestured to the banner, and the newly placed chain. "I should be bowing to you."

The dwarfs seemed flustered at Dinnidek's words, but they stopped bowing all the same. For an awkward moment, the dwarfs just stood there self-consciously, not sure what to do next. Din smiled and nodded toward the oldest of the three clansmen, the one who had recited the deeds of the fallen.

"I know you. Bulvi, isn't it?" The way Din said the family name sounded like 'bulv-eye.' The Bulvi family had joined the Daamuz clan shortly after the dwarfen exodus from Halpi. Many dwarfen families whose clan had been destroyed in the invasion were absorbed by the surviving clans in the chaotic aftermath. Dinnidek had personally met with each elder of these new families when they settled in Estacarr.

"That's me. Hammond Bulvi, at your service, my lord." Hammond introduced his companions as his nephews. Din clasped forearms with each dwarf in turn. "Thank you both for joining us in honoring my brother."

Din considered the two nephews, who had lost their father in the battle.

"It was our duty to pay honor to your father," said Din as he bowed deeply to the nephews in gratitude and turned to Hammond. "Tell me about your brother."

Hammond glanced at his nephews before answering. "His name was Huw, my lord. He was a baker by trade."

Hammond smiled as he spoke about his brother. How he was quick with a joke, how he valued family, how he saw cooking as a way to bring family together.

"He trained for the shield wall, like all clansmen should, and he was proud of his service. But he loved peace. When we joined up with your clan, he believed that we could find peace again."

"But Golloch ruined that, didn't he?" said one of the nephews.

"Yes," Rhyss scoffed, "he did."

"May Golloch rot in the Abyss," said Hammond. "When the news of conscription came, Huw and I knew we couldn't stay. We're... I'm... glad that we're back in Halpi, my lord. This is the best chance we have at a future for our family, even if it may cost us our lives." Hammond's voice got quiet. "Huw believed in it."

Din reached out and clasped Hammond on the shoulder.

"I would have liked to have met your brother. I wish I could have seen him build a life in Llyngyr Cadw." Din closed his eyes for a moment before continuing. "Thank you, Hammond Bulvi, for placing your trust in Clan Daamuz. Our clan is stronger because of you and your family, and I am in your debt."

Hammond and his nephews bowed. "No, my lord, we are in yours. You gave us a home when ours was destroyed. You gave us food and shelter.

But most importantly, you gave us hope."

"Yes, you did," said one of the nephews. "We'll see this through with you, my lord. Else my father's death will be for naught."

The second nephew nodded in agreement before gesturing to the great mound. "And I won't have those Abyssal scum desecrating my father's grave. This is our land. They can go back to the Abyss they love so much."

Hammond smiled fondly at his two young kinsmen's determination. Din's heart swelled with pride, and the melancholy that he'd been feeling was lifted, if only for a moment. Wordlessly, he bowed to the Bulvi family before taking his leave.

Rhyss walked silently next to him, letting Din process the conversation. The whistling of the wind vied with the sound of their footsteps on the dry ground. Din didn't have any particular destination in mind, he just felt better if he kept moving. He and Rhyss walked like ghosts through the battlefield, savoring the relative isolation. The Daamuz encampment was far off to the south, and the wind covered the normal commotion from the army. What was left of the Clan Helgwin forces was camped further away, separate from Clan Daamuz. Din could just make out some of the Helgwin clansmen, loading carts for their return trip.

Rhyss followed Din's gaze with a look of mild distaste. "Wish they were staying."

"Me too," agreed Din.

"Lots of brave words from Anfynn."

"Yes, but they've given enough." Din stopped walking and shielded his eyes from the glare of the late day sun to see the camp more clearly. A few of the closer tents seemed abandoned with open tent flaps blowing in the hot wind. A pair of dogs were cavorting around the camp with no sign of their handler. "Anfynn lost half his clansmen in the battle. He needs to get back and prepare Crafanc's defenses in case we fail."

"We have a better chance of succeeding if he's with us."

"True, but they have a home to protect, Rhyss. The ties of obligation can only extend so far." Rhyss crossed his arms and chewed on the inside of his lip. Din continued, "We owe them a deep debt of gratitude for what they've sacrificed for us. And Anfynn is offering to take in our wounded while we push forward."

"I know," said Rhyss, his tone softening a bit. "I'm just worried is all. We have one shot at this, Din. If we don't bring everything to bear, we may fail. And if we fail, both Daamuz and Helgwin will be done."

Din was silent as he resumed walking. He understood what was at stake, and he felt the same way, but what else could he do?

The two dwarfs moved on toward the birch forest and the Daamuz encampment. It was time to get back. Din purposefully headed to where

Veit and a team of engineers were making carts from the wreckage left on the battlefield. Din could hear Veit issuing orders and asking questions of his team. Three carts were laid out, in various states of repair. Veit himself knelt down on one leg by the side of a cart, his bad leg placed straight out to his side. The back end of the cart was jacked up on a pile of blocks to allow the wheels to spin freely. He was rocking a wheel back and forth as he fitted it to the axle, while an assistant stood nearby with a metal pin and a hammer. Din didn't want to disturb Veit, so he stopped a few feet away to allow the engineers to finish their work.

"Can you see it now?" asked Veit as he slowly maneuvered the wheel this way and that.

His assistant was peering down into a small hole in the inner rim of the wheel, looking for the corresponding hole through the axle to put the pin through.

"Hold on," the dwarf said. "Sorry, Veit, this light is making it tough to see. Bring it back a little," he said as he raised the pin. "A little more."

Veit very slowly and steadily turned the wheel, his eye on the other engineer for the sign that he'd found the spot.

"That's it!" the engineer exclaimed as his hand shot out to stop Veit from turning the wheel any further. He slowly dropped the pin into the hole, and he worked with Veit to rock the wheel until the pin dropped flush.

"Ha!" said Veit with some relief. "Nicely done, yes?"

The assistant smiled and gave the pin a few mild taps with his mallet to make the fitting snug. Veit grabbed the bed of the cart with both hands and pulled himself up with a mild groan. He gingerly placed his weight on his bad leg and shook the leg he'd been kneeling on.

"The pins and needles?" asked Rhyss as he approached the cart. He helped the other dwarfs hold the cart up while another pulled the wooden blocks that they'd used to jack the cart into the air. "That's the worst, isn't it?"

"Yes," said Veit as he shook his leg and stomped his foot on the ground a few times. "Good thing it usually goes away in a few seconds. Cormack says it has to do with blood not flowing to your feet."

Din smiled at Veit's explanation. Of course he'd asked Cormack about it. Veit wanted to know everything. "How many carts does this make, Veit?"

"Using the scraps from the leftover cannon chassis, combined with the pieces we could salvage from the Abyssal Dwarf camp, we've been able to make two dozen carts of various quality. Some of them can't carry much weight, but they should be good enough to transport our most wounded clansmen back to Crafanc." As he spoke, Veit limped over to the next cart in line.

"That's good," said Din. "Anything we can cob together will help."

"It's a mixed blessing, my lord," said Veit. "The Abyssal Dwarfs spiked our guns as they rolled our line, and I can't repair the cannons without specialized equipment, which I don't have. So, while I have plenty of wheels and wood to make carts for the wounded, it came at the expense of most of our guns. I still have the two pieces of field artillery that we commanded during the battle, plus a few more of Saorsi's light cannon, but that's it. I think we'll try to send the damaged gun barrels back to Crafanc on the sturdier carts, but we'll still need to abandon some of them here."

Veit grabbed the mallet from his assistant as he walked by.

"My turn to drive the pin," he said to the other engineer with a smile. "You took too long to find the hole last time."

The assistant rolled his eyes and knelt to begin putting the next wheel in place.

"Thank you, Veit," Din said. "As always, I appreciate all your efforts." He stepped closer so only Veit could hear. "And I know Diessa does as well."

The engineer blushed and patted Din on the arm before turning back to the task at hand.

"C'mon," said Veit to his crew. "We only have a few minutes of daylight left, yes?"

Dinnidek gathered Rhyss, and the two dwarfs left Veit to finish his work. Once they were far enough away, Rhyss whistled tunelessly. He didn't have to state the obvious. They had four cannons, five at most. It wouldn't be enough to take the hold. Din shook his head as he walked – they would have to figure something out. Din walked a few more steps in silence before whispering to himself, "We have no choice."

As they made their way through the camp, Din was stricken again by the number of empty tents. Normally the encampment would have been bustling with activity in the early evening, but now the camp felt like a ghost town. Din took note of a row of tents, meticulously laid out, everything just so. Each tent normally held a fist of dwarfs, five tents to a row. But Din could only see a few Ironclad busily prepping dinner for their cohort. Most of his clansmen were still busy preparing for tomorrow's march or tending to the battlefield. He tried to compare it to Anfynn's camp, but he faltered. The missing there were either dead or wounded.

Din unconsciously turned his feet toward the medical tents. The field hospital was situated within the makeshift palisade that ringed the camp, but still separate from the rows of tents that the warriors used. In the aftermath of the battle, the medical tent was full to bursting, and warriors that could walk were sent back to their fists to make room for the dwarfs with more dire injuries. Even so, wounded clansmen were lined up on rows of cots outside the tent entrance beneath the open air. Some of the dwarfs were conscious enough to talk or banter with the other dwarfs nearby, but most of them were either too exhausted or hurt to do anything except get what fitful rest they could. Din made sure to acknowledge each of the dwarfs in some way as he passed by.

Din stopped at the threshold of the tent to survey the scene. The field hospital was the largest tent in the army. Actually, it was three separate tents arrayed together, each thirty feet square and supported by its own birch tree trunk in the center. Where the tents butted against each other, the outer flaps had been rolled up to make a single space. Lamps placed throughout each of the 'rooms' provided the right amount of light. The first two rooms were full of wounded dwarfs, on cots or lying on blankets on the floor. These were the most severely wounded of his clansmen, almost all of them lying in fitful sleep with the help of soporific drugs. These dwarfs had suffered grievous injuries, and despite the low lamplight, Din noticed more than a few missing limbs or bloody bandages.

Din was more subdued as he walked slowly through the rows of maimed and mutilated dwarfs. He fought the desire to avert his eyes and forced himself to look upon his fellow clansmen. He bore witness to their sacrifice, not out of some perverse need to wallow in the pain, but to remind himself of what the clan had given so far, and what they'd be forced to give if they continued. Rhyss stopped before a pair of his rangers who were laid up sleeping in their cots. He gestured to Din that he'd be staying there for a while and to go on without him.

Cormack was at the far end of the tent, surrounded by lamps which bathed his work area in light. There was no hiding the exhaustion on the doctor's face as Din watched him in the glow of the fire. Dark circles hung below his eyes, which were tinged red from lack of sleep. He was working on Tordek, who was seated on a folding chair, wearing only a loose-fitting pair of pants, a pile of bloody bandages by his feet. Tordek's beard was pulled back, the ends loosely tied behind his neck to not get in the way of Cormack's work. Fresh bandages crossed his broad chest and covered a line just below the muscles there. Angry purple bruises spread all over the right of Tordek's torso, and the burly dwarf was hunched over toward that side, trying not to extend his ribcage.

"The fact that you're alive is a miracle, you know that right?" said Din quietly to his old friend as he acknowledged Cormack with a nod.

Tordek took in a few labored shallow breaths before answering. "I could say... the same... for you." The words came out slowly as he stole breaths between.

"Yeah," agreed Din with a smile, "I guess you could."

Cormack loosened Tordek's beard, and it fell forward to obscure the bandages and the bruises. Then he came around so that Tordek could see him.

"Remember what I told you, don't carry anything heavy for the next ten-day. You broke a lot of ribs, and even if the cuts on your side begin to heal, the bones will take time to knit together."

Tordek's right hand was busy propping him upright, so he waved his left hand at Cormack in a placating gesture.

"I'll be fine," he protested. "My dwarfen... breastplate... took most of... the shot. If it was... of human make... I'd be dead." Tordek tried to stand, but when he moved, he gasped, and a wince of pain flashed across his face. He slumped back down onto the chair with a growl.

"I know you won't listen," said Cormack, "but maybe he'll remind you."

Cormack gestured to Din with his thumb.

"He's not... the chief... of me," Tordek said with a weary smile.

"Actually..." said Cormack with a roll of his eyes.

Din chuckled and patted Tordek's shoulder. "Rest. We'll try again in a couple moments."

He turned to consider the other wounded dwarfs. The most seriously injured were kept here, nearest to Cormack so he could keep close tabs on them. All were sleeping, usually with the help of strong herbs. A few of the dwarfs had regrettably passed in the night, their lifeless faces covered by linen cloth.

"I believe the worst is over," remarked Cormack. "Those who still survive today will probably live."

He led Din over to a group of cots, and one dwarf in particular, who was lying on his back with his face turned away. The dwarf's arm had been removed near the shoulder, the stump heavily wrapped in bandages and tied down to his torso. As Din came around, Felwyr's face came clearly into view. Fel groaned and shifted in his sleep before settling back down. Cormack gently caressed Fel's head and 'shooshed' him soothingly.

"Not all of them will be whole, however. I tried to save the arm, but the bones were shattered beyond my skill to repair."

Over the past day, Din had been bombarded with visions of the dead and the dying. He'd begun to go numb to the pain, and he forced himself to keep looking, to stay engaged and not shut down. At the same time, he was careful not to wallow in self-pity or despondent sorrow. The clan needed him to be present. There would be time enough for processing the losses once they were finished. Seeing Fel like this, however, strained Din's resolve. Even in sleep, his friend's gaunt face was lined with pain, such a contrast to his normal light-hearted demeanor. If Rhyss was carrying nightmares from the battle, then how much more would Felwyr carry? Fel was a warrior, first and foremost. He had no other real skills to fall back on. He wasn't a baker by trade, like Huw Bulvi. As Cormack said, Felwyr would live, but he'd have to reforge a new identity within the clan. He'd essentially have to relearn how to live. Din stood speechless for a long while before closing his eyes.

There is no glory here, he thought. *There are no statues to dwarfs like Fel in the halls of Llyngyr Cadw.* He reached out and lightly touched Fel's head as he slept. *There should be.*

Din thanked Cormack and went to leave. Tordek saw him coming and held out his hand, silently expecting Din to help him up. Din shook his head and smiled at Tordek as he passed by.

"Do as Cormack says and take it easy." Tordek gave him a reproachful look, but Din kept his eyes on him as he backed out of the room. "I'm not just your chieftain, I'm your friend. Get some rest. We leave tomorrow, and I want you walking at my side."

Tordek waved him away with a smile, closed his eyes, and slumped back in the chair.

When Din exited the hospital, he found Diessa just wrapping up a conversation with Rhyss. Since the battle, Deese's deep connection with the spirits had waned, and she was returning to normal. Without the elemental connection, she had regained her sight and no longer used a blindfold. Din came up behind her as Rhyss disappeared between a pair of tents.

"Deese, do you have a minute?" he asked.

His sister turned with a smile and hugged him close before nodding 'yes' and gesturing for him to follow. The siblings walked silently for a bit, Diessa giving him space to formulate his thoughts. Dinnidek was still struggling with his emotions. A thousand impulses, ideas, and anxieties whirled around in his mind, and he was hoping that talking with Diessa would force some structure on it all.

"How have you been? We've barely spoken since the battle." He motioned toward her face. "It's nice to see your eyes again."

Diessa smiled.

"Yes, it's odd to have my normal sight back. But it's for the best. I can still feel the land, but I'm not in danger of being consumed by it, if you know what I mean." Din nodded as if he understood. The feelings were too foreign for him to truly relate, but he took Diessa's words at face value. "When the battle was over and the remaining elementals killed off the ratkin, I was completely exhausted. I came back to myself in a haze, and I couldn't process what I was seeing. I had gone from being connected with the world to feeling completely severed."

Din remembered finding her in the birch forest, fast asleep on the ground, surrounded by the surviving Stone Guard. Ratkin bodies were piled around her, a gruesome testament to their victory.

"But, as with most things, some rest and time set me right again. At least physically."

Din sniffed and nodded wordlessly. That was it, right there. The clan had taken their rest, and the ones blessed enough to survive had to decide what came next, both for themselves and for the clan as a whole. Din took a deep breath as he corrected himself. He, and he alone, was responsible for deciding for the clan. Everyone else just had to live with his decision. He sat in that feeling for a while, letting the gravity of it pull him down. He was the clan's leader, responsible for their well-being and their success. In this moment, he held the clan's survival in his hands. He felt comfortable with the weight of it, but he needed Diessa's perspective.

He let Diessa guide them as they walked, and she led them out of the camp, to the nearby birch forest. The hot evening breeze made the tall slim trunks creak as they swayed, and the leaves made a whooshing sound as they wriggled to and fro. The two walked along the forest's edge, the lights from the camp receding into the distance. Once away from the lamplight, their natural dwarfen dark vision turned the world into a monochrome vista of varying shades of gray.

Finally, Din broke the silence. "Diessa, before we came here, you advised me against coming back to Halpi. You had said that the price would be too high, that we were throwing away our chance at a peaceful life."

"Yes, I did. But I promised I would support you in any decision you made. I still will."

"I appreciate that." Din gathered his thoughts before he spoke again. "Do you still believe that I have the clan's best interest at heart?"

Din was surprised as he spoke the question. But now that he'd verbalized his fear, he waited with trepidation for Diessa to answer.

"I do," she said after a moment. Din exhaled with some relief at her answer. "I've seen how you've changed since we arrived, Din. I know this was never about personal glory, but I think a part of you was doing this to justify taking father's place as clan chief. And now, I don't see any of that. Instead, I see a leader who cares for his people and wants the best for them. Rhyss sees it too."

Dinnidek smiled at Deese's kind words. "Thank you. What does Daerun think?"

"I'm not sure. It's not the kind of thing that he would share with me. To be honest, I haven't seen him much since the battle. I think Felwyr's injury has shaken him."

Din felt a little guilty at Diessa's words. He had been busy with so many things that he hadn't spared much thought for Daerun.

Diessa turned into the forest, and they walked carefully amid the white birch trunks. The sounds of the camp faded away, leaving just the two of them to navigate their way. As they walked, the landscape changed. They passed more downed trees, and more charred branches littered the ground.

Finally, Diessa stopped at a small mound set in a clearing, a set of rocks piled up at its head. A blue ribbon was intertwined among the little cairn, a final token to Bruon, captain of the Stone Guard. The two stood reverently before Bruon's grave.

"I freed them from their oath, you know," said Diessa. She knelt and placed her hand on the ground. "I figured they'd given enough. I understand the sacrifice. Without them, I would be dead. And without me, the obsidian golems would have crushed Daerun's soldiers. Veit says it's simple logic."

Din knelt down beside Diessa to see her face clearly. A single tear rolled down her cheek as she continued.

"But it's a small consolation. I never asked for them to give their lives. It's not what I wanted."

She sniffed and wiped the tears from her eyes.

"You didn't demand it," Din agreed. "You didn't ask for it. They gave their lives freely, Deese. And you couldn't demand that they stay away."

"I know. And I know if they didn't die here, they could have died or been hurt while in the shield wall. It's just... there were so many casualties."

"Yes," whispered Din sadly.

"That's why we have to keep going," Diessa said, with a fierceness that surprised Din.

"What?" he asked, incredulously. "I figured that would be the reason you'd ask me to lead us back!"

The two siblings stood up to face each other.

"Don't get me wrong, Din. If you decided to turn around now, I wouldn't blame you. I'd support you with every fiber of my being. We could head back to Innyshwylt and try to build a new life with the survivors."

"Then why are you saying we need to push on? We've lost so many of our clansmen. We don't have enough cannons to force a breach in the gates. You remember the entrance to the hold, Deese. It's built into the very mountain."

"Because we won yesterday, Din. We destroyed their army and sent them fleeing. Half the camp is telling the story of how you killed Alborz."

"But I didn't do it. Not totally. Alborz was toying with me the whole time. Rorik's the one who should get the credit! Without his bullet, I'd be dead."

"Sure, but that's not the story, Din. The story is that you triumphed over our great nemesis and routed his army from the field. In the clan's eyes, you're a hero, and they believe in you now more than ever before." He tried to wave the sentiment away, but Diessa continued. "Things are better than you think, Din. The clan still believes in the cause, despite our losses."

Din thought back to his discussion with the Bulvis and how determined they were to keep going. He shared the conversation with Diessa. He related how they were still willing to fight for their future and how adamant they were that the future couldn't be found in Golloch's empire.

"There was a tinge of hate in their words, Deese. So much disdain for an arrogant king who only cared about his own glory. It was mixed with a burning need for revenge against the Abyssal Dwarfs who had stolen their home. And what else is revenge but hate with a purpose? It's like hate brought us here, Deese."

She considered that for a moment before answering. "The Earth Mother knows there's plenty of things for the clan to hate. I mean, there's plenty of things for us to hate too. The Abyssal Dwarfs, Golloch, our fellow clans who couldn't band together in time, the gods, even fate. But hate can only lead you so far. It can motivate a person, Din, but not an entire clan. Hate doesn't sustain you in the long run when things are bad. No, the real thing that motivated the Bulvis was hope. Hope that they could live in peace."

Diessa's words settled in Dinnidek's heart, and he knew they were true. He replayed the conversation again, but this time, he focused on other parts. Huw hadn't sailed across the High Sea of Bari to kill Abyssal Dwarfs. No, he came back to Halpi to be a baker. To give his sons a chance at a peaceful life, without having to die for Golloch.

As if reading his mind, Diessa went on, "We can't leave while the people still have hope. I know back in Estacarr I said that a leader protects the people from themselves, but I also believe that a leader's role is to rally the clan to achieve great things. That goes for times of peace and times of war. And right now, if you lead us back, then every death, every loss, will be in vain. It will be for nothing, Din. I can't go back to the families we left behind and see the looks on their faces when we arrive without their husbands, brothers, and sons."

Din saw the crowded hospital again in his mind. Saw the great mound with the clan banner tinged with blood. Diessa was right. He smiled at the irony. Diessa was perfectly describing how he was feeling, just from another perspective. Yes, there was loss. But the clan knew that was the price they would have to pay. He glanced down at the small cairn with the blue ribbon as his own words from a moment ago came back unbidden to his mind.

They gave their lives freely.

He hadn't led them here against their will. They had wanted to reclaim their home, and Din was helping them achieve it.

If he ordered the clan to retreat now while they still had the will to fight, he would be compromised as a leader forever more. The clan would constantly ask what would have happened if they'd just stayed. If they'd pushed on a little further. He'd be second-guessed for the rest of his life. And the clan may never have a chance to reclaim their homeland again. Din knew he couldn't live with himself if that happened.

Dinnidek embraced his sister and held her close as he took a few deep breaths. He let the emotions of the moment slowly ebb until he felt that he could talk again.

"You're right," he said as he let her go. He nodded shakily. "We'll go on. I knew that was the answer, but I dreaded it all the same. Thank you."

Diessa nodded in return. She grabbed his hand. "I'll follow you to the end, Din. And so will everyone else. All the way to the gates of Llyngyr Cadw."

"Yes," he said with a smile. And hopefully it wouldn't end there.

CHAPTER 23

"So that's when I fired," exclaimed Rorik as he pantomimed aiming his rifle. The dwarfen sentries around him stood in rapt attention as Rorik reached the crescendo of his story. They were congregating near the camp gates, their faces illuminated by a pair of lanterns which hung from the wooden palisade walls. "Hate to say it, but I missed and only got him in the shoulder. Lord Dinnidek was the one who finished the job. Cracked that bastard right across the head with the banner. Dropped him like a sack of potatoes." His audience chuckled as he brought his arms around in an exaggerated swing.

Daerun smiled along with the others at Rorik's antics. He had to admit, the sniper was an excellent storyteller if he had a drink or two in him. Dare had considered Rorik a little too stuffy for his liking, but since the battle, the two had been constant companions, making the rounds among the survivors. Talking and joking with his clansmen was Daerun's preferred way to keep the sadness at bay, but this time it didn't bring the usual solace. *Not the same without Fel,* he thought dolefully.

"I can imagine his ghost just floating there," said Rorik, "looking down with a stupid look on his face." He was laughing at the thought, and it made it hard for him to get the words out. "Well," he said in a low confused voice, his head cocked awkwardly to the side, "that was unexpected." The dwarfs sputtered and laughed along with him, and even Daerun snorted at how ridiculous it was. "Ah, yes. Let's raise a flask to Lord Dinnidek Daamuz, slayer of Alborz the Confused."

The sentries cheered and took pulls from their flasks, if they were lucky enough to have one. Like most provisions, the army's supply of liquor was getting low, and alcohol of any sort was hard to come by.

Dare nodded in approval at Rorik's toast. He hadn't drunk since the battle. He told himself he would rather his clansmen have what little remained, but that wasn't entirely true. His heart had been heavy the past two days, and he didn't feel up to joking the way he normally did. He would typically be the one telling the stories, but now he was content to be part of the audience. His somber attitude fought with his need to be among his clansmen, and it made him feel like an outsider in the crowd. It was a strange feeling for him, and it didn't help his melancholy mood.

"Yes," continued Rorik as he finished a long pull from his flask. "To Lord Dinnidek, may he rule in Llyngyr Cadw for generations!"

The sentries cheered again. Daerun smiled in appreciation at Rorik's words. According to Din, his brother would have been killed if Rorik hadn't shot Alborz when he did. Sure, Din had landed the lethal blow, but the real credit belonged to Rorik. However, the way the sharpshooter told it, Rorik's shot hadn't made much of a difference at all, and Din would have triumphed either way. Rorik's account put the glory squarely with Din, and he was sure to amplify the legend every time he told the story. When Daerun had asked Rorik why he chose to tell it that way, his answer had been simple. He had said with a shrug that he had missed, as if that explained it all. Daerun felt that Rorik probably had another agenda, but he didn't push the issue.

It doesn't make sense for him to one-up his employer, he thought a little cynically. *The clan needs a hero, and Rorik knows that it can't be an outsider, let alone an Imp. No, he's giving the glory to Dinnidek to keep up morale.*

As the dwarfs quieted down, one of the guards shouted in surprise and pointed out into the darkness. Daerun followed the gesture and saw a figure wrapped in a cloak, standing outside the gate at the edge of the lamplight. He wondered with some disquiet how someone could get past the outer sentries so easily. The guards' mood shifted quickly as they raised their weapons. Rorik stepped to the side to grab his rifle, behind the wall and outside of the intruder's field of vision.

Daerun calmly raised his hands and addressed the newcomer. "Hello there, friend. What can I do for you?"

Out of the corner of his eye, Dare saw Rorik silently pick up his rifle with his back to the palisade wall. As he raised it, he must have realized it wasn't loaded, because he shook his head and reversed his grip to hold it like a club. Dare spared him a sidelong look, and Rorik shrugged as if to say, 'what else do you want me to do?'

The figure took a small step forward into the light, revealing broad features, a long scraggly beard, and wild unkempt hair. Though parts of his face were obscured in darkness, his eyes glinted keenly in the light, beneath the shadow of his brow. Besides the cloak, he wore baggy breeches, an ill-fitting shirt, and sturdy boots. Daerun couldn't discern any weapons, but that didn't mean much. The strange dwarf cleared his throat.

"I bear a message from the Worm Lord."

Daerun made a subtle placating gesture toward Rorik. "Who is the message for, friend? Can you give it to us?"

"That depends on who you are."

Daerun was momentarily lost for words. The comment, though it could be taken as rude, made sense. Nonplussed, Dare chuckled at the stranger's cleverness.

"You have me there," he said. Rorik exaggeratedly rolled his eyes as he slowly lowered his rifle. "I am Daerun, thane of Clan Daamuz, third child of Drohzon. And who are you?"

The stranger ignored the question and instead bowed low.

"Master Daerun," he said, as if considering the name, "my lord will be pleased to know I spoke with you. He's aware that Lord Dinnidek and Lady Diessa both survived the battle, but he wasn't sure about you. Yes, he will be pleased."

Dare squinted in confusion at the dwarf, but he waited patiently for the stranger to continue. His father had taught him that when negotiating, there were times when the next person to talk would lose their leverage. He figured this was one of those times. The stranger seemed in no rush to speak, and the silence stretched awkwardly. The sentries, taking their lead from Daerun, stood ready at attention, but none of them moved as the tension built.

Finally, Rorik called out impatiently from behind the wall, "So, what's the message?"

Daerun couldn't help but smile at Rorik's outburst, and behind him, he heard the sentries exhale as the tension left them. However, the wild dwarf's face betrayed nothing.

"Can you give me the message, or should I call for my brother?" Dare asked respectfully.

"No, Master Daerun, I can give the message to you, if you wish." The emissary paused again for a long stretch, and Daerun was just about to prompt him on when he finally spoke. He stated the message in a formal manner that belied his disheveled appearance. "These are the words of the Worm Lord. To Lord Dinnidek Daamuz, first child of Drohzon, greetings. It is my pleasure to know that you, as well as your *siblings,* are alive. Congratulations on your victory over the Overmaster and his wicked host. It was my pleasure to lend what small support I could to aid you in your time of need. Please accept my apology for not taking direct part in the battle, for my forces, though highly skilled, are small in number. Rest assured that my army took great delight in hunting the orcs on the plain and are even now harrying the survivors as they return to Llyngyr Cadw.

"I know your quest, and I have a vested interest in its success, beyond my desire to scour the Abyssal Dwarfs from the face of Pannithor. I also know that you don't have enough troops to storm the gates of Llyngyr Cadw. In keeping with this, I would remind you that there is more than one way into your ancestral home. There are many tunnels that wind their way within the living rock. The Overmaster knew of most of them, but one such passage has remained hidden. The entryway I speak of used to lead to the old watchtower high atop the northwest peak of the Red Mountain. Since you used to reside there, I'm sure that you know of the tunnel of which I speak. The actual entrance is a narrow slit in the rock, cleverly obscured from prying eyes. It lies two hundred feet above the treeline and can only be discerned when you look straight upon it.

"I look forward to your eventual success and anticipate the day when our traitorous kin are pushed back into the fires of the Abyss. May the Earth Mother bless you.

"Thus speaks the Worm Lord."

The emissary stopped, and Daerun waited a few heartbeats before he spoke. "How do I know I can trust you?"

The herald gave Daerun an indulgent smile. "That is a bad question, Master Daerun. If I have good intentions, then I would state that I am trustworthy. Likewise, if I have malice in my heart, then I would also state that I am trustworthy. So, based on that, rest assured that you can trust me implicitly."

Daerun scoffed at the reply and instead took another tact. "How has the tunnel been kept hidden for all this time? Alborz had a decade to explore our home."

The messenger nodded sagely. "Now that is a better question. Before Drohzon Daamuz left Llyngyr Cadw, he had the tunnel sealed to hide it from the Abyssal Dwarfs. In the intervening years, the Worm Lord has constantly harassed the Overmaster's troops to keep them away from the mountain peaks."

Daerun considered the wild dwarf's words. There was something off in all this. "How does the Worm Lord know these things?"

The messenger spread his hands before him. "The Worm Lord knows many things, Master Daerun. We have been watching this land for the past ten years, spying on the Abyssal Dwarfs and their slaves. There is not much that happens in eastern Halpi that the Worm Lord doesn't know about. For example, we are aware that you only have a few cannons at your disposal. We know of your ally's intention to return to Crafanc. We also know of Lady Diessa's blindness." The emissary clasped his hands before him. "Please tell her the Worm Lord is pleased that she can see again." He gestured to the darkness all around him. "You were on guard for spies. Consider how much more information we have gotten from the brutish orcs or the careless ratkin over the years."

Instead of feeling reassured, the dwarf's response left Daerun with dozens more questions. He felt that the dwarf hadn't lied, but it was obvious he was keeping information to himself. Rorik had slowly come out from behind the wall while the emissary spoke and now stood just behind Daerun. The sharpshooter sounded bewildered as he asked, "Who are you?"

Daerun raised an eyebrow at the emissary expectantly.

"Do not think that the Free Dwarfs in Estacarr are the only survivors from the Abyssal Dwarf invasion, Master Rorik." The sniper inhaled quickly as the dwarf spoke his name. "At one time, I was a herald. Now I speak for the Worm Lord. There are scores of us, dispossessed, without family or clan."

The messenger took a step backward, into the darkness.

"Remember, the northwest peak of the Red Mountain, two hundred feet above the treeline. You will find the entrance there."

The dwarf stepped back again and bowed deeply to Daerun. As he came out of his bow, he continued to walk backward until he turned and dashed off into the darkness.

Rorik went to chase after him, but Dare grabbed his coat.

"No use for that," Dare said. He faintly heard a brock snuffling and growling as it receded into the distance. "He's not our enemy."

"Sure," agreed Rorik, "but I'm not quite sure he's our friend, either."

* * * * *

Dinnidek returned with Diessa to find the camp abuzz with activity. A sentry caught sight of the two siblings and ran over to them.

"Lord Dinnidek, Lady Diessa, Master Daerun is requesting your presence by the western gate."

Din's voice tightened in apprehension. "Is the camp in danger?"

"No, my lord," the sentry replied quickly, "he says he has urgent news to share. Do you happen to know the whereabouts of Captain Rhyss?"

Din shook his head no, and the messenger bowed and ran off. Din looked nervously at Diessa. She shrugged to show she was just as confused as he.

They arrived at the gate to find Rhyss already there, along with Rorik and Daerun. Veit limped up to the group, stopping to give Diessa a quick hug on the way.

"Do you have the maps?" Daerun asked Veit. The engineer answered by waving a roll of parchment that he held in his hand. Dare turned to a nearby sentry. "Is Anfynn on his way?"

"Yes, my lord. Anfynn said he'll be here shortly."

"Excellent," Dare replied. "Please escort him to the command tent when he arrives." The sentry nodded and turned his attention back to the darkness.

Daerun filled his siblings in on the strange envoy and his message. Din had a thousand questions but held his tongue for the moment. His mind raced as he marched away from the gates. Who were these dwarfs, and why had they waited so long to reveal themselves? Rhyss had told him about the Worm Lord and his movements, but who was he? Could they trust him? What if this was an Abyssal Dwarf trick? The questions became increasingly dire the further he went.

Finally, he could hold back no longer. "He said there was another way into Llyngyr Cadw?"

"How did Alborz not find it after all this time?" asked Diessa, clearly bursting at the seams as well.

"The herald said that Father sealed up one of the tunnels and hid it from the inside."

"What?" Din and Diessa both exclaimed at the same time. Din stopped and felt his heart beat faster at the news.

"I know." Daerun took him by the arm and pulled him along. "I had almost the same reaction."

"How did he know about Father?" Diessa asked.

"I don't know," Dare replied in mild frustration. "He said they knew all kinds of things, Deese. By the way, the Worm Lord says he's glad you're no longer blind."

This time, Diessa was the one who stopped. Dinnidek placed his hand gently on her back to get her moving again.

Din chewed his inner lip while he thought everything through. A spark of hope flared up inside him. He pulled Diessa close and whispered excitedly, "Do you think this Worm Lord knew our father? Did he actually speak with him? And if so, could Father still be alive?"

Diessa looked skeptically at Din in response.

"What?" she asked dismissively. "How could that be? It's been ten years, Din."

The two siblings stopped walking to give them some privacy from the others.

Din spoke with urgency in his voice. "Deese, listen, we've always assumed that Father died during the invasion, right? That he led a brave last stand to give us time to escape. But what if he survived?"

A torrent of thoughts and emotions began bubbling up at the very thought. It was both wonderful and frightening. Diessa's eyes softened as she considered her brother's words.

"Din," she said kindly, "if our father is alive, then why haven't we heard from him?" The simple question brought Din's excitement to a screeching halt as she continued. "No, if Father was alive, he would have done everything in his power to find us and become reunited with the clan. There's no way he would have abandoned us, Din."

Diessa was right, their father had sacrificed everything for them. He would never have abandoned them, not willingly. Din shook his head in sadness as the fleeting hope dissolved away. The two siblings walked slowly the rest of the way to the command tent, each lost in their own thoughts and emotions.

As they entered, Din reached out and grabbed Diessa's hand. In return, she gave him a sidelong look and a nervous smile.

"We'll talk later," she whispered and gave his hand a quick squeeze.

As she took a seat across from the door, Veit unrolled the maps of the hold in the center of the floor. The plans were drawn in clean, crisp lines with neat block writing in multiple locations. The depiction of the rooms within the center of the hold were well organized with multiple measurements shown here and there. Once outside the core halls and rooms, the map became more stylized, with winding tunnels and aboveground landmarks depicted in a more artistic manner. Rhyss stood near the tent entrance, gazing intently at the spot on the map with the tunnel entrance that Veit had marked with a red circle. Din quietly sat on the floor and calmed his mind as he waited for the meeting to get started.

Anfynn arrived with Kilvar and a younger dwarf who Din recognized but didn't know by name. The Warmaster doffed his helmet upon entering the tent and bowed to the assembled dwarfs before taking a seat near the entrance. Rhyss and Kilvar clasped forearms and greeted each other warmly, the Packmaster whispered something in Rhyss' ear before finding a spot to stand. Din could only make out the words, 'I'm sorry about,' and 'stayed.' Rhyss replied with a solemn nod and another clap on Kilvar's shoulder before turning his attention to Anfynn with a judgmental frown. Luckily, Anfynn was facing away and couldn't see Rhyss' stern expression.

"My lord Dinnidek," said Anfynn as he gestured to the young dwarf, "may I introduce Eswer, thane of Clan Helgwin."

Eswer nervously bowed in Dinnidek's general direction. Being seated, Din nodded in acknowledgment.

"Thane Eswer, we are honored by your presence. Please rise and feel at home among friends. We look forward to your wisdom during our council."

Eswer's cheeks flushed, and he hurriedly bowed again in response.

So young, thought Din. *He must have been recently promoted to thane. Makes sense, given the heavy losses Clan Helgwin sustained.* He smiled at Eswer to try to put him at ease, and the young dwarf anxiously grinned back before putting on a serious expression. *Of course, there was plenty of opportunity for glory, too. If I'm right, Eswer's rise is probably due to both.*

Anfynn's arrival filled the command tent to capacity, with everyone packed shoulder to shoulder to leave room for the map. Daerun raised his hand and waited for Din to formally cede the floor before he began to speak. Din gave him a tight smile and slightly bowed his head.

"Friends," Daerun began, "I want to thank you all for coming. We had a strange visitor to camp this evening." He gestured toward Kilvar. "Someone that I believe you've already met."

The Packmaster's eyes got wide as Daerun relayed his earlier conversation. For Dinnidek, this was the second time he'd heard the story, which helped to put it into more context. Rhyss had told him that the Worm Lord had been hunting the Abyssal Dwarfs. He knew they'd had an ally this entire time, why should this be such a big surprise?

Daerun finished with a description of the messenger and his strange manner of speech.

"Indeed," said Kilvar once Daerun was finished. "That's the one I met on the plain. Mysterious. Slightly impertinent."

"Smug bastard?" interrupted Rorik, breaking the tension.

"Yeah, that's him," replied Kilvar with a low laugh.

"So, Veit," said Din, gesturing to the map, "what do you know about this hidden entrance?"

Veit glanced around the room to make sure he had everyone's attention before pointing to the red circle.

"Well, the funny thing is that it isn't really 'hidden' at all. At least if you know what you're looking for." He traced a line from the red circle down to the interior of the hold. "This tunnel led to a wooden lookout tower situated on the mountain peak." He pointed at the red circle on the map.

"Right," Rhyss interjected, "but it was destroyed by the time I returned to Halpi." He stroked his beard in thought before he went on. "I assumed that the Abyssal Dwarfs had razed it to the ground."

"But what if it wasn't them?" asked Din. "What if it was Father? If he wanted the entrance to remain a secret, he would have destroyed the tower himself to not give the location away." It occurred to Din that if what he said was true, then his father knew he might lose their ancestral home. More importantly, his father had always planned for the clan to return.

Veit nodded at Din's suggestion.

"A valid point. Let's go on the assumption that Lord Drohzon had time to implement his plan." His finger traced a line from the northwest entrance down to the interior of the hold. "The tunnel, if I remember correctly, was only wide enough for one or two dwarfs at a time in some spots. It would take hours to get our army through there, even depleted as it is."

"Not to mention it would be simple to collapse the tunnel and cut you off if you were discovered," said Eswer. As soon as he was done speaking, the young thane looked around sheepishly, as if surprised at his own boldness. Anfynn turned his head so that only Din could see his face. He smiled wryly at Din as if to say, 'Youngsters, what else can you expect?' Din winked back in reply.

"Excellent point, Thane Eswer," said Dinnidek with an approving nod, which drew a relieved smile from the young dwarf. Eswer folded his arms across his chest a little more confidently. *If it's a good idea, it doesn't matter who says it,* Din thought, *as long as it gets said. How many good ideas have been lost out of modesty or decorum?*

"Right," Daerun said. "We'll have to distract the Abyssal Dwarf warriors inside the keep if we're going to have a chance of sneaking in the back way."

Anfynn nodded vigorously in reply as he stroked his beard. Din couldn't help but smile at Anfynn's demeanor. Even after taking such heavy losses, and stating his intention to return to Crafanc, the war leader's blood was up thinking about the battle to come.

"Lord Anfynn," asked Diessa, "do you still plan on taking our wounded with you to Crafanc?"

"Yes, my lady," replied Anfynn gravely as he came back to the present. "We won't be able to protect our home if we sustain more losses. But it is my pleasure to help in any other way we can. That includes caring for your wounded clansmen and sending supplies. I have already sent messengers to Crafanc to see if we can provide more cannons, but it will take some ten-days to transport them to Llyngyr Cadw."

Diessa gave a seated bow to Anfynn. "We understand, and we are in your debt, my lord."

Din noticed Kilvar kept his eyes down at the floor during the exchange, his face expressionless like a stone. It was obvious that not everyone agreed with Anfynn's decision.

"So," said Veit, "the other option is the front door."

He pointed to the eastern portion of the map, this time near the main entrance to the keep, which was flanked by high ground on either side. The area right before the gates was flat and wide. In more peaceful times, dwarfs and humans would be invited to set up their tents before the gates to trade their wares, while keeping outsiders from entering the hold. Veit traced his finger along the high ground that encircled this flat area.

"Numerous bolt holes and cannon emplacements encircle the entrance to the main gates. As you know, a frontal assault here, with our meager number of cannons, would be futile."

A tense quiet fell over the room. No one relished the idea of assaulting the gates, especially with no real artillery to speak of. It would be glorious suicide.

"Would it be possible to goad the Abyssal Dwarfs into another open battle?" asked Daerun. "It's a long shot, but what would it take to tempt them out of the hold?"

"Would have to be crazy to come out from behind those gates and fight," Rhyss replied. "It makes no sense to abandon the position. They could stay locked up in there for months while we starve."

"That's what we said about Alborz," said Dinnidek. "There was no way he would leave the high ground."

"True," agreed Rorik smugly, "and look where that got him."

The dwarfs chuckled at Rorik's words, but there was an undercurrent of tension. Everyone knew how close they'd come to disaster.

"How many troops do you think they have left?" asked Anfynn. "I mean, they lost thousands in the battle."

"Don't forget the ones the Worm Lord hunted down during the retreat," observed Kilvar. "I mean, assuming we can trust what the herald told us."

"Hard to tell, but it can't be that many," said Rhyss. "Further reason for them to stay safe behind the gates."

Rorik addressed Diessa politely, "Can you use the earth spirits to see what's going on inside the keep?"

Diessa's lips tightened into a thin line. "Sadly, no. I've tried, but there is an evil heaviness within the hold that stops me from seeing anything, at least from afar. I seem to have lost that deep connection with the spirits since the battle." She sighed and looked down at the ground. "It's for the best, I think. I couldn't stay connected like that and still keep my sense of self."

Rorik grunted in assent, and he went back to studying the map. "Shame," he whispered to himself, just loud enough for some of the dwarfs to hear.

Din's eyes narrowed as he considered the clan's options. "I don't think we can count on the Abyssal Dwarfs to come out. But we may not have to."

"What do you mean?" asked Dare.

"Well, we can't get the entire army in through the northwest tunnel. But we can send a small force in through there to gain entrance to the hold. We need to sneak in, so we have to force the Abyssal Dwarfs to put their attention elsewhere."

Veit nodded in comprehension. "I see it. While you're sneaking in through the back door, we'll be banging on the front door."

"But we just said that a frontal assault would be suicide," Daerun said, pointing at the killing ground before the gates.

"But you don't have to attack," interjected Rhyss. "You just have to look like you're going to."

"Exactly!" Din said excitedly. "We'll line the army up outside of cannon range, at the mouth of the valley. We'll act as if we're planning on laying siege to the hold. Then, under cover of darkness, we'll send a small force to enter the hold and open the gates from the inside."

Daerun sucked on his teeth and furrowed his brow. "Risky."

"Yes," agreed Din, "but I don't see a better plan."

Veit leaned low over the map, tracing the tunnel pathway to the interior of the hold. "If I remember correctly, the northwest tunnel leads to this section of the keep, near the workshops, gristmill, and bakery. There shouldn't be many people in this area if they're worried about an attack." He moved his finger further down the passageway. "Once past there, we'll have to go near the great hall to access the gates." He tapped his finger on the parchment. "If there's going to be trouble, we'll find it there."

Dinnidek looked up from the map to gaze at the assembled dwarfs in turn. Daerun and Rorik looked skeptical, while Rhyss stroked his beard deep in thought. Anfynn and his clansmen were more detached, but Din noted that Kilvar kept examining the mountain pathway near the cave entrance.

He's going to ask to stay, thought Din. *We'll see if Anfynn lets him.*

From behind him, he felt Diessa place her hand reassuringly on his shoulder. That small gesture was enough to give him the confidence to push ahead.

"Does anyone object to marching on Llyngyr Cadw?" He was surprised at how calm his demeanor was. This was the last step toward redemption or ruin for the clan. "I can order you to go, but you know that's not my nature. I need to know that you're all committed to this."

His gaze swept the room, and he locked eyes quickly with each of his friends in turn. He saw excitement, apprehension, and determination in equal measure, but there was no sign of fear or regret.

When he got to Anfynn, the two dwarfs shared a moment. Anfynn's eyes softened, and he cleared his throat before speaking.

"It's an audacious plan, Lord Dinnidek, just like all of your plans so far. I regret that I won't be able to join you."

Kilvar sighed audibly but kept his eyes to the ground. Din could see the tension around Anfynn's eyes, the distress in his countenance. It was obvious that Anfynn was torn about his decision, but Din understood that the clan came first. In the end, he had to do what was best for his people, even if it hurt.

"I understand," Din said gravely before switching to a lighter tone. "There will be plenty of opportunities to battle together once we've retaken our home. We'll have trade routes to protect and more clans to help by this time next year."

The tension left Anfynn's face at the understanding words. Din had acknowledged the tough choice the Warmaster had to make without blatantly calling attention to it. Anfynn smiled and raised his fist, a smoldering fire in his eyes. "Help more of our kin return? Push the traitors back to the Abyss? Establish trade and find peace again? Yes, we will, Lord Dinnidek. Yes, we will."

CHAPTER 24

Zareen carefully wrung out the bloody rag into the silver basin. The blood-tainted water fell into the waiting vessel, spreading red tendrils throughout the clear liquid. Zareen took a deep breath before rewetting the rag. He moved slowly, almost reverently, intensely intentional with every motion. As usual, his lab was hot, bordering on uncomfortable, and he relished the coolness of the blood-tinged water on his hands. The fire crackled steadily in the hearth behind him, occasionally flaring up with renewed vigor. He took another deep breath, and the rusty smell of blood filled his nostrils along with acrid chemical fumes which were strong enough to make his eyes burn. After a moment, he pulled the now soaking rag from the basin and turned back toward his brother.

Alborz was laid out on the laboratory table, wearing only his breeches. The skin on his bare chest was bruised and blotched in places, purple and blue hues spreading in ridges across his chest and below his waist. Zareen wasn't sure if the bruises were from the battle or the antlered nightmare which had held Alborz's body so tightly in its claws. The discoloration was worst around the right side of Alborz neck and temple where the killing blow had landed, centered on a cut that slashed the skin up and around his right eye. Alborz's head lolled unnaturally to the left, and his ruptured right eye was shut while his left stared lifelessly up at the ceiling.

Zareen held the wet rag in one hand and cradled Alborz's head up off the table. He ran the rag through his brother's hair, paying close attention to where it was matted with dried blood. He methodically stroked each lock of hair until the blood dissolved. He periodically stopped to rinse the rag, every time making sure to leave his hands in the water and take a few deep, cleansing breaths before continuing. His face was an implacable mask of seeming indifference while he worked away at Alborz's face and beard. On the surface, he was completely detached, and if there had been any onlookers, they would have thought that Alborz was just another corpse, and not Zareen's last connection to his old life. In contrast to his outer demeanor, Zareen's mind was filled with memories spanning back centuries.

In contrast to his outer demeanor, Zareen's mind was filled with memories spanning back centuries.

Images of when they were children flashed in his head. He remembered how even then Alborz's forceful charisma made him a natural leader that demanded attention and respect from the other children. His mind wandered to memories of Alborz teaching Zareen how to hold a sword.

As young Imperial thanes, they were expected to take their place in the shield wall. Alborz had been so patient with Zareen back then, demonstrating over and over how to hold his wrist, his thumb, just so. Zareen had been an awful student, and when he'd protested one too many times that he wasn't a warrior, Alborz had finally relented, but not before reminding Zareen that there was more than one way to rule.

He fought against a smile that threatened to curl his lip as he remembered the day that Alborz had asked their father to let Zareen train with the flame priests. Their father, the sole parent in their life after their mother's premature death, put up resistance at first, but even he could not resist Alborz's charismatic spell.

Neither of them would be where they were if it weren't for Alborz. Zareen was a quick study and rapidly gained a reputation for his keen intellect, and Alborz never missed a chance to trumpet his brother's accomplishments. Both of them were destined for greatness! Due to his renown, and his standing as the clan chief's son, Zareen was recruited to work with the clan engineers; and for a time, Zareen pursued both paths with equal rigor and intensity. For his part, Alborz was quickly becoming known as the greatest duelist in their clan, and it was whispered that he would one day be the youngest Warmaster in clan history.

Zareen stoically finished washing the blood and grime from Alborz. He dropped the rag in the red water with a splash and wiped at his eyes with the back of his hands. He went to his workbench and moved aside some of the vials and jars of chemicals to retrieve his surgical kit, a few needles of various sizes, some thin strong thread, and a scalpel. The fire continued to wax and wane with a pulsing regularity.

"Good," he said to himself aloud. "Not much time now."

He returned to Alborz and strapped on a pair of magnifying goggles before leaning in to peer at his brother's cuts.

"Yes, not much time." Zareen's voice had that sing-song quality that he used when he was engrossed in his work. "Need to work quickly."

He began to suture the wounds closed, meticulously working the needle deftly along the cut. His hands passed back and forth across his brother's face. In his mind, Zareen's hands were replaced with an older memory of his hands moving in complex patterns.

* * * * *

Zareen felt his teacher's intent gaze as the young dwarf manipulated the air. He had conjured the elemental spell thousands of times by now, but this time he was trying something different. He was pulling at an actual spirit of flame, not just the fire itself. His hands flew furiously, and at the crescendo, his hands erupted in a brief gout of sickly green fire that quickly faded away.

His eyes widened, and his mouth hung open in excitement. Normally the fires he conjured were red and orange, but this *green* fire had burned with a ravenous intensity. His excitement ceased as the old flame priest cursed and grabbed at Zareen's hands, admonishing him for his rashness.

"We do not summon the fire spirits this way," the priest had said with some severity.

"Why not?" Zareen asked, genuinely perplexed.

"Because the spirits do not exist to serve us, Zareen!" the priest exclaimed, as if the truth was so obvious that it wasn't worth mentioning.

"Why not?" Zareen asked again. "Do we not use the earth spirits in this way? We summon them and they do tasks for us. Why shouldn't the flame spirits?"

The priest looked shocked at the question and shook his head.

"The dwarfs and the spirits we commune with are partners, Zareen, working in harmony. We can't force them to obey, or else we risk corrupting that relationship and all of the works that come from it."

"Aren't we their masters? We give them shape and form. Without us, the spirits are less, weaker. Is this not so?"

The old priest responded by ending the lessons for the day. Zareen had left puzzled at the priest's anxious response. He hadn't asked anything unreasonable, had he?

Weeks passed, and Zareen received more and more scrutiny for his rogue experiments. He was furious when he found that word was spreading to the other priests that he couldn't be trusted.

Meanwhile Alborz, at his father's urging, had been persecuting a vendetta against a rival Imperial clan. He used spurious, but completely legal, pretenses to initiate duels with all the rival thanes. He publicly humiliated his enemies with his swordplay, taunting them during and afterward so that they lost further honor and standing. That should have ended it, but Alborz wanted to end the clan's power once and for all. One night, he resorted to starting a tavern fight with the rival chief's son that ended in bloodshed, and the chief's son eventually died of his wounds.

His father had summoned both the brothers, and as the two siblings were being berated, Zareen kept his eyes focused on the ground in front of him. Focusing back at the moment, Zareen heard his father yelling at him for his 'rash' experiments, demanding that he be more discrete from now on.

"Father," Alborz tried to interrupt, "Zareen's talent..."

"Silence!" Their father held up a single finger and brought himself inches before Alborz's face, who refused to flinch. "You are next! Killing that chief's son as you did? I cannot believe you!"

Their father turned away and exhaled deeply. The brothers stole a glance at each other before their father came back around, his gaze still hard and his eyes still fierce.

"I'm not mad about what you did, but about how you did it! You can't be so flagrant. Yes, what you did was completely legal, but the form matters!"

The point hit Zareen like a dart. It wasn't the deed. It was the fact that they'd been caught.

* * * * *

Zareen's mouth twitched, his hands continuing steadfast in their work, as he remembered that night. The brothers swore that they'd be more careful in the future, but it fell on deaf ears. Despite their protests, their father was severe in his punishment. Zareen would be pulled from the priesthood, and Alborz would be forced to pay the weregild, the blood payment, to the rival clan himself. Zareen always remembered that moment - Alborz, normally fiery and impassioned, became deathly quiet and left the room.

Two weeks later, their father was dead, assassinated by Alborz, with Zareen's help.

He and Alborz had outwardly mourned the loss of their father, but they knew it was for the good of their clan. It needed bold, strong, leaders destined for greatness. Not weak men willing to sacrifice ambition for grace.

Zareen's mouth twitched again, remembering how the clan, instead of embracing their new future, placed all of the suspicion on them. They were outcasts, refugees on the run. Their dreams of ruling their clan were nothing but ashes.

But, as Alborz had said, there was more than one way to rule...

Zareen finished his ministrations and cleaned his tools. He dropped the needles and the scalpel in jars of alcohol and replaced the thread on his work bench. He turned to a set of syringes and a large bladder filled with a sickly green ichor suspended on a stand at head height. He dragged the stand over to Alborz and led a tube from the bottom of the bladder to a small incision that he'd placed in Alborz's arm.

"Yes," he said, "there's more than one way to rule."

One to rule, echoed the voice in his head.

That was the crux of the problem, wasn't it? Only one person could truly rule Llyngyr Cadw. Zareen hadn't been ready to take on the responsibility, and Alborz hadn't been able to give up the honor. That's why the Immortal Guard had been killed. Their connection with Alborz, as leader of the hold, was the focus that fueled their power. Normally when an Overmaster was killed, there would be an obvious successor, either by decree, or by ruthless ambition. When Alborz passed on, and Zareen didn't embrace the title, that link was broken. Zareen sighed in sorrow at the waste, but he'd learned his lesson. He now understood what Alborz had been trying to teach him.

In the days since he'd returned, he had led the denizens of Llyngyr Cadw with a stronger hand. He needed to set a stern tone to do his work. He had been too indulgent before, too undisciplined. But not now. His troops now rightly feared Zareen's wrath, and none dared to disobey.

Zareen finished inserting the tubes into Alborz's arm and went back to retrieve the metal coils from the pulsing machine. The fires in the hearth throbbed with rhythmic intensity, like a giant's heartbeat. Zareen said a quick prayer to Ariagful as he lifted the metal implements from their hooks.

"M-Master Zareen," a ratkin burst into the room and bowed low. "The mongrel clan is pushing on to Llyngyr Cadw.

"Let them come," he said aloud. "They think that they've won? That the army they defeated was the extent of our power? They are mistaken."

Zareen smiled to himself. He had pulled back the gnorr armies from their positions in the tunnels, and even now they were preparing to crush Clan Daamuz when they arrived. The goblins and other vermin they were fighting were of no importance now. The only thing that mattered was destroying his brother's killer. A few squabbles had erupted between the different gnorr groups, but Zareen had used his remaining obsidian golems to ruthlessly restore order. They would be more than ready to wreak his vengeance upon the mongrel dwarfs when the time came.

"I will destroy them all," he ranted feverishly. "I will feed their bodies to Ariagful and spread their ashes on the wind so that their lamentations may be felt throughout the land. And once that's done, I'll hunt down this Worm Lord and do the same with him."

Zareen stared down into Alborz's face and caressed his brother's cheek. He spared a look around the room at the piles of Abyssal Dwarf bodies scattered haphazardly around the laboratory. Scores of corpses were piled waist high. He had been so engrossed in his work that he hadn't noticed them in some time. Small tubes led from each body to a central basin filled with reddish black viscera, with a single, larger tube leading out that fed directly into the inside of Alborz's thigh. Zareen placed the metal coils along his brother's leg and slowly walked back to the machine and its ornate copper crank.

With a final prayer, he gripped the crank with both hands and began slowly turning it, gradually picking up speed. Small sparks of lightning crackled along the wires toward Alborz, and the green ichor dripped slowly into his brother's arm.

The fires within the hearth flared rhythmically.

The viscera from the basin began to pump through the hose in time with the beating of the flames.

CHAPTER 25

Dinnidek strode ahead of the column with an infectious enthusiasm. He'd been anxious since the march began this morning, and it had only grown with each passing hour. Today they would reach the vale of Llyngyr Cadw and the great gates of his home. It was exhilarating. As the morning passed, the land had become increasingly familiar, and Din found himself reliving childhood adventures as each stand of trees or outcropping of rock brought back fond memories. The land had been greener back then, and it was obvious the toll that the Abyssal Dwarf occupation had taken on the foliage. The hot summer sun beat down on the column, which wound back through the damaged countryside along the old trade road that led to Crafanc and the Ironway. Despite the dreary surroundings, Dinnidek felt a youthful optimism soaring in his breast.

The land sloped steeply upward for a short way, and Din scrambled up the hill. He crested the last few feet before the ground leveled off and, with a last burst, jumped up onto a rocky ledge next to the roadway, where the entire vale of Llyngyr Cadw was laid out before him. For a moment, Dinnidek just stood with the blessed sun on his face and soaked in the feeling of accomplishment. They'd come home.

Before him, the roadway sloped gently down to the vale, nestled within the encircling arms of the Red Mountain. The land was covered in dead grass, but in Dinnidek's mind, he saw it as lush and green. The mountain stood tall and imposing, its bald head sticking up above its heavily wooded sides. The mountain itself wasn't red, but it got its name from the maple, dogwood, and oak trees that burst into blazing crimson in the fall. It would be a few ten-days before the trees began to turn.

The gates themselves were relatively small and unobtrusive, being only thirty feet high and just as wide, recessed into the mountainside. Dinnidek had always thought of them as the 'great gates,' but now that he was home again, he was taken with how modest they were in comparison to some of the great Imperial holds. The stone and iron doors stood stolidly closed before them, and Din could just make out the cannon emplacements that jealously guarded the entrance. He knew that the gate itself was surrounded by murder holes where defending troops could pour hot tar, boiling oil, or crossbow bolts into any assaulting force. Dinnidek hadn't been here when the gates fell, but he could imagine Alborz throwing hundreds of ratkin and orcs at the gates, backed by smoldering obsidian golems, until the defenders were overwhelmed. He shook his head at the thought of such callousness.

He would never be so wasteful with the lives of his fellow dwarfs.

The dwarfen column marched past him, and every now and then one of his clansmen would pause to take in the moment before being prodded on by his comrades. Din heard rustling behind him and turned to see Daerun scrambling up the rocks. He reached out a hand and hauled his brother up the last few feet to stand beside him. The outcropping was just big enough for the two of them to stand shoulder to shoulder, each lost in their own thoughts.

Dare put his hand on Dinnidek's shoulder affectionately.

"We did it," he said, the slightest hitch in his voice betraying his emotions. Din could only smile as those same emotions welled up in his throat. "Excellent work, big brother. Father would be proud."

Din cleared his throat and wiped an errant tear from his eye.

"Yes," he said with a sniff. "Mother would be proud too." Din gathered himself before continuing in a more light-hearted tone. "Of course, I hope it's a few centuries before they tell us in person."

The two brothers stood in satisfied silence for a long time as row after row of their clansmen filed past. Daerun pointed toward the head of the column, which had reached the valley floor, the warriors fanning out to make their fortified camp.

"This isn't how I expected to come home," he said somberly.

"Funny," Din responded with more steel in his voice, "if I'm being honest, this is exactly what I expected when we left." He turned toward his brother with a grim smile. "You remember Father's demeanor when he told us we had to leave. I knew he was protecting us. I mean, he said as much."

"I argued so hard with him," Dare scoffed.

"I remember," Din chuckled. "You swore up and down that you'd stay and slay every Abyssal Dwarf that dared to poke his nose in our valley."

"I was just saying what you were thinking," Dare said affectionately.

"Oh, I don't deny it. But we both knew Father would get his way."

"He always did," said Daerun with some admiration.

"Yeah, he had a will of steel."

"To match Mother's heart of gold."

Dinnidek smiled wryly at his brother's comment. "That was almost poetic, Dare. Corny, really."

Daerun blushed a little before looking back toward the gates. "Still true."

Dinnidek gestured toward the mountain. "It may be a little ragged, but home still looks the same from the outside."

"I bet it's a real mess inside."

"Not for long." Din's voice held a touch of iron. "Is Rhyss back yet from scouting the heights?"

"Not yet. Last message said he had encountered little resistance. Looks like the fiends are planning on hunkering down in there."

Din grunted in response. "Assuming Rhyss finds the lookout entrance unguarded, I've been considering who should be in the assault party."

"Who were you thinking?"

"Well, I'm thinking Rhyss and his rangers will be the main force. We'll need every Ironclad we have to be seen in front of the gates, and it wouldn't be unusual for the rangers to be missing from the shield wall." Dare nodded along in agreement. "I also think Diessa should go with me. If the tunnel is really sealed from the inside, we'll need her and the earth spirits for the final breakthrough into the hold."

"Sounds good," Daerun said as he clapped Dinnidek on the shoulder. "It's fitting that all three of us go in."

"Nice try, Dare," Din scoffed. "No, it will be two of us. You have to stay outside to lead the clan." Daerun started to protest, but Din spoke over him. "If this doesn't work, you'll be the new clan leader. We can't risk losing all three of us."

"I'm no leader," said Daerun in protest.

"What?" Din replied incredulously. "That is a load of mushrooms, and you know it. The clan respects you, Dare, and they'll follow you. In some ways, you're the leader they'll need if this goes sideways."

Dinnidek expected his brother to dig in his heels, but surprisingly, after a silent moment, Daerun just grunted in reply.

"Fine, but you be careful. I don't want to have to prove you right."

The end of the column marched by, and Din jumped down onto the ground, Daerun following close behind. The two brothers followed their clansmen down into the valley. The gates stood silent and formidable in stark contrast to the buzz of activity from the dwarfs. The Ironclad efficiently went to work, trading their swords for shovels and picks. A trench was already being dug across the mouth of the valley, and the sharpened wooden stakes found in each dwarf kit were placed to make a hedge of spikes facing the mountain. Tordek stood next to the clan banner, which he'd placed defiantly on a small rise to be seen by friend and foe alike. The march had been tough on him, and Din had repeatedly caught him wincing in pain as he carried the banner across his broad shoulders. Each time Din offered to help, Tordek waved him off with mild annoyance.

Further away, Veit was loudly directing the Ironclad in their work. His voice echoed off the surrounding arms of the mountain. "C'mon, hurry with those palisades! I want the trench at least as deep as my shoulders, yes?"

The dwarfs began singing an old tavern song to keep time as they dug, and Veit sang along and kept time with his off hand while he supervised the work.

Daerun pointed at the engineer. "You know he won't let Diessa go alone."

"I know," said Din. "I love him for it. He really cares deeply for her."

"And she for him," agreed Dare. "But I'll need him out here to man the cannons, such as they are. That being said, you should take some of his engineers with you, just in case Deese can't smash through the tunnel."

Dinnidek hadn't considered that, but it made good sense.

"Alright. But I want you to tell him he can't come with us. It's the price of leadership," Din said wryly. Daerun snorted in reply. "I want his best artillery crews out here with you, too. We only have a few cannons, so we might as well put our finest on them."

"It will be alright. We'll be on the defense. No need to get myself in trouble." Daerun sighed. "No, if things go according to plan, I should have a nice boring time of it until you open the front gate and let me in."

The two stopped to survey their army. Dinnidek was so intensely proud of what they'd accomplished, how they'd endured. He saw the dwarfs building make-shift fortifications with practiced efficiency and mastery. At their heart, that's what dwarfs were made for. They built. They created. It was the exact opposite of the Abyss and all it stood for. No nihilistic quest for dominion. No fake piety or hollow preening pride like the Basileans. Their work was pure. He imagined his ancestors hollowing out and finishing the first caves of Llyngyr Cadw. Making their homes as part of the living rock. The delight they must have shown in that original making. With a shake, he came back to the present and saw his clan, their numbers greatly diminished, digging in the earth outside of their home. So few had made it back.

Dinnidek spoke reverently, "Do you think it's worth it, Dare? All the loss? Even if we win, is this better than our lives in Estacarr?"

Daerun considered the question before answering.

"I still think so. I believe that we'd be lost as a clan under Golloch," he said with deep resentment. "No, Din, this is our only real chance at freedom."

Daerun chewed his lip for a moment, and his tone changed to something softer.

"It's a shame for the Imps that Golloch is their leader. I don't know whether he's the root cause, or a symptom of a greater problem, but it's crazy that our clan would rather be here, marooned and facing down an army of filth than spend another year in Estacarr."

Daerun kicked at the ground a few times and squinted into the distance.

"They'll see, eventually," said Din. "They'll have to, or they'll all be subsumed by one dwarf's ambition. By one dwarf's greed." He shook his head ruefully. "But if this works, if we regain our home? Golloch won't be able to control the Free Dwarfs. They'll come back here in droves."

The two brothers stood quietly, and Din's mind dreamed of a future where the Free Dwarfs were resettled in Halpi; but unlike last time, they worked together for mutual defense and prosperity. Seeing his clansmen working so hard, with their objective so close, it wasn't that hard to imagine.

"One last push?" Asked Din.

"Yes," nodded Daerun. "For redemption."

Din smiled and clenched his fist. "For freedom."

CHAPTER 26

"Remember," said Daerun to the assembled volunteers, "the objective is to get their attention, not storm the gates yourself." The Ironclad laughed at the idea, some nervously, others with more bravado. "When you get the signal, you'll advance along the ridgeline, toward the main gate. The minute they send out a sortie, what do you do?"

"We retreat," replied one of the Ironclad sergeants, "and head back to the main line."

"Exactly," said Dare. "If they open fire with their cannons, you fan out so you're not an easy target. If it's a sortie, stick together and get your butts back here as fast as you can. I don't want anyone playing hero and getting killed. Understood?"

The group acknowledged the command.

One of the Ironclad raised his hand with a question. "What if they don't react?"

"Then you keep advancing up the ridge but stay out of the killing field before the gates. Remember, our people are breaking in the back door. If things go according to plan, they'll sneak in, take the gates, and open them for us. So keep your eyes on the gates. If they open, and you see friendly faces, rush in. The rest of us will be right behind you."

Daerun pointed to a rocky outcropping located halfway between them and the main gates.

"In the meantime, you remember the forward gun emplacements built into the ridgeline? Based on their silence so far, we believe that they've been abandoned. You'll move to the closest one and make sure it's out of commission." He pointed to a pair of engineers in the back of the crowd. "If by some chance the emplacements are still occupied, the sappers will fix it quick."

One of the engineers called out, "We'll have the explosives in our packs, so don't stand too close."

Another round of nervous laughter rippled through the dwarfs, but Dare noticed several of the Ironclad unobtrusively take a few steps away from the sappers all the same.

Daerun raised his hammer in salute. The volunteers nodded and raised their weapons in return. "The Earth Mother watch over you. And be careful!"

With that, Daerun dismissed the volunteers, and they marched off north to get into position. He watched them go with a strange sense of foreboding. He would rather be marching with them, opposed to standing in the back lines when there was work to be done. He shook his head ruefully. He felt more comfortable leading from the front. But that was a luxury he couldn't indulge in anymore. He turned away from the departing column and considered the valley instead. The dwarfen fortifications spanned the entire width of the valley, anchored on both sides to the rocky ridges that encircled the flat plains before the gates. The plain was completely barren, with only a few crows circling lazily above the dry and dusty ground. Llyngyr Cadw was so tantalizingly close. The gates were less than a half a mile away. But they might as well be on the other side of Pannithor.

Daerun studied the hold with a mixture of gratitude and frustration.

"Nothing," he said to himself in mild disbelief. "Over twenty-four hours and still nothing."

Tordek, who was standing nearby with the clan banner, just grunted in reply. The stalwart bodyguard held the banner pole with his left hand, away from his bruises, the bottom braced against his foot. The past few days, he'd stubbornly kept pace on the march, but Daerun saw the exhaustion on Tordek's face when they stopped to rest. Even now, Tordek was too proud to show any discomfort. His only sign of weakness was that he hunched to his right, as if afraid to stretch out the ribs on that side.

Daerun kept his eyes on the hold and shook his head in puzzlement. The fiends had to know they were there. The Daamuz army hadn't tried to make it a secret, after all. They'd been busy building their fortifications out in the open for the past day.

"What are they doing in there?"

He knew he shouldn't complain. Every hour that passed before the Abyssal Dwarfs came out to play was another hour they had to set up their defenses. The dwarfs had dug a long, deep trench across the mouth of the valley, the dirt piled high on the opposite bank with sharpened stakes pointing menacingly toward the keep. Veit had made sure that the embankment was high enough for the dwarfs to hide behind and give them some shelter from the enemy artillery. The loosely packed earth would also absorb most of the impact from the cannonballs and allow them to sink into the ground instead of careening through the dwarfen ranks.

Daerun and Veit had worried that the fiends would open fire on the dwarfs while they were building their entrenchments, and they'd kept one tense eye on the gates the entire time. But the fortress had stood silent, as if the besieging dwarfs were beneath its notice. The dwarfs had spent the entire evening on high alert for an ambush, a raid, anything, but the gates stood implacably sealed. The army, under Veit's guidance, had even had time to erect a pair of redoubts overnight, earthen mounds piled almost ten feet high and reinforced with timber walls and a wooden platform. He'd ordered the cannons to be placed on one and amassed the remaining clan Ironwatch on the other. Daerun would have to thank Anfynn for giving the army their remaining ammunition before departing – assuming he ever saw him again.

Daerun was struck by how fatalistic that thought was. He realized that this was where Fel would say something witty to lighten the mood. But Felwyr was on his way to Crafanc to rest, and hopefully recover. Dare remembered Felwyr lying in bed with the remains of his arm heavily wrapped, his face drawn in pain. His mind jumped to Fel's rescuer, and he saw Bruon's charred body, smoking and unrecognizable. Dare shook his head and sighed. When he'd spoken to Dinnidek yesterday, he was optimistic, downright determined. It was hard to stay down when he was talking with his brother. But since then, a pall had descended on Daerun's mood.

He spat into the dust with distaste. "It will be nice to get this over with."

Again, Tordek grunted in reply. Dinnidek had left a few hours ago with Rhyss, Diessa, and the rest of the raiding party. If things went according to plan, they'd break into the hold while the Abyssal Dwarf army was focused on Daerun. But the plan wouldn't work if the fiends didn't take the bait. Daerun had hoped that all the construction would have brought on some sort of response, but apparently it wouldn't be that easy. He needed some sign, some reassurance, that the Abyssal Dwarfs were watching. Daerun shouted at the gates accusingly, "You're not playing along!"

"Abyssals and traitors," said Rorik wryly from behind him, "you can't expect them to do anything right."

The sharpshooter was walking nonchalantly toward him, his rifle slung across both his shoulders, his arms draped above him over the barrel and the stock.

Daerun snorted in mild amusement. "I know, what was I thinking?"

Dare noticed that Rorik's clothes were clean, as opposed his own, which were caked in grime. It was clear that Rorik had avoided the dirty work of building the fortifications. Daerun pointed at Rorik's boots with a wry smile.

"You have a little scuff there on your toe. You may want to clean that off."

Rorik looked down and smiled at the tone in Daerun's voice. "You're not paying me to dig, Master Daerun." Rorik unslung his rifle and leaned it up against the nearby wooden palisade before joining it with a sigh. "You are supposedly paying me to kill Abyssal Dwarfs, but so far that includes a lot of standing around."

Daerun leaned on the wall next to him and gazed at the valley, a still and desolate no man's land.

"So far." Daerun absently cracked his knuckles and nodded toward the hold. "You'll have plenty to do once we get those gates open."

"Maybe they'll just hide behind their walls and wait for us to go away? I mean, that's what I would do," Rorik said with a shrug. "Either way, there can't be many remaining in there."

"True, but it wouldn't take many soldiers to hold us off." Dare slapped the palisade in mild frustration. He rubbed his temples and squinted his eyes. "It makes Din's mission that much more important. For him to succeed, we need to keep the fiend's attention on us. They could be watching us the entire time, we just wouldn't know it."

Daerun looked toward the assault party, which was just getting into position.

"The problem is that we have to be sure."

"Agreed," nodded Rorik. "And the only way to be sure is to have them shoot at us." He arched his eyebrow. "Lovely."

"Yeah," Daerun sighed. "It's not the best."

"So, what next, Master Daerun?"

"It's time we knocked on the door," Dare answered. He turned toward the southern redoubt where Veit was fussing over the small artillery battery. He called over a messenger. "Have Veit open fire, sparingly. I know the cannons are too weak to do any real damage at this range, but I want to get their attention."

The messenger saluted and ran off. Daerun waved to a nearby musician to have him give the signal for the raid to begin. A long horn call echoed off the surrounding mountainside, followed by two short notes.

The assault party advanced cautiously over the embankment and marched quickly along the base of the northern ridge. Daerun kept one eye on them and the other on the hold. He had the musician nearby in case he had to signal an early retreat, but so far there was no reaction from the Abyssal Dwarfs. A lone cannon blast sounded from the southern redoubt. Daerun followed the cannonball as it arced across the sky and hit the mountainside, just south of the gate with an ineffectual puff of smoke and debris. Another pair of cannons fired a minute later with similar results.

The assault party continued their advance for what seemed like an eternity. Dare knew the dwarfs were moving quickly, but at this distance, it looked like they were crawling along the base of the ridge. Veit fired another volley at the walls. Daerun clenched his fist tightly with the tension. It felt like the entire army was holding its breath for something, anything to happen. The gates of Llyngyr Cadw seemed to be holding its breath as well, standing perfectly still and serene. The dwarfs might as well have been bugs crawling along the back of some giant, leathery beast. Beside him, Rorik watched their progress through the scope of his rifle. The sound of Veit's cannons punctuated the stillness every few moments, but the relative silence in the valley made the sound all the more jarring.

The assault party made it to the base of the forward emplacement and scrambled up the rocks. They fanned out and stayed out of the line of sight from the emplacement windows. Normally, there would have been a shelf of rock just below the gun ports, but that was destroyed when the keep had fallen, and apparently the Abyssal Dwarfs hadn't bothered to make repairs. Three of the dwarfs climbed the last few feet, and Daerun could just see one of them throw a bag into the small, thin window before they all slid as fast as they could down the slope. A second later, smoke and debris belched from the opening like dragon fire, followed by the sound of the explosion a split second later.

Long seconds went by and there was still no sign from the hold as the dwarfs regrouped at the base of the ridge.

"Uff'ran," Daerun cursed and stared at the sky with mounting frustration. They were running out of time. He contemplated forming a second, larger attack force, when Rorik tapped him on the shoulder and pointed at the hold.

The gates had started to open.

The twin doors swung slowly outward, revealing nothing but a yawning blackness that contrasted against the sun-drenched sky outside. Daerun bit the inside of his cheek in anticipation. He prayed to the Earth Mother that he'd see Rhyss excitedly waving back to them.

The doors finished opening, and for a moment, silence reigned over the field. Llyngyr Cadw held its breath, along with the throng of dwarfs waiting outside.

Frenzied screams echoed from within the Red Mountain, and columns of Abyssal Halfbreeds erupted from the hold. Scores of the abominations emerged from the gates, and without hesitation, they galloped forward to engage the assault party. Daerun waved for the musician to signal the retreat, but the dwarfs had already begun running back to the safety of the dwarfen line. The halfbreeds recklessly sped toward them, and Daerun could tell it would be a close race. Meanwhile, more orcs and ratkin marched from the gates. Dare smiled to himself. If the Abyssal Dwarfs emptied their hold to come fight, all the better. It would be easier for Dinnidek to take the gates if all the defenders were busy.

Rorik ran off to the northern redoubt to take command of his snipers who were stationed there. Daerun turned back to the retreating assault party and slapped his leg in agitation as the halfbreeds sped across the plain. It would be close. A salvo of cannon fire sounded from behind Daerun, and the ground before the halfbreeds erupted with dirt and debris, momentarily disrupting their charge.

"Quick thinking, Veit," Daerun said to himself. The dwarfs kept running for their lives, but Veit seemed to have bought them the precious moments they needed.

Daerun spared a glance toward the gates. He expected to see a few ratkin stationed to cover the halfbreeds once their sortie was complete. But instead, the plain was filling with hundreds of ratkin and orcs. They were already formed up in ranks and were marching slowly toward the dwarfs. This was more than a sortie.

The dwarfs to the north cheered as the assault party made it back to the safety of their fortifications. Daerun saw the Ironwatch on the northern redoubt pour fire into the halfbreeds, driving them off. Veit fired another cannon volley, this time into the massing ratkin. The shots got swallowed up in the densely packed enemy formation, and Daerun couldn't make out what effect, if any, the artillery had. And still, more and more troops emerged from the hold.

As if in reply, the cannon ports around the gates exploded with fire, and the shots groaned and whistled across the sky before raining down on the dwarfs. The palisade erupted all along the line, and the dwarfs took shelter from the splintered wood and flying debris. Daerun resisted the urge to duck down behind the palisade, and he instead raised his axe and shouted to his clansmen.

"Stand fast! Stand fast!"

After the initial volley, a continuous cannonade belched from the hold, keeping the dwarfs pinned down. It was just as well. The valley was now filled with a mass of ratkin and orcs, with more still coming. A pack of obsidian golems strode out of the gates, black smoke billowing from their molten flesh and polluting the hot summer sky. Daerun stared in growing disbelief.

"Where did all these troops come from?" he shouted to Tordek in frustration.

"Doesn't matter," yelled Tordek above the thunderous artillery barrage. "Looks like we finally got their attention."

"Yay for us," Dare responded sardonically.

This made no sense. Where had the Abyssal Dwarfs gotten all these reinforcements? Dare looked up and down the line. The Ironclad were showing no signs of wavering. They'd faced artillery barrages like this before. But they were heavily outnumbered. Daerun felt a hollow feeling growing in his gut. They were in trouble.

He locked eyes with Tordek, and the bodyguard's steady gaze calmed Dare's nerves. Tordek just simply nodded, as if to remind Dare that this had all been part of the plan, more or less. Dare walked toward Tordek and leaned in so that he could be heard above the artillery.

"Let's get to the northern redoubt. We'll lead the defense from there."

Tordek nodded, turned with a wince, and trotted off northward. Daerun steeled himself. He had wanted to lead from the front. He was going to get his wish.

* * * * *

Diessa reached her hand out and gently brushed against the low scrub trees that covered the mountain at this elevation. The small green leaves on the alpine bushes were surprisingly soft, and the feel of them soothed Diessa's nerves as she steadily ascended the Red Mountain. Even at this altitude, the mountain breezes were hot and still, as if the very sky was holding its breath. Rhyss led the raiding party, comprised of almost two hundred rangers and a few engineers, hiking in single file through the twisting herd path. Gwel, who she had resummoned earlier that morning, made his own way a few feet off the path, flowing effortlessly between the densely packed foliage. She figured that it was fitting to have the land's help in this final assault, and Gwel was small enough to not attract too much attention as they snuck along.

She needn't have worried. The mountainside was desolate, with no signs of enemy sentries. It seemed like the deranged herald had been speaking the truth that the Abyssal Dwarfs hadn't discovered this back entry into the hold. Diessa had puzzled over the situation and still had her reservations. The whole thing seemed like the perfect trap.

The dwarfs crested above the treeline, and the ground changed to bald stone. The column scrambled quickly now, trying to keep their exposure to a minimum. In her memory, she could see the wooden watch tower standing tall and proud above the mountain slopes. She studied the ground, looking for signs of the old structure, but there were none. She thought that there would be something left, but even the stone foundations had been smoothed over to blend into the mountain rocks. Diessa wondered how the survivors had managed to destroy the tower so completely. Had they accomplished it just before the Abyssal Dwarfs laid siege to the hold? Or had one of the stone priests escaped and used the earth spirits to cover their tracks?

"There it is," said Rhyss warily from up ahead as he pointed to a natural cleft in the rock. Dinnidek, who had been following just behind Rhyss, ran forward to stand before the opening. Din took off his helmet and held it loosely at his side while he wiped his brow with the back of his other hand. He stood there, gazing into the entrance with a look of solemnity that touched Diessa deeply. She stopped a few feet away and paused to give Dinnidek the space he needed. Din's hand slowly relaxed, and he accidentally dropped the helmet. It hit the ground and made a loud clanging sound that rattled Din out of his reverie. He looked back at Rhyss and Diessa sheepishly before leaning over to pick it back up.

Mike Rossi

"Um, sorry," he blushed as he spoke.

For a moment, Diessa had a feeling of deja-vu. Had she seen something like this before?

Diessa reached out and patted Din's shoulder affectionately. "It's okay," she whispered. "It's a lot, isn't it?"

Din just nodded and took a deep breath while he kept his eyes on the crevasse. Gwel wandered forward and poked his little head around the side of the entrance to look inside. He turned back to Rhyss and shook his head 'no' with a shrug.

"Looks like he doesn't see anything," observed Diessa.

Rhyss silently signaled to the closest fist of rangers, and they readied their equipment to enter the tunnel. The engineers, meanwhile, huddled together. They carried a bundle of small explosives that would be used if the elementals couldn't break through. Because of their dangerous cargo, they'd be bringing up the rear. Gwel cautiously entered the tunnel. As the spirit stepped out of the sunlight, Diessa felt something tugging at her mind. She closed her eyes, and as she did, she saw the tunnel clearly, despite the dark.

"He's sharing his sight with me," she said with a delighted smile.

"Good," said Rhyss approvingly. "Can you ask him to scout ahead a bit?"

Gwel moved deeper into the tunnel. The floor was uneven and full of broken rocks which jutted out from the walls at odd angles. The elemental deftly maneuvered a dozen yards in before the tunnel turned sharply to the left. As he turned the corner, Gwel saw that the tunnel ended abruptly at a wall of large boulders. Gwel sent Diessa a vision of the dwarfs standing away from the tunnel entrance.

"Gwel's at the end of the tunnel," said Diessa. "He wants us to stand back."

The closest dwarfs backed away without question, except Rhyss, who stood off to the side, his back to a large boulder. Diessa saw through Gwel's eyes as the small elemental approached the cave-in, closer and closer to the wall of jumbled stone. As he contacted the wall, Diessa stopped seeing through Gwel's eyes, but instead she *felt* what he was doing. She sensed Gwel meld into the stones, and then he stretched? Expanded? The feeling was so alien that Diessa couldn't put words to it. Gwel's spirit extended slowly into the boulders that blocked the passageway, and then, in an instant, Gwel's consciousness leaped away, into the surrounding bedrock. The boulders were pulled down into the floor, or were sucked up into the tunnel ceiling, leaving a small entry for the dwarfs to squeeze through. Outside, the ground shook, and a whoosh of dusty air belched from the tunnel entrance, showering the ground and a few of the closer dwarfs with pebbles and detritus.

"Sweet Earth Mother," exclaimed one of the engineers. "If the little bugger can do that, what do you need us for?"

Diessa laughed as Gwel resumed his original shape and came back up the tunnel. He waved his small arms and bowed, inviting the dwarfs to follow him in. Without waiting for a response, he turned and made his way deeper into the mountain. On Rhyss' signal, a score of rangers entered the tunnel, some with small, hooded lanterns carried in their off-hands.

The low boom of cannon fire carried to them from the valley below. A few moments later, the sounds intensified to an unrelenting thunder that rolled and echoed between the mountaintops.

"Looks like Dare has their attention," Dinnidek said with a nervous smile. "Everything is going according to plan."

Diessa clasped his hand and gave it a quick squeeze. Din took one more deep breath in, exhaled strongly, and walked purposefully into the tunnel. Diessa gazed into the yawning darkness, rubbed her hands together in nervous anticipation, and took the final fateful steps back into her home.

* * * * *

Rorik calmly exhaled and fired. Through his scope, he saw the orc sergeant clutch his abdomen, slump over, and fall off his gore. He pulled his rifle down and hurriedly began to reload. From his position at the northern redoubt, Rorik had a commanding view of the battlefield. Fighting raged all along the line, but the dwarfs were holding firm behind their embankment, for now. Behind the initial wave, the valley teemed with ratkin and orcs pushing relentlessly forward to overrun the dwarfs.

"I don't care what Master Daerun says," Rorik declared, "there's no way this was part of the plan."

The enemy were packed together so tightly that Rorik couldn't miss. He still scanned the battlefield for quality targets, but if he happened to shoot wide, his bullet would simply kill another slave in its stead.

The Wyverns were interspersed among the other Ironwatch, flowing from spot to spot along the ramparts to get a better bead on their targets. Rorik approached the closest pair of sharpshooters and pulled them close enough to be heard over the roar of battle.

"Keep your packs close, gents," he said as he gestured toward the eastern trade road. "We're in over our heads, and if this gets bad, I want us ready to retreat back to Crafanc. If we get separated, we'll meet up at the place where we made camp two days' march east of here. Got it?" Rorik didn't wait for an answer before he pointed at the next pair of snipers further down the line. "Go spread the word, but don't be too overt. Hurry now and bring your packs."

The Wyverns saluted and trotted off. Rorik turned back to the pressing matter of killing all of the ratkin. He swept the field, looking for targets. Fulgria knew there were plenty to choose from. A horde of orcs were advancing hard to the north, and they crashed into the dwarfen palisade with a savage fury.

Rorik bellowed to the Ironwatch all around him, "To the north!" They didn't fall under his command, but the dwarfs knew a bad situation when they saw it. The gunners ran to the northern end of the palisade and fired indiscriminately into the orcish flank. Even at that far distance, the volleys had an effect, and scores of orcs fell, oblivious to where their doom had come from.

The attack momentarily abated, but a fresh mass of orcs surged forward to carry on the assault. The Ironwatch continued firing their murderous rain into this new threat, but this time, the charge rammed home. Rorik watched in fascination as a troop of orcs recklessly threw their bodies against the Ironclad atop the embankment. Within seconds they were butchered, but their suicidal charge disrupted the shield wall enough for more orcs to press the advantage and plunge into the opening. The dwarfs were pushed back from the high ground, and in other places the line bowed dangerously. Rorik exhorted the Ironwatch to keep up their fire. He concentrated on his breathing to keep calm while he 'tsked' in agitation. This wasn't the worst situation he'd been in. But it was close.

Horns blared, and Rorik saw Daerun lead his reserves to reinforce the northern end of the line. The dwarfen thane commanded the counter charge himself, and he ran up the embankment and crashed into the mass of orcs, his Shieldbreakers just behind him. For a few long moments, Rorik lost sight of Daerun within the confused swirling melee. The Shieldbreakers smashed the orcs and forced them back down the embankment, choking the defensive ditch with orcish dead. As the orcs fell back, Daerun emerged from the chaos. Dare caved in an orc's chest with his great hammer and kicked his foe down the earthen slope. The orc's body got hung up on a few of the wooden stakes, and it hung there as a grisly warning to its fellows. The Ironwatch let out a cheer and sniped at the fleeing orcs.

Well, thought Rorik, *that was close.*

He wiped his brow with his sleeve and turned back to the south. His sense of relief was brief. A horde of ratkin were assaulting the shield wall positioned before the southern redoubt. The dwarfen line there was holding its own, but it couldn't last for long. A series of explosions erupted all around the redoubt. The Abyssal Dwarf artillery was finding its range. A group of obsidian golems were coming up behind the ratkin. With a sinking feeling, Rorik realized that the orc assault to the north had been a distraction. The real push was to the south. He 'tsked' a few times before he directed the

Wyverns to begin firing into this new threat. He glanced down at the pack by his feet before raising his rifle for another shot.

* * * * *

It had been ten years since Rhyss had walked this tunnel. In his memory, the finished stone walls glowed with the light of small oil lamps, spaced evenly along its pathway, wide enough to accommodate two dwarfs walking side by side. Back then, the tunnel had seemed bright, almost cheery, with the steady flames of the lamps dancing subtly across the clean, dry stonework. Now the tunnel was damp and cold, the lanterns hung dark and neglected from loose metal hooks. Their golden light was replaced with the faint green and blue glow of phosphorescent moss that grew on the ceiling and the cracks on the floor. It made the tunnel feel eerie, and even though Rhyss was technically coming home, he felt like he was descending into an unknown realm of wispy shadows.

Rhyss was near the front of the main column, with only the advance scouts roving ahead. Gwel walked a dozen paces in front of him. He was surprised at how fast the little earth spirit could move, given how small his legs were. At one point, Rhyss tried to match Gwel step for step, but even though his strides were much longer, he still couldn't catch the elemental. Eventually he stopped trying to understand it and just chalked it up to magic. Rhyss tried to remember how long the tunnel had felt back then, but he found that his memory couldn't decide if the passage was much longer or shorter than today. It added to the surreal feeling.

As they turned a gentle corner, Rhyss saw a signal from his rangers who had scouted further down the tunnel. Two tight beams of light reflected off the opposite wall from where the tunnel had turned, so even though the rangers were out of sight, their silent signal carried. Rhyss raised his fist to tell the column to stop and studied the long and short bursts of light. His advance scouts had found a finished stone wall that sealed off the tunnel.

Good thing they're using the lanterns, Rhyss thought to himself. *If that wall abuts the hold, we don't want the fiends to hear us from the other side.* That would be the trickiest part. They'd have to move fast to avoid getting bottled up in the tunnel.

Diessa came up next to Rhyss and whispered, "Gwel says there's a wall up ahead. Want me to have him open it?"

Gwel had pulled his disappearing stone trick two more times during their journey, each time with a rumble and cloud of dust.

"I don't think so," Rhyss answered thoughtfully. "I believe the hall is on the other side of the wall. Don't want to make too much noise if we can help it."

Diessa nodded in understanding before she closed her eyes and became very still. Rhyss assumed she was communing with Gwel. Meanwhile, the rangers who had been marching behind caught up to them. Within a few moments, the passage was crowded with dwarfs patiently waiting for their next move. It made Rhyss feel cramped. He kept running through their options regarding what they'd do if they were discovered. There wasn't much room to maneuver, so most of his plans devolved into 'fight and push forward.' There was no telling what was on the other side of the wall, and the danger of the unknown, combined with the menacing feeling from his old home, was setting him on edge.

Diessa abruptly opened her eyes. "We're good. The hallway on the other side of the wall is empty."

"What?" asked Rhyss. "How do you know?"

"Gwel told me." She smiled. Rhyss was about to ask her how Gwel knew, but she anticipated his question and cut him off. "He looked through the wall. It's made of stone after all."

Rhyss sighed in relief. "Can Gwel open it up?"

"Sure. He's waiting for you by the wall. Give him the signal and he'll let you in."

She began rummaging through a satchel at her side as she spoke. She pulled out a set of geodes and some chalk and piled them into her left hand. Rhyss gave her a quizzical look, but she just handed the geodes to him and smiled.

"I'm going to summon some help." She closed her satchel and retrieved the items from Rhyss before turning back up the tunnel. She called over her shoulder as she maneuvered between the waiting rangers. "I'll join you in a few minutes. Don't wait for me!"

Rhyss watched her go with a smile. *She's changed somehow,* he thought. *Stronger. More confident. It suits her.*

He began organizing his rangers for the assault and pulled two fists of dwarfs with him to the end of the tunnel. Gwel was waiting there, leaning against the wall with his little arms crossed, as if he was impatient to get started. Rhyss walked next to him and placed his hand on the elemental's stone shoulder.

"I hear you," he said. "I'm anxious to get in there as well."

"As am I," said Dinnidek from behind him. Rhyss turned back to see Din standing among the rangers, his axe out and ready. Rhyss was about to ask him if he was sure he didn't want the rangers to sweep the hallway before he entered, but Dinnidek interrupted him. "I'm going in, Rhyss. You can't make me wait."

Rhyss snorted. He was getting tired of Daamuz siblings cutting him off. Rhyss reflected that it was a good thing that Daerun wasn't there. He'd be jostling with Din to see who would get in first. Rhyss nodded at Din in acquiescence.

"Of course, my lord," he said with an exaggerated tone.

Din rolled his eyes at having been 'm'lorded,' but he didn't move. After a moment, Rhyss took the hint and shifted his focus to his troops. The rangers were lined up ready to go, with their cadre of engineers further back up the hallway. He nodded in satisfaction and turned to Gwel.

"We're ready, little one." He gestured to the wall. "After you."

Gwel bowed, walked up to the wall, and melted into it. The small stones that made up his body clattered to the ground in a lifeless heap, and he simply disappeared. It occurred to Rhyss that he probably shouldn't be standing so close to the wall in case it shattered like the others. He ordered everyone back as he kept his eyes on the stone. The dwarfs had only stepped back a few paces before the wall seemed to shimmer? Melt? It was hard to describe. It seemed to bow out, away from them, and then the very stones just walked away from them. It was as if the wall itself came alive, and as it 'stepped' away from where it had stood, it coalesced into an eight foot tall humanoid shape. An opening appeared in the void where the stones used to be, and Rhyss could see the hallway that led to the old bakery. The elemental strode to the opposite end of the hallway, leaned against the wall, and folded its arms.

"Show off," said Rhyss as he came to the entrance.

Rhyss checked down the hallway for any danger and, seeing none, he stepped aside to give Dinnidek the honor of entering Llyngyr Cadw. Din came up next to him and peered around the corner to see the hallway for himself. Once he was sure it was clear, Dinnidek took a deep breath and strode forward, the rest of the rangers following close behind. Rhyss jumped into line right after them.

"Welcome home," he whispered and tightened the grip on his axes.

* * * * *

"Get that grapeshot loaded! No time!" Veit screamed at his artillery crew.

The dwarfs worked frantically in the face of the sea of ratkin surging toward them. The Ironclad stationed at the palisade had tightened up their formation in response to the furious assault. From his vantage atop the southern redoubt, Veit could tell that the line was barely holding. In some spots, the dwarfen warriors couldn't do anything except lock shields and dig in their heels. The attacks were coming so quickly and from so many angles that there was no room or time to swing their axes for a counterattack. Hordes of ratkin choked the plains before the palisade, a chittering screeching mob whipped into a frothing frenzy by the Abyssal Dwarf slave drivers. The cacophony of battle was almost overwhelming. It was so loud that his ears couldn't process it, and Veit felt it in his chest more than he heard it. The crew was under so much stress that they were on the borderline between simply moving fast and giving in to rushed panic. Veit knew that panic meant mistakes, and mistakes led to untimely explosions.

Veit pulled one of the gun crew close and shouted in his ear. "Elevate the guns five degrees. We're gonna relieve the pressure, yes?"

Veit pointed out toward the masses of ratkin warriors past the defensive ditch. The gunner followed Veit's finger and nodded in understanding before rushing toward the cannon and turning the small crank at the rear of the chassis. Veit limped over to the next of his three guns. Within moments, all the cannons were sighted and ready. Veit caught all the crews' attention and raised his cane into the air. He gave one last glance at the chaos below and signaled for the cannons to fire.

Smoke and fire burst forth from the cannons, and a barrage of shrapnel cut through the ratkin in front of the redoubt. Scores of vermin fell, their bodies shredded instantly. The ratkin let out a cry of despair and pain, as if the enemy army was one giant organism fighting for survival. The pressure on the Ironclad momentarily abated, and the dwarfs took the opportunity to cut down the ratkin at the palisade. The enemy fell back in confusion.

Veit screamed for his crews to reload, but they didn't need to be told. He looked at the ammunition stores and his heart fluttered. This would be their last round of grapeshot. After that, they had a few loose shots remaining, but not enough for a concerted salvo. Veit limped to the closest cannon, hefted a swabbing pole, and helped to load the gun. The cannon barrels were getting hot and were in danger of warping if the dwarfs kept up their pace. But there was no choice. Veit swabbed out the barrel, and the water hissed as the bundle of wet rags touched the blackened insides of the cannon. When he was done, he rammed the charge into the barrel and prayed that the gun was cool enough to not inadvertently ignite the powder. Lastly, the crew carefully loaded the bundle of grapeshot.

Veit had been so engrossed in loading the gun that he hadn't spared a look at the battlefield, though he'd been dimly aware that the ratkin still hadn't renewed their attack. When he finally whirled around to survey the enemy, he understood why they'd held off. A pack of obsidian golems were rumbling inexorably toward the southern end of the dwarfen line. The ratkin had regrouped and were advancing behind the smoking behemoths, using their giant bulky bodies as cover against the dwarfen fire. The lead golem was already out of the blast radius of the southernmost gun, and the grapeshot wouldn't be as effective as the six-pound balls they normally fired. There was no time to pull together a coordinated response. Veit could only shout, point at the golems, and hope the crew understood.

Luckily, they did. Two of the cannons fired their payload of grapeshot into one of the golems, which took the brunt of the fire. Though the ammunition was smaller, there was plenty of it, and the obsidian golem's rocky black skin shattered in multiple spots before its leg crumbled away and it fell to the ground. The third fired a few seconds later, and it cut a bloody swath into the ratkin that had been hiding behind the fallen golem.

The remaining obsidian golems barreled forward. One of them leaped forward over the defensive ditch and landed in the midst of the Ironclad shield wall, crushing the wooden palisade and dwarfen warriors alike. The other golem traversed the ditch easily and scattered the defenders with sweeps of its giant smoldering arms. The dwarfs had no choice but to fall back, and Veit watched helplessly as the ratkin poured into the hole in the line.

Veit grabbed the closest crewman and together they swiveled their gun toward this new threat. He ordered the crew to prepare to fire and pointed at the last of the six pounder balls. Without waiting for a response, he ran to the remaining cannons. He grabbed some crew and pulled them close.

"We'll have to spike the guns." He pointed at a pouch that hung from each of the chassis, containing a pin and a small hammer. Instead of letting the guns fall into enemy hands, the crews would hammer the pins into the firing holes. The pins were designed to fit snugly and could only be removed by a blacksmith. It turned Veit's stomach to have to do it, but what choice did they have?

He limped back to the southern cannon and peered over the edge of the rampart. The Ironclad had recovered from the initial shock but were forced to make an orderly retreat. Their backs were to the redoubt, and the ratkin were flooding the area. Without help, the ratkin would be able to maneuver around the Ironclad to the dwarfen rear.

Then the line collapses, he thought in frustration. Having cleared the area, the remaining pair of obsidian golems stood behind the masses of ratkin preparing for another push. They were so tall that their heads were even with the top of the redoubt.

Veit limped next to the cannon and grabbed the firing wick from a crew member. "Get out of here! Gather up the rest and make for the northern redoubt. We can't do anything else useful here."

No time to wait to see if they'd follow his orders. If they decided to stay and die, it was on them. Meanwhile, Veit cut the firing wick down as far as possible with his pocketknife. Then he stood by the cannon and sighted as best he could from beside the barrel. He smiled a little manically to himself as he worked. It was ironic that he told everyone to leave, but here he was, manning the cannon all the same. He just couldn't follow his own advice.

Some leader he was.

The larger of the two golems kept swaying back and forth as it swung its giant arms to attack the nearby dwarfs. Veit studied how the behemoth moved, and after a few seconds, he felt he had it down. The arms swung to the right, the head moved to the left a moment after. He closed one of his eyes and stared down the barrel, the giant jet stone head swinging into view over and over. He watched the arms and counted. Left. Right. There it was. And... now.

He touched the fire to the stub of wick. A split second later, the cannon fired and the cannonball struck the golem square in the face. The monster's head exploded, firing bits of jagged black stone into the ratkin, doing as much damage as a cannister shot. The golem's headless body toppled backward lifeless to the ground, crushing the nearby vermin and buying the dwarfs precious seconds to regroup.

The last obsidian golem stared down at his comrade's corpse then looked up, directly at the cannon, and Veit. It raised its arms in the air and opened its red-hot magma filled mouth in a silent howl. The pit of Veit's stomach felt hollow as terror took hold. The golem dropped its arms and rushed straight for the redoubt. Veit didn't have time to pick up his cane, he just turned and ran, the rush of adrenaline covering the pain in his leg. Just when he reached the middle of the platform, there was a mighty crash from behind him. The platform shook violently, making Veit trip and fall flat on his back. He lay there, staring at the sky, struggling to breathe. More crashes sounded from behind him, and the platform pitched wildly downward in front of him. The sky rotated up as the ground soared into view and he started to slide down the platform. He spread his limbs to slow his descent and slid the last few feet to the ground. He twisted his body to take most of the brunt on his good leg, but he still landed hard on the bad one. He screamed in pain and fear.

He took a second to recover and laid back against the platform, now at a forty-five-degree angle. He looked up to see giant black fingers curl around the end of the wooden planks at the other end of the platform. Veit knew enough about fulcrums to predict what would come next. His eyes widened in panic and he dove forward, off the wooden platform and onto the ground. He landed awkwardly on his side and continued to frantically roll away. The golem pulled down on the planks on its side, and the wood near Veit 'whooshed' up into the air, just missing him. He rolled onto his hands and knees and painfully regained his feet to scramble away to safety. Behind him came a crash of timbers and splintered wood.

Sweet Earth Mother, that was close! he thought. He took a moment to shake off the feeling of vertigo, then tremblingly stood, favoring his good leg. Having finally gained his feet, he quickly limped away to join the Ironclad as they retreated toward the northern redoubt, still on shaky legs. *I should have listened to my own advice.*

Up ahead, he saw his engineers reach the relative safety of the dwarfen lines. He glanced behind him at the wreckage that used to be the redoubt, cannon parts strewn among the chunks of obsidian.

No artillery, he thought anxiously. He shook his head and limped to join the rest of his clan.

* * * * *

Rhyss and his rangers padded down the corridor, Dinnidek in the lead. It had been several minutes since they breached the wall, and he'd been on high alert for signs of the Abyssal Dwarfs, but so far, they'd found nothing. The hold was strangely empty. Where were all the soldiers and slaves? Rhyss heard the muffled sounds of cannon fire, so obviously their plan had worked to pull the fiend's attention to the front gates. But there were usually people still wandering the halls on important errands. Now, there was nothing. It was as if the entire hold were laser focused on the dwarfs outside. It was unsettling.

The rangers nearest to Rhyss passed by a side corridor which led to the bakery. Din had checked for immediate threats before continuing toward the main hall but hadn't explored further. Rhyss stopped and peered down the darkened corridor, listening for signs of trouble. Nothing. He debated just moving on, but he figured it was better to be safe than sorry. It wouldn't do to have an errant servant emerge and scream the alarm. He motioned for a fist of rangers to follow him and quietly stalked toward the bakery.

Rhyss's breathing came quick, and he strained to hear any tell-tale signs of the enemy above the rushing of this blood in his ears. The corridor seemed to stretch on forever. He stopped intermittently to listen, but he couldn't hear anything over the shuffling of the main column of dwarfs. It struck him that even though the dwarfs were trying to be silent, all these warriors gathered together could only be so quiet. He came to a bend in the corridor and raised a fist to signal the other rangers to hold their position. He knelt down and poked his head out cautiously to get a better view.

The door to the bakery was partially open, revealing a darkened room piled high with... something... bags of food, maybe? He couldn't tell from this angle. He motioned for the rangers to follow and rushed toward the door. He closed the distance quickly and readied his axes as he burst through the entryway. After a tense second, Rhyss realized that there was no one in the room. No one living, anyway.

This used to be the bakery, he thought in disgust. The large oven lay cold and still, completely devoid of wood, coals, or even ash. The space where the bakers had worked was replaced with a workbench cluttered with vials of foul chemicals. Bizarre machinery was built into what used to be the larder. What he'd mistaken for large sacks were actually dozens of Abyssal Dwarf bodies, piled high and reeking of death and decay. Blood stained the floor, the walls, the benches and tables, everything. The charnel smell filled his nostrils and left a tang on his tongue. He lowered his axes, fighting the growing revulsion within him, and stepped closer to investigate the grisly scene. The carcasses seemed sallow, sunken, drained of their viscera. Nothing more than dried husks. Dozens of tubes led from the bodies to a bowl, sunken into the middle of the floor and stained with thick dried blood. A pair of tubes snaked from the bowl up to a table, held in place with a pair of clamps. Whatever those tubes had fed wasn't present anymore, and Rhyss had no desire to find out what it was.

Bile rose in his throat, and he motioned the rangers back to the main corridor. His pride demanded that he be the last one to leave, but it was a close call between his pride and his guts. Thankfully, he kept the retching at bay long enough to rejoin the main group and pushed his way to the front of the line. He took a few deep breaths and forcibly blew the air from his nose to clear his nostrils of the smell.

The booms of the artillery had intensified to a constant thrum by the time he caught up to Dinnidek. The dwarfs were clustered at a T intersection in the tunnels. Din held his finger to his lips and pointed toward the tunnel leading to the main gates and the sound of cannon fire. The tunnel would head east and split, one passage widening out and heading down toward the gate, and one passage going upward and splitting to the various gun emplacements that guarded the entrance. The other way led to the great hall, the central seat of power within the hold.

Din leaned in close and whispered in Rhyss' ear, "The advance scouts say that the gates are full of fiends and ratkin. Too many there for us to take. From the sounds of things, the Abyssal Dwarfs conjured themselves up a whole new army. Daerun is in trouble." Rhyss growled low in response. Bad news all around. "We could head to the main hall and see if the Abyssal commanders are there. If we can kill them, maybe we can sow enough confusion to still carry the day."

Rhyss gazed at the tunnel leading to the gates. He looked back up the corridor, and he saw the pack of engineers standing together in the hallway.

"I have an idea," he whispered back.

* * * * *

Rhyss silently counted off ten rangers to follow Dinnidek, who stepped out into the hallway, away from the main group and toward the main hall. Rhyss silently ordered the rest of the rangers to head toward the main gates with hand signals. One of the engineers gave him a puzzled look, and he realized they couldn't understand what he was saying. He'd have to do this the old-fashioned way.

The rangers were already moving to obey, and as the engineers got close, Rhyss pulled one aside. "Follow the rangers," he whispered. "They're going to lead you to the cannons. You're going to silence those guns."

The engineer gave a thumbs up and followed the main body down to the gates. Rhyss waited until the last of the rangers passed and watched them go with some trepidation. If he was wrong, if there was a large force of ratkin or fiends around those guns, he may have just sent his clansmen to their deaths. He exhaled nervously and moved quickly to catch up with Din. As he traveled the corridor, again he was taken aback at how alien the keep felt. The scene in the bakery had shaken him deeply, and it was reinforced by the black and red banners hanging on the walls and the twisted statues lining the corridor with a strange, repulsive beauty. The keep had once been a warm and inviting shrine to their great clan, now it was a temple to cruelty.

A clang of metal broke the eerie silence, and Rhyss ran the last few meters up the tunnel. He barreled into the main hall to see Dinnidek standing tall, surrounded by a fist of rangers. Like the rest of the keep, the hall had been changed to suit the Abyssal Dwarfs' tastes. The giant mural, the frescoes, even the dais and the great throne, had all been removed to be replaced with sterile black and red tiles on the floor and banners on the walls. The room was dark and dimly lit, and Rhyss could just make out an Iron-caster, pale and blond, adorned in blackened steel plate armor, surrounded by four hulking ratkin. The vermin were giant, almost twice the height of a dwarf, with warped mechanical contraptions fused on to the ends of their arms. Some of the arms had ornate canisters with hoses leading to nozzles with small green flames on the end, while other arms ended in prongs that crackled with infernal energy. The ratkin were unnaturally muscular, and the skin of their heads seemed to be stretched in places to cover their strangely enlarged skulls. An obsidian golem hulked behind the Iron-caster, its long arms spread wide, knuckles dragging on the floor.

Rhyss wished he'd brought three dozen more rangers. Dinnidek, meanwhile, stared defiantly at the Iron-caster and raised his axe into the air.

"I've come with my people to reclaim our home. Your time here is at an end, fiend!" He released his grip on the haft of the great axe and caught it with a sweep and a flourish.

For a moment, the Iron-caster stood completely still, the only sound being the low electric hum from the surrounding ratkin's enhanced limbs.

Suddenly he began to laugh, softly at first, but steadily growing into a mad cackle that echoed off the walls and dome of the great hall. The rangers fanned out and drew their crossbows to take aim at the ratkin, but still the Iron-caster laughed. Rhyss slunk unobtrusively in along the wall. Finally, the infernal sorcerer quieted down, and with a flourish of his hand, he spoke with a voice that was surprisingly high and thin.

"I think not." He swept his arm in a grand gesture that took in the entire keep. "This is mine now. This land bends to my will. Even now, your clan warriors are being slaughtered before the very walls of their home. A fitting end for a disgraced clan."

The Abyssal Dwarf's voice took on a tinge of madness as he continued.

"I am the ruler of Llyngyr Cadw, not some mongrel cur with delusions of grandeur."

"I killed the last traitor who claimed to rule Llyngyr Cadw," replied Dinnidek as he pointed his axe at the Iron-caster. "I can kill you too."

The Abyssal Dwarf sneered wickedly. "Is that so?"

A figure emerged from behind the obsidian golem, adorned in ceremonial white-lacquered armor with a crimson hooded cloak hiding his face. He walked slowly, purposefully forward, and stood before the Iron-caster, facing Dinnidek. He brought his hands up and pulled back his hood to reveal a shock of ragged blond hair, a wicked scar over his right temple, and one glassy green eye. The dwarf's skin was sallow, with blue and green veins pulsating just beneath his papery skin, and one eye sewn closed. It was the Overmaster.

Alborz was alive.

* * * * *

Daerun watched the southern redoubt fall with a growing sense of foreboding. Despite facing an army conjured out of nowhere, despite being outnumbered, the thought that the dwarfs might lose hadn't entered his mind. But the fiends and their slaves had breached the defensive line, and things were looking bad. He knew he couldn't let it show, but inside, he was worried that Din might win the gates just to watch his clan get destroyed.

Dare pulled Rorik over to where Tordek was standing. He gestured to the south. "I'm going to handle things over there. You stay here and pour all the fire you can into the last obsidian golem. As for the ratkin, keep them pinned."

Rorik gave a thumbs up, slung his pack over his shoulder, and started organizing the Ironwatch. Daerun pulled in Tordek and pointed down at the platform.

"We rally here, understand? This redoubt is ours. If it falls, we fall."

Tordek rapped the bottom of the banner pole onto the wooden planks of the redoubt and nodded grimly.

Daerun came off the redoubt at a run and gathered the last of his Shieldbreakers. Without words, he pointed at the obsidian golem standing within the ruins of the southern redoubt before charging toward it. The Shieldbreakers followed without hesitation. As he closed in, he passed dwarfs fleeing from the south.

"Rally at the northern redoubt and stand firm!" he shouted as he passed. "Stand firm!"

The sight of Daerun and the Shieldbreakers charging back into danger emboldened the Ironclad. Some headed for the northern redoubt, while others turned to fight.

The obsidian golem saw the dwarfs approaching and slammed its smoking fists into the ground in challenge. It rose to its full height and took a giant slow stride toward the dwarfs.

"The right leg! That's the target!" Daerun yelled.

The closest Shieldbreakers acknowledged the order and slowed their charge. They'd let the golem take that last step forward and then the dwarfs would commit. No use getting ahead of everyone and getting stepped on for your trouble. He briefly thought that this would be a lot easier if Diessa were here, but she was busy cleaning out the hold from the inside. He just had to keep the army together and buy them time.

The ratkin surrounding the golem kept out of its path as well. They were moving to outflank the dwarfs and encircle them, but some of the Ironclad who had rallied moved in and extended the line to counter it. They didn't have to win. They just had to hold. Meanwhile, sparks flashed off the golem's face and chest. The bullets were doing their work, and small cracks appeared in the obsidian skin. The golem took a final step forward and planted its right foot into the ground.

"Wait for it!" Daerun screamed to his clansmen.

The golem swung its arm in a wide arc to sweep the dwarfs away. Some of the more eager Shieldbreakers had kept charging and were effortlessly batted aside by a giant stone fist, bodies shattered by the impact. The remaining dwarfs had the presence of mind to wait for the deadly swing to carry past before they pounced forward and swarmed the golem's right leg.

Daerun smashed the golem's knee with his double handed weapon. The metal head of the hammer struck the unyielding stone of the golem's skin, and the impact reverberated up Daerun's arms, causing his hands to go numb. A dozen Shieldbreakers clustered around the leg, striking it in the ankle and the shin. Daerun got in one more strike before the golem raised its foot into the air.

"Run!" Daerun screamed, and the Shieldbreakers scattered.

The foot came down with a crash that shook the ground. Daerun found himself behind the golem, and he immediately swung around and struck the monster behind the calf. Chips of razor-sharp black stone splintered away, revealing red smoky magma underneath. He could feel the heat emanating from the wound.

Daerun looked between the golem's legs and saw a dwarf hacking away at the creature's foot. Without warning, the golem's palm smashed down on the dwarf, instantly crushing him to death. He never saw it coming. Dare roared and struck the wounded calf again and again. The golem seemed to finally feel the damage and slowly turned toward Daerun. Its face was riddled with cracks and divots. The bullets were striking so fast that sparks were raining down from the side of its head like molten rain. A large chunk of stone fell from its face and shattered on the ground below. Magma poured from the wound and cascaded down the golem's shoulder. Daerun jumped back to avoid the molten river as the ground hissed and popped. The golem raised its arm to strike at Daerun but faltered. Its leg gave way, and it crashed down in a lifeless heap, an arm landing just feet away from where Daerun was standing.

The dwarfs shouted in triumph and rushed forward to press their advantage against the ratkin. The closest vermin fell back in confusion, and the Shieldbreakers made to push forward. But they pulled up short. The ratkin came streaming from around the base of the southern redoubt. They had formed ranks and presented a wall of spears to the dwarfs. Daerun rallied his Shieldbreakers into a defensive formation. He considered the odds. Less than a handful of dwarfs against all those vermin? A part of him wanted to recklessly rush forward to make the ratkin pay a heavy price. But then what? He'd be leading his clansmen to a glorious death, but it was death all the same.

He shook his head 'no' and called to his clansmen. "Form up for withdrawal. There are too many of them, boys."

The Shieldbreakers tightened up and started walking steadily back, still facing the ratkin. Daerun shouldered his hammer and pulled out his battle horn. The vermin surged forward, hungry to butcher the dwarfs.

"Stick together!" Dare yelled. "On my signal, make for the redoubt, fast as you can. We make our stand there behind the Ironclad!"

Daerun raised his horn and blew a clear note. In the face of the horde of ratkin, the dwarfs fled. The ratkin phalanx was too far away to catch them, but it would be close. As Daerun ran, he looked up in relief at the redoubt to see Rorik and the Ironwatch. He put his head down and sprinted for safety, the crackle of gunfire overhead. He stole a quick glance behind him and saw ratkin in the front line fall and writhe on the ground.

The Ironclad opened their ranks to allow the Shieldbreakers past.

Daerun rushed between a pair of dwarfen warriors and immediately turned to rally his troops. The relentless gunfire continued from above, mowing down ratkin by the dozen, but it wouldn't be enough to stop them. There were just too many. Once the last Shieldbreakers had passed, the Ironclad locked their shields into a defensive shield wall and shouted their defiance. The Shieldbreakers stationed themselves just behind to butcher any who broke through. The ratkin continued to pour into the gaps in the shattered fortifications, and soon the redoubt and the northern part of the line was an oasis in a sea of enemies. Dare heard Tordek bellow in his deep bass voice for the dwarfs to stand firm. The dwarfs obeyed and adopted their 'mountain formation,' warriors forming a set of outward facing concentric rings.

The ratkin, facing an unbroken line of shields and axe blades, paused to gather themselves for another charge. They'd pay a deadly price if they engaged the dwarfs, but the dwarfs would pay the ultimate price.

Daerun cursed. This was bad. "Hold fast, boys! This is our home!"

The dwarfs shouted the clan name and banged their axes on their shields. Their cries echoed off of the slope of the Red Mountain and filled the valley with their determination. Dare looked back over his shoulder and saw Tordek wincing as he waved the clan banner high. Rorik was pulling the gunners into groups, pointing out targets for their last precious shots. Finally, Veit pushed his way to the front of the line and locked eyes with Daerun. Veit gestured at the clan warriors, and in the midst of certain doom, he smiled. Not a tragic, fey smile that reflected their doom, but a smile full of pride and power. In that moment, Daerun shared in that pride.

We didn't come all this way to fail, he thought grimly. *As long as one of us survives, the clan survives with us.*

Veit, as if he was reading Daerun's mind, nodded solemnly, pulled out his last pistol and gestured with his chin toward the enemy. Dare nodded back and turned to face the horde of ratkin.

"Come on," he taunted the slaves, "let's get this started!"

The ratkin gathered their courage, but they were wary of the dwarfen clansmen. They had numbers, but no one wanted to be the first to meet their death against the shieldwall. For a moment, the ratkin froze, and a quiet fell over this part of the battlefield.

From far off, Daerun felt a subtle shift in the enemy morale. A commotion erupted from a spot behind the Abyssal Dwarf army along the southern ridgeline, near the base of the Red Mountain. Daerun could just see over the wooden palisade to the site of the ruckus. The orcs in that part of the plain had stopped advancing and were turned to fight an unseen menace. The trees along the ridge obscured his view, but Daerun watched those very trees begin to sway and fall. It looked like an avalanche was rolling down the ridge as giant boulders tumbled to crush the Abyssal slaves beneath them.

Daerun stood transfixed as more and more of the encircling ratkin's attention was pulled toward this new threat. He squinted in that direction, trying hard to decipher what was happening.

Suddenly, scores of dwarfs erupted from the treeline down onto the plain below, some mounted on brocks, others rushing forward on foot, wielding pairs of whirling axes. It was an army of berserkers. The feral dwarfs crashed into the enemy with a fury and sent the orcs reeling back in confusion.

From behind, Dare could just make out a group of rangers along the treeline, dressed in maroon and brown. They fired volley after volley of crossbow bolts into the orcs, sowing further confusion. A wave of palpable relief washed over Daerun. Kilvar and his ranger had stayed to fight after all. Daerun wondered if Anfynn knew that Kilvar was here.

Another wave of boulders rolled down onto the orcs to break their formation and disrupt the lines. Daerun noticed that the boulders, once they stopped rolling, didn't just stay put. The rocks continued to move, and some of them stood on four stubby legs, like giant, headless stone mastiffs. The earth elementals turned and barreled through the orcs like giant playful dogs, scattering them. Daerun had never seen elementals behave this way. The brock riders pushed into the gaps and cut the enemy down in droves. The shock of impact left nothing but confusion and chaos among the Abyssal Dwarfs and their slaves.

Lastly, a giant brown bear, eight feet tall at the shoulder, and almost twice as long, emerged from the woods. Over half a mile away, Daerun could still hear the beast's deafening roar as it thundered a challenge at the orcs. The sunlight shone and glinted off armor plates lining the bear's shoulders, chest, and head. A regal dwarf sat astride the great beast, wearing an ornate helmet adorned with sweeping stag horns and armor of bones. The rider spurred the bear forward, and they plunged into the mass of orcs.

Daerun raised his arms and gave a shout that turned into a whoop of joy. His clansmen took up the cheer, and now it was the ratkin's turn to look worried.

The Worm Lord had come to fight.

* * * * *

Dinnidek stood stunned, his racing heartbeat thrumming in his ears. He couldn't process what he was seeing. It was impossible.

I killed him. The thought kept repeating over and over in his mind. He remembered the clan banner smashing the side of Alborz's head, the Overmaster's skull at an odd angle above his snapped neck. There was no way he could have lived through that. None. The memory brought back a rush of emotions that threatened to overwhelm Dinnidek. He re-lived the terror and fatalistic dread that had coursed through him during the fight. The Overmaster had toyed with him, mocked him, and left him prostrate before him in the dust. It was a miracle that Dinnidek had survived. Seeing Alborz alive made him feel powerless, as if all the struggle, all their accomplishments, were for naught. As if anything they did was just a temporary victory against an encroaching chaos, a devouring evil, that could not be denied.

"Ariagful is a goddess who gives power to her servants," said Zareen with a fervent zeal. "Not like your feeble Earth Mother, who does nothing but weep and lament for her people." He motioned toward the twisted ratkin, the obsidian golem, and lastly at Alborz. "Your goddess holds no sway here, cur."

Dinnidek intensely studied Alborz. The Overmaster stood unnaturally still, with one hand on the pommel of his sword, the other hanging loosely at his side. His chest lacked the steady rise and fall that signaled breathing, and his green eye stared dully straight ahead, his dilated pupils betraying no comprehension of the world around him. Din let out a small exhale of relief – Alborz wasn't truly alive after all. Before Din could relax, Alborz shifted his gaze to look directly at him. They locked eyes, and Din felt a shock roll through him. Alborz's green eye flared brightly with an intense fire. It felt as if Alborz was looking ravenously at his fear and pain, laying it bare for him to consume. Dinnidek flinched back before that hungry and remorseless gaze. Alborz grunted and drew his sword. He swept it before him in an arcing flourish before raising it in a silent salute. Dinnidek stepped back defensively and raised his axe shakily in response. Alborz took a fluid half step toward Din, the aggression in his movements reflected in his fiery eye, but completely at odds with the slack, impassive look upon his face.

Zareen barked a harsh word and snapped his fingers, freezing Alborz in midstride. Alborz's eye flared for a second before dying down to a smoldering emerald ember. Din's eyes widened in confusion at this turn of events. Zareen sneered at Din's consternation.

"Ah yes," the Iron-caster said mockingly. "Since your last meeting, there has been a shift in the balance of power. It's only fitting, really. I have imbued Alborz with the power of Ariagful, and in return, my brother serves me now."

Zareen looked upon Alborz, and for the briefest moment, Din saw a surprising fondness in Zareen's gaze, whether for his brother or the goddess he worshiped, Din couldn't tell. In a flash, it was replaced by a cruel sneer. His voice became frenzied once again.

"In the end, Ariagful will consume all, and all will bend to my will, including you and your mongrel clan. It's a pity that we never found your father's body. He would have made an ideal vessel for Ariagful. To watch him butcher his own children would have been the perfect sacrifice. But alas, I'll have to settle for watching Alborz destroy you instead."

As Zareen spoke, Din's feelings of powerlessness were replaced with a smoldering anger. He gripped his axe so tightly that his knuckles popped. He growled deeply, and his breathing became shallower. The growing rage threatened to consume him. He felt himself losing control, like he had at the beach. He wanted to embrace the anger as a way to destroy his enemies once and for all, but a small voice within him warned him not to give in to his rage, but instead to cling to what really made him strong: his family, his clan, his friends. He had tried to use anger as a weapon before, and it had left him hollow, weak, and ultimately alone. He couldn't make that same mistake again.

The tension in Din's mind was mirrored within the great hall. Each side stood warily, waiting for the other to make a move. The room was eerily silent, save for the low electric hum of the ratkin's mechanical contraptions. Din concentrated on slowing his breathing and willed his hands to relax. As the red haze left his sight, his vision broadened to encompass the entire great hall. He noticed Rhyss out of the corner of his eye, slowly creeping forward within the shadows that clung to the walls. Zareen had been so intent on Dinnidek that he'd been blind to everything else. Din kept his eyes locked on Zareen, so as not to give Rhyss away; but despite himself, the corner of his mouth twitched in a slight smile.

In response, Zareen's eyes became hard, and his lip curled up in a matching sneer. "You dare to mock me, cur!"

He raised his arm, and his hand became wreathed with green flame that matched the flashing emerald fire within Alborz's good eye.

"Kill them! Burn them to ash!"

Zareen swung his hand, and a gout of green fire shot toward Dinnidek and the rangers. Matching flames blossomed from the ratkin's mechanical arms, sending a rolling conflagration toward the dwarfs. The attack was so fast that Dinnidek didn't have time to consciously react. He heard Rhyss scream the word 'No!' as the wall of fire raced across the great hall. Din's eyes widened in sudden panic, and he instinctively knelt to cover his body as best he could with his shield. There was nothing else to do. His only thought in that moment was the certainty that he was about to die.

Dinnidek's eyes were clenched shut, so he could only feel what happened next. The stone floor that he knelt upon tilted below him. The tiles between him and Zareen surged upward, like a rolling wave, and pushed him backward. He opened his eyes in surprise and tumbled to land flat on his back. From his vantage point on the ground, he saw a wall of stone had sprung up from the floor to protect him. Everything else was green flames that poured over the wall and flared throughout the hall. The light was blinding, and the heat from the sorcerous fire sucked the air out of Dinnidek's lungs. He tried to scream, but it came out as a sickly wheeze. And then, in an instant, the fire was gone, leaving an eerie silence.

Din lay panting, trying to get his wits about him. The rangers he'd been with were scattered across the floor, safely behind the wall. They all moved groggily, clutching weapons with shaky hands. Din rolled over to all fours to get to his feet. A powerful voice echoed within the great hall and brought Din fully back to his senses.

"Enough of your ranting, fiend! Take your fire back to the Abyss. I'll show you the power of stone!"

Diessa strode confidently into the hall with Gwel, who was back to his normal size. She gestured for Din to stand up and winked at him with a shaky smile that belied her show of audacity. Din scrambled to stand and whirled toward the stone wall in time to see it dissolve back into the floor. As the stone receded, Dinnidek saw Zareen, surrounded by his slaves, standing with a stunned look of fury. Part of the wall didn't sink back, but instead, it reformed into a tall humanoid shape with a pair of giant mica orbs for eyes. The ratkin shot more flame from their arms, but the elemental batted the fireballs away effortlessly, Diessa mimicking its motions with almost careless waves of her hands.

"Good work, Joro," Diessa said as she patted the elemental's leg. The earth spirit looked down at Diessa and nodded slowly.

Zareen screeched incoherently, and his minions sprang forward to attack. The obsidian golem stood up to its full height and stepped over Zareen to come at the dwarfs. Electricity arced wildly between the prongs on the ratkin's mechanical arms. In response, Joro put his shoulder down and charged the golem while Gwel sank down into the floor and disappeared. The rangers fanned out and shot their crossbows at the ratkin, leaving Dinnidek suddenly alone in the middle of the hall.

Alborz charged at Dinnidek with supernatural speed. Where before his face had been slack, now the fires in his eye lit his face in a wrathful glow that highlighted a visage filled with hate. Din raised his shield and prepared to face Alborz one more time.

* * * * *

The Iron-caster shot a bolt of flame at Rhyss, sending the ranger captain diving for cover. The green fire hit the wall, lighting the tapestry on fire. Rhyss rushed forward on all fours to escape the hungry blaze and hid behind a statue of a stylized female dwarf wreathed in flame. Another fireball hit the wall closer to Rhyss, causing him to flinch back with a curse. Rhyss pulled out his crossbow and loaded it with a practiced, smooth motion. He was still shaken from Din's close call with the wall of fire and was running on pure instinct.

Gotta kill the biggest thing first, he thought. That would be the obsidian golem. He shook his head. *Nope, that's too big. Think a little smaller.* The mechanical ratkin were the next biggest problem. The weapons grafted onto their arms would make a mess out of the dwarfs if they could produce a second wall of fire.

Rhyss took a few quick breaths and poked his head out from behind the statue. Zareen was walking closer, flanked by a pair of the giant ratkin. Behind the Iron-caster, the hall was a tangle of chaos. Joro was locked in combat with the obsidian golem in the center of the hall. Diessa knelt down and punched the ground with her fist, and a wave of energy undulated across the floor up into Joro's body, giving him renewed vigor. Farther away, Alborz was pushing Din back with a lightning quick attack. Amid the confusion, his rangers fired shots at the remaining ratkin, never staying in one place for long. Zareen raised his arms and his hands wreathed in flame, sending Rhyss back behind the statue for cover just in time. The place where his head had been exploded in green fire.

What to do? The Iron-caster and his ratkin bodyguards were creeping closer. He looked around for another piece of cover to jump to, but the next few statues were too far away. There was nowhere to run. Rhyss' mind jumped to a detail that he'd initially missed. The ratkin both had flamethrower arms, comprised of a tank of vile liquid with hoses leading to a trigger mechanism next to a lit flame where the fingers would have been. Presumably, the liquid would fire, pass over the flame, and shoot forward. It was a clever mechanism, Rhyss thought with a hint of panic as he heard Zareen's footsteps come closer. He didn't have time to consider his nascent calling as an engineer. He had only seconds before he would be cooked to a crisp. And then, Rhyss' brain snapped all the pieces together.

It would be a tricky shot, and he'd probably only have one chance.

Another fireball exploded against the far wall, spattering Rhyss' boots with green flame. He stomped his feet against the ground to put the fire out, but it was sticky somehow and didn't easily tamp out like normal fire. He heard Zareen's voice, eerily close.

"There's nowhere to run, mongrel."

The Iron-caster was right. Rhyss was out of options. He looked to his right, away from where Zareen was approaching. All clear. He checked his crossbow one more time, breathed in deeply, and held it for a second to steady himself.

He sprang up to his right with a yell, trying to keep the statue between him and the Iron-caster. The two ratkin were waiting for him. They lifted their hulking arms, prepared to bathe Rhyss in fire. He saw the little flames at the ends of the flame throwers, and the hoses. The ratkin were slower than Rhyss, imprecise and brutish due to their muscular physique. The ranger captain aimed his crossbow and fired his shot in one smooth motion.

In that split second, time slowed down for Rhyss, and his world narrowed down to the crossbow quarrel as it whizzed through the air. He had aimed for the ratkin to his right, if for no other reason than because it was slightly closer. The quarrel struck the beast in the forearm, nicking the hose. The ratkin fired the flamethrower, but instead of a jet of green burning ichor, the volatile liquid dribbled from the hose and coated the beast's arm. In an instant, the ratkin bellowed in pain as its arm became a parody of the Iron-caster's. Green fire raced up its limb and touched the tank mounted on its triceps. The other ratkin bodyguard stopped to look at his compatriot and took a step back in fear, fouling its own shot. Rhyss' eyes widened in primal panic, and he ducked back behind the statue, only to see Zareen waiting for him on the other side. Rhyss stopped short, with nowhere left to run.

Zareen smiled and pointed at Rhyss.

Rhyss heard a strange hissing that sounded like a whining tea kettle. It blew a note that rose sharply from low to high.

Then the world exploded.

Rhyss instinctively flinched away and dropped to his knees behind the statue as the shock rolled through him. A second blast flared an instant later. The sound was so loud that it didn't register as sound, just pure vibration that blew the air from his lungs. Even though his eyes were closed, the flare of green light still nearly blinded him.

It took Rhyss a few seconds to realize that he was still alive. He forced himself to take in a ragged breath. Then another. The ringing in his ears made him deaf. He opened his eyes and blinked away the afterimages. He shook his head and numbly tried to draw his axe, ready to defend himself from the Iron-caster. Ironically, the statue of Ariagful had shielded Rhyss from the brunt of the blast. In contrast, Zareen was lying crumpled beside the wall a few feet away.

Serves him right, Rhyss thought groggily.

With a start, he remembered that there was a bigger battle going on, and he took a few shaky steps out from behind the statue.

A sickly green and brown spot marred the floor where the two ratkin had stood. One of his rangers was lying prone on his back in the middle of the hall, knocked unconscious or worse, and dangerously close to the titans who were still fighting as if nothing untoward had happened. Rhyss stumbled toward the ranger and grabbed him with both hands behind the collar. He pulled him back to safety on shaky legs as the obsidian golem cinched up the elemental around the waist with its elongated powerful arms and tried to hoist him up. Rhyss leaned the ranger up against the wall and checked his breathing. He was still alive, thank the Earth Mother. He turned back in time to see the elemental headbutt the golem, smashing its forehead into its face, snapping its head back and up. The golem stood half a head taller, but the earth spirit followed up the strike by pulling his left arm into his torso and regrowing it up above where the golem's arm clung to his waist, freeing it. The elemental's palm pushed up into the golem's jaw, keeping it 'looking' up at the ceiling, and not allowing it to regain its footing. With a powerful step forward, it threw the golem off-balance, sending it tumbling to the floor with a mighty crash.

As the titans moved away from the center of the hall, Rhyss saw Dinnidek falling back before Alborz. It was clear that whatever the Overmaster had become, he was more than a match for Din. He drew his second axe and rushed to help his friend.

* * * * *

Dinnidek recovered from the explosion just in time to block Alborz's strike with his shield. The impact pushed him back, and he stumbled, barely regaining his balance before his shield absorbed another hit. He went to swing his axe in a riposte, but Alborz's sword was already coming back for a third strike. Din deflected it with his axe, and he barely held on to his weapon. Alborz wasn't moving as fluidly as he'd been last time they'd fought. There were strange pauses interspersed between his motions. To make up for it, Alborz was considerably stronger than he'd been before. So far, Din had been able to keep Alborz at bay, but he'd been forced to take a purely defensive stance. Through it all, Alborz's eye had pulsed with a hungry green light, his face impassive and his mouth closed in a tight thin line. It was unnatural and added to Din's growing sense of unease.

Alborz was just too strong for Din to chance leaving himself open. Din would be done for if the fiend got a clean cut in, but he couldn't fight defensively like this forever. Din tried to push his foe back with his shield to create room, but the Overmaster set his feet, and Din ineffectually bounced off. He brought his shield down to block a low thrust from Alborz, and he saw Rhyss running across the hall toward him. Din feinted with his axe, hoping to keep his foe's attention. It worked. The Overmaster parried the axe and switched his line of attack to push the sword blade down the axe haft, sending the sword point at Din's stomach. Din jumped back and knocked the sword down with the edge of his shield. Alborz was stretched forward from his sword thrust, abdomen exposed, when Rhyss arrived.

The ranger captain slammed one of his hand axes to wedge within Alborz's ribcage. The attack would have killed any foe, at least any foe that was truly alive. The fiend looked down at the axe, the handle sticking out wildly and shaking in response to his movements, and casually brushed at it with his free hand. The axe fell to the floor with a clang, its blade stained with the barest hint of blood. He turned toward Rhyss and opened his mouth, revealing a wicked green glow. A flash of flame flicked from Alborz's mouth, aimed at Rhyss' face. Rhyss dropped to his stomach to avoid the fire and snatched up his axe before springing back to his feet.

"Bah, enough with the green fire!" he yelled.

Din sunk his axe into Alborz's side when his back was turned, but it had the same results. Alborz barely registered the hit; his only reaction was from the physical impact of the blow.

"He's not alive!" Din yelled.

"Figured that," replied Rhyss as he jumped back away from another sword thrust. Din hacked again into Alborz's side, hoping to hit a vital organ, but it had the same effect as before. Alborz turned, mouth open, and shot fire at Din, who brought his shield up just in time to deflect it.

"We can't beat him like this," yelled Din from behind his shield. If Alborz didn't have organs, if he didn't pump blood, then they'd have to find another way to stop him. "We'll have to butcher him instead. Attack the structure!"

Rhyss grunted in reply and reset his axes. "Left leg!"

Din blocked another attack with his shield. "My left or yours?"

Rhyss sprang to the side to avoid Alborz's backswing. "My left, your right!"

Din came down on Alborz's right thigh with a solid hit from his axe. It cut through the meat of the muscle but stopped hard on Alborz's femur. He had just enough time to remove his axe before Alborz blasted him with more fire. He scrambled back and away, his axe arm severely burnt where his leather bracer failed to cover. Rhyss struck Alborz in the same thigh, this time on the other side. Alborz smashed down with his sword to strike at Rhyss' outstretched arm. The attack was so fast that Rhyss had to drop his axe to get his arm back to safety. Din struck Alborz in the back of the thigh, near the hamstring, and this seemed to do the trick. Alborz's leg went rigidly straight, making him stand unnaturally tall. Rhyss swung his second axe into the inside of Alborz's knee, sending the Overmaster to the ground.

Din raised his axe to start hacking away at the body when Alborz looked upward at him and opened his mouth, sending a fountain of fire up into the air. Din flinched back and covered his face while Rhyss reflexively fell backward to avoid the gout of flame. Din was about to re-engage when a fireball flew past, just missing his face. He followed the shot back to see Zareen, leaning up against the statue of Ariagful, his one arm bent at an odd angle. His other arm, however, held multiple small balls of green fire.

"Go!" yelled Rhyss as he stood back up. "Take care of him. I'll handle Alborz. You already killed him once, anyway."

Din checked to make sure Rhyss was alright, took one more look at Alborz's prone form, and dashed off toward Zareen.

As Din ran across the hall, he saw flashes of the chaos all around him. Joro had taken the golem to the ground and was sitting across its chest, pummeling it in the face with his massive fists. The golem's legs were twitching with every crushing strike. Diessa stood nearby, channeling energy into Joro to make him stronger. The rangers were embroiled in a desperate melee with the last mutant ratkin. The ratkin touched one of the rangers with his electrified prongs, blowing the dwarf off his feet and back into his mates. Diessa shouted an oath to the Earth Mother and her eyes flared with light. A second later, a pair of stone hands rose from the ground to grab the ratkin's legs. The remaining rangers took down the ratkin in a rush.

Zareen saw Din coming and forced himself to stand tall. He screamed a prayer to Ariagful and winced in pain as he raised both his arms, now wrapped in flame. Zareen thrust out his open palms and shot a beam of green fire. Din ducked his head down behind his shield and continued to rush forward. The fire hit his shield and washed over the rim, cascading over his dragon helm. Unlike last time, the fire didn't come in a burst, but in a steady stream that pushed him back and slowed him down until he was reduced to a plodding walk, leaning forward against the flames as if he was walking into a mighty gale.

He heard Zareen screaming, ranting his hatred at him as he got closer. "Your clan is nothing! Even if you best me, you won't survive the winter, cur. Your clan will starve before the Abyss comes to devour you utterly. Ariagful will sate her hunger upon your people, leaving nothing but ashes and sorrow!"

The force of the fire grew as Zareen vented his wicked loathing. Din was pushing forward with all his might against the weight of the vile sorcery. The inside of his shield was getting hot, and the hair within his helmet was starting to burn. He braced the shield with both hands and took another step forward. He was close, but still out of reach of Zareen. He kept his head down, afraid to look up and risk being hit with the flames. The shield wobbled in his hands and pitched so that the bottom tilted in toward his thighs. The flames went from cascading over the top of the shield, to under the bottom, bathing his shins in fire. Din screamed in pain as the fire impacted his chainmail and leather greaves. He wanted to flinch away, but if he gave in, he'd be burnt to ashes. He could only stand there and endure the searing heat, head down behind his shield, staring at the ground with his legs shaking in pain and weariness.

Then, suddenly, the pain eased. Din saw Gwel rise out of the floor by his feet. He was using his body as a shield to protect Din from the flames. The little earth spirit had taken a wide and squat form this time to cover the most area. He gave a slight wave of his right hand before turning his face directly into the fire. Din took a labored step forward, and Gwel kept pace, keeping his head and upraised arms even with the bottom of Din's shield. Din took another step and caught his breath to gather his energy for another push. Zareen screamed and called on Ariagful to destroy his foe, but it was for naught. Din took one more step forward, and he could see the tip of Zareen's boot.

The pressure on the shield was intense. Din pulled his axe hand away free, and his one arm wasn't strong enough to keep the shield held out in front of him. It smashed back into the brim of his helmet and bottom of his thighs, but Din held his ground. He smelled his hair burning within his helmet, and his limbs were tingling with pain everywhere. He let his axe hand drop down to his side. His entire world had been reduced to the back of his shield and the burning green fire. He carefully spun the axe blade so that it faced Zareen and set his feet for one last push. He thrust forward with all his might, Gwel now helping to support the shield with his little hands. It was just enough. Din took the half step forward, and he could see Zareen's leg from under his shield.

He swung his axe in a quick chop to strike Zareen on his inner thigh. The Iron-caster howled in pain, and the fire abruptly stopped. With the pressure from the fire gone, Din suddenly rushed forward and slammed Zareen with his shield, sending him sprawling to the floor. Din pounced forward to finish his enemy once and for all. Zareen snarled at Din and raised his hands, but the flames had died out.

His sorcerous powers were gone. Ariagful had forsaken him.

Zareen wailed in comprehension at his goddess's betrayal. The look of hatred and disdain on his face was replaced with sheer panic as Din swung the axe down and struck the killing blow.

Din stood over his fallen foe and took a few deep breaths, his body wracked with pain from the burns. He turned slowly to take in the great hall. Joro stood tall over the remains of the obsidian golem, Diessa next to him, leaning on his leg. The surviving rangers were just finishing off the last ratkin. And finally, Rhyss was standing over the body of what had been Alborz. There was silence. Even the thunder of the artillery had stopped. The fighting was over.

They'd won.

Dinnidek collapsed onto the floor and gazed up at the great hall. His body was so exhausted that he could do nothing but smile in triumph. The last thing he noticed before he passed out from the pain was an area on the wall where the plaster covering had been blasted away. Behind the cracks, Din could just make out the head of his great-great-grandfather, standing triumphantly over the body of a giant white dragon.

* * * * *

The dwarf next to Daerun fell, clutching the spear buried in his belly. Dare hammered the ratkin holding the weapon across its snout, crushing its face and sending bits of teeth and blood spattering over its fellows. The stricken dwarf struggled to stand, but he remained hunched over, curled into a ball around his mortal wound. Daerun and the nearby Shieldbreakers stepped forward to stand over the body, while soldiers in the rear ranks pulled the wounded dwarf back to safety. The dwarf grunted in agony as he was dragged back behind the line. The Shieldbreakers, meanwhile, smashed the ratkin back with their great hammers to create some space. The vermin retreated, leaving dozens of bodies behind on the grass.

Dare wiped his brow with the back of his hand and let his hammer rest at his side. The dwarfs were clustered around the northern redoubt in concentric defensive rings that the ratkin couldn't penetrate. But they were encircled by the press of enemies swarming around them. There were too many to attempt a breakout.

Daerun heard Rorik calling to the Wyverns from above him on the redoubt. He would call out a target and the closest Wyverns would call it back.

"Red banner!" Rorik yelled.

"Red banner," they echoed.

In the brief respite, Dare scanned the enemy ranks. In the rear was a red banner, held by a giant ratkin. He heard the crack of rifles and the giant ratkin spun and fell, taking the banner with it. Meanwhile, Veit was directing the remaining Ironwatch to fire volleys into the advancing vermin, disrupting their charge and giving the Shieldbreakers a fighting chance.

Daerun spared a look across the valley to where the Worm Lord was fighting. The orcs on that flank had recovered from the initial assault and were reforming their lines to repel the berserkers. The Worm Lord's army was highly skilled and rock hard, but heavily outnumbered. At least their arrival had spared Daerun's army from being overwhelmed. Fighting on two fronts, the orcs and ratkin couldn't destroy either of the dwarf armies, but in return, the dwarfs couldn't make any headway. The field was a stalemate for now, but the dwarfs were being ground down. Daerun gazed back to the wounded dwarf. Every clansman that fell was precious, in stark contrast to the teeming sea of vermin. If Daerun's position fell, it would spell the doom of the dwarfs.

At least that infernal artillery has stopped, Dare thought. *Probably don't want to risk hitting their own troops.*

The ratkin had gathered themselves for another push, and the closest line of vermin lowered their spears and charged forward with a screeching, chittering war cry.

"They want another round, boys!" Daerun yelled to his troops. The Ironclad in the rear ranks strode forward and locked their shields to repel the wall of spear points, while the Shieldbreakers stepped back to crush any ratkin that managed to break through the line. From above, the Ironwatch fired a volley at close range into the charging ratkin. Some of the vermin in the front ranks fell, their fellows stepping over them or tripping to be trampled by the ratkin in the rear ranks. The ratkin charged, sending the dwarfs back a step, but the shield wall held. A few dwarfs reeled back with wounds on their legs or arms where stray spearpoints had snuck between the shields, but their places in the line were quickly filled by the second line of dwarfs. Daerun watched nervously, alert for any sign of weakness along the shield wall. The dwarfs held their ground, but only just. Despite Daerun's bluster, the dwarfs couldn't keep this up all day. The ratkin seemed endless, and the dwarfs would eventually break.

It was then that Dare heard the artillery begin firing again from the hold. Were the Abyssal Dwarfs firing at the redoubt, even though the ratkin were so close?

Callous bastards, he thought, *throwing away the lives of their troops.*

He glanced up, waiting for the rain of destruction that was sure to come. He heard the whistling sounds of the artillery, but the shells didn't land near him at all. Instead, explosions blossomed amid the ratkin arrayed on the plain in front of the dwarfen trench, sending bodies flying into the air. A second barrage landed among the enemy ranks, and they cried out in growing panic and despair. For all his relief, Daerun couldn't understand what he was seeing. Had the gun crews misread the ranges? No, once was a mistake. Twice was what? Treachery? Or a miracle? The cannons were intermittent at first, but soon a steady rain of destruction fell on the ratkin. The vermin on the plain stopped their assault and began retreating to the hold, but the gates were closed.

Daerun shouted in triumph as he realized that Dinnidek had taken the gates and the gun emplacements. The plain was a swirling chaotic mass of Abyssal slaves being brutally slain by the artillery from the hold, while the Worm Lord and Daerun's armies hemmed them in.

"Yes! Daamuz! Daamuz!" Dare yelled his clan name with a fervor that swept through his fellow clansmen like lightning.

Meanwhile, Tordek bellowed for the dwarfs to hold fast and keep their positions. The ratkin's attack on the redoubt ebbed and eventually stopped as the vermin saw the carnage on the plain. Another volley from the Ironwatch broke the ratkin morale, and they fled back up the eastern road. Meanwhile, the ratkin further out were sent into a frenzy, and they threw themselves against the dwarfen formations in panic, trying desperately to escape the relentless artillery barrage, but they were no match for the disciplined dwarfs. Eventually the vermin ceased their futile attacks and ran for safety. The order to hold echoed throughout the dwarfen ranks as the ratkin on the plain ran past them. Here and there, wherever the ratkin tried to rally around some banner or leader, Rorik would order the Wyverns to fire. The packleader or the banner would fall, spreading panic and discord throughout the mob.

Soon, most of the enemy had left the plain, scattered to the four winds. The gun emplacements fell silent, and the dwarfs held the field. Daerun sighed in relief and leaned on his hammer while his troops whooped and celebrated.

Daerun climbed the redoubt to survey the scene. The ground before the gates was chewed up by the artillery and choked with enemy bodies. It was a grisly testament to their victory. Veit came to stand beside him and pointed at the front gates, which were slowly opening. Rorik stepped forward and sighted the opening through his scope. A small figure wearing the Daamuz clan colors stepped out from behind the great stone door, but Dare couldn't make out any other details at this distance.

"Looks like one of ours," said Rorik. Daerun smiled broadly and patted Rorik on the back. The gate opened wider to reveal a giant earth elemental pushing the door aside.

"Thank the Earth Mother," whispered Veit, just loud enough for Daerun to hear.

"Yes," replied Daerun, shooting Veit a relieved smile. The elemental was testament that Diessa had survived.

Dare looked at the dwarfen bodies scattered around the redoubt. His sister was alive, but he couldn't shake the sadness at seeing so many of his clansmen lying dead before the gates of Llyngyr Cadw. They had been so close to coming home.

A tap on the shoulder from Veit brought Daerun back to himself. The Worm Lord's army had arrayed itself on the plain, while Kilvar's rangers were coming to join Daerun's forces. After a few moments, some of the berserkers began retreating into the woods from whence they came. The Worm Lord sat astride his giant bear, his bone armor and great stag helm giving him a menacing and regal bearing. He was flanked by a stone priest with wild white hair, standing within the upraised palm of what seemed to be a giant stone hand, the fingers curled up behind him, and a lone dwarf on a brock with a ragged cloak. The dwarfs were too far away to converse with, so Daerun raised his hand in a gesture of greeting and gratitude.

The Worm Lord stood tall in his saddle and raised his axe in a return salute. Daerun expected him to approach so that they could talk, but instead, the old dwarf stayed frozen in place. After a heartbeat, the Worm Lord released his grip on the haft of the great axe and caught it quickly, giving it a swift sweep and a flourish before abruptly turning to rejoin his army.

Daerun's heart skipped a beat at the Worm Lord's salute. By the time he recovered, the Worm Lord was almost to the treeline. Daerun could only stand there numbly, his next word coming out in a whisper.

"Father?"

CHAPTER 27

"In keeping with our grand plan to wrest the Halpi Peninsula from the forces of the Abyss, Clan Daamuz, working closely with agents of our grand empire..." Daerun cleared his throat as if the words he was speaking were threatening to choke him.

Dinnidek, seated on the dais within the restored great hall, snorted in annoyance along with his brother. "I knew you couldn't get through the whole thing without cringing. Go on, let's hear the rest of this drivel." He waved his hand to Daerun to continue reading the Imperial decree.

Daerun shook his head in disbelief as he went on. "Where was I? Right... Clan Daamuz, working closely with agents of our grand empire, and under our direct auspices as the right imperial majesty, established a beachhead by retaking the ancient hold of Llyngyr Cadw." Dare raised his eyes from the parchment with a look of mild shock. "Oh, come on. How can anyone believe this tripe?"

"I'm not surprised," rumbled Tordek from his usual spot behind Dinnidek's seat.

"Me neither," agreed Rhyss. "The minute we succeeded, he had to act as if the whole plan was his idea. Every good thing in the Empire happens because Golloch wills it."

"Yes," agreed Din, "and he can't call us traitors because he'll have to contend with the rest of the Free Dwarfs in exile. It wouldn't do to have a group of disgruntled traitors scattered everywhere. Very shrewd." Dinnidek scratched at his beard thinking of how their success here was playing in the halls of power back in Caeryn Golloch.

"Shrewd indeed," agreed Dare as he went back to the decree. "And so, let it be known that I, High King Golloch, do formally allow Sveri Egilax to proceed with an invasion of the Halpi Peninsula, with my full support. Let all dwarf refugees answer the call for freedom and muster yourselves for the crusade ahead, in full knowledge and comfort that you step forth as one dwarfen people, under one great leader." Dare couldn't help keep his hands from shaking in anger at the end. "Very subtle, that last part."

"Very subtle," agreed Din with a weary sigh. "Though the wording there is very clever. It's hard to tell who he is referring to as the 'one great leader.' It could be Sveri, it could be Golloch, depending on the bias of the reader." Din shook his head and his voice became more pensive. "I was so worried about us being hunted as traitors that I didn't think that we would be used as propaganda for that self-righteous windbag. I almost think being labeled a traitor would have been better than being labeled an accomplice. And now Golloch is lapping up every scrap of reflected glory that he can. Typical."

"And sad," agreed Rhyss. "He'll sanction the crusade, but we'll see how much help he actually gives."

"True," agreed Dare. "He'll allow them all to leave, but probably won't spend any of the empire's blood or treasure to see it through." Silence reigned in the hall as the three dwarfs reflected on the decree and what it meant. After a few moments, Daerun crumpled the parchment in his hands and threw it onto the nearby brazier to be burned to ash.

"If Sveri can muster our people," opined Din, "and bring them home, it could be everything that we've dreamed of." He thought back to Anfynn, just a few months ago, proclaiming that their deeds would be a call for the Free Dwarfs to regain their purpose, to come home and wrest their lands from the Abyss. He had been right, just not in the way that they had envisioned it. There was no use worrying about it now. The alloy was cast. They could only wait to see how strong it could be forged. He shook his head and sighed in resignation.

A herald entered the hall and bowed in deference before announcing that the delegation from Crafanc had arrived and was waiting in the anteroom. Tordek waved to the herald to allow them in, and Dinnidek stood up from his seat and descended the dais to personally greet his guests, Daerun and Rhyss close behind. "Welcome, friends! You honor us with your presence. Please, make yourself at home in our halls."

Anfynn, Kilvar, and the rest of the delegation from Crafanc bowed deeply in gratitude as the two brothers approached. Anfynn came out of his bow with a broad smile on his face and clasped Din's forearm before pulling him in for a hug. Dinnidek winced as the Warmaster put pressure on his burnt skin, but he tried to hide his discomfort to spare Anfynn any embarrassment. It had been two months since Alborz had burnt his arm, and it was slow healing. Din's legs were worse. Cormack had to apply new bandages and salves every few days, and the pained and puckered skin on his shins was still hot to the touch. Din subtly shook his forearm as he disengaged from the embrace. He was worried he'd have the same issue with Kilvar, but Rhyss spared him the trouble. The ranger captain abandoned all decorum as he called to his friend and trotted across the hall before lifting the packmaster up in a bearhug.

"How was the trip?" Daerun asked.

"Easy," Anfynn replied in his low gravelly voice. "We only saw one or two orcs, and those were at a distance. Every time, it gets a little easier. Trade is picking up, and the east-west road is getting more secure every day."

Dare nodded in approval at the news.

"We have you to thank for that," said Dinnidek with a smile. He gestured toward Rhyss and Kilvar, who were excitedly trading stories. "With your rangers helping Rhyss, we've been able to keep the Abyssal slaves out of the valley. It's no small feat."

Anfynn smiled as he stroked his beard contentedly. "It's as you said, Lord Dinnidek. One day, trade will flow between our holds. We'll be a bulwark against the evils of the Abyss, and our people will return in force. That starts with us working together. We won't forget the lessons the invasion taught us."

Daerun stomped his foot in agreement at Anfynn's words. A servant came into the hall to offer the guests beer and light fare. Anfynn smiled and picked up a tankard of ale from the servant's tray before the two brothers took theirs. Anfynn raised his tankard to the Daamuz brothers and took a deep draught.

"Oh, that's not bad," he said with some surprise. A split second later, Anfynn realized how his tone must have sounded. "Sorry, it's just that it's only been a few ten-days since you opened the brewery up."

"Priorities," replied Daerun with a wink as he raised his tankard.

"And how have you been, Master Daerun?" Anfynn asked. "I noticed you and your Shieldbreakers escorting a group of your people past Crafanc about a ten-day ago. It would seem that Captain Saorsi has delivered the rest of your clan from Innyshwylt. Did you get a chance to see her?" He asked the last question with a sly wink.

Daerun blushed at the question and took the opportunity to take a drink before replying. "Why, yes, yes I did. The captain is a lovely conversationalist."

Anfynn rolled his eyes. "Yes, she's both those things. Good for you," he said with a lop-sided grin.

Dinnidek snorted and changed the subject. "It's good to have our people reunited. To be honest, it will be nice to hear the sound of children again. It's been too long. We're stronger together, even if there are fewer of us."

Din gestured toward the clan banner, which hung high behind the dais from cables suspended from the ceiling. Hundreds of chains, each holding small mementos to the fallen dwarfs, hung from the banner. A set of bullseye lanterns were aimed at the chains, reflecting the light into thousands of glinting motes that floated across the walls of the great hall. Anfynn looked down in respect at the mention of the dead.

"Luckily," Din continued, "between the goods Captain Saorsi sends us, and the limited foraging we've been able to do, we should have just enough food to get us through the winter. Hopefully, by next year, the mushroom fields in the lower caves will be fully developed."

At the mention of the underground caves, Anfynn looked pensive. "What about the tunnel defenses? Have you had any trouble from below?"

"Some," said Dinnidek, "but nothing that we couldn't handle. We've heard rumors of free tribes of ratkin that broke away from the Abyssal Dwarfs and are now establishing themselves under the mountains to the west." Anfynn clenched his fist at the news. "It could be bad, but it could also be an opportunity. A divided enemy can only help us. Either way, we've sealed off most of the tunnels and put guards on all the underground pathways. It may be months before we can reclaim parts of the underway. Until then, we'll have to keep the overland routes open."

Anfynn considered the problem for a moment. "We'll make arrangements for the coming winter. If the weather is bad, you may find yourself isolated for months on end. Can't have that."

"I whole-heartedly agree," said Din. He'd have to talk about retrofitting the carts, perhaps with skids to turn them into sleds. He studied the problem in the back of his mind while distractedly tracing the outline of his forearm burn with his finger.

As if on cue, Veit entered the hall with Diessa and a pair of young dwarfs, dressed in blue tunics emblazoned with a red mountain on a white circle. Deese dismissed the two junior stone priests before joining the group. She bowed low to the Warmaster, the end of her honey-colored braid just brushing the floor. Veit, meanwhile, went searching for a tankard of ale before returning to the group. He raised the stein to Anfynn and took a long drink.

"Ah," the engineer said with relish, "I needed that." He wiped his lips with the back of his sleeve and turned to Dinnidek. "The new watchtower is complete, my lord. Joro finished placing the roof an hour ago, and my builders have finished the interior work."

"Excellent news, and please give Joro our thanks, Diessa."

"I will," answered Deese as she stifled a yawn. "My apologies," she said with a shake of her head, "it's been a long day."

"No, I'm sorry, Deese. There's no need for us to stand," said Dinnidek. He clapped Anfynn on the shoulder before gesturing toward a group of seats on the dais set in a semi-circle, allowing Dinnidek to speak comfortably with his guests. The only other chair on the dais was the ornately carved throne, adorned with friezes and inlays depicting dragons in flight. Din waited for the other dwarfs to be seated before he took his place on one of the smaller chairs, making sure to rest his burnt forearm gingerly on his lap. Tordek took his customary place behind Din. Anfynn arched an eyebrow in surprise and his eyes glanced toward the empty throne.

Din's lip curled up in a slight smile at the unspoken question and he nodded toward the throne.

"That's not my seat yet," he said, as if that explained everything. Daerun nodded in silent approval, while Diessa sighed in exasperation. Anfynn looked quizzically at the three siblings and gestured for them to go on.

Daerun spoke first. "We believe our father is still alive. Dinnidek doesn't want to formally assume the throne until we're sure."

Diessa scoffed, "Even if he is alive, our father would want Dinnidek to be proclaimed chieftain." Her tone reflected that the siblings had been having this argument for a while.

Anfynn raised his hands in surprise. "Drohzon could be alive? This is the first I've heard the news. How can you be sure?"

"I saw him, after the battle at the gates," said Daerun. "The Worm Lord saluted me with his axe the same way that father used to."

"And the same way as Lord Dinnidek," observed Veit.

Diessa smiled at Din. "I remember when you were young. You would practice that sweep and flourish move for hours. You wanted to be just like him."

Din acknowledged the comment with a smile and waved his hand airily. "Both my brother and sister are correct. Our father would have wanted me to be chieftain, but if there's a chance that he's alive, I don't feel right taking the throne. In the meantime, I am the head of Clan Daamuz, just like before."

Veit pointed up at the restored mural with the white dragon. "The clues were right in front of us, really. We always assumed the Worm Lord's name was spelled with an 'O', but what if it was a 'Y'? If Drohzon is alive, taking the title of Wyrm Lord makes much more sense."

"Yes," said Anfynn, "but if Lord Drohzon is alive, why hasn't he come back to Llyngyr Cadw? Why hasn't he reunited with his clan?"

"I don't know," said Din, "but we intend to find out."

"Speaking of," said Rhyss as he and Kilvar approached the group, "Kilvar and I have gathered our best rangers together. We'll be ready to depart in two days."

"The Wyrm Lord's people are clever," said Kilvar, "but they won't be able to hide from us forever." He looked at Anfynn. "Assuming I have your leave to join Captain Rhyss, my lord."

Anfynn arched his eyebrow. "Oh, you're asking permission, now? Just make sure you're back by the equinox. Winter is coming, and our two holds will need you both to lead the patrols."

"My thanks, Lord Anfynn," said Din. "I appreciate your support on such a personal errand."

"Sure, it's personal, but it's also good planning," opined Rhyss. "Whether or not Drohzon is the Wyrm Lord, we haven't heard anything from his people since the battle before the gates. Establishing contact for mutual cooperation this winter is important if we're going to survive. The Abyssal Dwarfs haven't gone away. It's only a matter of time before they return."

"Let them come," declared Anfynn as he drained the last of his beer. "We'll be ready this time."

Daerun banged his beer stein against the arm of his seat before rising. "Please excuse me Lord Anfynn," he said with a bow. "I believe Felwyr traveled with you from Crafanc. We have some catching up to do."

He descended the dais and crossed the hall with a definite spring in his step.

Dinnidek watched Daerun leave the hall with a feeling of contentment. In this moment, he wanted to share Anfynn's optimism. Here in his ancestral hold with his people finally reunited, it was easy to feel confident, to forget the sacrifices the clan had made to be truly free. He thought of Felwyr, and the countless other dwarfs who had suffered grievous injuries that they would carry for the rest of their days. He looked up at the dragon mural, hundreds of tiny lights reflected from the mementos of his clansmen slowly moving over its surface. Each light was a departed spirit, watching over the clan, sharing in its triumphs, and sustaining it through its tragedies.

The next few years would be tough. It would be a long cold season, and they'd have to use all of their resourcefulness and industriousness to survive their first winter home. Who knew how long it would take the remaining Free Dwarf refugees to return to Halpi. The Abyssal Dwarfs and their slaves were roaming outside their door, hungry to destroy the Free Dwarfs and stamp their light from the world. The free ratkin and the goblins would be probing the dwarfen underground defenses, gnawing at the roots of the mountains. And Golloch was still out there, probably secretly stewing in anger over the clan's perceived betrayal, despite the spin he had put on the clan's success. There was no telling what the High King would do to avenge his wounded pride. No, they had plenty of enemies.

But they had plenty of friends, too.

Din gazed at the assembled dwarfs in the throne room, and his heart warmed at their camaraderie and their strength. Great warriors and stalwart leaders, clever builders, and wise women. Din smiled to himself, closed his eyes, and decided it would be enough.

Look for more books from Winged Hussar Publishing, LLC – E-books, paperbacks and Limited-Edition hardcovers. The best in history, science fiction and fantasy at:

https://www. wingedhussarpublishing.com

https://www.whpsupplyroom.com

or follow us on Facebook at:

Winged Hussar Publishing LLC

Or on twitter at:

WingHusPubLLC

For information and upcoming publications

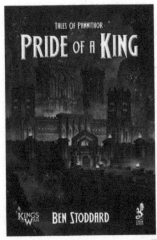

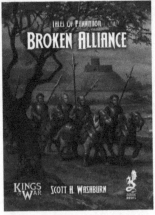

About the Author

Mike Rossi is an enthusiastic gamer, professional engineer (wizard), long time martial artist (monk), aging hiker (ranger), avid reader (mage), and now first time author. He resides in Upstate New York with his wife, three kids and bajillion cats.